"A rough and tumble Western with heart."
—Kathe Robin, *Romantic Times*

Bay drew her into his arms . . .

"You're still nervous of me," Bay said. "Let's see if we can do something about that."

This was it. He was going to kiss her now, and that would be the end of her, and all she could do was stand there, waiting for her downfall to begin.

He held her eyes with his, and they stood there a long moment. His fingers massaged the small of her back, and Mariah fought the urge to relax against him.

As she stood there like a fool, waiting and wanting, and trying not to want, Bay brought his other hand up and cupped her chin. His thumb brushed across her lips, sending a tremor of pleasure down her spine, and then his mouth skimmed the same path before he set her away.

It took her a moment to realize the kiss was over, that the brief contact was all he had planned.

"Good night, Mariah Hoag." He strode off toward the barn. Confused by his sudden retreat, Mariah stood there, her lips tingling with the traces of Bay's touch . . .

DIAMOND WILDFLOWER ROMANCE

A breathtaking line of searing romance novels . . .
where destiny meets desire in the untamed fury
of the American West

More praise for Lisa Hendrix:

". . . it's remarkably easy to become caught up in the lives of the people who inhabit *Drifter's Moon*. A darned good book."
—*Affaire de Coeur*

Also by Lisa Hendrix

HOSTAGE HEART

Drifter's Moon

Lisa Hendrix

DIAMOND BOOKS, NEW YORK

If you purchased this book without a cover, you should be aware that this book is stolen property. It was reported as "unsold and destroyed" to the publisher, and neither the author nor the publisher has received any payment for this "stripped book."

This book is a Diamond original edition,
and has never been previously published.

DRIFTER'S MOON

A Diamond Book / published by arrangement with
the author

PRINTING HISTORY
Diamond edition / January 1995

All rights reserved.
Copyright © 1995 by Lisa Hendrix.
This book may not be reproduced in whole or in part,
by mimeograph or any other means, without permission.
For information address: The Berkley Publishing Group,
200 Madison Avenue, New York, New York 10016.

ISBN: 0-7865-0070-0

Diamond Books are published by The Berkley Publishing Group,
200 Madison Avenue, New York, New York 10016.
DIAMOND and the "D" design are trademarks belonging
to Charter Communications, Inc.

PRINTED IN THE UNITED STATES OF AMERICA

10 9 8 7 6 5 4 3 2 1

To my mom,
who had the good sense to give birth in Kansas.
I love you.

Chapter One

Chase County,
Kansas, 1874

MARIAH KNEW WHAT was happening the instant she heard the sound. Bawling cattle and splintering wood could only mean one thing. She abruptly stopped churning and straightened up enough to peer through the dusty square of window glass.

"Oh, Lord, the corn." She jumped up, the butter forgotten, and darted to the door.

"What is it, dear?" her mother asked from the chair where she'd been dozing.

"Cattle, Mama. Longhorns. They've pushed down the fence again. There must be a thousand of them."

"Where's the dog?"

"Asleep."

Mariah poked a toe at the scruffy form stretched out in the shade just outside the door. Clyde rose, shook the dust off his speckled tan back, then looked expectantly at Mariah. She pointed toward the field. "Do your job, lazy. Get out there and run them off. Go on. Get 'em."

Clyde rushed off, barking enthusiastically, and slipped through a gap in the low fieldstone wall that separated the farm yard from the crops. Small as he was, he nearly disappeared in the young corn. Mariah tracked him by watching him leap over the rows jack rabbit–style.

Acasta Hoag joined her daughter in the doorway to watch, and Mariah slipped an arm around her mother's slim waist.

Mariah felt the bony ridges of ribs beneath her fingers and glanced down, frowning. Still too thin, she thought to herself. *So fragile.*

Clyde apparently decided that a rear attack made sense. He rushed a bunch of cows, driving them deeper into the field and toward the house. More young corn went down.

Clyde suddenly stopped dead in the middle of the field as a big bull, a particularly rangy creature with one broken horn and splotches of brownish red on his dirty white hide, turned and lowered his head. Dog and bull stared at each other, then the longhorn snorted and pawed at the ground belligerently. Seconds later, Clyde grovelled at Mariah's feet.

"You pathetic, worthless animal. This is just what we got you for, and you haven't carried your weight since the day I rescued you." Scolding, Mariah dragged Clyde back toward the wall and the shifting mass of horned raiders, but he'd have no part of it. Spotted pink belly up, he whimpered like a wounded puppy.

Disgusted, Mariah ordered the dog into the lean-to shed beside the barn. "Sit in there and think of a reason why I should feed you tonight," she said, and slammed the door shut.

A loud shriek drowned out Clyde's whine. Mariah turned and saw her mother scrambling back through the same gap in the stone wall that the dog had used. A steer with a set of horns the width of a barn door tried to follow her.

"Leave her alone. Go on, get." Mariah ran to the wall, yelling and ripping off her apron as she went. She whipped the apron across the steer's muzzle, and the wall shuddered as a ton of beef rattled horn against stone on its far side. Mariah snapped the apron again. The steer tossed his head in frustration, then trotted off to join the others in demolishing more of the corn crop.

"Come on, before he remembers how big he is and just walks over the top." Mariah reached for her mother's trembling hands and helped her back toward the house. Bright, feverish circles spotted her mother's cheeks, and Mariah's stomach tightened with concern. "What on earth were you doing? You know you're still supposed to be resting. Father's going to have a conniption if he finds out I let you start chasing after cows."

"Nonsense, child." Mrs. Hoag straightened and brushed her daughter's hand off. "I thought I could shoo them away."

"Those aren't milk cows, Mama," Mariah said in exasperation. "Now, into bed, where you can't get into trouble."

"Not while those monsters eat our entire crop. Why is it these things always happen when your father and brother are away?"

Why indeed? Mariah had her own suspicions on the subject, but she kept them to herself. Speculation would only upset her mother. "We'll be fine. I can chase them off on the horse."

"By yourself? Fiddle. Stop coddling me. I'm fine, dear, really."

"I know, Mama, I know."

With her mother tucked into a chair just outside the door where she could watch the field—a compromise that satisfied neither of them—Mariah tugged on a pair of her brother's worn trousers beneath her skirts, tied on her bonnet, then hurried to the barn and threw a bridle and the battered saddle on her old horse. Barely more than a pony, the little sorrel was hardly a match for the longhorns, but since Father and James had taken the other horses, Mariah didn't have much choice. For once, Mama didn't object that she was riding astride instead of a ladylike side-saddle.

A few minutes later, Mariah sat facing the bull that had stared down Clyde, feeling a sudden empathy for the pup's reluctance. This was not one of the gentle milking shorthorns her family kept. The tip of the bull's good horn had a polished look to it, like it had been carefully sharpened for battle, and the cast in his eyes said he'd be happy to use it on anyone who disturbed him. All around him, cows and steers milled through the young corn, brandishing equally impressive weapons. Even if there weren't a thousand of them—more like fifty or sixty—they made a terrifying sight.

The bull apparently decided the little horse posed no threat and turned to nip the top off of a deep green corn stalk. Mariah glanced across the field, sizing up the distance and direction of the broken section of fence. About half the cattle were in a bunch near the gap. She quietly circled the sorrel behind them and started driving them toward the hole. They went easily, and she felt a rush of pride and relief when the last one stepped over the remains of the fence.

The feeling didn't last long.

No sooner had she turned toward the bull and his remaining herd, than the other cows meandered back into the field.

"All right, so you want to stay together," Mariah said aloud. The bull lifted his head warily. "I can manage that. Get on there."

Mariah swung the end of her rope in a wide circle out to the side, like she'd seen drovers do. The familiar action must have convinced the animals she knew what she was doing, as they bunched up and moved in the direction she intended. Once again, she smiled with satisfaction as the herd moved toward the gap in the fence.

Once again, that satisfaction proved premature. The bull hesitated at the line of debris that marked the downed fence, then veered off to the left. The herd followed close behind him, circling back into the field where they quickly drifted apart.

Mariah considered a series of names for the bull and his harem, but refrained from using them aloud. A lady never curses, her mother always said.

"But then, ladies seldom wear their brothers' pants to drive cattle," Mariah mumbled. She began gathering the herd again.

She had the cattle all together and moving toward the gap when she noticed two men cutting across the creek, up past the far corner of the pasture. She recognized neither of them, but their weathered hats and dusty gear said cowboy. One of them led a string of three horses.

One of the cows broke away, and Mariah rode her down and nudged her back into the group. When she looked up again, the man with the horses had disappeared into the cottonwoods along the creek bank, but the other, the taller of the two, had stopped to watch. He sat his big blue roan with ease, and Mariah hoped he'd stayed to help. Surely he'd have the knack of moving cattle. But he just sat there, and she could see a flash of white teeth as a grin lifted the corners of his mouth.

So he'd stayed to laugh instead of help. Fine. Mariah felt her spine stiffen. Fine. Well, she had more to worry about than being some fellow's amusement. She whipped the rope around again.

The herd trotted obediently toward the hole in the fence, but once again the bull refused to cross the downed fence and circled back into the corn, taking the cows and steers with him.

Sudden tears prickled the back of Mariah's eyes. At this rate, the cows wouldn't have to eat the corn to ruin the crop: every stalk would be trampled into the ground. Without a crop, they couldn't make the mortgage. They'd lose the farm and have to move again and. . . .

"I thought you had them that time." The deep, glossy baritone slipped in between Mariah's thoughts, and she glanced up. Her audience now sat his tall horse less than a dozen feet away. "Would you accept some help from a stranger, ma'am?"

Mariah didn't quite trust her voice to be free of the tears, so she just nodded.

"I'll get that bull around. You bring that bunch up along the fence line." The cowboy reached for the neatly looped lariat that hung by his knee and nudged his horse into action.

She could see the difference in the herd immediately, even as she went about following the stranger's instructions. The cattle seemed to *know* they were at the mercy of a real drover. The roan's long legs let him and his rider out-maneuver the rangy longhorns. The man had the whole herd together in the amount of time it took Mariah to coax half a dozen sullen cows out of a corner.

"Now move out there on the left flank," the cowboy directed. "When I tell you, start making a lot of noise and wave that rope of yours around."

He whooped, and the herd started toward the break at a good clip, he and the roan working to keep them bunched tight. Mariah trotted her pony out along the left flank.

Just before the fence, the cowboy began cursing.

The storm of profanity brought Mariah to a standstill, but it galvanized the herd. The cattle bolted for the gap in the fence.

"Now," the cowboy yelled.

His order plus the sight of the bull, trying once more to break away, shocked Mariah into action. She hollered and swung the rope end toward the bull. Eyes rolling, the bull sheered away from her, hopped over the debris, and pounded away. Every cow and steer followed.

Mariah continued to shout as she and the sorrel chased the cattle across the open grassland. Her bonnet slipped back on her head, and out of the corner of her eye, she glimpsed the trampled corn. Her frustration boiled up, and running the cows off the corn just wasn't enough. She dug her heels into the sorrel's side and tore on after the longhorns, determined to drive them so far beyond Hoag property they'd never find their way back.

About the time they hit the far side of the nearest rise, she realized the cowboy was even with her, then passing her. She pushed her horse harder, and suddenly they were racing, the little sorrel against the big blue roan, Mariah against the stranger, just for the joy of the wind in her hair. The white-eyed cattle were briefly forgotten in the pounding of hooves against earth.

Then the man swung his mount away, and Mariah saw the bluff ahead. She whooped wildly one more time, and the cattle plunged down the ledge and into the deep grass below. She pulled the sorrel up short at the bluff's edge. The cattle bawled and struck out across the narrow valley, their horns scything through the tall bluestem and sunflowers, and toward a rooftop just visible on the far hill.

"Go on, you miserable creatures. Run right up on McKenzie's front porch." Mariah shouted the curse exultantly, the energy of the chase still rich in her blood. She shook her fist at the fleeing cattle, and then laughed with the sheer joy of victory. The sorrel did a little hop and settled down, his sweat-flaked sides heaving.

The roan turned a couple of tight circles as his rider brought him under control, then settled next to the sorrel. While the horses snuffled at each other, the cowboy pulled off his Stetson to mop at his forehead with his sleeve, revealing hair so black it shone with iridescence, like a blackbird's wings in the sun. "Not your herd, I take it."

"No, they're not, and if I find out McK . . ." Mariah stopped, suddenly conscious of the fact that she was talking to a stranger. This man might work for anyone, including John

McKenzie—though that didn't seem likely given the help she'd just received from him.

"You think you know who did it?" he asked.

"Maybe. But I won't make accusations until I know for sure."

"That's probably wise," he agreed. "Words can be pretty powerful."

"So I noticed."

To give the man credit, he tried to look guilty, but the crinkles around those pewter eyes told Mariah he was laughing at her again. He sat close enough that she could count those tiny lines: five on the right side, but only three on the left.

Probably from that cocky, crooked grin, Mariah thought.

"Sometimes you just have to cuss them to get them to move," he offered in explanation. "Especially when they're fresh off the trail like that bunch. However, you do have my apologies, ma'am."

"Miss," Mariah corrected automatically, then flushed at the way he lifted one eyebrow with interest.

She suddenly realized just how tall her rescuer was, sitting there on his big gelding, especially with her on the sorrel pony like some child. A touch of her heels and a gentle tug backed the sorrel away a half dozen steps, where she didn't have to tilt her head back so far to look up at the man. "Miss Mariah Hoag," she continued when she felt safe.

"Bay Jackson," he said.

"Well, Mr. Jackson. I'll accept your apology if you'll accept my thanks." Mariah turned her horse back toward the farm, and Bay reined his mount in alongside her.

"It was no trouble. And it's just plain Bay," he said conversationally.

Mariah let his over-familiarity hang in her silence, but for some reason, she found herself watching the slight movement of his knee and thigh as he rode. The gently worn canvas of his pants looked like it was molded over bronze, and he rode so closely that it seemed likely their legs might brush against each other. The idea didn't seem all that unattractive.

"How do you know they're fresh off the trail?" she asked, trying to distract herself.

"I've eaten my share of dust behind herds just like that one," he said. "Those cattle carry Texas brands and a fairly recent trail brand, but nothing that looked like a fresh local mark. By the way, I noticed a lot of ticks on them."

"Spanish fever," Mariah said, mostly to herself. Sounded like a McKenzie stunt all right. Now they'd have to keep their own cows well away from that field until after the first hard frost in the fall.

They soon reached the mangled field. Mariah dismounted, tied the sorrel to a section of the fence that still stood, and took a good look at the damage. It was both better and worse than she'd thought. Three full spans of her father's fence lay on the ground, two broken posts among the shattered boards, but much of the corn was only bent.

Bay Jackson swung off his horse and left him ground tethered. He straightened a stalk of corn, then used a booted toe to tamp a mound of earth around the base to hold it up.

"I thought cowboys didn't like farming," Mariah said.

"They don't, but rescuing fair maidens comes in a whole different category." He went on to a second plant, and Mariah quickly started on a row of her own. "Besides, I don't ride herd all the time."

"Oh? What do you do, then?"

"A little of this, a little of that. Some horse trading now and then. Whatever I get the urge to do. You're lucky. Another time or two through this field and there wouldn't have been enough corn left for the crows."

"Don't I know." She suddenly recalled the way he'd sat there, just laughing at her, and snapped, "You might have helped me sooner."

"You might have asked."

He was right, of course, and that didn't make it sit any better. Mariah grabbed the stub of a broken stalk and yanked it out of the ground.

It took them better than an hour to rescue what they could of the corn, and when they finished, Mariah surveyed the field with some sense of hope. With any luck, the propped plants would survive, but even if they didn't, they might still have a good crop—provided nothing else went wrong. She picked her way back over the broken fence. With Papa and Jimmy not due home for days, she'd have to put that right, which meant digging post holes. Her shoulders ached at the thought of it.

Bay caught up with her as she was about to mount and bent to give her a leg up. Mariah hesitated, then stepped into his laced fingers and swung into the worn saddle.

"Thank you, Mr. Jackson," she said to the top of his hat. "And thank you for the help with the cattle and all."

"You're welcome, Miss Hoag." The hat tilted back, and Mariah found herself staring down into his eyes, which weren't particularly far away considering how short her horse stood and how tall Bay Jackson was. That cockeyed grin spread over his face again, drawing her eyes to the firm curve of his lips. *If I was of a mind to,* she thought, *I could kiss him right on the mouth, just by leaning over a few inches.*

Good grief, what was she thinking? Mariah felt her cheeks warm to a red hot glow beneath his unwavering gaze. The only reasonable course was to get away from this man before she embarrassed herself completely. She wheeled her horse toward the house, but something inside her apparently didn't want to get away quite yet.

"We have a good well," she heard herself blurt. "You and your mount are welcome to as much water as you need before you go on."

"I think I'll take you up on that. Thank you, Miss Hoag," Bay said.

He was laughing at her again. Mariah was certain of it, even though she refused, absolutely refused, to so much as peek in his direction.

When they turned through the front gate a few moments later, Mariah groaned inwardly at the sight of her mother straightening her shawl. She'd forgotten about Mama being outside. Now she couldn't make up for her impulsiveness by hustling Bay to the pump and leaving him to fend for himself and be on his way.

So when they had the horses settled, she did the mannerly thing and led Bay over to her mother.

"Jackson." Acasta Hoag's face lit with interest as Mariah

introduced Bay. "A distinguished name in the part of the country from which we come. I don't suppose you're kin."

"No, ma'am. The General's no relation, more's the pity," Bay said. "My mother's people are from New Orleans, though. I'm sorry to intrude, but—"

"Hardly an intrusion when you were so much help. Would you like some lemonade? I'm afraid the lemons aren't very good, but our well water is sweet and cold."

"That sounds fine, ma'am. Thank you."

Acasta excused herself and Mariah, and the two women slipped into the tiny frame house.

Mariah dropped her voice to a whisper. "Mama, you can't—"

"Let's use the crystal and the good serving tray." Acasta opened the cracked glass door of the old corner cabinet that held the vestiges of another life. The hinges squeaked loudly from lack of use. "He seems like such a nice young man, and it's so good having callers."

"Mother—" Mariah began again, but then she saw the sparkle in her mother's eyes and she softened. "It is a treat, isn't it? I think Jimmy left a few ginger snaps. I'll set them out."

"That's my dear." Acasta leaned over and pressed a quick kiss to her daughter's cheek. "Now, please remove those pants. I don't want him thinking you're a hoyden."

He probably already did after that little race, but Mariah nodded. "Of course."

By the time Mariah put the tray together, she'd fallen into her mother's good spirits. In the old days—the days before the gray and blue uniforms had stormed back and forth over Virginia's hills—they'd had callers nearly every day. Mariah had only been a child, but she still remembered the elaborate tea cakes and the big silver service. Of course, they had visitors here in Kansas, too, just not so often, and always the same few neighbors, over and over. It was easy to understand her mother's excitement at having someone new to entertain.

Truth be told, Mariah admitted, she felt a certain excitement herself, a fact which didn't especially please her. She had no business getting all stirred up over a man who'd be riding off in an hour. Nonetheless, she blotted a damp cloth over her face to take the glow off, and gave her cheeks a quick pinch before she carried the tray outside and sat it on the stool by her mother's chair.

Over the tart lemonade, Mariah surreptitiously sized up Bay Jackson, trying to convince herself that there was no reason for her to react quite so strongly to him.

He certainly was handsome, no question of that, sitting there in the shade with his sun darkened cheeks and his carved, square jaw. He'd troubled himself to scrub up while they were getting the lemonade, and the cut crystal julep glasses her mother had insisted on using—the only three left from a huge set they'd once owned—didn't look out of place in his hand. He spoke well, ignoring that one outburst directed at the cattle, and under the coating of dust, his clothes and gear looked pretty fine, too.

Maybe too fine. If anything, he seemed a little too polished for the average cowhand.

Taking pride in himself doesn't make the man bad, another voice argued.

That would be Mama, Mariah thought—just like it had been Mama's words, drilled in for years, that had prompted Mariah to invite this stranger back to the house against her better judgement: "When in doubt, always choose to do the kind thing. And above all, be a lady."

Mama was always a lady. Mariah glanced at her mother's flaxen hair. Even here in Kansas, even ill, Acasta kept it neatly twisted into a chignon and caught in a crocheted net, a feat Mariah could never manage with her own wild, golden mane. Instead, the curls escaped every braid or ribbon in which she tried to contain them and swirled out in the near constant breeze that ruffled the tall grasses of the Flint Hills. No matter how hard Mariah tried, she always looked disheveled. Jimmy had once told her it was definitely not the hair of a lady.

Of course, the thoughts she'd been having about Bay Jackson would go to prove her brother's point. Very unladylike to think about kissing a total stranger.

"No, ma'am," Bay said in answer to one of Acasta's

questions. "I'm just passing through. I have a little business to take care of in the area, then I'll be headed out."

"Home?" Acasta asked.

"No, ma'am." Bay looked south across the gentle swell of prairie and his eyes narrowed a little. "Home is pretty much anywhere my friend and I throw our bedrolls down."

"What happened to that friend of yours, by the way?" Mariah asked. "I'm surprised he didn't join you for the laugh."

"*Mariah*." Acasta began to scold, but Bay interrupted.

"He was chuckling pretty hard as he left," he said with a grin. "Actually, he offered to help, but I sent him on. I figured a woman on her own wouldn't be happy seeing two strange men riding down on her. We didn't see any menfolk around, and I didn't want to frighten you."

Acasta nodded thoughtfully. "That was considerate of you. I am always concerned when we're here alone. Mr. Hoag and my son won't be back until next week sometime."

"You shouldn't leave your fence down that long," Bay said. "If whoever owns those longhorns doesn't round them up, they may come back looking for easy pickings."

"I can fix it," Mariah said. Really, she wished her mother hadn't told a complete stranger there would be no men around for a week or more. Especially not this stranger.

"It seems we always have such problems when Cornelius goes off," Acasta said. "I just don't know what we'd do if anything else happened to our crop."

"I'd be happy to come by tomorrow and put your fence up for you," Bay offered.

"We couldn't ask you to do that," Mariah said. "Honestly, I can fix it. My brother and I did most of the work to begin with."

After the trouble she'd had with those few cows, she didn't want the man thinking she was totally useless. And she *could* fix it. She had before.

"It concerns me so, not having a man on the property," Acasta continued. "You know, I thought I heard a wolf last night."

"It was just a coyote, Mother, and it was a good two or three miles off."

"As long as I've been here, they still make the shivers run up and down my spine," Acasta said. She looked out over the hills, her eyebrows knitted in a frown. "If we could just hire someone on for a few days. Are you looking for work, Mr. Jackson?"

Oh, Lord, no. Mariah straightened with a start. Couldn't her mother see the kind of man Bay Jackson was, the way he looked at her? "Mama, we can't, he has business. You heard him."

"It would just be until your father comes back. My mind would be so much more at ease."

"We don't have the money to pay anyone," Mariah argued.

Bay leaned toward her mother. "I'll work for bed and board, provided I can have a few hours free when I want for my own business."

Acasta brightened immediately, even as Mariah blanched. The idea of having the man around for nigh onto a week made every nerve in her body jangle with an uncomfortable mix of anticipation and warning.

"We'd be most grateful, Mr. Jackson. You'll have to sleep in the barn, of course, but we set a hearty table. And you can have whatever time you need for yourself, provided you're around at night."

"Sounds fair. I'd better go catch up to my friend and let him know I'll be staying here for a few days." Bay rose and made motions to go. "Thank you for the lemonade and cookies, ladies. I'll be back at sunup."

"Not this evening?" Acasta sounded disappointed.

"I doubt I can arrange things with my friend and still get back before dark. But I promise I'll be at work first thing in the morning."

He took a moment to check over his horse, lifting one stirrup to snug up the girth.

When her mother began gathering the glasses onto the tray, Mariah sidled over towards Bay. "You don't have to do this," she whispered.

"I know." He flipped the stirrup down and turned to face her, a slight lift to one corner of his mouth. He shifted his weight forward a fraction, so his breath, faintly lemony, fanned her cheeks and lips. "I want to."

He didn't even touch her, yet it felt like somebody had lit a match in her middle. For an instant, Mariah stood there, shocked by the sudden intensity of whatever the sensation was. She didn't have a name to put to it. All she knew was that it frightened and excited her all in one rush.

"You'll eat breakfast with us, then," Acasta said from her place in the shade.

"Yes, ma'am." Bay swung up into his saddle. The horse nickered at his sudden weight. "See you ladies tomorrow. Good bye, ma'am." He tilted the brim of his hat with one finger. "Miss Hoag."

As Mariah watched the roan's ground-eating lopes carry him out of sight, a bark drew her attention toward the barn. She hustled over to the lean-to and pushed the door open. Clyde came bounding out, ears cocked forward and tail wagging furiously, and Mariah bent down to give him a pat and the promised apology.

"You're still worthless, you know," she added, smiling, when he licked her hand. She rose and returned to where her mother sat happily in her rocker.

"That Mr. Jackson is a nice young gentleman," Acasta said, before Mariah could get a word out. "Good manners, and a pleasant way about him. There's always a special manner to people from New Orleans."

Mariah flicked a spice-scented crumb from the tea towel that covered the tray and kept her tongue. He hadn't said *he* was from New Orleans, he'd said his mother's people were. And whatever her mother thought, cowboys were not southern gentlemen, especially not this drifter—no matter if he did say ma'am and take off his hat to be introduced, no matter if he did have family in Louisiana and a trace of Dixie sang in the deep drawl of his voice.

Besides, she'd clearly seen him wink at her as he'd ridden off.

Serendipity, that's what it was.

Bay grinned to himself and turned Cajun to follow Eli's tracks along the creek.

He'd been thinking things might go a little smoother if he could check out the mood in the area and the Hoag farm looked ideal: far enough from any neighbors that no one was likely to spot him, but with two decent sources of gossip sitting right there. They might not get many visitors, but Bay would bet a dollar to a dime that they squeezed every drop of news out of the ones they did get.

It also hadn't escaped him that Miss Mariah Hoag apparently held strong opinions about John McKenzie. In fact, the possibility of getting her to tell him just what mischief the old man had been up to in the past dozen years had been an added inducement to hire on.

The real attraction, though, was those quick, emerald eyes. He thought he'd seen something like desire in them, almost from the start, but those last few moments had been the corker. She might as well have asked him to kiss her—and he might as well enjoy himself while he reconnoitered.

Bay grinned again. Yep, he very much wanted to find out if the woman held as much promise as her eyes seemed to. And in return for a pleasant and informative week, he vowed to himself, he'd give the Hoags fair value in his work.

A thin line of smoke curled skyward between the cottonwood leaves about a quarter of a mile ahead. That would be Eli boiling up some coffee.

He would get a kick out of how neatly things had worked out, Bay thought.

They had some planning to do and the extra horses to get rid of, but all in all, this had turned out to be a fine afternoon.

Damned fine.

Yep, serendipity.

Chapter Two

TRUE TO HIS word, Bay Jackson rode through the gate at first light, just as Mariah headed out, lantern in hand, to milk the cow. Her stomach knotted at the sight of him. She'd been hoping he'd change his mind and just keep riding on with his friend—that is, part of her had hoped. The rest of her ignored the subtle currents of danger that eddied from the man and stood there smiling softly in the half light.

With the dawn sky behind him, he was hardly more than a shadow, like the delicate, old cut paper silhouette portraits of Grandmother and Grandfather Hoag that hung over her bed— except that this silhouette, all hard angles and carved features, was far from delicate, and its eyes picked up the glow of the lantern's light to give the shadow life. Mariah felt gooseflesh run down her arms, and they had nothing to do with the morning chill.

Tail low and ears back, Clyde scurried between his mistress and the stranger.

"Hush," Mariah scolded at the dog's low, warning growl. Then she added under her breath, "Why in blazes didn't you get brave yesterday and save us all some trouble?" She grabbed the scruff of Clyde's neck and held him while Bay dismounted.

Bay tied his horse to a post and reached under the flap of one saddlebag to pull something out before he approached. A few feet from Mariah, he stopped and tugged one leather glove off, then squatted down and held his bare hand out to the dog. "Come here, fellow. I've got a little jerky for you. I'm not going to hurt you."

Clyde sniffed at the air then dropped to his belly. Mariah let him go, and he crawled over to investigate the newcomer and his offering. The jerky disappeared with a chew and a gulp.

"That's a boy," Bay said, but when he reached to scratch the pup's ear, Clyde nipped at his hand and dodged away a few feet. There he stood, wagging his tail apologetically, looking at Bay like he expected another handout.

"I'm sorry, did he bite you?"

"No." Bay glanced at Mariah. "He just can't decide if he likes me or not. He must be your dog."

That grin again. Blast the man. Mariah could only hope that he thought the color in her cheeks came from the glow of sunrise that reddened the eastern horizon. A pained *moo* from the direction of the barn gave her the excuse she needed to leave.

"I've got to do the milking." She picked up the pail and started backing toward the barn. "You can put your horse in the stock pen and your gear in the barn. The tools are mostly in the shed, and I think Papa has some extra posts and board in there, too. I'll have breakfast ready in about an hour. It'd be a help if you could draw some water, but just set it by the door and please don't wake my mother. She had a bad night."

Having said all that needed to be said, she turned to make her escape.

"Good morning to you, too, Miss Hoag." Bay's low chuckle followed her into the barn, gently mocking, yet bringing an unwilling smile to Mariah's lips as she lifted the lantern onto the iron hook by the door.

She led the cow out of her box stall and snubbed her up to a post in the lantern's circle of light, then plunked the milking stool at the animal's side. The cow's rear foot came up with a jerk and a kick, and the stool sailed past Mariah's shin. It landed with a thunk against the wall.

"Hush, Peach, hush. Hush, sweet thing, that was my fault." Mariah crooned to the cow as she fetched the stool back. "I didn't tell you what I was doing." She dropped her voice to a conspiratorial whisper and leaned toward the cow's ear. "That Bay Jackson has me all discombobulated. He's about the handsomest man I ever saw, and when he looks at me . . ."

Mariah shook herself. "I swear, I get the most outlandish thoughts about the man."

The cow gave her a wise, brown-eyed stare and *moo*ed.

"You're right," Mariah said, brushing a piece of straw off the cow's nose. "He's a drifter, and that probably means he's no good. But I vow, I'm glad he'll only be here a few days. He can't cause much trouble in that short time. Besides, Mama's around."

Feeling much relieved by this bit of logic, Mariah stroked the cow's silky flank and moved quietly into position on the milking stool. She pulled the pail around and rubbed her hands briskly to warm them, then reached down, patted the cow's bulging udder, and curled her fingers around the long teats. "There we go. See, he didn't make me forget everything. We'll be just fine."

"Lands, but I hate cooking once summer comes. The house just gets too hot. I feel like a steamed oyster." Mariah set the plates on the table she'd dragged outside in the shade, then mopped at her forehead and cheeks with the hem of her apron.

"I'm sorry, child," her mother said. "If I was up to it . . ."

"I didn't mean it that way, Mama. I just hope we can add on a separate kitchen soon."

"At least we have good shade around here on the side."

Mariah nodded. She could see Bay's yellow shirt at the far end of the field as he set a fence post into place. She'd been watching him all morning between chores, enjoying the safety of distance. Now the sun stood high, and the ham hocks and beans were cooked so tender they about fell apart, and she had to call him in for lunch.

Kind of like calling the serpent out of the tree in Eden, Mariah thought, like asking to be tempted. She reached for the bar to sound the dinner bell and gave the triangle three sharp whacks. Bay waved in answer and started for the house.

Mariah braved the heat once more to fill plates for Bay and her mother. On a day this warm, they didn't need the whole kettle of beans sitting in front of them, steaming away. She carried them to the table and went back for her own food. She ducked into the house just as Bay came around the corner of the barn. Just that glimpse of him set her pulse thumping in her ears.

Out of self-protection, Mariah loitered in the blistering heat. Her plate sat, full, on the warming shelf until she thought surely Bay must be at the table, sitting next to her mother where he could do no damage. Her gathered apron made a convenient pot holder for the scorching metal plate, and she darted out into the relative cool of the noon sun.

Unfortunately, Bay stepped back from the washbowl just as she passed. She avoided a collision, but bubbling juice from the beans slopped over the edge of the plate and splashed onto his left side.

"Ow. Damn!" Bay ripped his shirttail out and twisted to get it away from his skin. "Criminintly, that burns."

Mariah slammed the plate down next to the wash bowl and grabbed the pitcher. She sloshed the contents over Bay, soaking him from shoulder to boot.

His eyes widened with shock, then a pained sort of humor. "Well, that's cool enough."

"I'm sorry." Mariah began blotting at his sleeve with her apron. "I can't believe I did that. I'm so sorry."

"Are you all right, Mr. Jackson?" Acasta called from the table.

"Fine, ma'am." Bay backed away, still holding his shirt out from his body. "Or at least I will be when I get into some dry clothes. Why don't you let that dinner cool down a little while I change. I don't think I can stand a burnt tongue, too."

"Bring those things back and I'll launder them tomorrow," Mariah said. "I'm so sorry."

She apologized again when Bay reappeared in a fresh blue shirt and canvas pants, but he waved it off and started his dinner. It was Acasta who noticed him wince when he handed his empty plate to Mariah at the end of the meal.

"Lift your shirt," she ordered, and Mariah recognized the tone of voice that had cowed her and James into swallowing a dose of kerosene and molasses each spring for years. Bay looked at Acasta, then Mariah. He lifted his shirt.

"Please get the salve and some binding, Mariah dear," Acasta instructed, her voice once again genteel.

Mariah stood there, staring at the muscles that rippled down Bay's side and across the stretch of ribs and belly that the raised shirt exposed. She'd never seen that part of a man naked before. Papa wouldn't think of undressing where she could see him, and even Jimmy kept his back to her when he had to change his shirt in her presence—at least he had since he got big enough to think himself a man—and he usually had his undershirt on anyway.

So she stared, completely fascinated by the lean, taut flesh. A minute passed before she became aware of the angry pink burn discoloring a palm size patch at Bay's waist.

"Mariah," Acasta repeated. "Hurry, child."

Mariah started, her gaze shifting guiltily. She spun away before her mother noticed what she'd been doing.

When she returned with the pot of goose grease and yarrow, however, Bay gave her a look that told her *he'd* noticed. She stared hard at the back of her mother's head and tried not to see anything else to fuel her imagination.

Fortunately, it only took Acasta a few minutes to grease and bandage the burn, and Bay refused to be coddled. Mariah fussed with re-rolling the strips of bandage until he left to go back out to the fence, then she sank onto a stool.

That was it, she resolved. If she was going to make an ass of herself every time the man was around, she'd just avoid him as much as possible. And she'd never, *never*, let him catch her anywhere alone. No telling what she might do—or let him do.

It would be unutterably stupid to let herself get caught up with a drifter. She'd just keep that in mind every time he gave her that look. Besides, she reminded herself, he'd only be here a few days, then he'd be gone.

The sun came up the next morning in an ill temper, and by noon the metal rivets on Bay's canvas pants had heated to the point where they scorched his skin, like he was sitting too close to a fire instead of digging post holes on a June day. Even the dark cloth of his shirt felt fiery against the tender patch on his side. He'd stripped off the bandage that morning when the wrapping of linen got uncomfortably warm. Now he wished he had it back, to provide a buffer between himself and the hot blue cloth. Maybe he'd ask for a new one when he went in for dinner.

Maybe this time Mariah would do the wrapping. He grinned to himself.

Getting burned last night had almost been worth it, just to catch that look in Mariah's eyes while her mother bandaged him. It was the same expression he'd seen when she'd looked down at him after they'd run off the longhorns, all female and self-aware.

Bay stabbed the post hole digger into the ground and heard a metallic clang. Swearing mildly, he poked around, trying to find the rock's edges to see how big a problem he faced. He heard a noise and glanced up just in time to catch Mariah coming up between the rows, frowning.

"You didn't come for the bell," she said curtly.

Bay straightened, wiped the sweat off his forehead with his sleeve, and enjoyed a long look at Mariah. Lord, she was pretty. Not in the fashionable way, what with her broad, high cheeks and squarish jaw, but in a way that belonged with this land. Strong as most men, from the work she did. Proud. With that untamed hair and skin all gold and pink where the sun touched her.

"I wanted to get this post in before I stopped," he said. "You didn't have to bring dinner out."

"Mama was afraid you'd starve." The aroma of fried ham drifted out of the basket in Mariah's hand, and she held it out to him. "Besides, she feels guilty, knowing we're not paying you. She says she'll understand if you want to move on as soon as the fence is done."

"Does she, now?" Bay stepped closer and looked straight down at her. "Don't take offense, but I don't believe you."

Mariah bristled. "Are you calling me a liar?"

"Tsk, tsk. Not exactly. I just think you're the one offering to let me go. I make you nervous, Miss Hoag."

"Rubbish." Color flared in Mariah's cheeks, and she thrust the basket into his hands. "What's taking you so long with this, anyway? I thought you'd have it done yesterday."

"So did I, but I found a couple more posts loose. I thought

DRIFTER'S MOON

I might as well set them right. It will save you trouble down the road."

Mariah shifted awkwardly. "Thank you."

Bay made no comment, but carried the basket over next to the big oak bucket full of water he'd hauled out for himself early that morning. He tipped the bucket to spill some water over his grimy hands and scrubbed them vigorously, then splashed his face. The cool water only took the surface dirt off, but at least the remaining layer of thin mud felt cooler.

After drying off with the big red kerchief from around his neck, Bay sat down, settled with his back against the heavy limestone post that marked the corner of the field, and opened up the basket. "Ham, potatoes, new carrots in butter, hush puppies. Looks good. A man can hardly claim to be underpaid on this job."

Mariah didn't say anything, but the ghost of a smile showed Bay she received the honest compliment well. She proceeded to stand there—much too long for manners—watching him drape his kerchief for a lap cloth and organize his meal. He saw the exact instant it dawned on her that she was staring again. Lips thin, she whirled and started to stomp off toward the house.

"Mariah."

It was the first time he'd said her name, and the single, quiet word stopped her between the rows of corn. She stood there, her back to Bay, waiting.

"Sit and talk to me while I eat." He made his tone half request, half command.

It worked. Mariah chose to perch on the remains of an old cottonwood stump, near his outstretched legs. Clearly skittish, she pulled her feet in close, and tucked her skirt around her legs so neatly he could see only the worn toes of her black shoes. The position put her eyes just at his level. She squinted at the sun, which burned down on the top of her head.

"I should have worn my bonnet," she muttered, raising a hand to shade her face.

"Wear this." Bay leaned over and popped his Stetson onto her head.

"Oh, I can't." Mariah removed the hat, but Bay dug into his

meal and refused to take the Stetson back. After a time, she gave in, shrugged, and put the hat back on gingerly. Being too big, it settled low on her forehead, its wide brim providing more than enough shade. "Thank you. Again. I seem to be saying that a lot."

Between mouthfuls, Bay traced a circle over the plate with his fork. "You're a good cook, Mariah Hoag."

"I had to learn young," she said. "After Mama took sick."

"What's wrong with her?"

"The doctor isn't sure. Maybe too much strain. She's kind of . . . fragile."

Plain sickly was more like it—possibly consumptive. Bay had already seen just how much of the farm's back-breaking work fell on Mariah's shoulders, and not just the women's work, either. Maybe it wasn't so bad when her father and brother were home, but he suspected she still worked too hard. Unless life brought her some relief, she'd wind up like her mother, worn out and sickly.

"How did you folks come to settle here?"

"We got burnt out," she said simply, and it was explanation enough. Burnt out, taxed out, or otherwise Reconstructed out, whatever the particulars, the West was thick with displaced Rebs, despite the loyalty clause in the Homestead Act. It might keep Confederates and sympathizers from filing for free land, but it didn't keep them from buying some. He'd heard the story a hundred times, but he listened to Mariah's version thoughtfully. "It kind of broke Mama's health," she said. "Papa thought she'd do better if we started fresh someplace. As soon as he could fix things, we headed west."

"He picked a hell of a place for a farm."

"He said it didn't matter if Kansas was a free state as long as there was land we could afford."

Bay laughed. "I can see his point, but what I meant was, the Flint Hills raise better cattle than corn."

"We do fine."

"The last time I was around these parts, Jack McKenzie was running his stock up this way."

"Maybe, but he hadn't bothered to file on it or pre-empt it. We filed and then we paid up, so it's ours. Ours. Nobody's going to make us move again, ever." Mariah's voice suddenly shook with fury.

"Whoa, whoa. Nobody said you had to."

Mariah stared down at her hands. Bay realized she had her nails dug into her palms. She took a pair of deep breaths to calm herself, and Bay leaned forward a little, his face intent. This was the sort of thing he was after. "McKenzie's trying to run you off, isn't he?"

She looked up, suspicion in her bright emerald eyes. "Do you work for him?"

"No." Bay looked her straight in the eye, relieved that he could say it truthfully. So far, he'd scrupulously avoided saying anything untrue to these people, especially Mariah. "I don't. I wouldn't work for anyone who could make you that mad."

She considered him a long moment, then sighed. Her hands relaxed, and Bay saw the whitish crescents where she'd pressed her nails into her palms. "We've been here since '66, and he's been trying to run us off ever since. He still calls us squatters, and in his mind that justifies everything."

"What's he done?" *This time*, Bay added to himself.

"He started off threatening us, driving his cattle across the fields, having his men sit out on the hill watching, that sort of thing. We lost a couple of horses. Then there was stray gunfire that just missed Papa and Jimmy out in the field one time. The second year, there was a wildfire that took out most everything except the house and barn. We're not sure he caused it, but between the natural troubles and the ones McKenzie caused, poor Mama never even had a chance to get better. When he realized we wouldn't scare off, he started trying to aggravate us out, doing every picky-ass little thing he can think of." Mariah clapped her hand over her mouth. "Mama would have a fit if she heard me use such language."

"Fortunately, I'm not your Mama, and I've heard women use worse."

"*Women*, not ladies," Mariah noted, but then she smiled that little quarter smile of hers again. "I keep trying to be a lady for Mama's sake, but it doesn't always work. Oh, my, I shouldn't say things like that, either. But you are easy to talk to, Mr. Jackson."

It occurred to Bay that the only time he'd seen her laugh or even smile full out was when they'd run off the cattle. He swore silently at the kind of life that could make a young woman so miserly with her smiles.

"Anyway, over the years, we've had every kind of so-called bad luck you can imagine, from broken wagon axles to missing mail orders. I have chased cows and pigs all over these hills. Papa had to take a bank loan just to make repairs last fall—that's the mortgage. And now this. . . ." She looked down the fence line. "We put the fence up in the first place because he wouldn't see to his cows, but this makes the fourth time it's been knocked down. Three thousand acres just isn't enough for him."

"You're sure McKenzie's behind it all?"

"If you mean, are we going-to-the-sheriff sure? No. That's partly why I didn't want to say anything out loud the other day. But as far as knowing he did it, well if he didn't, I'd be surprised. Besides, we're not the only ones, or even the first. According to what we've heard, he used the drought back in '60 to take over a couple of places. He's got the best spring in this part of the county—never slacked off a day—and he didn't share even when people started going thirsty."

Bay nodded. He remembered all too clearly. "Doesn't sound like he's too popular."

"Neither were his boys. Chips off the old block, folks say. I think they must have beat up every boy in the area before they ran off to the war. Anyway, McKenzie's still greedy with water, uses it to get his way. Papa had to hire a lawyer from Topeka to get our water rights straightened out. That's where part of the mortgage money went, and even so, we only got about a tenth of what we're entitled to. Papa says it's because we're Confederate and the water board's all Yankees. About the worst thing, though, at least for Mama, is the drummers. The only ones who stop are the ones who haven't been by McKenzie's first, which is hardly any. I think he pays them not to come."

"No wonder your mother was so anxious to pour lemonade down my throat." Bay popped a hush puppy in his mouth and chewed thoughtfully. "Your nearest neighbors are what two, three miles off?"

"Old Mr. Quincy's place is about that, but it's not just how far, it's how many. One of us walks over to Birley for the mail once a week, but there are only a half dozen people that ever get around to visit. We hardly ever see anyone different unless we get over to Bazaar or up to Cottonwood Falls, and with Mama sick so much . . . well, if you hadn't finagled a job first, she might have tied you to the chair just for fresh company." Mariah stared toward the house a long moment. "You wouldn't know it looking at this place, but we used to have one of the prettiest houses around Martinsville, and Mama was a very popular hostess. She kept the house filled with flowers and people and . . . and, well, things were different."

Bay's mind wandered to another house, also filled with flowers and life. Different. So different, it hardly seemed like the same lifetime.

"It was a long time ago," Mariah said, echoing his thoughts. Suddenly she looked embarrassed, as if uncomfortable that she'd said so much. She waved off the memories that neither of them needed or wanted. "Sounds silly doesn't it, what with flowers growing all over the hills this time of year? It just seems like there isn't enough time to pick them." She jumped up and brushed her skirts off. "In fact, I shouldn't waste any more time out here. I've only got the ironing half done, and I've still got hoeing to do. And I want to put up some green plums to use in place of olives."

Bay shook himself out of his reverie and set his plate aside, then stood up, too. "So you think McKenzie brought those longhorns around to add to your trouble."

"We're well east of the line," Mariah pointed out, referring to the quarantine that tried to keep Texas cattle and their tick fever away from the more susceptible farm livestock. "Someone brought them here on purpose, and I can't think of anyone more likely—McKenzie runs a longhorn cross that he claims is immune to the fever. Besides, something made them push through that fence. That corn hasn't even begun to set ears yet. Why would they want it?"

Bay shrugged. "There's no accounting for what a longhorn wants. Tell you what. I'm taking some time tomorrow to take care of a few things. I can nose around, see if I can find out where those animals belong. Maybe McKenzie is behind it and maybe not, but at least you'll know for sure."

"That'd be fine. Just don't say anything in front of my mother. She gets upset every time she hears the name McKenzie anymore, and she doesn't need that." Mariah edged away, but Bay followed her. He stopped her with a touch on her arm and she turned. With his hat on, she had to tilt her head back to look up at him, which put her in the perfect position to be kissed, a situation he hadn't calculated, but decided to use to his advantage. He trailed his fingers up her arm and over her shoulder until he found the soft skin just above her collar. She gasped, her lips parting enticingly, and he lowered his head.

As he did, a flash of shadow and light on the hill caught his attention. Bay glanced sideways, then froze, inches from his goal.

"What the . . . ?" Bay stared toward the road, shaking his head in disbelief. "Naw, it can't be."

"What?" she asked.

"I think I've been out in the sun too long." He shook his head again. The figure was still there, barrelling straight down the hill toward them. "It looks to me like Thor the Thunder God is riding over the hill on the biggest damned war horse I've ever seen."

Mariah whirled out of Bay's grasp. "Nikolai."

"Who?"

"Nikolai Jensen. He's . . . he's a friend."

And the size of two. Bay gaped as the blond giant slid down off the big, dappled draft horse that he rode like a saddle pony. The man must have been close to seven feet tall, a full head taller than Bay himself—and a tremendous head it was, too, one that fit the rest of the towering body. It didn't take a professor to spot Nikolai's frown through his full reddish blond beard and mustache, or to realize what, or rather who, caused it.

Mariah gave Nikolai one of her quick, faint smiles.

"Who is he?" Nikolai demanded bluntly, his heavy accent thick with disapproval.

"Our hired man," Mariah explained, still a little breathless from the almost-kiss. "Just until Papa's home. Some cattle knocked the fence down, and we needed some help. Mama wanted someone around."

And so did you, Bay thought as Mariah studiously avoided his gaze.

He smiled blandly and extended a hand to Nikolai. "Bay Jackson."

"Nikolai Jensen. I am courting Mariah. Two years now." He took Bay's hand and bore down hard.

Bay dipped his chin a fraction, acknowledging the warning, and a note of amusement flickered across his face. He tightened his grip a notch and watched Nikolai frown.

A smith, Bay judged, or maybe a mason, by the size of the man's fist and the calluses lining his palm. He squeezed a little harder. Both men's knuckles turned white. Bay kept his gaze fixed on Nikolai's face, watching for the slightest sign this show would go further.

"Nikolai," Mariah said sharply, and the Norwegian's hold slackened immediately. Bay retrieved his numbed fingers and felt them tingle as the blood ran back in. "What are you doing here in the middle of the week? Did something happen at the quarry?"

Stone cutter. Bay mentally patted himself on the back.

"I asked Mr. Clements for part of the day special. There is something I must tell you and your mama."

"Then you'd better walk me to the house. I was going anyway."

No you weren't. You were going to let me kiss you. Bay wondered if she let Thor kiss her. Maybe so. Maybe she let him do more. That could explain why a man would bother to court a woman for two years without marrying her.

Nikolai glared at Bay, then at Mariah—at her head, more specifically.

His hat. Lord, no wonder the brute was ready to arm wrestle him. Bay had to hold back a laugh as Mariah ripped the hat off and practically threw it at him.

"Thank you very much for the loan," she said quickly. "There are a few cookies in the bottom of the basket, so I'll leave it for now. Please remember to bring it back."

* * *

How could she have forgotten Nikolai?

Mariah asked herself the same question over and over as he walked her back to the house, his horse clumping along behind. He'd ridden over every second Saturday for two years and she'd enjoyed his company. They all did, just as they all counted on him for his help and advice. He cared enough for her to forfeit most of a day's wages to bring some kind of news, yet she hadn't given him a solitary thought since Bay Jackson had started cussing cattle.

She spent most of the walk back once more telling Nikolai why they'd hired Bay. Her explanation just made him more agitated.

"You should have sent a message to me," Nikolai grumbled. He glanced back at the field where Bay worked, a distant blue form against the green. "I would fix your fence, you know this."

"You have your own work to do," Mariah said reasonably. It sounded hollow, even to her. After years spent cutting stone, Nikolai Jensen could probably handle the work on three farms plus the quarry without breaking a sweat, provided the sun stayed up long enough. He should have been the first person to come to mind when they needed help.

"So you have this stranger to do it," he said. "This is not good, I think. Tell him to go, and I will do any work you need."

"Mama already promised him bed and board. She won't go back on that now."

"I will talk to her," Nikolai said.

He talked and talked, in the thick Norwegian accent that ten years in America had barely touched, but it did little good. Acasta Hoag might be sickly, but she could be stubborn as a jenny mule when the mood hit her. To Mariah's relief, Nikolai didn't mention to her mother what he'd seen between her and Bay, which made her think he'd noticed nothing awry but the hat. He subsided into an incomprehensible grumble.

Acasta patted his hand. "There, now, what's brought you out here this time of the week?"

"I asked for today to have off. There has been trouble. I

knew Mr. Hoag and Jim went to Wichita, and I thought you should hear, so you be careful."

"Nikolai, hurry up and get it out before you give Mama the vapors." Mariah stood up and fanned her mother, who had blanched.

"I am sorry, Mrs. Hoag." Concern creased Nikolai's ruddy face. "There was a robbery down by Matfield Green, two nights ago. They took three horses from Creelors."

"How awful. Was anyone hurt?" Mariah asked.

"No, but they scared Mrs. Creelor bad, so she takes to her bed. I am worried for you, so I asked to have the time to come see all is good. You will keep your animals close, yes, so no one sees them and thinks they are easy to steal."

"That's probably a good idea. We'll tell Mr. Jackson to take care of that," Acasta said, apparently oblivious to Nikolai's discomfort over Bay's presence. "And I will ask him to be sure to keep his rifle handy."

Once again, he frowned toward the field where Bay worked. "I guess maybe it's good he is here, so you are not alone," he admitted.

Mariah deflected the conversation to more usual topics, both for her mother's sake and to appease Nikolai. The ironing lay untouched while she took the afternoon to sit with her beau—not that she minded avoiding the chore, in this heat. She invited Nikolai to stay for supper, as he usually did when he visited on Saturdays, but he made excuses about the long ride home and having to be back at the quarry early the next morning. He left before Bay came in from the fields, with a reminder that he'd next see her for Independence Day in Cottonwood Falls.

"I swear," her mother said, watching Nikolai go. "He makes such a sight on that horse of his. They're both so huge. I never can get over it."

"Bay said he looked like Thor on a charger."

Acasta considered the idea, then smiled. "Thor had longer hair, I think, but Nikolai does have that big hammer. I wonder if he'd carry it in a pageant if we could get the smith to make him one of those helmets with the horns." She smiled at her own flight of fancy. "Let's see about supper."

*   *   *

Bay not only brought the basket back, he brought it back full of flowers: an armload of purple coneflowers he must have waded into the prairie grass to hunt. He handed the bouquet to Acasta with a flourish and a pretty word—and a meaningful glance in Mariah's direction.

"I used to have a bonnet just this color," Acasta said as she arranged some of the flowers in the big, blue-speckled enamel pitcher. "You do know how to make an old woman smile, Mr. Jackson."

But Mariah understood he meant them as much for her as for her mother. Long after Bay had excused himself to go bed down in the barn and Acasta had dozed off over a book, Mariah sat in the dim glow of a candle and let their wild scent wash over her.

Bay disappeared the next day before noon with barely a word of explanation and certainly nothing that gave any indication of the business that drew him away. As she finished the ironing and canned the plums, Mariah tried to concentrate on Nikolai and on her relief that she didn't have to face Bay for a few hours, but every sound made her glance toward the gate to see if he'd come back.

When twilight shadowed the prairie hills with purple and charcoal and he still hadn't returned, Mariah left his stew on the warming shelf over the stove and went to sit with her mother in the cooling breeze.

A distant yipping coyote deepened the furrows between Acasta's brows.

"He'll be back, Mama."

Acasta settled back and nodded in rhythm with the rocker, but they both sat there in the gathering dark, planning the next day's chores, until the shadow of a horse appeared beyond the gate. Mariah thought of Nikolai's warning and reached for the cool blue barrel of the shotgun that leaned just inside the door.

"It's me, ladies," Bay called out through the dark. "Sorry I'm late."

"No trouble at all, Mr. Jackson," Acasta said. "Mariah set aside a plate for you."

"I appreciate that."

Mariah started to rise, but Bay waved her off. "That's all right, I'll get it myself." He turned the roan toward the corral. "It's safer."

Mariah groaned. "You're not going to let me forget that, are you?" she called out after him.

"Nope."

It took Bay a good quarter of an hour to water and feed the roan and get him settled, during which time Mariah and her mother moved inside. With the fire dying back and the door and windows open, the house was nearly bearable. Mariah laid out his supper, then pulled out the new sprigged muslin dress she was making to finish some of the hand work. As Bay tucked into his supper like he hadn't eaten all day, Mariah and her mother consulted over the fancy pleating. Bay finally slowed down on second helpings.

"You mentioned you have family in New Orleans," Acasta said. "Have your travels ever taken you down that way?"

"I was actually born there," Bay answered. "Have you ever visited the city?"

"Just once, many, many years ago," Acasta said.

Mariah looked up from the pleats and gave her mother a quizzical look. "I didn't know that."

"It was before your father and I married. Your grandmother thought I might find better prospects away from Charlottesville— that's where I was brought up, Mr. Jackson—and she was afraid Cornelius would turn up if we didn't go quite a way off."

"Papa courted you that hard?"

"Yes, indeed, child. Mother wanted to ship me to France, but Father wouldn't allow it. They compromised on New Orleans." Acasta's eyes twinkled with remembered adventure. "Cornelius turned up there within a week."

"Papa followed you clear to Louisiana? How romantic. Why haven't you ever told Jimmy and me about this?"

"Children don't need to know their parents' youthful indiscretions. Your brother especially doesn't need wild ideas in his head. I keep expecting him to run off as it is."

"How old is your son?" Bay asked.

"Seventeen. I'm afraid he doesn't appreciate farm life. All he can think of is heading farther west."

"He has gold fever," Mariah added for Bay's benefit.

"He's not the only boy who can make that claim," Bay said, and suddenly the conversation took off in a new direction. He kept them entertained for better than an hour with stories of fortunes found and lost in the rowdy gold camps of the Rockies.

Mariah stitched while she listened and watched, and she had a sudden hunch that he'd been one of the lucky ones. Not once did he say "I found gold," but the energy in his hands as he told the stories made her suspect he had, as did the recollection of the expensive saddle and gear that rested in the barn. The longer his stories stretched, the more they told her something else, too—he seldom stayed in one place for long.

"Well," said Acasta at last. "It all sounds so very dangerous and exciting. I do hope you'll keep all this to yourself when my son, James, is about."

"That I will, ma'am, if I even run into him," Bay said. He yawned heartily and rose. "I'd better excuse myself and let you get some rest. Good night, ladies."

As it had the past two nights, the house seemed to diminish when he walked out the door, turn smaller and duller, and the women quickly headed for bed. Mariah brushed out her mother's cornsilk hair and braided it for the night, then helped her settle into bed with her book and her spoonful of medicine.

Outside, a familiar, metallic squeak told her Bay was at the pump.

Acasta glanced up from her reading. "Why don't you go out and get the water for morning while Mr. Jackson has the pump primed?"

Mariah turned away before her mother could see how much the idea pleased her. She told herself it was because she'd been waiting for the chance to ask Bay what he'd found out about the longhorns.

"I'll be right back." Mariah slipped out the door, leaving it cracked a few inches just to be safe. The squeaking stopped, and the splash of water into the bucket trailed off.

She could just make out Bay in the wedges of lantern light

that leaked out the door and around the curtains, and she almost wished she couldn't. He looked dark and lean and dangerous, standing there by the wall waiting for her, every bit the opposite of fair Nikolai.

While he filled her bucket, Mariah asked her question quickly, in a murmur that wouldn't carry back into the house.

"The cattle aren't McKenzie's," Bay answered. "It turned out they belong to a fellow a little south of here, at least that's where I found them. It seems one of your neighbors decided he'd just ignore the quarantine line. He wasn't very pleased to have me nosing around. I pointed out you all weren't very happy either. He promised to get his animals dipped, and he sent you this, to make up for the fence."

Bay dug into his shirt pocket and came out with gold: a three dollar gold piece, to be exact, a rarity with the country running on greenbacks for so many years. He held it out until Mariah reached for it, then laid it on her outstretched palm. She flinched at the soft brush of his fingers across her skin, as though he'd touched her more intimately.

"You're still nervous of me," Bay said. He took her hand between his two and curled her fingers around the coin, then pulled her a little closer. "Let's see if we can do something about that."

Chapter Three

THIS WAS IT. He was going to kiss her now, and that would be the end of her, and all she could do was stand there, waiting for her downfall to begin.

Bay drew her into his arms, shifting one hand to slide it around her waist and secure his hold. He held her eyes with his, and they stood there a long moment. His fingers gently massaged the small of her back, and Mariah fought the urge to relax against him.

Think of Nikolai, she told herself, but the image of the stonecutter's blonde hair faded in her mind while Bay's reflected moonlight with black brilliance. *Think of Nikolai*, she tried again, but the recollection of his occasional kisses paled against the anticipation of what Bay's might do to her senses.

As she stood there like a fool, waiting and wanting, and trying not to want, Bay brought his other hand up and cupped her chin. His thumb brushed across her lips, sending a tremor of pleasure down her spine, and then his mouth skimmed the same path before he set her away.

It took her a moment to realize the kiss was over, that the brief contact was all he planned, and by then he had grabbed the pail at his feet.

"Good night, Mariah Hoag." He strode off toward the barn. The closing door echoed woodenly behind him.

Confused by his sudden retreat, Mariah stood there, her lips tingling with the traces of Bay's touch. Her fist began to hurt. She glanced down, found herself holding the coin, gripping it like life itself.

* * *

Lips set in a thin grin, Bay pushed the barn door open a crack, just enough to see Mariah standing there, still, staring at the coin he'd dropped into her palm.

Twin slivers of lamplight from the house and barn poured across the farm yard, meeting at Mariah, touching the curves of her body with gilt. Bay traced the highlights in his imagination: Slender neck to shoulder; high, delicate breasts; waist narrow enough to span with his hands.

I could be touching those places. Bay felt the heaviness in his thighs and groin as his body responded, and he let the door frame take his weight. It creaked.

Mariah started, glanced up to meet his eyes, then darted toward the house like a frightened doe.

So she was still skittish, but because of innocence or loyalty to that big stonecutter? Either way, Bay realized, he really wanted the girl, so much that he had trouble thinking of anything else when she was within reach.

The dog, which had followed Mariah out from the house, trotted into the barn.

"Get locked out, fellow?" Bay asked. The dog sat down and started chewing at the tip of his tail.

Bay unbuckled his gun belt and looped it over the end post of the nearest stall, then stripped off his shirt and began scrubbing away the day's grime. He'd barely finished toweling off when the pup scrambled to his feet, ears forward, growling. Cajun and Mariah's little sorrel began to nicker in agitation. Something scuffed in the dust outside the barn. Bay reached for his pistol and ducked into a corner just as the door pushed open.

A low whistle, barely audible, echoed through the barn. A battered felt hat popped around the door, followed by a head and beard of unkempt red hair. The man's blue eyes found Bay without hesitation, and he broke into a grin.

"Whoa, boy. Don't go shooting your partner."

Clyde growled again and wuffed a low warning.

"Don't go sneaking up in the middle of the night. Hush, Clyde." His own hackles slowly relaxing, Bay stepped out into the light and slipped the gun back into the hanging holster.

"Get in here and shut that door, Eli. I don't want you waking up the ladies."

Eli Hightower gave Bay a slant-eyed look as he latched the door. He let Clyde sniff at his boot. "Looked to me like you were doing real well waking up one of them for yourself."

"Nosy sun of a gun, aren't you?"

"Can't help it if you've got no sense, spooning with her right out in the open like that." Eli hitched his thumbs into his waistband and rocked back on his heels. "You said you weren't going to get tangled up with that gal, and the first time I come around, there you are, tangling."

"That was barely a kiss, friend. You've been on the trail too long."

Eli laughed, then hoisted himself up onto a barrel for a seat. "Just remember who dragged who along and then told him to make himself scarce. By the by, I sold those horses over to Emporia, like you suggested. Have you found out anything useful?"

Bay shrugged and leaned against a post. "I rode around the edges of the ranch today."

"You see him?"

"I made a point of not seeing anyone. Heard a nice little tale, though." Bay summarized Mariah's story, Eli all the while nodding his head.

"You think she's right, that the old man's behind their troubles?" Eli asked.

"I do."

"And these Hoags—they aren't going to leave?"

Bay shook his head with certainty. "No. I doubt there's a power on this earth that could yank Mariah Hoag off this farm. Her roots are already so deep in this country they're part of the bedrock."

"Hang on. I've got things confused. I thought we were talking about the girl."

"We are," Bay said.

"Then how come she's the one that's going to say whether they leave?"

"Her mother's a little . . . " Bay considered and chose Mariah's word. ". . . fragile. I'd guess Mariah's the one that keeps her father and brother on their toes. She works like a son of a gun."

"Wouldn't be the first woman who made a place go. I've been off the farm a while, but it looks to me like they're almost making it."

"Almost. Fifty or hundred miles east, maybe into Missouri, and they'd have a good, solid place. The problem is, Hoag's been here eight years, and he's still trying to farm this place pretty much as if he was in Virginia. He hasn't learned, and this land doesn't forgive folks who won't learn. I doubt they'll ever get past almost, unless Mariah figures out what they need to change."

"And then all that extra trouble, too. It's a wonder her mama is the only one that's give out." Eli gave Bay another skewed look. "That little gal's probably looking for some help that'll stick around."

Bay had already considered this. "Actually, I think she's found some. She's got this big Viking sniffing around. He tried to break my hand the other day, just because she and I were talking."

Eli snorted. "I know the kind of talking you do with women. You just watch yourself. You don't need a jealous beau or righteous papa coming after you. You remember that fellow back in Bannock . . ."

"I remember," Bay said, but it didn't stop Eli.

While his friend rattled on with his dire warning, Bay considered Thor, no, what was his name, Nikolai. As desperately as Mariah wanted to stay on this land—and she did, though Bay couldn't image why—she probably hoped Thor could help her keep the farm together. And he just might have the expertise to do it—though if he did, Bay wondered why he hadn't straightened Hoag out already.

What this family needed was a hero, someone to handle their problems with Jack McKenzie and get their farm on track. Bay frowned. If she expected *him* to contribute to the effort, she had another think coming.

"I'm not about to get myself shot," Bay said when Eli finished the last gruesome detail.

"Well, you watch out," Eli groused. "Next thing you know, she'll be asking you to settle down."

"Hardly. Don't worry, my friend, I won't leave you to ride off on your own. And I'll give her fair warning before I kiss her again."

He would, too. Sweet as it would be to tumble Mariah into the hay, she had to know she would never hold him here. He'd had women offer their bodies much more freely—and with a lot more skill—and not one had held him for more than a few weeks. The minute he finished up his business here, he'd leave Chase County far behind. Permanently.

Still, a part of Bay hoped she didn't take his warning too seriously.

"When is it your husband's due back?" Bay asked over breakfast the next morning.

"Cornelius thought by Monday." Acasta drizzled a stream of honey into her tea. "Are you anxious to be going, Mr. Jackson?"

"No more than usual. The road always has a hold on me. I like finding out what's around the next bend."

He's going, Mariah thought, and something like panic squeezed her chest.

Of course he was going. Bay Jackson was a drifter. She'd known that from the start, even before Mama made her unreasoned offer to hire him on. That's why Mariah had decided to stay away from him in the first place.

"Were you able to finish your business so soon?" Acasta asked.

"No, ma'am. I'll probably stay in the area for another week or so, but not much past that."

Mariah stood by the side table, the milk pitcher dripping on her toes and the bare wood floor. At the table, Bay discussed his departure casually, his eyes resting on her. Embarrassed at her meandering thoughts, Mariah stepped to the table, and started pouring.

Bay cradled his cup in one fist while Mariah poured for him. His thumb moved slightly, tracing the rim, and suddenly her lips tingled where he'd brushed over them the night before.

She moved quickly to return the pitcher to the side table before she began to tremble.

"Are you all right, child?" Acasta asked.

"Just a little catch in my arm," Mariah fibbed. She shook her hand out like she needed to work out a crick. "I must have slept on it."

At that, the uneven crinkles appeared around Bay's eyes, and Mariah had to turn away.

She didn't understand. She'd been courted, even before Nikolai, and no one had made her this nervous—but then, Bay wasn't courting her, exactly. She tried once more to turn her mind to Nikolai, good, safe, reliable, *settled* Nikolai with his honorable intentions.

If only Bay would finish and go out to work, then she'd be fine. Then she could scrub the floor or scour a pot clean, and the work would give her the discipline that hours of restless tossing in the night had not.

Blast him anyway, for turning her life upside down, for making her want something she could never have, something she shouldn't even imagine having.

"I'd appreciate a piece of that bread," Bay said.

Mariah cut three thick slices of bread from the loaf, then carried it to the table, board and all. "Here you go."

She plunked the bread board down in front of Bay. The fat oak slab split straight down the middle.

"Oh, no." Mariah grabbed at the bread and caught it before it hit the floor. "I'm sorry, Mama."

"Old Will made that for us," Acasta said softly. She looked stunned, as though something far beyond the value of the board had been broken. Mariah understood: another scrap of the old life vanished. A little scrap, granted, but Mama seemed to feel each loss more deeply than the last.

Acasta squared her shoulders. "It's just an old bread board. We'll have a new one when your father gets around to it."

Mariah quietly found a plate for the bread and set the pieces of the board outside the door. A few minutes later, Bay finished his meal and excused himself.

By mid-morning, every pot shone. The worn flooring in the house reeked of pine tar soap. Even the jars and boxes on the shelves looked fresh from the store, so thoroughly had she dusted and polished. Mariah searched for something else to keep herself safely inside, away from Bay, but the heat building inside the little house told her the garden would suffer if she didn't tend to the watering.

The problem was, Bay was right out there, working in the shade cast by the barn and the young sycamore at its southeast corner. He'd hauled her father's green carpenter's box out of the tool shed right after breakfast, then come in and taken out the chair he'd been sitting in the past few meals. It wobbled, she knew, as it had for months. Mariah stood at the window, trying to pretend she wasn't watching him fix it, while she fidgeted with the lid to a canister.

She heard her mother moving around behind her and quickly turned away from the window, but Acasta was already peering out.

"He's such an industrious young man. We could use more like him around here," said her mother.

"He's not the settling kind, Mama. He's a drifter and probably a gambler and heaven knows what else. I'll be glad when he's gone." *Liar*. Mariah ignored her mother's raised eyebrows.

"Looks like the cabbages are starting to wilt," Acasta said after a bit.

"I know. I was just going to water. It's getting awfully close in here. Would you like to move your sewing out into the shade?"

"That sounds fine, dear."

There, a chaperon. Mariah set her mother's rocker out, got her settled with some mending, and went to get the buckets.

Bay popped the lid back onto the glue pot with the heel of his hand and met Mariah at the pump. "It's getting too hot for you to be doing that all by yourself. I'll help."

So she pumped and he hauled, and the sight of him nearly did her in. Each time Bay lifted the two full buckets, his blue shirt pulled tight across his shoulders and chest, and Mariah once again thought of cloth over bronze, like someone had dressed a statue. What was worse, she now knew just how sculpted those muscles were, different from Nikolai's sheer bulk, and the recollection of how she knew brought as much heat to her blood as the midday sun. Oh, God, he was going away soon, and she wanted him to kiss her until—

"That's enough," Mariah said. She stopped pumping to blot at her face with her sleeve, pretending the flush in her cheeks came from the sun and the work. "I've got to get dinner. I hope cold ham will do."

Bay nodded and she escaped to the house, and if she exchanged another dozen words with him the rest of the day, Mariah couldn't recall them.

Late in the afternoon she looked up from where she was hoeing out in the corn and caught him standing by the corner of the corral, staring out toward the western horizon. He held his bridle in his hands, and the restless way his hands ran over the leather straps echoed his words at breakfast. All she could think of was how those hands would feel on her skin.

Katydids and crickets trilled in full voice, trying to outdo each other in the darkness, nearly drowning out the sounds of the stock moving around in the corral. Mariah stared at the little stack of clothes: a yellow shirt and a pair of canvas pants, neatly ironed and folded. Bay's clothes. They'd been sitting there on the shelf for two days. Last night, she'd honestly forgotten to give them to him.

Tonight, she'd remembered, though. Tonight, she'd seen him look straight at them, and neither of them had said a word before he strolled off to the barn after supper.

She'd gone about her business, straightening up, getting the coffee pot ready for morning, setting a pan of milk out to clabber for biscuits. Now she stood at the side table, the washbowl and pitcher at hand, sponging herself clean and staring at Bay's clothes.

Mariah rebuttoned her dress and sat down at the table while her mother readied herself for bed. A coyote sat on a hill just up the way, and his occasional howling, so close to the house, made Acasta nervous. Mariah was grateful that the medicine Dr. Bloom had given her mother for her dry night cough made her groggy.

In the moments before her mother slipped into sleep, Mariah stood up.

"Mama."

"Mmm?"

"Mr. Jackson forgot his clean clothes again. I'm going to carry them out to the barn."

"All right, child. . . . Come . . . right back." Acasta's words drifted out the door behind Mariah.

Clyde started to follow her across the yard, but she pushed him away with the side of her foot. He skulked back to his place by the door.

The temperature had barely dropped since midday, but the night breeze found wisps of damp hair along Mariah's neck and cooled her. She hugged the clothes to her chest as she neared the barn. The door stood open a foot or so. She slipped through the space without a sound.

Bay had hung the lantern so that it threw its light in a circle just inside the door where Mariah stood. Beyond, the barn held only shadows, but she felt him watching her.

"I brought your clothes," she said finally and tossed them onto a nearby barrel.

One of the shadows moved and took a human shape. Bay stepped out of the back of the barn, to the edge of the light. His hair, damp from washing up, curled in black ringlets around his ears. He had no shirt on. His skin shone deep gold, not as brown as his face and hands, but darker than she'd imagined from the glimpse she'd had. The lantern glow showed her every detail of him, from the hollows of his neck, over the broad swell of his chest with its sprinkling of black, curling hair, to the ridges of his belly down to the button waist of his trousers. Mariah felt the breath stick in her lungs and thought for an instant that she would faint.

Bay moved forward as silently as a hunter, as though he was stalking her. He stopped directly in front of her, less than a yard away. The lantern light picked up the smoky gray of his eyes and gave them a vaguely yellow cast, the color of the flat, angry bottoms of the thunder clouds that often boiled over the hills.

Suddenly she understood.

"You're like a storm," she whispered. "Blow in, do your worst, and blow out again."

"I never claimed to be anything else."

"No. You warned me. And I'm still here. Some people might say I'm not too smart about storms." *What on earth was she doing, saying such a provocative thing?* Mariah hurried to set her story straight. "I got caught out on the hills one time. I was daydreaming. When I looked up, the sky was blacker than the inside of this barn. I started to run for home, and then it was like something grabbed hold of me, some kind of . . . power from the storm. I turned around and faced into the wind, and the lightning struck the hills all around, and then the rain started, sheets of it, and I—"

This was even worse. Mariah's voice trailed off into embarrassed silence as she realized what she was about to reveal.

"And you what?" Bay asked softly. He stepped closer.

"Nothing. I just . . . nothing." She squinted off into the shadows over Bay's shoulder.

He took another step and leaned toward her so his lips brushed her temple. She felt the heat radiating off his bare chest and caught the sharp, clean, male scent of him.

"And you what?" he repeated more firmly. His breath stirred past her ear and made a shiver run the length of her spine.

The hair on her neck lifted, but she ignored the warning, just as she had during the storm when the lightning struck close. She'd never told anyone, and the sudden need to tell Bay the whole story, the need to challenge him the way she had the storm, outweighed whatever crumbs of common sense she had left.

She blurted the words. "I shucked off my clothes, that's what. Every stitch. I stood there in the rain and the wind like some heathen, until the storm blew on over the ridge."

Bay stood there, unmoving, for the longest time, until Mariah began to think he must be embarrassed for her, or maybe disgusted at her brazenness, but something in her took one more try at making him understand. "Sometimes things are just . . . hard. Sometimes I get so tired I feel like I can't take another step. But then I think about that storm, and how pure it felt on my skin."

Her cheeks began to burn under the unblinking intensity of his gaze. Mariah turned toward the door. "This was a mistake."

His hands clamped down on her shoulders, almost brutal in their firmness, and he spun her back to him.

"No. Not a mistake."

And then she saw his face, really saw it. Saw the raw, taut hunger in it, a clarification of the vague wanting that filled her, for just an instant before he lowered his mouth toward hers.

She should stop him, she knew. Only a harlot would behave this way with a man, only a Jezebel would say such things to a man and then let him kiss her, but the first touch of his lips sent a shock of recognition jolting through her body. Mariah gasped, and his tongue slipped past her open lips, taking possession. She lifted up onto her toes, anxious to press against him, to feel the strength in his tall, lean body, to slip her arms around his neck and hold him so the kiss would go on.

He wouldn't allow it. Twisting his lips free, he burrowed one hand in the tangle of her hair and tugged her head back, so her neck arched for the kisses he strung down her throat. He paused over the pulse that hammered just above the collar of her gingham dress, his lips moving hungrily over the tender skin.

She felt his free hand wander down her back and over the curve of her hips, then back up along her waist and ribs, up to places he had no business touching.

He'll stop if I tell him to, but the very thought made Mariah feel safe to let him go a little further. *Just a little more*, she thought, *then I'll tell him to stop*.

His palm brushed boldly over her breasts, once, then twice, and through the cloth of her bodice and shimmy, Mariah felt the searing warmth. She buried her head against his shoulder, her lips moving with little whimpers of pleasure. He tasted of salt and lye soap.

Just a little more, a tiny bit more.

Except he caught the peak of her breast between thumb and forefinger and teased it to a throbbing point, and the rush of pleasure made her not want him to stop at all—not when she felt his fingers move to the buttons of her dress and then her chemise, not even when his breath touched the newly bared skin and his kisses moved into the valley between her breasts.

Mariah's knees threatened to turn to liquid. As she swayed, Bay slipped one arm around her waist to support her. With his other hand, he dipped into her open neckline, flicking over her nipple once more before he tugged the cloth aside, baring her to his heated gaze.

"Mariah," he whispered, and she waited, so impatient now, for whatever came next. Oh, she wanted to know what came next. But Bay froze.

His head came up. He released her, his attention suddenly elsewhere. It took Mariah a second to hear Clyde raising a ruckus outside, another to realize her own nakedness. She fumbled at her buttons.

"Is that hound of yours likely to bark at the wind?" he asked.

Mariah shook her head.

"Stay here until I see who or what's out there." Bay reached for his rifle. "Put that lantern out."

She realized he was thinking of the robbers Nikolai had reported. *Oh, Nikolai.* Moving in a daze, Mariah obeyed, then watched Bay slip out the door. She heard the soft crunch of gravel as he moved away across the yard.

Dear Lord, what was I doing? Mariah leaned against the door frame, earlier passion dissolving into guilt and mortification. What she was doing to Nikolai was bad enough, but what if someone had hurt Mama while she was out here letting Bay do those terrible, wonderful, sinful things?

Mariah peered out the door. The yard was empty, but off between the garden and the chicken coop, Clyde stood barking ferociously into the night.

Beyond the dog, she caught a glimpse of movement. Man shaped. Robbers or Bay?

Suddenly she didn't know which was more dangerous. She didn't care. She pushed the door open and ran for the house. Behind her, the door slammed against the side of the barn like a gunshot. She didn't look back.

A man and a barking dog proved too much. The badger retreated with a snap and a snarl into the night, the wide, hoary stripes down his sides marking his path until he disappeared into the shadows. No chickens tonight.

Bay scouted around the henhouse to make sure the badger was the only problem. He'd just finished the circuit when he heard the barn door slam and, a few seconds later, the quieter click of the front door catch.

So, Mariah had vanished as well. He cursed aloud at Clyde and the badger and headed back, the weight of his unquenched desire and the loss he felt leaving him in a foul mood.

He waited until it grew clear she wasn't coming back, then flopped onto the neat pile of hay and blankets that made his makeshift bed. It took a while to get himself under control enough to consider Mariah's visit.

He'd expected her. They'd had some mysterious but definite communication there in the house, and he'd known she'd come to him with the clothes as an excuse. But that tale about the storm—now *that* had thrown him. Was it simple truth, or her way of telling him she'd already had a lover? The storm might mean Nikolai—after all, Bay himself had come up with the nickname of Thor, the Thunder God.

Bay grimaced at the idea of Mariah in the big mason's arms. No. She had to mean a real storm. He *wanted* it to be a real storm.

But why? There would be less risk to him if she wasn't a virgin. She would be more available. The whole thing might be easier to sort out if he could get past the image of her standing on a hillside, naked, as the lightning flashed around her. But he couldn't get past it, and he drifted off to sleep with that picture in his mind.

The rooster started crowing much too early, and Bay lazed in his blankets a few minutes, his head still thick with dreams of Mariah. The cow bawling to be milked reminded him that the golden-haired heathen herself would be coming out in a few minutes. He tugged on his shirt and boots and waylaid her at the barn door with a quick kiss. She kissed him back, for the barest moment, then pulled away.

"Don't," she said quietly.

Bay released her, even though the strain in her voice made

him think she wished he wouldn't. He began rolling up his cuffs.

"What did I do?" he asked.

"Nothing. Just . . . just please go do your chores. I really have to milk the cow now."

"And you don't want me around. You're afraid I'll remind you of this."

He caught her and kissed her again, deeply, and when she swayed a little, he took advantage of the motion and tugged her to him. Her breasts lifted against his chest as she sighed. He couldn't resist taking the weight of one in his palm, and her shudder of pleasure as he circled the crest with his thumb told him he hadn't misjudged. She wanted him.

But it was daylight, and her mother was undoubtedly awake in the house. Reluctant as a kid giving up a candy stick, Bay released her and broke the kiss.

She raised her hand to touch her lips. They had a smudged look that made Bay's chest tighten with an absurd desire to keep them looking that way for as long as he stayed around.

"You can't do that," Mariah muttered. "I can't. There's Nikolai and . . ." She glanced up, meeting his eyes for the first time that morning. Color crept into her cheeks, and her emerald gaze accused, even though her voice came out calm and matter-of-fact. "And you'll be leaving."

So that was it. Bay nodded, but he reached out to trace the hollow of her cheek with one finger. "Okay. I won't take anything you're not willing to give."

He wasn't quite sure why he made that promise—or where he found the wherewithal to walk out of the barn then.

Breakfast unnerved him. Mariah moved and talked and worked as easily and competently as always, but when she reached for a canister on a high shelf, the long, curved line of her torso ignited Bay's imagination. He bolted his meal down and excused himself before his body betrayed him.

Throughout his morning's work, he remained conscious of Mariah and where she moved about the house and yard. He finally retreated into the narrow stand of trees down by the creek, where he repaired a gap in the tiny spillway irrigation dam that supplied water for the little orchard and the patch of tobacco Hoag was trying to raise for a cash crop. While he was at it, he lectured himself aloud on behaving like an adult instead of a randy kid, confident the steady gurgle of water over the two foot fall would drown his voice before it carried to the house.

Noon came around, and Bay jammed a final stone into its notch in the dam and strolled back toward the house. He came around the corner of the house to the sight of a gaudy red peddler's wagon standing in the yard.

Mariah was busy poring through the contents of a basket that sat on the back step of the wagon. Two voices, Mrs. Hoag's and some man's, issued through the open door of the house.

Bay walked up behind Mariah. "I see at least one drummer made it past the blockade."

She turned, eyes bright, and a few strands of golden hair, warm and fragrant from the sun, brushed across his cheek. Bay caught a wisp between thumb and forefinger. It felt like silk, and he wondered how it would look spread over a pillow in the moonlight.

He wanted her, and for a moment, he saw that same desire reflected in her eyes. At least he thought he saw it, and then it passed and she shifted away warily. The lock slipped through his fingers.

"He has a lot of fine books," she said, gesturing toward the side of the wagon. "I helped him carry some in to show Mama, so she doesn't have to stand out here in the sun."

"With a little lemonade and some of that applesauce cake from last night, he ought to be good for a whole afternoon of visiting." Bay glanced down into the basket. It was full to the brim with a rainbow of ribbon and clouds of edging lace wrapped on long bobbins. Mariah's hand rested on a spool of brilliant green satin ribbon that she'd pulled to the top.

"It's too bad, both of you turning up at the same time. I wish he'd come around after harvest." She glanced down regretfully. Her fingertip traced the edge of the ribbon, then she sighed and pushed the spool down in with the others. "He has a lot of pretty things."

None of which she could afford, Bay realized. "Let's see if

he's got a recent Kansas City newspaper tucked in with the Twain."

"I think I saw one," she said. She started around the corner of the wagon, Bay close behind her, enjoying the gentle sway of her skirts.

Movement in the doorway of the Hoags' tiny house caught Bay's eye. A man came out, beaming through a straggly brown beard and looking oddly familiar.

"I'll be right back with that, ma'am," he said. The voice struck Bay as familiar, too.

"Here," Mariah said. Bay looked toward the wagon, saw for the first time the name painted on its side in yellow, DOUGLAS STUTT. He had just put the name together with the face behind the beard when the drummer got to the wagon.

"Find anything you want, miss? How about you, sir?" Puzzlement crinkled the man's eyes, then recognition. Bay lifted a finger to shush him, but it was too late.

Stutt snapped to attention, four long years of military service suddenly in play. A grin the size of Connecticut split his face as he touched his hat brim with a sloppy salute.

"Black Jack—I mean, Captain McKenzie. Good to see you, sir!"

Chapter Four

THE BEGINNINGS OF a smile faded from Mariah's lips. Her fingers curled around the book she'd pulled down from the peddler's shelf.

"McKenzie?" The name caught in her throat like the thick summer air. "You must be mistaken. This is Mr. Jackson, our hired hand."

But even as she said it, she saw Bay standing there at the corner of the wagon, his hand half raised as though he was trying to push the name away, and she knew there was no mistake.

The drummer looked from Bay to Mariah and back again several times, then cleared his throat noisily. "Yes'm. I must be. This fellow just—"

"Never mind, Trooper." Bay finally moved, stepping forward and holding his hand out in greeting. "You always had a better memory for faces than I did. Good to see you." The two men shook hands and thumped each other on the shoulder.

"Almost didn't recognize you without those black muttonchops of yours. Then I remembered a young pup of a lieutenant that showed up with . . ." Stutt's voice trailed off as Bay removed his hat and turned to Mariah.

"Bayard Jackson McKenzie," he said in precise formal manner, as though introducing himself at a cotillion. "John McKenzie is my father."

"Jackson," she whispered. "The one they called Young Jack." Oh, God, he was a McKenzie and she'd let him touch her like that. Anger erupted just behind the humiliation that turned her cheeks to flame.

"If you'll just let me explain," he began.

Mariah backed away from Bay's lying charm. "You're a McKenzie. That's all I need to hear. It explains it all, every bit. God, you must have been laughing last night."

"It's not like that, Mariah. I—"

"Damn you!" The book in her hand sailed across the space between them. It clipped Bay's jaw and flopped to the ground behind him.

"Tarnation, miss. That book costs six bits." Stutt hustled to retrieve the volume and dusted it with his sleeve.

The man's presence shocked Mariah. She'd forgotten him.

"Mariah, listen to me." Bay reached for her hand.

She jerked away. "You have five minutes to get off this property, *McKenzie*, or I swear, I'll blow your backside so full of lead they'll be able to melt you for cannon fodder. Mr. Stutt, I apologize for throwing your book. Please get whatever my mother wanted and come back inside. And I'll trouble you not to mention any of this to her." She accused Bay with her eyes and voice. "She is ill. She doesn't need to be upset."

The drummer stared at her blankly.

"Mr. Stutt," Mariah repeated.

"Yes'm. I mean, I'll be right with you." He shelved the book, then scurried around the other side of the wagon. "I'll just get this other box, here."

She glared Bay into continued silence. For once he didn't have that crooked grin on his face. In fact, he looked like he might even be sorry. Then she noticed the way his brows lifted at the ends, and the line of his nose, and how his jaw worked with agitation—just like John McKenzie's. She must have been blind, not to see it before.

As soon as Stutt came back around the wagon, she headed for the house.

Behind her, she heard Stutt's footsteps scuffle to a stop. "I ain't clear about what's going on here, Cap'n, but I sure am sorry."

"Not your fault, Stutt."

"Four minutes," Mariah said clearly, and walked on toward the house. By the time she hit the door, she had herself composed.

DRIFTER'S MOON 55

Douglas Stutt wasn't quite as successful, stumbling through his sales patter, but Acasta was so engrossed in the contents of his notions box that she didn't seem to notice.

I should have seen it, Mariah berated herself again as her mother examined a pair of sewing shears. Turn his black hair red, put a beard on him, and he'd be the image of John McKenzie. What she'd thought was a crooked grin was just the McKenzie smirk. She listened for the sounds of him riding out and tried to think of what to tell her mother.

The four minutes passed, and another four, and she still hadn't heard him leave. "Excuse me, Mama. Mr. Stutt. I left something outside."

The shotgun stood by the door. She grabbed it by the barrel quietly as she walked out, shielding the motion—and the gun—with her skirts.

The blue roan stood tied to the corral fence, with a full set of gear strapped on behind the saddle. After a moment, Bay came out of the lean-to shed. He had a flat, cloth-wrapped bundle under his arm.

She aimed the gun and cocked it. "Your time's up."

"So it is." His face was flat, unreadable. He shrugged and walked toward her, stopping just a foot or two beyond the end of the gun. "Put that thing down. You're not going to shoot me."

Sorely as he tempted her, Mariah knew he was right. She slowly lowered the gun.

"I intended to give your mother this at supper tonight." Bay held out his package. "Don't deny it to her because of how you feel about me."

"She's going to feel just the same," Mariah said, but she took the stiff bundle.

Bay gathered his reins up, stuck a toe into his stirrup, and hoisted himself into the saddle. Mariah found herself looking up at Bay, and for a moment, her body recalled the feel of his as he held her and kissed her and made her want—

"Get off our land," she ordered.

"You're going to let me explain to you sooner or later," Bay said with a certainty that matched her own that she'd never listen to another word from him again. He pointed at the package. "Give that to your mother."

He rode out the gate and, no surprise to Mariah, turned toward his father's house. She watched until his square shoulders and Stetson disappeared in the waves of tall grass.

His leaving drained the fury out of Mariah. The weights of the shotgun and the package dragged at her arms. She walked back toward the house, careful to stay out of her mother's line of sight.

She leaned the shotgun near the washstand and started to peel away the flour sacking that wrapped Bay's gift, then stopped.

By the feel of it, he'd made her mother a new bread board, blast him anyway. Nothing a McKenzie could give was important enough to bother her mother with. Besides, Bay's disappearance would be hard enough to explain.

He was gone.

No, worse: he had never been. That Bay had been another McKenzie scheme.

Mariah fought down a sob that balled up in the back of her throat, then dropped the board into the space behind the washstand and poked at it until not a scrap of white showed. Wiping her sweaty hands against her skirt, she walked into the house.

Mama and Mr. Stutt sat at the table with glasses of lemonade and a row of fancy embroidery scissors laid out between them. They both looked up.

"Is everything all right, child?" Acasta asked.

To Mariah, it felt like each of those scissors had plunged into her heart. "Fine, Mama. Everything's fine."

Mariah watched her mother drizzle honey into a cup of chamomile tea. The dust from the peddler's departing wagon had long since settled, and the sun sat low enough in the western sky to turn the hills orange-gold, but the sob of rage and humiliation and loss still hung there in the back of her throat, on the verge of bursting out.

"I wonder where Mr. Jackson's gotten himself off to," Acasta said. "I don't believe I've seen him since before lunch.

Do you suppose he's gone off on more of his mysterious business?"

"Yes. No. I . . ." Mariah struggled for the words that had been eluding her all afternoon. "He's gone, Mama. For good."

"Gone? But I don't understand. He promised to stay until your father and brother come home."

Mariah pulled a chair over next to her mother and sat down. Somehow, she had to find the will to stay calm, to keep her mother calm. "He probably would have. I, um, I told him to leave."

Acasta's eyes widened with surprise. "Why on earth would you do that? You know I—"

"I caught him lying. About who he is and why he was here. Mr. Stutt recognized him, from the war I guess, and said his name before Bay had a chance to warn him. It turns out he's not just the drifter he claimed to be, and I told him to get off our land. I know you thought a lot of him. I'm sorry he let you down."

Mariah mentally crossed her fingers, hoping her story would satisfy her mother, but Acasta was too sharp.

"That's some pretty fancy dancing around his name, daughter. If he's not Bay Jackson, just who is he?"

"It doesn't matter. The important thing is that we found him out before he did us any harm. And it's only a couple of days until Papa and Jimmy come home."

"Mariah . . ."

"Bay McKenzie," she muttered. "I'm sorry I ever let him onto our land."

A spasm twisted her mother's face, an echo of all the pain and trouble John McKenzie had caused them over the past eight years, and in that instant, the only thing Mariah felt for him or his son was pure hatred, acid enough to burn away the lump in her throat.

Acasta took a deep breath, and the look passed. She swirled her cup of tea a few times before she spoke. "I used to be such a good judge of character."

"Don't blame yourself, Mama. He fooled me, too."

"What do you suppose he was up to?"

"He's a McKenzie," Mariah said bitterly. "He was probably

looking for ways to help his father, trying to find some new way to ruin us." *By ruining me.* Mariah got up quickly and went to the side table, before her mother could notice her hands trembling or see the high color that washed her skin.

The silence in the room stretched out, broken only by the slosh of water as Mariah poured some water into the wash basin. She splashed a little over her cheeks in a vain effort to rinse away the stain of embarrassment and guilt, then blotted the moisture away with a nubby towel.

"I don't think so," Acasta said.

"What?"

"I don't think Mr. J—Bay was trying to help John McKenzie."

Mariah whirled to face her. "Mama, how can you sit there and defend the man! He lied from the first minute he opened his mouth. He sat out in the field and talked to me about McKenzie like he barely knew him."

"Maybe he does barely know him. From what I understand, he's been gone for nearly fifteen years. And as for my defending him, other than misleading us—"

"Lying."

"All right, child. He prevaricated. But other than that, he did nothing more terrible than help us when I asked him. He didn't have to fix our fence, much less put it up better than it was to start. He put in a lot of hard work around here. He was polite and every bit the gentleman."

"Bull." Mariah blurted the word, then instantly wished she hadn't. "I'm sorry, Mama. I know you don't like me to use such language."

Acasta dipped her head slightly, accepting the apology, but her eyes never left Mariah's. "More to the point, however, is why you said it. Did he . . ." She hesitated. "Did he take liberties with you?"

God help me, I gave them to him freely. Mariah wanted to melt into a puddle and run out through the cracks in the floor. She tried distraction instead. "He's a liar. I just don't see how you can call him a gentleman when he's lied to us."

"Don't dissemble with me, young lady. I've seen the way you two look at each other."

"Mama . . ."

"Did he try to take advantage of you?"

Surrendering to the terrier tone in her mother's voice, Mariah pressed her hands to her burning cheeks. "He kissed me."

"And?"

"Isn't that enough, Mama? He kissed me, and I enjoyed it and kissed him back."

"Ah." Acasta turned a little to stare out the window, but she looked so quietly relieved that Mariah knew she'd accepted her half-truth.

Damn you, Bay McKenzie, for making me lie to my mother on top of everything else.

They stayed that way for a long time, Acasta staring out the window, Mariah leaning back against the side table, her hands still covering her cheeks.

Finally, Acasta pushed to her feet and stepped around to face her daughter. She tugged Mariah's hands down.

"A young woman deserves a stolen kiss now and again, especially from a man as handsome as Bay." She leaned close, so their foreheads touched. "However, I think perhaps we'd better keep that part of it from your father. He's going to have enough to swallow. What you're going to have to decide now is whether you're more angry at Bay or yourself. And what you're going to do about Nikolai."

"Nothing. Keep seeing him. I might as well. The Bay that kissed me claimed to be a drifter. Now he's gone, that's all."

The sob welled up again without warning. Mariah spun away from her mother and scooped up the now tepid cup of tea.

"I'll get you some hot water for a fresh cup, then dish up supper."

No. I won't cry. Not over him. Not over someone who could try to use me to get to this farm.

She fought the tears and she thought she'd won, until she reached to lift the big iron kettle. The tears spilled off her lashes onto the stove top and vanished with a hiss of steam.

Work. That was the cure, and Mariah flung herself into it the next morning. By breakfast, she'd milked, fed and watered the animals, gathered eggs, split an armload of kindling, hung the bedding out to air, put a batch of bread to rise, and weeded the garden.

After breakfast, she attacked the floors. Her mother watched, a knowing, if slightly worried, expression on her face.

"You just scrubbed that floor down to fresh wood two days ago," Acasta said.

"It's dirty again."

As she swept and scrubbed, Mariah kept an equal eye on Acasta. Her mother's sunken cheeks and blue-circled eyes spoke of the sleepless night they'd both spent. She blamed Bay: If her mother got sick again, he'd have hell to pay.

Just after nine, she heard the jangling approach of a team. Hoping her father was back early, she hustled to the door in time to see the red drummer's wagon turn through the gate.

"It's Mr. Stutt," she said.

"Why, I wonder what he's doing back here?" Acasta laid aside the sock she was darning, and lifted a hand to check her hair. Mariah knew her own was a mess and didn't bother.

The wagon rolled up in front of the house, and Mr. Stutt set the brake and hopped down. "May I come in for a bit, Miss Hoag?"

"Certainly, although I doubt it will do you any good. We can't afford those embroidery scissors any more today than we could yesterday."

"What, no long lost uncles have left you money since then?" Mr. Stutt asked in mock surprise. He chuckled at his own joke. "Actually, I don't expect you to buy. I just need to have a word with you and your mother."

Mariah suddenly felt wary. She wanted to block the door, but her mother's voice rang out clear from behind her.

"By all means, Mr. Stutt. Do come in. Mariah, there's some coffee left from breakfast, isn't there?"

The drummer removed his wide-brimmed straw hat and stepped inside. "Thank you kindly, ladies, but I really can't stay. I just have a message."

"From *him*?" Mariah demanded. "You tell your Captain McKenzie he can take his messages to Hades."

"Mariah, really," Acasta said. "I will not have you talking to a visitor that way. It's not Mr. Stutt's fault if you're angry. The least you can do is listen to him."

Stutt cleared his throat. "Actually, the message is, uh, for you, Mrs. Hoag."

"Good. Then I don't have to stay." Mariah started past Mr. Stutt.

"He said I should ask you if your daughter gave you the package he left," Stutt said quickly.

Mariah stopped in her tracks. She didn't have to see her mother's disapproving stare; she could feel it, burning two round holes in the shoulders of her dress.

"Yes, ma'am," she muttered. "I'll get it."

A fine layer of dust settled on Acasta's skirt as she unwound the flour-sacking a few minutes later. Mariah watched, her lips pressed together in frustration.

"It's my old bread board," Acasta said. Her face glowed with delight as she traced the pattern of carved acorns that edged the board, and Mariah knew Bay had gone a long way—too far, probably—in winning her mother's forgiveness by this one act. "He's put it back good as new."

"Not quite, ma'am," Stutt corrected. "He said to tell you not to get it wet, more than to damp wipe it, since the glue might not hold. But it should be fine for cutting bread."

"Yes. Yes, it will be." Acasta's voice hitched a little, like she was on the verge of tears. "It's silly, but this old thing means a lot to me."

"He thought it might."

She fingered the carving a little more. "Was there anything else, Mr. Stutt?"

"No, ma'am."

"No pretty apology?" Mariah asked bitterly.

"He said that had best come from his own lips."

"I'd sooner listen to a hog squeal at butchering time. Tell him I'm keeping the gun loaded until I hear he's left the county."

Mariah didn't stay to hear her mother scold her. She pushed past Stutt and headed out to water the vegetables.

She'd already finished the row of onions when the peddler came out. He waited for her by the pump.

Mariah ran a suspicious eye up and down him as she came back for more water. "Is there something you want?"

"I'd be obliged if I could top off my barrel again. Since I was coming back this way, I figured I didn't have to use creek water."

"Go ahead." Mariah set the bucket under the spigot, and he started pumping. "Just why did you come back, anyway? Surely not for the sake of telling my mother about that bread board."

"As a point of fact, yes, I did. But I would have turned back anyway, even if he hadn't given me the message to bring. You see, the captain stopped me after I left here yesterday afternoon and asked me not to go on up to his pa's place. Said he'd take it as a personal favor if I'd just skip the McKenzie ranch permanent-like and take you folks on as regular customers."

Mariah didn't want to admit how much that would mean to Mama, so she took refuge in sarcasm. "And all he has to do is ask?"

"Yes'm," he said. He gave the pump handle another stroke and deftly switched buckets in mid-stream. "I'd do anything for that man. He was about the best cavalry officer ever wore Union blue."

"That holds little sway with me, Mr. Stutt. I saw the kind of men you Yankees had for officers."

"Good and bad, just like your side, miss. Captain McKenzie was one of the good ones."

"Then he's changed."

Stutt gave her a keen look, then shook his head. "Excuse me for saying so, but you're mighty young and fine looking to be so hard."

"McKenzies made me that way," she answered sharply. "Your buckets are full."

He hauled the buckets over to his wagon, and tilted them into the keg that rode strapped to the back corner. He popped the lid back on, then returned the buckets. He stood there, staring at Mariah for a minute.

"Yep," he muttered to himself. "Green as bottle glass."

"Is there something *else*, Mr. Stutt?"

"Yes'm. This." He fished into his coat pocket and came out

with a bobbin of emerald ribbon. Mariah recognized the expensive satin she'd admired—and rejected as too dear—the day before. He held it out to her. "For you, miss."

"I don't want it."

"He said you'd say that. I'm supposed to leave it anyhow. Go on. It's bought and paid for. You might as well have it."

When Mariah wouldn't take it, he went over and tossed the reel into the stool by the front door, then climbed up to his wagon seat.

"He said it matched your eyes—it does, by the by—and that it will look nice with the new dress you're working up." He sorted out the reins and popped the brake handle. "There's something else too, let me think. Oh, he said Thor would probably like it."

The wagon moved off with a jerk and a rattle of pots and cutlery, leaving Mariah standing there in the heat and dust, feeling about two inches tall.

"I should be back through about harvest time," the peddler called back. "Tell your mama if she saves up for the scissors she wants, I'll throw in a fancy china thimble."

Mariah stared after him, fuming. Didn't that take the cake? The one drummer willing to stop at the farm, and Bay McKenzie was behind it. Of course, they were two of a kind, as far as she could see: Full of polite words and kindnesses one minute, making a fool of you the next. She'd have to watch the man every minute when he came back.

A glimpse of green caught her eye as she turned back to her work.

If she was as hard as Douglas Stutt thought she was, she'd just toss the ribbon into the creek and watch it float off, but she wasn't, so she let it lay while she filled the buckets over and over for the cabbages and peas and string beans and carrots. The noon hour found her frowning as she carried the ribbon inside and stuffed it deep into her sewing basket.

Her mother, bless her heart, kept quiet.

"Jeez-us," Eli said.

Bay understood his friend's awe. He'd had much the same reaction a few days before when he'd sat in some heavy brush on the far side of the creek and stared at the result of John McKenzie's preoccupation with becoming a man of substance. On top of the hill sat a complex of buildings and corrals and paddocks to rival the finest spreads he'd ever seen.

The stone house comes as no shock; the workmen had just started the foundations before Bay rode off in '61, and he'd seen the plans often enough that he could probably walk through it blindfolded. But the reality of it, planted there just below the hilltop and surrounded by various barns and outbuildings, all cut from the same native limestone, had left him shaking his head. The place looked like it belonged on the banks of the Potomac, among the other monuments.

"Jeez-us," Eli repeated.

"John McKenzie never went in for half measures," Bay said. "He always did want to be laird."

His fingers automatically brushed the grip of his pistol as his eyes flickered down to check the rifle in the scabbard at his right knee. He smiled at himself, and at Eli, who also reached forward to touch the butt of his own rifle. Years of riding into unfamiliar situations had left them both cautious.

An easy chuckle escaped him. "They're not going to shoot the prodigal son, friend. Let's go find out what the old man has to say when he sees me."

"You sure you don't want to go up there by yourself?" Eli asked. "I mean, it being so long and all, it seems like your pa might want to see you by your lonesome."

"This won't be your typical family reunion."

"But I thought the whole reason we came all this way was to let you get things settled with your pa before he passes on. That Nalley fellow you ran into in Cheyenne—"

"—said he got broken up in a fall, that's all. I doubt it had a lick of effect on his temper." Bay kicked Cajun into a canter and heard his friend fall in just behind. A handsome red stallion in an outlying pen trumpeted a challenge to their mounts as they passed. "He's probably still mad I ran off."

Up close, the ranch impressed Eli beyond swearing.

Bay slowed as he passed under the tall gate. MCKENZIE AND SONS, the board read, just as it had thirteen years ago. That gate had been the last thing Bay had seen of the ranch.

A young hand who'd been lounging against the post jumped to his feet, a belligerent lift to one corner of his mouth.

"Do something for you gentlemen?" he asked.

The kid probably had orders not to let anybody through the gate who looked like they'd take a shot at the boss. Bay put on his captain's manner. "We're here to see John McKenzie. Can you tell us where to find him?"

"Up at the house," the boy said, relaxing at the sound of authority. "Probably on the porch, if it's like most mornings, but it ain't a good idea to disturb him."

Bay touched the brim of his hat with a finger and nudged his mount in the right direction.

"Foreman does the actual hirin'," the boy called after them.

A knot of unease formed in Bay's belly. The idea of John McKenzie passing control to another man was alien.

The porch stretched the full width of the two story house, its overshot roof supported on carved stone pillars fit for a Grecian temple. Three men sat on one end of the porch in high-backed chairs. Two had the well-cut clothes and air of lawyers or bankers. The other was a gaunt, silver-haired man with a crooked leg and a full set of muttonchop whiskers. Behind him, a woman in serviceable gray serge covered by a sparkling white pinafore briskly shook out and folded a lap robe. She appeared to be scolding, though her words didn't carry.

Visitors, Bay registered, then the invalid looked up and blue eyes met gray, and the unease bloomed into the shock of disbelief. *No*.

Ignoring the protests of the woman, the man pushed to his feet and hobbled a few pained steps to the edge of the veranda. The morning sun picked up a few red strands in his wavy silver hair as he lifted one hand to block the glare.

That's not my father, Bay's guts screamed as he worked to keep his face neutral. *That walking skeleton is not the man who used to toss me up in the air until I wanted to puke.*

Ted Nalley's description hadn't prepared him for this. He'd always thought of his father like one of the Greek gods described in his schoolbooks: larger than life in both good and bad, lusty, and most of all, invincible. All through Bay's childhood and youth, the universe had spun around John

McKenzie. Neither the war nor the gold camps nor years of drifting had been able to shake that out of his system. Truth be told, that was part of why he'd come home, to rid himself of the myth. But not this way.

The man wobbled a little and reached for the support of one of the stone pillars. The woman started forward.

"Keep your bloody hands off me, Mrs. Shaw," the man snapped. "Get out of here, all of you."

The angry Scots brogue rang, and Bay knew.

The other men rose. One spoke. "We'll just wait for you inside."

"You do that." The old man softened his tone a little. "Would you serve breakfast, Mrs. Shaw? Save mine, I'll be speaking with this young buck for a bit."

The housekeeper hesitated.

"Go on. I'll be fine." He directed his next comment to Bay. "Not likely to let me keel over, are you laddie? Not when you come all this way to surprise your old father."

The nurse and the men glanced at each other, then beat a quick retreat.

John McKenzie gave his son a long, hard look. "I see you brought a friend. Afraid to face me alone, are you?"

"It always pays a man to have someone guarding his back when he deals with you."

John's cheeks darkened with anger, then his face relaxed into a smile. "You've grown up well, laddie." He hobbled back to his chair, eased himself down, and reached for a cut glass decanter that sat on the table next to him. He poured a tumbler full and lifted it toward Bay. "Don't look so sour. It's good Scotch whiskey."

"When did you start drinking at seven o'clock in the morning?"

"When I started needing to." He slapped the knee of the crooked leg. "Did you see that big old bay stallion as you came in? He tossed me to hell and back, then trounced me for good measure. I should have had him cut years ago, but damn if he doesn't sire the finest foals you've ever seen. Now, come on down from that horse and tell me what you've been up to for thirteen years, Jack boy."

"It's Bay, now, and talking can wait. You've got business with those gents. Get it done, and then we'll talk."

"They're staying a few days."

Just as well, Bay felt. He needed the time to come to grips with his father's fall from godhood. "I'll be here."

"Good. Good." John looked pleased. "Pick whatever rooms you want, you and your friend. There's plenty of space in the south wing."

"No thanks. We'll bunk out with the men." Bay caught Eli's pained groan as he turned his mount toward the outbuildings.

"Nonsense. You're my son." John's voice rose as they rode away. "I want you in the house, where you belong. I'll not have you acting like some common hand."

Cajun sidestepped fretfully. Bay looked down, found his fist tight around his reins. He loosened his grip and thumped the gelding's neck to settle him.

Eli brought his mare up alongside, his eyebrows lifted in a question.

"Damn, you're my own flesh and blood!" John shouted behind them. "Family!"

Bay's answer came out in a barely audible mutter between gritted teeth. "You should have worried about that years ago."

"I hear the wagon." Mariah abandoned the mess of new peas she'd been shelling and went to the door. "It's Papa."

She ran outside. Her father set the brake and hopped down from the bench seat of the heavy farm wagon, then snatched her up to whirl her around. "There's my girl."

"Oh, Papa, I'm glad you're home." She gave him a big kiss on the cheek and released him to her mother.

"I am, too, Cornelius."

"Acasta, love of my life."

His greeting to his wife was just as enthusiastic, if slightly less rambunctious. Mariah had always loved the sight of her father kissing her mother. His sandy brown head always bent over her mother's pale gold for much too long to be proper. It was the one unladylike thing her mother did, letting her husband kiss her with so much passion in front of just about anyone but the preacher. "Scandalous," some called it. "How can she let him behave that way?"

Out of love, Mariah thought, watching them. She had always wanted a husband who kissed her like that.

Like Bay did, a voice whispered in her head, and suddenly she had to turn away from her parents. Bay McKenzie's attempted seductions had nothing to do with love.

"Makes a man want to go on more trips, if he gets a greeting like this when he gets back." He said the same thing every time he came home.

"Did James stop over at the Martins'?" Acasta asked. Aurelia Martin was the one thing they all suspected might keep Jimmy in Chase County past the age of eighteen.

"Not exactly. He stayed in Wichita. Oh, now, don't get all worried." Her father gave his wife a wink and a squeeze. "Come on inside and I'll tell you what your son's up to. Pour your old father a cup of coffee, please, Mariah."

He waited until they were all settled around the table, then took a big swig of coffee. "It's fine to be home. Now, about James. I want to start off by telling you, again, not to worry, Acasta. The boy's fine. In fact, he got himself a job."

"A paying job?" Mariah asked.

"A real, paying job. Some fellow he met at the stockyard hired him on."

"Wichita's such a rough town." Acasta's voice quivered a little. "And it's so far away."

"I know that, wife. I just drove every mile of the way." Cornelius took another sip of coffee. "But he'll be working outside of town, mostly, and it's not as bad as the newspapers would have us believe. Look at it in a positive light: The boy's finally showing a little responsibility. He said this fellow that hired him is building a new holding pen and chute. He wanted a few extra hands to help out. The job only lasts until they're finished."

"That doesn't sound like the kind of thing Jimmy would like," Mariah said skeptically. "He always grumbles so about doing fence work or carpentry."

"There's a difference between working for your own father and working for wages. He'll do fine."

"I just wonder if he'll come home when the work's done," Acasta said, echoing Mariah's thoughts.

"Of course he will. Now for some real news." Cornelius pulled his money purse out of his deep pocket, and spilled the wadded contents across the table grandly. "Look what I managed to get for that load of walnut."

The women spent a few minutes excitedly smoothing and counting bills.

"A hundred and seven dollars!" Mariah said.

"Some fellow's putting up a hotel for the drovers and buyers," her father said, smiling broadly. "He's trying to make it as fancy as that place of McCoy's up in Abilene, and he wanted the walnut for his card room. When he found out someone else was interested, he offered fifty cents a board foot for every scrap I had."

"It's a shame we can't figure out a way to raise a crop of walnut trees in a year, like corn," Acasta said. "We'd be rich as Croesus."

"I'll be happy just to pay off the mortgage. Well," Cornelius shrugged his shoulders a few times to loosen up. "I need to take care of the wagon."

It took him longer than it should, and when he came in he had a scowl on his face.

"What happened to the corn?" he demanded.

Mariah looked to her mother, but Acasta signalled her to start. "Some cattle got into it."

"Ours?"

"No, sir. They belonged to some fellow south of here. He gave us three dollars for the trouble. They were Texas longhorns and they had ticks, so we'll have to keep our cows off the stubble until winter."

"You did a fine job fixing up the fence."

"I didn't do it, Papa."

She told the story as briefly as possible, her mother adding a few well-chosen words in Bay's behalf to defuse her husband's anger. Still, when they finally revealed Bay's last name, his knuckles whitened from squeezing the back of the chair so hard. Mariah thought vaguely that it was a good thing

Bay had fixed it, or else it would have come apart in her father's hands.

"Son of a . . ." Cornelius bit off the sentence and dropped onto the chair. He smacked the table with his fist. His coffee cup rocked wildly, then settled. "I can't believe he had the gall to send his boy onto my property. Are you sure he didn't cause any mischief?"

Acasta looked at Mariah, then to her husband. "No trouble at all. Odd as it seems, he was a perfect gentleman."

Chapter Five

BAY AVOIDED HIS father for two days.

It wasn't hard, except for convincing the foreman he really meant to work with the regular hands. Once he and Eli proved they knew one end of a horse from the other, they had their pick of chores. Bay simply chose the ones farthest from the house.

Eli tagged along obligingly until it came to packing an orphaned calf across his saddle, so they could find a fresh cow that might be willing to take it.

"Nope. Don't want him ruinin' my new boots."

"Those boots haven't been new for a good six months." Bay took a final look at the dead cow and swung up onto his roan. "Looks like she bled too much after she had him. Well, if you won't pack him, boost him up to me."

Eli scooped up the bawler and they arranged him in front of Bay. The calf struggled briefly, and one tiny hoof clipped Eli in the shoulder.

"Going to be a mean little bull."

"Steer," Bay corrected. "He's too scrawny for seed stock."

It took them most of the afternoon to find a cow with a full udder and no calf, and another couple of hours to coax her into nursing the newborn. They watched until they were satisfied she'd mother the calf, and by the time they got back to the bunkhouse, the crew were lined up along the board and trestle tables outside, deep into their supper. They tied their horses, washed up, and headed for the chow line.

Bay watched the cook heap Eli's plate with potatoes and stew and biscuits, then held out his own.

"Nope." Cookie folded his arms across his chest. Gravy dripped off his ladle and ran down the seam of his stained pants. "Mr. McKenzie says you're to eat up at the house tonight."

Two tables full of noisy, hungry cowboys fell silent. They all knew who Bay was, of course. Not a man had asked him a single question about his background, which meant whispers had gone through the crew, probably before he'd gotten his blankets rolled out on the bunk. They'd all been friendly, but they were clearly waiting to see what would happen between the big boss and his son.

Well, now they'd all find out. The tin plate clinked as Bay dropped it back on the stack. He nodded at the cook. "Hope that woman up at the house makes biscuits as good as yours. Thanks for the message."

The cook shrugged and went back to stirring his stew. "Sure."

Eli left his plate on the end of the table and followed Bay into the bunkhouse. "Suppose those lawyer-fellows are still up there?"

"I imagine they are." Bay dug into his gear for a clean shirt and pants and started to strip down. He wished he felt as careless as his words sounded. "I expected this. He never thought I'd be back, but now that I'm here, he wants to show me off to his guests. It's also his way of showing me he's still in charge. By damn, I'll do what he says, even if he has to starve me to make the point."

"And you're going to go along with it?"

"Only because it suits me." Bay grabbed a washrag and some soap and gave himself a quick once over to take the stink of the day's work off. No use sitting down to a decent dinner smelling like that calf. "He's been locked up with those gents for long enough to tell me they're up to something. I'm curious. Maybe I can find out what they're up to over a glass of whiskey."

"It's no never-mind to me, but I thought this trip was about settling the past."

"It is. We may get around to that this evening, too."

Eli shrugged. "I guess you know what you're doing."

Maybe, and maybe not. Bay pulled on the fresh clothes and found the one clean bandanna he had left, a dark blue one. Folded neatly and knotted at his throat, it made a passable tie against the yellow shirt. He ratted through his gear for the small, leather-bound journal he kept. A piece of paper tucked inside the front cover went into his pocket. As a final step, he checked himself in the battered mirror that all the hands shared. Other than a shadow of whiskers, he made a passable appearance. He'd look better in a suit, of course, but both of his were in a trunk in Denver. At least everything looked like it had seen an iron, thanks to Mariah.

A slow smile played over his face as he recalled the same shirt and pants lying on a shelf in the Hoags' house, while he and Mariah pretended to forget them. Suddenly he wanted to see her, to put that smudged look back on her lips and see if he could get her to forgive him.

Eli walked up behind Bay, his thumbs hooked in his waistband. "Your hide isn't worth a plugged nickel on that farm, I'd vow, 'specially not with her daddy and her brother home."

Bay grimaced. "How'd you now what I was thinking about?"

"Last time I saw you in that shirt, it was an inch thick with trail dust. Stands to reason she's the one that washed it. And then there's that fool grin on your face. I warned you not to tangle with that girl."

"Oh, go on and eat. Your stew's getting cold."

Bay left his friend outside at the table and headed for the house, the fool grin now a pensive frown. He still wanted to explain himself to Mariah—and to her mother, for that matter. Being tarred with the same brush as his father was as distasteful now as it had been as a kid. Somehow or other, he'd have to find a way past the Hoag men before he left.

Which meant he didn't have much time, if tonight went the way he hoped. He focused his attention on the house and on the man waiting inside.

At the front door he reminded himself that he was the son of the house and walked in without knocking. Muffled voices coming from the hall to the right would have told him where the dining room was even if he didn't know the floor plan inside out. He headed directly for it without slowing to look around. He didn't want some trace of the past to make him sentimental—or angry—at this point.

A ladder-back chair sat at the head of the hallway, and what lay across it made him stop. Bay shook his head at the black jacket and tie. Clothing had never mattered much to John McKenzie unless it served some purpose like showing off money or power.

This was definitely a play for power. Bay put on the jacket, probably an old one of his father's. It fit, or close enough, though it looked peculiar with his canvas pants and yellow shirt. Grinning, he went ahead and replaced his kerchief with the tie. No harm in letting his father think he'd won another round. It would put him off guard, and it might make dinner less unpleasant.

Sure enough, John McKenzie broke into a triumphant smile when Bay walked into the dining room. "There you are, boy. We were about to go ahead without you. Gentlemen, let me introduce you to my son, Ja—Bayard, come home at last."

Bay tried to keep his hackles down as he went through the motions of meeting Freemont, Wallace and Putnam. The first two were lawyers, the third, a banker from Cottonwood Falls.

"Bay," he corrected when Wallace called him "Mr. McKenzie." His father frowned, and continued frowning until Bay slid into the place conspicuously left open at his right side.

The woman in gray, Mrs. Shaw, appeared almost immediately with the first course of potato soup. Bay shook the folds from the heavy Irish linen napkin, and laid it across his lap. When he looked up, his father was staring at him.

"It's good to have you at the table again, boy." John stuck his hand out awkwardly. The mix of pride and joy and sadness in his eyes caught Bay off guard and he took the offered hand. They shook, father and son again for the moment.

A discreet cough made them both start with embarrassment and release their brief hold on the past.

"So, Mr. McK—Bay," the banker, Putnam, began. "Your father says you haven't joined us before because you've been working around the ranch. Getting your hand back in, so to speak. What do you think?"

So that was it. He was supposed to be part of the united front of McKenzie and Son.

Bay knew the role. He'd played it often enough when he was growing up. He wished he knew what his father was up to this time. He had half a mind to let the old man sink on his own, but the gambler in him said he should play along for now.

"It's going to take more than two or three days to see all of the changes my father has put in place. The most obvious thing, of course is that we've moved away from horses and more into cattle. I can see both good and bad in that, but it looks like the land's handling it well. The bluestem up in the north end is nearly as healthy as when we put up our first soddy."

"That's because I rotate the herds," John said, drawing a circle over his bowl with his spoon. "Keep the big louts moving about, like we did the sheep back home, so they don't tear up the sod. You have to do that when you've not got open land all around for grazing. I told you that years ago, did I not, boy? Always keep them moving."

Bay nodded. Using that "we" had made his father sit up straighter.

"That takes a lot of land if you're going to have any size herd," Freeman said.

"Have I not been telling you so." He glanced toward Bay. "But enough of business at the table, especially with my boy here for the first time in years. How about if you tell these gentlemen all the places you've been since the war, son."

He said it as if he'd already heard the stories himself.

Bay had to smile at his father's way of digging, though he felt more than a little frustration at having the conversation cut short just when it was going to get informative. There was nothing to do about it now.

"Let's see, first I headed for Montana."

So the rest of the evening went, Bay spinning tales, the others listening and asking questions that led off into still more tales. His father's housekeeper moved in and out, filling and clearing dishes, until the only things left on the table were shot glasses and the bottle of Scotch whiskey that had been a fixture of every dinner Bay could remember. Every now and again he caught himself thinking of the last time he'd told some of the same stories. Mariah's face swam into his mind, and he imagined her gold curls dancing in the light of the brass chandelier overhead.

Eventually the bottle ran dry, and Freemont and company excused themselves to bed.

"Just a minute, gents. I'll see you along." John hoisted himself to his feet, pain twisting his face as he straightened, and hobbled after them. "The place is yours, boy. Do what you like. Good night."

Bay stared at the open door as the mismatched footsteps faded, leaving him alone in the empty dining room.

"You old son of a gun," he muttered, then burst out laughing. That's what he got for assuming he could work John McKenzie for information. He'd been out-foxed by a master.

Mrs. Shaw stuck her head in from the pantry. "Will there be anything else, Mr. McKenzie?"

"It's Bay, and no. Thanks." He tossed back the dregs in his glass, stripped off the jacket and tie, and left them lying over his chair. "Good night."

He had every intention of going straight back to the bunkhouse, but a glimpse of his mother's portrait pulled him into the front parlor.

His mother had commissioned it on a whim when he was about eight years old, long before they'd moved to Kansas. The artist had been a student in New Orleans, desperate for cash, but he'd had a skill beyond most. Bay could look into the canvas and hear his mother's laugh and the rustle of her favorite pink taffeta ball gown.

"Your papa will like it. Now you keep it a secret for maman, all right?"

He hadn't seen it when he'd gone in. Just as well, really. There would be more traces of her scattered throughout the house, a daguerreotype here, a china demitasse there. Somewhere, he suspected, in one of the bedrooms, would be her tortoise shell dressing set. He wanted to find them all, follow his mother's memory from room to room like a bread crumb trail back to a happy family.

And that, he knew, was what his father was hoping for, leaving him alone in the house. Damn him, he was still using her.

He headed for the darkened bunkhouse, playing over the events of the evening.

So, besides a fresh lesson in just how manipulative John McKenzie could be, all he had come away with tonight was a sense that he'd better stick around the ranch long enough to find out just what his father was conniving this time. The only hint was that it had something to do with land.

But then, it always did.

"I'm so glad Mr. Quincy agreed to see to the animals." Acasta glowed with good spirits, her cheeks a healthier shade than Mariah had seen in months, despite the long wagon ride into town and the dust that rolled up around the heavy wheels. "I think I'd forgotten how much I missed the hustle and bustle of town."

"They're going full out." Mariah pointed at the ornate limestone courthouse, the pride of the county since its completion nine months earlier. They'd driven all the way around town just so they could come straight down Broadway from the north and get the best view. "Just look at all the bunting."

"It's quite festive," Acasta said. "I do believe Independence Day is my favorite holiday anymore."

"Not Jeff Davis's birthday?" Cornelius asked, putting an arm around his wife's shoulders.

She gave him a soft smile. "It doesn't carry the same charm it used to."

"Fortunately, love of my life, you do."

"Oh, pshaw. Anyway, I like the way Independence Day falls in the middle of the summer, especially when it's a Saturday like this year. I enjoy the picnicking and the band music."

"*Yankee* music," Cornelius pointed out in mock disgust. "*Yankee Doodle. The Battle Hymn of the Republic.*"

"I'll just have to sing a chorus of *Dixie* tomorrow to even things out."

"Mama, you wouldn't dare. There are people here who would lynch us." As far as they were from Lawrence, both in time and distance, Mariah knew that the memory of Quantrell's brutal raid smoldered in the old timers' souls. Not that she could blame them for clinging to the anger: the Raiders had hunted down hundreds of men in the night and slaughtered them like so many animals.

"Why not? After all, the Yankees won. They can't begrudge us a song or two." Acasta saw her husband's and daughter's concerned faces and broke out laughing. "Oh, of course I'm not going to sing. At least, not yet. We'll give them a few years, and then I'll organize a Southern Ladies Chorus to do it right."

Cornelius gave his wife an affectionate squeeze and flicked the reins just to remind the horses he was there. "There's Annie Richardson going into the general store."

Acasta laid her hand on her husband's arm. "Stop, dear. Mariah, go on and see if she'd like some company."

"I thought I'd help you settle in at the Flowers'," Mariah said, "since Papa's going by the bank and all."

"Nonsense," her father said, pulling the team to a halt. "She doesn't need help to take a nap, which is all she is going to do this afternoon. I'll see to her. There's no need for you to spend your whole trip with us old folks. You go on and have fun."

Mariah gave her mother a quick peck on the cheek and clambered down over the wheel. "I'll see you at supper time."

"Do you have any pin money, child?"

"Yes, ma'am." She waved and watched the wagon roll off.

Staying at the Flowers' had become a tradition for their rare overnight trips into Cottonwood Falls. Not only did Georgina set an especially hearty table, she raised big gray and white geese for their feathers and down. Her pillows and tickings slept like clouds, a treat after jangling into town on a heavy farm wagon.

Mariah exchanged greetings with the old gents on the bench out front and paused to let her eyes adjust to the darkness within the store. Aromas of licorice and apples, kerosene and fresh-ground coffee wafted through the open door, a heady mix.

Inside, Annie picked over a counter stacked with bolts of cloth. She'd been the first girl to make friends with Mariah when they'd moved to Kansas, and they had remained best friends after the Richardsons had moved into town.

Annie looked up from a bolt of cotton and her grin turned her ruddy cheeks into ripe peaches. "Mariah Hoag. Just the person I need. Come on in here and help me pick out material for my wedding dress."

"Wedding?"

"Right after harvest. I want you to stand up for me."

"Oh, Annie!"

The two women hugged and launched into an afternoon's worth of fussing over cloth and style interspersed with excited questions and answers. By the time they left the store, Mariah had all the details of Henry's proposal and Annie owned twelve yards of sparkling white cotton batiste and enough ribbon to tie the courthouse in a bow, all thoroughly wrapped in brown paper to keep it pristine.

"Have you seen Nikolai yet?" Annie asked as they loitered in the shade outside the store.

"No. Not yet."

Fortunately, her friend misread the relief in her voice and went on happily, "Is he hiring a buggy to take you sparking again tomorrow night?"

"We did *not* go sparking last year, and we won't this year either."

"Mmm-hmmm," Annie said noncommittally. "Celia says he goes into the bank every week after he gets his pay at the quarry. He's saving up for something. I bet he's going to talk to your pa soon."

Mariah's stomach churned with guilt. Nikolai had mentioned over a year ago—no, exactly a year, when they'd been out on that buggy ride Annie was talking about—that he had his eye on a house and some land over near Elmdale. The implication, of course, was that he intended to marry her. With his work at the quarry, they'd avoid the insecurity that plagued most of the farmers in these parts.

She wanted that secure future, she really did. She shook her head, unsure why she had put it all in jeopardy for the likes of Bay McKenzie.

"Well, if he hurries up, we can have a double wedding.

Lands, I've got to get." Annie gave her a big hug and started backing away reluctantly. "Henry's supposed to meet me over at the gazebo to take me home. Oh, I almost forgot. I'm having a quilting at the end of the month, for my wedding chest. Remind me tomorrow and I'll tell you the particulars."

"I will. Go on, now, before Henry thinks you've found another beau."

"Not me. Bye." Annie blew a kiss and hustled off toward the courthouse.

No, not Annie, Mariah told herself. She keeps her clothes on in the rain, and she wouldn't let another man kiss her, either. Convinced her guilt must be blazoned across her chest like the Scarlet Letter in the book, she ducked her head and started briskly toward the Flowers' neat two story clapboard house.

She had turned west onto Main and was just passing the livery when a familiar voice issued from the double doors.

"I told the smith to go ahead and do all four feet," Bay said. "I might as well hit the trail with him freshly shod. Anyway, his boy will bring Cajun over when he's done, and you can reach me at the Doolittle House if you need to."

Mariah heard the livery man's muffled response from deep inside the stable, but her mind had closed down. *He's going.* She forced her feet to keep moving, even when Bay stepped into the sun directly in front of her.

One black eyebrow lifted in surprise. "Mariah."

His voice sounded just as it had that day in the cornfield, the first time he'd said her name. Her heels scuffed in the dust as she fought the alternate urges to stop or to turn and run. She hesitated, gathering her emotions close, then stepped firmly around him.

He followed her, and with his long legs there wasn't much chance she was going to out-walk him.

"My horse threw a shoe on the way into town," he said conversationally. "I already had to hike three miles. Can we sit down someplace?"

"There's a liar's bench up at Ferry and Watson's, Mr. McKenzie. Feel free."

"I'm not going to leave you alone until you let me explain."

"You had several days to say your piece, but you didn't see fit to do so."

"That was a mistake."

"Mistake?" Anger blazed up and Mariah stopped and faced him down. "You call a week's worth of lies a mistake? I can't even remember how many times we talked about John McKenzie and his dirty dealings, and every time you sat there and pretended to sympathize."

"It wasn't pretense."

"Oh, no, of course not. You just forgot to mention you were trying to accomplish the same thing as your father. I didn't think anyone could get more despicable than John McKenzie, but I hadn't counted on his son."

"What are you talking about?"

"Butter wouldn't melt in your mouth, would it? Damn you McKenzies. Well, it wouldn't have worked. You still wouldn't have gotten the land, even if you'd managed to finish what you started in the barn."

"For god's sake, Mariah, you can't believe I'd stoop to that." His face reddened like she'd slapped him, and she felt a perverse pleasure in knowing that she could wound him.

"I do," she said. "What I can't believe is that I was about to give—"

Mariah bit her lip, aghast at what she was about to admit in her effort to hurt him more. Aurelia Martin's pretty round face suddenly swam into focus over Bay's shoulder, her mouth an *O* of shock.

Mariah looked around hastily. Aurelia wasn't the only one watching the scene. Back at the livery, the stableman and another, redheaded man had come out to investigate the racket, and several other townsfolk had paused in their traffic along the street. She felt the pulse pound in her temples as mortification struck. She wanted to run straight to the river and drown herself.

Instead, she lifted her chin and glared at Bay with all the loathing he deserved. He stared right back at her, disbelief on his face, and something else, too, that reached right down into her soul and made her want to hide herself in his arms. She started shaking.

"Mariah!" Nikolai's voice boomed down the street, but she couldn't pull her eyes away until he was actually beside her. "What is going on? Mr. Jackson?"

"His name's not Jackson. It's McKenzie." She saw Nikolai's fists bunch up and hastily hooked a hand around his arm. "Don't. He's not worth the trouble and I was just telling him as much." She found a smile someplace and made her voice bright. "Would you walk me over to Mr. and Mrs. Flowers' house, please? Mama and Papa are probably waiting for me."

"This isn't over, Mariah," Bay said softly.

She dug her nails into Nikolai's forearm and started walking.

Bay wanted to grab her back and set her straight, but the good citizens of Cottonwood Falls had had enough entertainment for one afternoon. Tomorrow he'd have the whole day to catch her away from her family and old Thor.

Bay turned to see Eli, whose face registered something between amusement and concern. He stabbed a finger in his direction. "Don't say a word."

His friend held up his hands in mute surrender. The livery man felt no such compunctions.

"Whew. I'd hate to be in your boots, mister."

There was a sneer of obscenity behind the words. Bay felt like planting his fist in the man's face, but that wouldn't do Mariah's reputation any good.

So he shrugged. "I would, too, if it was as bad as it sounded. It's all just a misunderstanding. She and her mama were going to give me a dollar for fixing their fence, till she found out who I am." Close enough to the truth, if anyone bothered to snoop. "I guess they had a little trouble with my old man while I was gone. The name McKenzie sets her off."

"Like a Roman candle, not that I can blame her." The man looked disappointed, and Bay knew he'd squelched some of the impending rumors. "You just better hope she doesn't turn that beau of hers loose on you. He's got the biggest hands I've ever seen." He held his own large fist up for contemplation; it didn't come close to Nikolai's.

"He doesn't strike me as the fighting kind," Eli said.

"He generally ain't, but any man'll fight given the right reason."

On that warning, they took their leave and strolled toward the business section of town. Bay tipped his hat to the moon-faced little blonde who eyed him with trepidation from the stoop of the print shop. She reddened and hurried inside.

"My, my, my." Eli tsked. "You're just making all the girls swoon today."

The tension drained out of Bay's shoulders and he chuckled. "It's a gift, friend. It's a gift."

"I suppose we're going to hang around for the fun tomorrow."

"The bank's closed already, so we might as well. Besides, we can't deprive the ladies of our companionship on the anniversary of our nation's birth."

Eli gave Bay a sour look. "Do me a favor, pard. Just watch the fireworks. Don't make any."

Chapter Six

GETTING TO MARIAH turned out to be like trying to outflank General Nate Forrest. Between her father and her beau, she managed to keep herself well out of reach. Bay was stymied.

And she knew it, too. He caught her glancing his way at the brass band concert, where she wedged herself onto a bench between her father and Thor. He spotted her deliberately looking the other way at the courthouse, where Nikolai loomed next to her during the speechifying and the dramatic reading of the Declaration of Independence. Now, at the pie feed, Bay stood off to one side while she continued her show of holiday gaiety at a trestle table shared with her folks, her beau, and two other families.

"I haven't come under so many 'civilizing influences' in one day since I left Ohio," Eli said. Pale, sticky juice trickled onto his beard as he scooped another forkful of gooseberry pie into his mouth. He daubed at the drip with his thumb. "The way these nesters are moving west, there won't be a place for a man to raise cattle or a little hell in another ten years."

"You being more interested in the hell-raising," Bay observed. Mariah's parents excused themselves and walked off toward their wagon. Nikolai didn't budge.

Bay leaned against the trunk of a young elm, watching Mariah. The happy-go-lucky act she'd been performing all day was beginning to give way under her constant awareness of his presence, and frankly, he found it encouraging. Every time Nikolai leaned close, Mariah backed off a little. Every time he reached for her hand, she found something to do that required two hands and pulled away. She flinched when their arms brushed accidentally. Old Thor had put Bay's presence together with Mariah's reticence and was beginning to look like his namesake, thunder darkening his brow, but he stuck with Mariah until she got up to take her turn behind the serving table. Then, apparently considering her safely guarded, he made a beeline toward the privy out back.

Bay grinned. "I think I want some pie after all."

"That boy's going to come back pretty quick," Eli warned. "And she's not going to like it if you start another scene. Give it up."

"She started that fracas in the street, not me. Besides, all she has to do to avoid a scene is agree to talk to me." Bay lifted his hat and combed his fingers through his hair before setting it back.

"Run it by me one more time why you're so set on this. About the time you get her to forgive you, we'll be riding out of here."

"Because I don't like leaving things the way they are."

"The way things are is fine. She's got her beau. You're going to leave. We have plenty of time to get down to Santa Fe before fall. Why mess with . . ." His voice faded as Bay meandered off across the lawn.

A little careful maneuvering kept a knot of people between him and her until he reached the table. He waited in their lee while Mariah made change for a woman, then deftly slid into the open spot directly in front of her when she looked down to slice another pie.

When she looked up, she blanched. A long moment passed while she collected herself.

"Apple, sweet potato, plum, gooseberry, or mince?" she asked finally.

"You already made mincemeat of me," he said, and thought he detected a hint of smile around her eyes before she remembered how angry she was.

"What do you want, Mr. McKenzie?"

"It's Bay. Ten minutes of your time."

"I'm busy. And I don't want to hear any of your excuses." She asked the next man back what he wanted and efficiently cut him a piece of apple pie. As she reached past Bay to hand the pie over and collect the two bits, he resisted the urge to catch her hand and tug her across the table into his arms. She frowned. "Don't you have better things to do than hang over the pies?"

Bay shook his head. "Did you bake for this feed?"

"No."

"That's a shame. You're a good cook. I especially enjoy the way you serve beans."

This time her eyes definitely crinkled with amusement. Bay leaned over the table. "Ten minutes, Mariah."

"I . . ." She squared her shoulders and shook her head stubbornly. A few strands of gold escaped from the hank of hair at her neck and wafted around her ears, and he remembered how soft it felt twined around his fingers. "I told you, I'm busy."

"Well, then, I guess we'll just have the conversation here." Bay put a hand down on either side of a plum pie with a sugar-glazed crust. The move put his face a foot or so from hers.

"Stop it," she hissed. The woman working next to her gave them a sideways glance.

Bay felt the next fellow push up in line behind him. He ignored the man, his attention drawn to the bloom of heat in Mariah's cheeks and down into the modest neckline of her dress. His imagination carried it farther.

"I only want to talk," he said, acutely aware that he was lying to her for sure this time. He wanted a damned sight more than talk just now, but he'd settle. He'd even risk making her madder if it would get her away from this crowd and give him his chance to explain. He gambled and pushed a little harder. "Ten minutes in private, or right here and now. But I am going to have my say. Your choice."

"Ja, her choice," came a heavy voice over his shoulder. "Her choice is no."

Bay straightened and turned to find himself in the awkward, and unusual, position of looking up to another man—a very annoyed man by the frown on his face. Thor stood practically on the toe of his boots.

"Jensen."

"Mac-Kenzie." It sounded like a swear word, and Bay wondered just how much Mariah had told him besides his name.

"There are others waiting and you gentlemen are blocking the table," Mariah said, her voice a little tight, but otherwise clear. "Kindly move on."

Bay nodded and backed off a couple of yards before he turned and walked away. He kept his head cocked enough to see the brute and led the way toward the edge of the crowd. Heads swiveled to follow them.

When they'd gone far enough to be out of hearing, Bay stopped and faced Jensen. The big mason could probably hit like a pile driver. Bay had a feeling he was going to find out in the next few seconds. He tensed, ready to block the blow.

"The only way you talk to her is to come through me." Nikolai's voice rumbled like a runaway freight wagon. "You are bigger than most men, but I think I can break you pretty easy, no? You take off your gun, we see if you still want ten minutes."

"I bet he will." Eli left his position by the elm and came up to one side. "See, if he takes his gun off, I've still got mine. I'm not going to let you beat his head in, no matter how much he might deserve it."

Nikolai sneered. "You hide behind your friend."

"He's got a mind of his own," Bay said. "If you really want a fight, I'll tell him to go, but you'd better think about how Mariah's going to react to you and I bashing on each other in public."

Watching Nikolai change his mind was like watching a snowdrift melt. It happened gradually, from head to foot, each muscle in turn relaxing as the thought travelled the length of his body.

"Ja, you are right," he admitted. "But I do not like you, Mac-Kenzie. Not from the start, when I see the way you look at my Mariah."

"You've been courting her for two years, but that doesn't mean she's yours."

"You so sure?" Nikolai looked smug, sure of his right of possession, and Bay thought again of Mariah and her thunderstorm. She must have meant Thor. His hands balled into fists and he eyed the big man's jaw with a sudden, intense need to beat him bloody. Nikolai saved himself by fishing into his pocket and pulling out his watch to check the time. "We go now, but I warn you, stay away. Next time, maybe no one is around, eh?"

He strode off across the cropped grass, bellowing, "Mariah, time to go."

She passed her serving knife on to the next woman and joined him, but Bay fancied she moved unwillingly. And as they went off toward the buggies parked on the far side of the school, she looked back over her shoulder. He wished he was closer, to see what her eyes held, but just the fact that she bothered to look encouraged him.

Beside him, Eli whistled like a sky rocket going into the air and threw his hands up in a mock explosion. "I guess we don't need to hang around for the fireworks this evening."

"You think that was pretty good, do you?" Bay thumped him on the shoulder jovially. An idea had come into his head. "Friend, the fireworks haven't even begun."

"Nikolai's back to take you to the dance." Acasta's voice came from the door behind her, and Mariah turned, her smile more for her mother than for the news she brought.

"He's early. Tell him I'll be a few more minutes. I don't even have my corset laced."

"I don't think there's a hurry. He seems perfectly happy to sit and talk with your father. Georgina set out some cider and cookies. Let me help you with that."

"Thank you, Mama."

A few minutes later, Mariah stood eyeing herself in the vanity mirror while her mother arranged the draped overskirt of the new sprigged muslin. That overskirt had given her fits when she was sewing, but the flattering way it draped certainly made it worth the trouble.

The bodice was a different matter. She'd fit it snug, but she hadn't realized quite how snug until now—or how much her corset pushed her breasts up into the open neckline.

She raised a hand to the vee, covering the fullness of bosom exposed there. "I'd better put the insert in."

"Let me see." Acasta tugged her hand away and gave her a thorough looking over. "Nonsense. For church, of course, you want the neckline filled in, but this is evening and a party."

"But Mama, it's so . . . shocking."

"Only in Kansas, child. And perhaps Boston. You're just not used to it because you've never had a nice ball gown, but this is not terribly revealing. I assure you, I used to wear lower." Acasta raised her chin proudly. "In fact, I still would if I had anywhere to go. Now, let's see what we can do with that hair of yours."

Skilled fingers tamed the mass—temporarily, at least—into a loose chignon that set off Mariah's cheekbones and left her eyes looking large.

"There," Acasta said with satisfaction. "I know it won't last through the dancing, so I tied the front back with a ribbon before I pinned the rest. When the bottom comes loose, just brush it through with your fingers and you should still look nice."

Mrs. Flowers stuck her head in the door. "My, you look lovely. Would you like to use some of my face powder or maybe a drop of toilet water?"

"Oh, that's so kind of you, Georgina," Acasta said before Mariah had a chance to refuse. Their hostess quickly returned with her dressing tray, and the two women set about powdering and perfuming to their hearts' content.

"Acasta." Her father's voice boomed up the stairs. "What are you doing to that girl? Send her down and let us see her."

"Just a moment, Cornelius." Acasta daubed at Mariah's nose and cheeks one more time. "Now pinch, child, and moisten your lips."

Mariah did as she was told, then tried to check herself in the mirror, but her mother held out her skirts and blocked her view. "You're not accustomed to face powder, either. Just let Nikolai's eyes tell you how you look."

They told her she looked fine. In fact, they said he was delighted with the way she looked, as did her father's, although he looked mildly disturbed by the amount of skin her neckline exposed. Mariah caught him lifting one eyebrow toward her mother, who nodded her head and smiled.

"It was worth the waiting," Nikolai said with a smile.

"Thank you, kind sir."

"You two go on and enjoy the box supper," her father said. "We'll meet you later at the courthouse. Your mother tells me she may feel up to a couple of dances tonight, especially if I can get them to play a waltz."

"I'm sure they will. Later, then." Mariah gave her mother a quick hug, and followed Nikolai out to the trim black livery buggy.

Since he'd dropped her off after the pie feed, he'd been hard at work weaving red and blue ribbons into the white mare's mane. Tiny flags already hung from the headstall, fluttering as the mare tossed her head. He'd changed into a fresh white shirt that contrasted brilliantly with his black pants and red suspenders. His sleeves were rolled up, showing the corded muscles in his forearms. His flat-brimmed straw hat lay on the leather seat, its usual black band replaced by a red, white and blue one. He scooped the hat up as he climbed up beside her, popped it on his head and flicked the reins. The mare started off.

"It is a good night," he said with sureness. "A good night."

Mariah took a deep breath, trying to rid herself of the uneasy feeling that rose as soon as they left her parents behind. Nikolai had been uncharacteristically silent bringing her home after his encounter with Bay, apparently too angry to grumble. Now he showed up with the buggy decked out in style, and there was something in him she hadn't seen before, a certain determination.

Her instincts proved right when, instead of turning toward the picnic grounds with the other buggies, he veered west, across Spring Creek and onto the Elmdale Road.

"We need to talk," was all he'd say when she questioned the detour, but two or three miles later he still hadn't spoken a word. Mariah's uneasiness grew.

Finally, he stopped at the top of Osage Hill, not far from a seasonal creek that ran north into the Cottonwood River. He looped the reins around the whip socket and sat for a long time, looking over the village and the curving sweep of river below.

Mariah remained motionless beside him, her hands folded in her lap.

Nikolai finally turned to her. The late sun drew out the red in his blonde hair and beard, turning them to fire. "You are very pretty in that dress, Mariah. The ribbons match your eyes."

Thor will like it, Bay had said through his messenger.

"Very pretty eyes," Nikolai repeated, his voice soft and thick. His arms moved around her. "Too pretty."

Then, abruptly, he was kissing her, first gently and then with more ardor, his lips bruising, his tongue probing. Mariah parted her lips and felt his tongue sweep into her mouth. Nikolai had never kissed her so ardently before. She waited for the same warmth that had flooded through her when Bay did it.

It didn't come.

The willingness to press into his arms and kiss back just didn't come, and she suddenly wasn't sure if it ever really had. Kissing Nikolai had always been, as it was now, pleasant, but not thrilling. She hadn't known to expect more until Bay. She sat there, trying to make sense of the difference, so distracted she missed the change in Nikolai.

He pushed away from her, his lips set into a thin line, and muttered something in Norwegian. "What is the matter with you?" he demanded.

She looked at him, helpless to explain. "I don't know. I just . . . didn't expect . . ."

"No. Not just now when we kiss. You have been like this all day, even before the pie feed. It is him. Mac-Kenzie."

It would do no good to deny it. "He's so persistent. Showing up everyplace we go. He claims he just wants to apologize, but he won't take my word that I don't want to hear his excuses."

"Ja. Ja." He pounded his fist into his palm. The heavy smack, like stone striking stiff leather, startled the horse, and the buggy jerked forward a few yards. "I can fix."

"Nikolai, don't. Promise you won't fight him."

"I cannot promise this." He looked once more down the hill toward Elmdale, the determination clear on his face. "He said you are not mine. Why, Mariah?"

Because I'm a fool without the sense to stay out of a storm. "To taunt you."

Nikolai nodded, accepting her reasoning. "I can fix this, too." He pointed at a whitewashed frame house tucked into the burr oak grove at the bottom of the hill, nearly invisible in the creeping dusk. "You see that house down there? What do you think?"

Mariah began to pleat the overskirt of her dress, gathering even half-inch folds across her knees. "It looks nice. It's hard to say from here."

"We will come and look again in the light. Maybe tomorrow after church. But it is not important. The land is good, and after, I can build bigger."

"After?" she asked dully.

"After we are married." He didn't give her a chance to think, but slipped onto one knee in the foot well. The move put his blue eyes on the same level as hers, and she could see the intensity in them. "I talked to your papa today while I was waiting for you. I do not know the right way to say it, but I want you to be my wife."

Oh, God, she'd been waiting for this for months. Nikolai. Steady, hard-working, reliable. He'd hold his own land and help her father keep his. He'd be a considerate husband. He'd provide well, and he would stay in Chase County forever. He'd once told her that he'd known it was home from the first day he'd come to cut stone for the courthouse.

"Even with my work, it will not be easy," he said. "But I will take care of you, you and your parents. And when he hears we are promised, that I am responsible for you, Mac-Kenzie will leave you alone."

The mention of Bay's name broke the dream. Nikolai deserved a temperate wife, one who ran from lightning and could commit with all her being. She had to find that in herself first.

She groped for words. "I am honored that you ask, Nikolai, and I want to—"

"Good. Good." His broad smile broke her heart.

"I want to *eventually*. But I'm not ready. Not now. And you're not either. You weren't going to ask me to marry you yet. I know you. Brave soul, you decided this is the best way to protect me from Bay McKenzie. That's not a reason to make a marriage."

"No. But it is not the only reason I want to marry you. I have strong feelings in my heart for you, Mariah, and I want you as a man wants his woman."

Mariah pressed her hands to her flaming cheeks. "You mustn't say such things."

Nikolai touched her hand gently. "It is not right to say, but it is true. Soon you will be my wife, and you will understand."

Heaven help her, she understood already, more than she should. Nikolai must never know that when she thought about a man wanting her and about wanting back, it was Bay's face that came into her mind.

"Take me back to town, please." She couldn't meet his eyes.

The seat springs creaked as he shifted and settled his weight. "Ja. It is getting dark. Your papa will shoot me, I think, if we do not come to the fireworks."

His hands tightened around the reins and the muscles in his forearms bunched and rippled.

Thor. She could almost see him with the hammer, and she felt ashamed.

Thor might be a god, but the name also carried a heavy dose of mockery. Nikolai was a good man; he didn't deserve that, and yet she couldn't help thinking of it. It had kept popping into her head all day, especially when she'd seen him looking Bay's way with thunder in his eyes.

Never again would she think of him simply as Nikolai. Another mark Bay had put on her life.

They drove in near silence back toward town. Behind them, the sun slipped toward the horizon, until the shadow of the horse and buggy stretched out ahead like a serpent, with Nikolai's hat on its head. Mariah let her mind drift as the shapes wavered and changed over the uneven road. She was startled when two horsemen appeared at the tip of the shadow.

Bay. Mariah recognized the way he sat his roan and the slant of his hat an instant before his eyes found hers in the gloom. She imagined the other man was his friend, the one who'd been with him the first day.

Nikolai was a second or two behind her. "Damn him." He

lifted the buggy whip out of its holder and clucked to the mare to speed up, but Bay and his friend blocked the middle of the road. The buggy jolted to a stop.

"Get out of our way," Nikolai said.

"Ten minutes," Bay said. His eyes never left hers.

Mariah straightened. "No."

"I told you, this isn't over until you hear me out."

"I told *you* no."

"Then you don't leave me much choice." Bay pulled out his pistol and let it rest across his knee, not aimed at them, but a clear threat nonetheless. "Get out of the buggy."

"No." Nikolai and Mariah spoke almost together. Nikolai added, "Go to hell."

"I'm bound to. But I'm talking to her before I do." He aimed the pistol at Nikolai's head.

Mariah gasped. "Don't. For God's sake, Bay."

Swearing fervently in Norwegian, Nikolai jumped out of the buggy. He put up a hand to help Mariah down.

"Not you, Mariah. Just your . . . friend, there."

"So. I am down." Nikolai turned on Bay and advanced a few steps, his fists high. "You ready? Put away your gun and come down here with me. No one is here to watch."

Bay shook his head. "I have no intention of fighting you. I'm just going to borrow your buggy and take Miss Hoag for a ride."

"You'll do no such thing," Mariah said.

"I will. Move away, Jensen."

Nikolai balked. "I will not let her go with a horse thief."

"Tell him, Mariah."

"He's right," she said. "You're acting like a common criminal."

"You generally get what you expect from people. I don't see as I lose any ground with you by playing highwayman."

Nikolai spat on the ground. "Bastard Mac-Kenzie."

"That's my father. Now move off before my finger gets restless."

A hardness underlined Bay's careless words, a hardness that warned Mariah he was losing patience. "You'd better do as he says, Nikolai."

"No. I not leave you."

"He's not going to hurt me," she said with certainty. "But I'm worried about you. Go on, I'll be fine."

Muttering curses in two languages, Nikolai backed out into the pasture a little ways.

"Farther," Bay said, motioning with his pistol. "Go sit on that stump out there and turn your back. Eli will keep an eye on you." Nikolai looked at Mariah and then at the pistol, and obeyed.

Bay rode his horse around in back of the buggy. Mariah refused to look, but she heard sounds like he was tying the animal to the back. A moment later, he hopped up beside her. She kept her eyes on the white mare and her decorations.

Bay yelled out toward the field. "She and the buggy will be safe and sound in town when you get there."

"Ten minutes, you said," Nikolai shouted. "If she is not back in ten minutes, then I come find you and crack your head like a green walnut."

"No, you won't, boy," Eli said. "You'll just sit there 'til I say you get up."

"My father and mother are waiting for me," Mariah said. "They'll worry. Mama—"

"Will think you're out spooning with Thor and lost track of the time. You'll only be a few minutes late." He found the reins and gave them a snap. As the mare started forward, he hollered to Nikolai over his shoulder, "You're only about two and a half miles out. If you hustle once Eli turns you loose, you and Mariah can enjoy most of the dance."

Nikolai roared his fury out over the hills, but Bay just clucked at the mare, moving her into a brisk trot. He gave Mariah a sideways glance. "What, nothing from you?"

"I . . . you . . ." She was shaking so hard with rage she couldn't form words.

"What? Bastard? Liar? Thief? Between the two of you, I think you've covered everything."

"Damn you! You were going to shoot him!"

Bay pulled the pistol out of his holster and tossed it on her lap. "You once threatened to fill my butt full of lead. Here. The first one's on me."

The heavy Smith and Wesson dragged at her skirts. She trapped it between her hands and sat there staring down at the blue gleam of the barrel. In the deepest wells of her anger, at him, at John McKenzie, at everything back to the first Yankee trooper that rode through the vegetable garden, she suspected there lived something that could shoot a man. She'd felt its black touch a few times, and she'd rather keep it in the hole.

She handed the gun back to Bay. He pointed the barrel skyward and pulled the trigger. The only sound was a metallic click.

"It's not loaded," she said.

"Nope. Neither's Eli's. 'Course Thor doesn't know that."

"What would you have done if he had come at you?"

"Done my best to beat his head in. Tried to keep him from doing the same to me."

She sat for a long time as the light faded, listening to the roan and the mare nicker back and forth to each other as they moved into the evening. At a fork where Bay should have gone straight, he turned right instead. She didn't say a word. Both roads led to town; this one just took a few minutes longer. Around them the prairie buzzed with insects settling down for the night, punctuated by the distant pop of the firecrackers that had been rattling the windows all day.

It still wasn't quite dark when a low boom rolled across the hills. Like every year, she had to see the circle of sparks falling over town, blue as the wings of dragonflies, before she knew it was the first of the skyrockets and not a cannon and the war all over again.

"They set the first one off early to give everyone a chance to get to the show," she said to fill the silence after. "Give me your pocket watch."

He handed it over. "Does this mean you're going to listen to me?"

"It means I'm not sure who's the biggest fool here." She flicked the watch open and peered at the face. She could barely make out the delicate black hands in the dusk.

"Twenty minutes past nine," she said. "All right, Mr. McKenzie. You have your ten minutes."

Chapter Seven

"THAT'S THE FIRST thing we're going to get straight," Bay said firmly, yanking the buggy to a halt. "I'm getting blasted tired of hearing 'McKenzie,' especially from you and in that tone of voice."

Mariah looked at him like he was a lunatic. "That's your name."

"Maybe, but before Doug Stutt walked up to that wagon, the last two men to call me McKenzie were the colonel that accepted my resignation of commission and the quartermaster that gave me my final pay packet."

"You're saying you've been going by Jackson?"

"For nine years." He could almost see her anger shrink as she absorbed the fact. "You can ask Eli if you don't believe me. He's known me since Montana and hadn't even heard the name until I asked him to ride back here with me. Or I can give you the name of a banker in Denver who's got my accounts. As Bay Jackson."

"Well, you're back in Chase County now. People know you as John McKenzie's son."

"I'm well aware of that. Leave it at Bay. Without the sneer."

"Why?"

"Because it's my name, damn it all."

"No, I mean why Jackson? Why *not* McKenzie? You certainly act like him, taking what you want, when you want it, helping him get—"

"And that's the next thing," he interrupted. "Where the devil did you get the idea my seducing you had anything to do with my father?"

99

"You didn't seduce me," she snapped. "But as I said, it wouldn't have done any good if you had. After all we've been through, it will take more than shame and embarrassment to make us pack up and slink off."

She turned her back on him, dismissing him, and that didn't go far to sweeten Bay's mood. He grabbed her by the shoulders and turned her back, forcing her to face him.

"First off, I don't use women that way," he said harshly. "Second, I haven't had anything to do with the old . . . with him since I left in '61."

"Humph," she snorted. "He's been telling people you write. He said you were out in Wyoming, starting a new ranch. Extending the family fortunes."

"Well, he lied. I've never sent so much as a letter since the day I left. I hadn't even seen him yet when I met you, and I didn't see him until after you threw me off the property."

"Oh," she said. There was a long silence in which he listened to the sound of her uneven breathing. "Then why *did* you come back?"

"I happened to be in Cheyenne the same time Ted Nalley went through on his way to Oregon, and we ran into each other in a hotel lobby. Oh, yes, I misspoke myself earlier. He called me McKenzie, too, but Eli wasn't around. Anyway, Ted told me about the accident my father had."

"That would have been a long time ago."

"Last fall. It took me a while to decide to come." He found himself still holding her, unwilling to turn her loose now that he had her. He shifted to put her into the crook of one arm, more like a girl he was courting than one he'd basically kidnapped. The change brought his thigh alongside hers, and he pulled her close enough that the curls escaping her bun tickled his cheek and chin. His body responded with startling immediacy.

He turned his mind back to the topic at hand with difficulty. "When I got here I wanted to scout around a little before I went to the house, find out if my father was still up to the same stunts. By the time I knew he was, you'd made it pretty clear you wouldn't tolerate a McKenzie on your land, even to help out—and before you start to argue, you *needed* the help. I figured I'd be done and out of your hair before you found out."

"And then Mr. Stutt showed up, and I wouldn't let you get a word in edgewise," she finished the story.

"Not a syllable."

In town, the fireworks show started in earnest. Ephemeral flowers colored the sky, followed a few seconds later by an uneven tattoo of explosions. From his lead behind the buggy, Cajun whinnied with excitement.

"We'd better go," Bay said. "We don't want your mother to fret."

Between the stars and the skyrockets, there was enough light to manage the road without the headlamps. Bay handled the reins one-handed, enjoying the rare pleasure of driving with a young woman tucked up against his side, even if she held herself stiff as a courthouse statue and hadn't quite forgiven him yet.

"You still haven't told me why you changed your name," she said. "And why didn't you come home after the fighting?"

He didn't want to get into this. "You've dealt with my father. Describe him."

"Greedy, obsessed. And arrogant," she added, including Bay with her tone.

He glanced toward Mariah, ready to ask if that weren't enough, but she was finally looking up at him. Her eyes were luminous in the darkness, like deep pools in the woods, not green, not black, and he plunged in before he thought about it.

"He's that and more. I fought a hundred fights for his name before I could admit to myself just how bad he was. When the war came along, he saw it as 'a lovely chance to make money off people's foolishness.'" Bay mimicked his father's brogue with bitterness. "My brother had had it with him and left. We got one letter, saying he'd taken a commission in the Second Cavalry, Union. The next day my father sent me and a couple of hands to Missouri, to deliver a string of horses to a Confederate raider."

"So many families got caught up in the war on different sides," she said softly. "You can't blame him for that."

"I wouldn't, if it was for some principle, but he never owned slaves, and he thought the Rebs were crazy for starting a fight they couldn't win. This was for money, pure and simple. To consolidate the land. To build that damned manor house of his." Bay's teeth grated as he clenched his jaw. "He was selling horses to both sides."

"Dear lord."

"I stole the whole string and delivered them to the first Union cavalry unit I could find. Those horses bought me a spot as a trooper, and I worked my way up to Captain through field promotions."

"And your brother was killed."

Apparently his father hadn't lied about that. Bay felt the tightness in his throat that always came when he thought about Johnny, even after all these years. "At Opequon. I often wondered if the man that killed him was riding one of my father's horses."

"Oh, Bay." Mariah reached up and touched his cheek. Her fingers lay cool against his skin, and he turned his head a little, letting his lips brush her palm. She leaned her head onto his shoulder, and he savored the pressure as he got his emotions under control.

"I heard stories about Montana," he continued, hoping the later memories would help. "After the war, I headed out there. One night I won a claim in a card game. My cards, Eli's money. We worked it a little. When we hit, we named it the Jacks High—*Jackson* and Hightower—hired a good manager and headed off for the next adventure. The money from the claim lets us do pretty much what we want."

There was another long silence before Mariah spoke. "Why did you come back here?"

Bay shook his head. "Now that I'm here, I'm not sure. I planned to confront my father, about Johnny and all the miserable things he did, but have you seen him since his accident? He's a broken old man. I know in my head he's as mean as ever, yet every time I think of giving him hell, I get the guilts."

"Well, I don't," she said, lifting her head. "I'll do it for you."

A rocket burst brightly overhead. They had reached the edge of town, and the glittering stars seemed to rain down around the buggy, highlighting the half serious look on her face.

Bay's chuckle was as much release as amusement. "I do believe you would, Miss Hoag. However, this is one fight I intend to finish myself."

"Speaking of fights," she began. "I've heard how you used to beat up the boys around here. I want you to promise that you won't fight Nikolai."

"It's his idea, not mine. Okay, okay," he conceded before she could start in. He had no intention of fighting anyway. He hadn't done that in years. "If he doesn't swing first, I won't. How's that?"

"Tolerable," she said, and he begrudged Thor the concern she showed.

They passed the first whitewashed houses, and Bay turned onto one of the side streets that eventually led up behind the livery. He pulled the buggy into the deep shadow of an overhanging elm and turned to her.

Maybe it was the dark, but she seemed to be staring just past his left ear. It disconcerted him and made his ear itch, and he tugged at the offending lobe and looked away. This was ridiculous. He felt like a moonstruck boy, wanting to kiss her and being uncertain of how she'd react.

No, he had a pretty good idea how she'd react. It was himself he wasn't sure of, all of a sudden. He didn't want any entanglements, especially not here and now.

The courthouse bell tolled twice and strains of the Grand March wafted between the businesses and houses. The dance had started. He'd have to let her go soon.

"So," she said carefully, "you didn't lie to me about your name, and you weren't trying to use me to get to our land."

"That about sizes it up."

"It doesn't excuse what you did do."

"And just what is that?"

"Made me . . . I don't know." She looked away, then back, this time meeting his gaze. "Why *did* you try to seduce me?"

The artless question took his breath away, and with his breath went the uncertainty. Bay tightened his arm, pulling Mariah closer. He buried his nose in her hair. She smelled of perfume, some mix of flowers and sweet musk that made him think of things feminine and lacy, a delicious contrast to the sturdy woman in his arms.

"That's an easy question to answer," he said. "Probably the easiest one you've asked all evening."

He tilted her chin up and kissed her gently, intending to leave it at that, but when she freely opened her lips to let his tongue slide past, his reaction was explosive. Suddenly he couldn't get enough of her, probing until he garnered a moan of pleasure from deep in her throat, until her tongue lifted to battle his to see who could cause the most pleasure. Abandoning that skirmish before either of them won, he touched kisses over her face, then recaptured her mouth and teased her again, until she slipped her arms around his neck and leaned against him in surrender.

Flush with victory and increasing desire, he found the pulse point just beneath her ear where the perfume clung and nuzzled it until she tilted her head back to give him better access. He caught her head in his palms, and her hair tumbled loose and spilled over his hands. Her sigh as he nipped at the soft skin just below her jaw made him smile, and he worked his way down her throat, looking for more sensitive spots.

He pulled a strand of loose curls over her shoulder, letting its silkiness stroke the area he'd just kissed and drape lower across her bosom. All during the drive he'd tried unsuccessfully to keep his eyes off the lush rise of breasts that her dress revealed.

Now he revelled in the recollection of how they looked uncovered, letting his fingers drift with the curls into the shadowed vee he could no longer see in the dark. Her heart thudded against the back of his fingers, and she lifted into the touch, offering herself. He found the budding hardness he was searching for and teased it to a peak beneath her clothing, while he let his other hand drift lower, over the confines of corset, until he found the softness of her thighs swathed in her muslin skirt. He kissed her again, nibbling at her lips while he continued to taunt her with his fingertips. A gentle push set her knees apart a little, and he began a slow, careful exploration back upward that ended when she dug her fingers into his shoulders.

Her gasp drew a groan from his own lips. God, he could feel

the heat of her, even through the layers of cloth. The part of his mind that wasn't telling him he ought to stop while he was ahead, tried to think of a place nearby where he could go with her, where he could rid her of those skirts and touch her freely, and where he could find out how far they could drive each other before he had to lose himself in her.

One of the horses nickered. Someone giggled. Caught in Mariah's magic, Bay thought it strange that she would make such a sound.

Then he heard someone shush the giggler and smelled burning punk and had just a second to release Mariah and grab for the reins.

A string of ladyfingers exploded under the buggy. The mare reared back and lunged forward, dragging them into the moonlight. Cajun screamed. The buggy scraped sideways with his frantic efforts to pull away. Mariah snatched for a handhold.

Bay heard boyish laughter and caught a glimpse of three striped shirts dodging between shrubbery like jackrabbits as he fought the mare. "Whoa, girl, whoa. Cajun, I'm here. Settle down, boy, take it easy."

"I can handle the buggy," Mariah said, reaching for the reins. "Get your horse."

"He's used to gunfire," Bay said, and sure enough, Cajun was already calming. The mare responded to the reins and the gelding's low whinny and began to settle, too.

Bay looked at Mariah and she looked back, and they both started to laugh, full belly laughs that rocked them and made the horses start dancing again.

Then Mariah's laughter faded, too quickly, and her eyes widened. She pressed her hands to her cheeks. "Sweet heavens, what am I doing? Sitting here in the middle of town, in an open buggy, letting someone like you . . ."

"Not someone *like* me. Me." Arousal still clung to his body like cobwebs, tangled with the sudden anger he felt at her accusative tone. "Me, Mariah."

"You, then."

"A man who wants you very much."

Mariah looked away into the night as the strains of the first waltz rippled down the alley. "I've got to get to that dance. And to Nikolai. He wants me, too."

"Mariah," Bay said, keeping his voice reasonable against all his deepest instincts. He waited until she finally turned back to him.

"I could lie to get you to see me again," he said. "I could tell you I'll stay and help you save your farm. But I won't. I'm not that kind of hero. I haven't stayed in one place more than six months since I left the army."

She raised her chin a fraction. "Nikolai asked me to marry him tonight."

"I'm not going to do that, Mariah."

Her breath was fast and harsh. He knew she was angry at the truth. "My whole life is turning upside down, and you're to blame."

"Then either tell me to go to the devil or take things as they come." He started to put his arms back around her, to remind her with a kiss that "things" could be pleasant.

"*You* take things as they come." She shoved at him, hard.

The push caught Bay off guard and he tumbled off the buggy seat, half-catching himself by the front wheel.

"I have no intention of being just one more in the string of women you leave in every town." Mariah snatched up the buggy whip and held it high. "Now untie your horse and let me get back to my life."

A moment later, the buggy lurched off down the street, carrying her away and leaving him standing alone with his horse.

"I think that went pretty well," he told Cajun wryly as he knocked the dust off his clothes. She hadn't actually sent him to hell, after all, and as strong as she was, she could probably do it.

He hadn't really expected the evening to end very much differently. The original plan called for forgiveness and a sweet good night kiss from Mariah before he let her go off to the dance. So he'd ended up in the dust after the kiss. But what a kiss. . . .

Given the state of things, there was nothing to be done but head for his rendezvous with Eli.

He managed to keep to his good intentions for a few minutes, long enough to ride around to the livery to pick up the gear he'd left. But the music from the courthouse was clearer there, and the man on duty kept grumbling about missing the fun, until Bay could see nothing but Mariah twirling through a waltz in Thor's arms.

"Hell," he told himself, standing in the middle of Main, on the very spot where she'd sliced into him the day before. "He probably can't even dance."

He grinned. Then she'd need a partner who could.

But first he was going to find those boys.

"There you are." Annie Richardson dragged her fiancé, Henry, through the crowd to where Mariah stood just inside the double doors of the courthouse. "Your pa was just asking if I'd seen you. Where have you been?"

"We went out driving." Mariah left it at that, but Annie broke into a secretive grin.

"I *told* you Nikolai was going to take you sparking. Where is he?"

"He'll be along in a little bit." Mariah grew uncomfortable under Annie's continued assessing stare. "What?"

"Well? You look so solemn but your cheeks are glowing like anything. What happened? Did he already ask you?"

"You're a Nosy Nellie," Henry interrupted with an affectionate but firm hand on Annie's shoulder. "If she has anything she wants to tell you, she will. Now come on. The lemonade is thataway."

"If he did, I want every detail," Annie called back as Henry led her off.

Mariah nodded distractedly, already searching the swirl of Sunday-best clothes inside for her parents.

She didn't find them until the music ended. Mama might be starting to worry, but not so much she wouldn't enjoy her waltz. Mariah took a deep breath as her parents made their way toward her.

"You're late," Cornelius said.

"We lost track of time," Mariah said, conscious of echoing Bay's words. "I'm sorry."

"Sorry is not enough, young lady. You made your mother worry."

"Oh, Cornelius, hush," Acasta interrupted. "You were more upset than I was. She's here and she's fine. Besides, you know very well what they were doing—just exactly what we did at the same age. Where is Nikolai, by the by?"

"He'll be along in a little," Mariah repeated uncomfortably. "I just wanted to find you right off and let you know we were all right, so you could go on home. You look a little tired, Mama."

Her mother did look a little flush from dancing, but in actuality, Mariah wanted them gone before Nikolai made it to town. It would be bad enough trying to explain things to him and calm him down. Telling her parents would have to wait until tomorrow, when she'd had time to come to grips with everything herself.

Her father came down on her side. "Mariah may be right. I know you're having a wonderful time, my love, but I don't want you to wear yourself out. We'll tell you goodnight now, daughter, but I expect you back right after *Good Night Ladies*. No more losing track of time."

"No, sir." She gave them each a hug and said good night, then watched her father lead her mother toward the door. She watched long enough to wave and make sure they were really gone, then breathed a sigh of relief. That made one less thing she had to worry about tonight. She pushed her way over to the refreshment tables that stood at the end of one hall.

"Where's that big Norwegian of yours?" Michael Skinner asked as she tried to tuck herself into a cluster of wallflowers a few minutes later.

Lands, why had she stayed inside? She should have gone back out and waited in the buggy until she saw Nikolai coming down the road. For that matter, she *should* have driven out after him, but she couldn't bring herself to face him any sooner than she had to. "He'll be along."

"Then there's time for a dance or two."

Maybe that would be better than standing around waiting for the next shoe to drop, even if it put her at risk from Mike's notorious toe-crunching two-step. She set her cup of punch aside. "I do believe there is."

She avoided a broken toe and, at the end of the dance, broke away from Mike long enough to scan the crowd for Nikolai. Behind her, Mike asked a question. She turned back to her partner.

And found Bay, standing next to him.

Her jaw dropped open. She spluttered, but nothing came out.

His lips lifted in that crooked grin. "I believe the proper response is, 'I'd be delighted.'" He held his arms up in dance position.

A good score of townsfolk turned to stare with open curiosity. If she had a lick of sense, she'd put an end to this now by walking off.

"I'd be delighted," she said like a dullard, and let him swing her away into the schottische, fully aware of the whispers that followed them around the floor.

Bay put his mouth to her ear conspiratorially. "I don't think they expected a McKenzie and a Hoag to dance so well together."

"They don't even expect us to *talk* civilly. What are you doing here?" she demanded under her breath. "I told you I want you gone."

Bay lead her through an intricate turn that ended with Mariah firmly in his arms, one of her hands drawn securely behind her waist and the other locked against his chest. "I didn't take you seriously. Actions speak louder than words, I'm told, but you, Miss Hoag, send conflicting messages."

"I'd have thought pushing you out of the buggy would make things pretty clear."

"Alone, it might have, but considering what your lips said a few minutes earlier . . ."

"*Shut up*. People will hear you and talk."

"To Thor, you mean?" He said it lightly and wore the same fixed smile, but the crinkles around his eyes faded.

"Yes. You promised not to fight with Nikolai and then you go and show up here where you know he's going to be."

"More to the point, where I knew *you* were going to be. You don't have to worry, I'll be gone before he shows up. But before then I intend to dance with every unmarried woman I have time for. No one will think anything of this little spin. You'll just be one of the 'string.'"

Mariah glared defiantly, but having her own words thrown back in her face stung more than she wanted to admit. She ignored the sick feeling in her stomach and Bay's further attempts at conversation as he led her around the floor.

The latter attempt was not very successful, considering how aware of him she was. Whatever her mind told her about the man, her body was dead set on enjoying this dance.

Every time he stepped in close, always a little closer than propriety allowed, the places he'd touched earlier throbbed back to life. Her sense of loss when he dipped his head and walked away so easily at the end of the dance nearly made her go after him. Only Mike Skinner's reappearance saved her from completing her performance as the town's biggest fool.

She thought the simple reel that followed would allow her to get her balance back, but she got caught up in watching Bay turn his charms on Mary Elizabeth Williams. When each couple finished their turn at the head of the line, they worked their way toward the foot by way of a grand allemande through all the other couples. Twice she had to take Bay's hand and let him go.

Just like I would in real life, she told herself. He was doing her a favor, giving her the ammunition to work up a good rage to substitute for the one she'd been nurturing all week, the one he'd talked her out of in the buggy.

So where was it?

She suffered through three more dances, three more partners for Bay, every one eating a little deeper into her efforts to lock her heart away where he couldn't break it.

"Fire in the hole!"

Mariah and Mike both looked up at the quarryman's call. She spotted three faces hanging over the walnut railing three floors up. One of the boys dropped what seemed to be a long reddish snake.

"Watch it!"

Mike shoved her sideways when the first of a yard-long string of firecrackers exploded in mid-air. Couples scattered.

Then the string hit the floor and fell apart, and all hell broke loose. A dozen crackers suddenly exploded in unison. Girls and women screamed. Men shouted. Sulfur and shredded paper filled the air. The crowd rushed for the outside doors.

Surrounded by smoke and sparks, Mariah ducked and ran for the shelter of the stairs. A hand grabbed her and pulled her around a corner and through an open door. The door closed with a solid crack.

"Are you all right?" Bay asked.

Mariah nodded and pushed her hair out of her face. A scrap of red paper drifted to the floor. "This is an office. How did you get in here?"

"It wasn't locked." Bay kept hold of her arm.

"It's them kids," a man outside shouted over the last few pops. "Up there in the bell tower."

"Get 'em," others chorused.

"Sounds like they're about to pay the piper," Bay said. "Young fools. They were only supposed to set off one or two."

She suddenly put it together. "Those were the same boys that threw the crackers under the buggy. You're behind this somehow, aren't you?"

"Guilty," he answered. "They . . . ahem, *volunteered* to stand picket duty and let me know when they spotted Thor coming down the street. I'd be happy to confess my further sins, but I've got about two minutes if I want to avoid a public brawl, and there's something I want to see and something I want to say."

"Keep it to yourself. I'm not interested." Mariah tried to pull away, but his fingers tightened around her arm.

"I think you will be." Bay's weight carried her back against the wall, until the full length of his body pressed against her and she couldn't avoid his descending mouth.

He kissed her, briefly but thoroughly, and heaven help her, she loved every bit of it even as she mentally listed all the reasons she shouldn't. When he finished, Bay leaned back, his gaze fixed on her mouth, and a slow grin spread across his face. He cupped a hand under her jaw and let his thumb drag across her bruised lips.

"Yes," he said, nodding to himself. He grazed her cheek with a kiss and put his lips next to her ear. His voice was barely a murmur. She had to strain to hear, and that let the words go straight into her heart.

"I do not have a string of women in every town. I am very selective."

Bay released her, crossed to the open window, and threw one leg over the ledge. "Good night, Mariah."

And he was gone, just like that. Just like he would be after . . .

After nothing.

She would not let him do this to her. She wouldn't.

She'd be practical, like she always had been until Bay drifted into her life. She'd get through the evening, she'd work hard for the next few weeks, and when she'd purged herself of this nonsense, she would accept Nikolai's proposal. Everything would be fine.

The glass in the window sash served as a mirror as she brushed through her disheveled hair with her fingers. A few more scraps of paper fell out, as did five hairpins that had survived thus far. She scooped them up and tucked them in, more to keep track of the pins than to hold her hair.

There. Her color was a little high, but she'd do.

Nikolai would never know.

Chapter Eight

"LET ME SEE." Eli started counting off on his fingers. "In one evening, you stole a rig—"

"Borrowed it," Bay corrected. They turned on the road toward Cottonwood Station and the railroad tracks.

"—shanghaied that girl—"

"Convinced her to take a ride."

"—at gunpoint. Then you arranged for some boys to drop enough black powder into the middle of that dance to take out a stump—"

"That was *their* idea. I only asked for one small pop."

"—just so you could dance one dance with a female who's told you to go to Hades more than once."

"Actually, I danced with several young ladies."

"So there's likely more than one man peeved at you. I should have gone to ground as soon as you promised fireworks," Eli said.

"Then you would have missed the fun. And you know that's why you ride with me."

Eli laughed and nodded. "That big old boy was madder than a stepped-on rattler. He's going to be after you for sure, now."

"You've earned his love, too," Bay pointed out. "Thanks, by the way."

Eli dipped his head in acknowledgment.

They rode in silence for a few minutes. Bay heard the music from the courthouse start up again. They must have caught the boys.

"How much farther have we got to go?" Eli asked.

"A mile or so past the station. If I remember right, there's a good spot back in the woods along there."

Silence again, then Eli cleared his throat. "For all the trouble we went to, I hope she at least forgave you."

Bay considered. "Sort of."

"*Sort of* enough that you can drop this now and move on?"

"I'm not through with my father yet," Bay said, deflecting the question. "I still want to find out what those lawyers were doing out at the house. Remember? That's what we came to town for."

"I guess I lost track of that in all the excitement. Just how long do you suppose all this finding out is going to take?"

The sarcasm in Eli's tone rolled off Bay as he recalled Mariah's face in the last instant before he'd dropped out the window: well kissed, stunned, openly hungry for more in spite of herself.

Bay's answer spoke as much to her as to Eli: "As long as it takes."

Sunday morning the pastor spoke for nearly an hour on the Ten Commandments, focusing particularly on "Thou shalt not lie," of which, he said, he had noted a lot of violations in the young in the past few months.

Mariah could have sworn he looked directly at her for inspiration.

Of course, she rationalized, he couldn't be. They only came to this church once or twice a year, when they came to town for some other reason. He couldn't possibly know anything about her personal sins. Still, she said a silent thank you when he moved on to "Thou shalt not steal," a topic about which she felt more secure.

"I had intended to speak only on the Ninth Commandment," the reverend continued after he'd sermonized on stealing for another good bit. "However, I felt it necessary to go back to review what we discussed last week. Many of you may know why. For those who don't, two more horses were stolen last night."

A buzz went through the pews.

"The thieves hit the Johnson place over by Cottonwood

Station last night or early this morning. There was no confrontation and no one hurt, for which we can be thankful. According to the report I got from Frank"—the pastor gestured toward a man in the front pew that Mariah didn't know—"there may have been three men this time, although it isn't clear from the tracks whether the third party actually was with the thieves or just happened to pass by. The sheriff again asks all of you to keep an eye out for strangers. And now I'd like to offer a prayer for the victims, and ask that the thieves, whoever they are, receive their just reward. Soon."

"I know strangers," Nikolai muttered as the members of the congregation bowed their heads.

Mariah glanced over. His rock-scarred hands knotted and unknotted, as though he were strangling someone.

After service, the congregation broke up into small groups on the church steps and lawn. Naturally enough, the topic of conversation tended toward the thieves. Mariah chatted long enough for politeness, then tugged Nikolai aside, well away from her parents.

"What strangers?" she asked.

"Mac-Kenzie and his friend."

"That's a terrible accusation. And ridiculous, too."

"Why?" Nikolai demanded. "They have come just when the thieving starts. And you said they had extra horses, the first time you saw them. Where are the horses?"

"I don't know. Sold, I guess. Or up at the ranch."

"Ja, maybe. And maybe they were Mr. Creelor's horses, I think."

"*I* think you're still upset about last night."

"Ja. Last night, when they *stole* the horse and buggy. And you."

"*Keep your voice down.*" Mariah scanned the area quickly to make sure no one might have heard. "I don't want you upsetting Mama."

Nikolai frowned. "You still did not tell what happened?"

"Shhh. No."

"This is not good, Mariah."

"I intend to tell them. It's just that Mama's having such a

nice time, I don't want to ruin it. And unless you want the whole town to find out, kindly keep quiet."

"Maybe it is better if they do find out, to make sure he steals no more horses. I would like to know what he did after he ran away from the dance last night."

"Went back to the Doolittle House and went to bed, if he had any sense. And he didn't run away. He left so the two of you wouldn't fight."

"Or so he could steal the Johnsons' horses."

"Shush. Don't you dare speculate aloud about something like that when you have no proof."

Nikolai looked perturbed. "What is 'speculate'?"

"Supposing about things you have no place supposing about, especially not when they could get a man hung. You just keep your opinions of Bay McKenzie to yourself, because that's all they are."

"What he did last night is not opinion. Is truth. Truth your mama and papa should know. Then I would still like to know what he did after the dance."

"Nikolai . . ."

He nodded, as if to himself. "I make deal. You tell your mama and papa all about last night, and I will not 'speculate' to other people for now."

"Fine," Mariah agreed, though she knew she could never tell *all* about last night. She modified her promise. "I'll tell them about Bay taking the buggy. And what he said to me about why he came back."

"I think I need to hear that again, too. I come with you."

"There's no reason . . ."

"Ja. One good reason. To make sure you tell them. You go say to your father to wait, so I can ride with you to the turnoff. I get my horse."

After stealing a glimpse of Mariah and her family leaving church and heading for home, Bay spent most of Sunday afternoon making his brand-new, store-bought suit look less new and considerably less store-bought. There was nothing like a crisp, pressed jacket and sharply creased pants to mark a man as a cheap dandy in cow country, and by the time he finished, there wasn't a detectable crease left in the pants. Another night rolled under his head completed the effect: The suit could pass for one of the well-worn tailor-mades that the town's merchants wore—appropriate for the prodigal son of the local cattle baron.

Monday morning, he appeared at the bank a half-hour after opening.

"Good to see you again, Mr. McKenzie." Clarence Putnam shook Bay's hand with enthusiasm.

Bay let the McKenzie stand without comment. It served his purpose to have the banker link him with his father. "I hope I'm not interrupting anything."

"No, no. Of course not. Please, have a seat. What can I do for you?"

"Bring me up to date on the financial end of McKenzie and Sons."

Putnam pursed his lips. "I'm afraid our policy on confidentiality is very specific."

"Good. I'd hate to think you bandied our business around town."

"Then you understand I can't just lay your father's accounts open to you." The banker splayed his hands apologetically.

"No, I don't." Bay let his voice carry a fair layer of irritation as he stretched the truth to its breaking point. "I thought it was clear at dinner last week that I am back as an active participant in the ranch. I'm not asking to withdraw money at this point, just for your expertise on a few matters."

"Of course, of course. It's just that without authorization—"

Bay rose and started for the door. "Fine. I thought that since I was in town anyway, I might as well take full advantage of my time, but it can wait until I get back in a couple of weeks. I'll have my father draft a letter for you."

"Sit down, sit down." So urgent was Putnam's effort to pacify Bay that he stubbed his toe on the leg of his desk as he came after him. The pen rattled in its holder. "Since you're only asking for information . . . Well, we always try to accommodate our clients. What is it you want to know?"

Bay settled back into his chair and watched the banker do the same. "Everything, sooner or later, but let's start with the expansion properties. I'd like to be a little clearer on where things stand."

"Certainly." The banker motioned for a clerk to come over, and he gave the man a few brisk orders. "Your father's attorneys are handling the paperwork, of course, but I can give you a pretty good outline of his plans."

A few minutes later, Bay rolled the plat map out across the desk.

"Here." Putnam put a finger on the map. "This big piece up at the north end, east of Clements. I thought we had it, but the owner is balking. Frankly, he would rather sell to someone other than your father."

"I'm sure you or my father will find a way to encourage the sale," Bay said.

"Possibly." Putnam shrugged modestly, as though Bay had given him some kind of compliment, then pointed out several more parcels bordering the ranch.

All together, they'd add a third again to the ranch. The extent of his father's planned expansion floored Bay. John McKenzie couldn't get around to see the property he had. How on earth did he plan to handle that much ranch? And to what end? It wasn't like he had family to pass it on to—at least none willing to take it. Putnam kept talking while Bay contemplated his father's greed.

"And then there's this piece here," Putnam said, pointing to a quarter section that made a notch in the ranch's southeastern border like a missing tooth in a smile. "He's been after this one for several years now."

"The Hoag place," Bay said. He ground his teeth with his effort to keep calm. "It's hardly worth the effort he's put into getting his hands on it."

"But it's a particular challenge to him, since it's taken him so long to secure it. Fortunately, the stalemate will end soon."

Bay ran through what he'd absorbed about the Hoags' troubles and hazarded a guess. "I take it you don't think they're going to make their mortgage."

"They're good people, but sadly . . ." Putnam touched his fingertips together and shrugged in a most un-sad way. "No. I don't think they will."

"Then you undoubtedly want it off your hands."

"Your father and I have discussed that. However, Mr. Hoag very shrewdly negotiated a rider to the note that prevents us from transferring the paper to any local private party unless the loan is actually in foreclosure. I think he realized your father might move to buy it."

Good for him, Bay thought. Unfortunately, his father was a master of finding his way around such riders. He put himself in his father's shoes and gambled. "I believe my father has spoken to you about the possibility of an out-of-state firm purchasing the note."

"Yes," Putnam said carefully. "However, he hadn't yet . . ."

"The problem has been resolved. I know a firm that would be interested."

"Would this firm have a McKenzie as part owner?"

"I think it's better not to ask too many questions in a case like this." Bay returned Putnam's knowing smile. "What do you need from . . . the buyer?"

"Basic information. And a wire or draft of the funds to cover the purchase of course. I have the procedure here someplace. Let me see . . . " Putnam went through his knee drawer and came out with a neatly penned list. "Here you go."

Bay scanned the instructions. "None of this is a problem. If the telegraph operator cooperates, we should be able to handle everything by closing today."

"Is there a hurry?"

"Let's just say I'd like to give my father a present to celebrate my homecoming."

Mariah trudged toward the house with the hoe over her shoulder. Ahead of her, brown and yellow grasshoppers leapt randomly, like beads of water sizzling in a hot skillet. She escaped them only when she reached the stone wall and slipped through the opening into the barren farmyard. She leaned the hoe against the wall and flicked a single tiny hopper off her skirt.

Mama stuck her head out the door. "Is your father coming?"

"He says he got too far behind, taking two days away so

soon after being gone to Wichita. He wants to eat out in the field. What are you doing in there?"

"Making a batch of biscuits, and don't look so put out. It feels good to be cooking again, even if it's just soda biscuits."

"I heard you promise Papa you'd rest today."

"And I will. Just as soon as I slip this pan in the oven."

Mariah washed up quickly and went in to her mother. "You go sit down, and I'll get a basket ready to take to Papa."

"Come sit down for a minute. We haven't had a chance to talk alone since you told us what happened Saturday night, and you have to wait for the biscuits anyway."

"There's nothing to talk about," Mariah said, but her mother motioned her toward a chair.

"I have a hard time believing that," Acasta said. "Your father told me Nikolai spoke to him about marrying you. I assume that's why the two of you were out driving to begin with."

"He showed me the place he wants to buy," Mariah admitted. "Over by Elmdale."

"Then he proposed?"

Mariah nodded and added quietly, "I told him no."

"Ah," her mother said. "I take it Bay McKenzie had something to do with that?"

"Nikolai made it pretty clear that he asked because he's jealous of Bay and thinks that marrying me will keep him away."

"I can hardly blame him, although I doubt that after two years, you can attribute his proposal solely to jealousy. Is that the only reason you said no?"

Mariah glanced up, ready to add to her stack of lies, but her mother's clear blue eyes expected truth. She looked away. "It was at the time."

"Bay kissed you again. When he had you in the buggy." More statement than question.

Mariah nodded.

"Did he do more than that?"

"No, ma'am." Mariah heard her voice getting very small.

"Did you tell Nikolai this time?"

"No. You said yourself, a stolen kiss isn't so bad."

"If that's all it is, no. But I look at all the pain in your eyes, child, and I have the feeling it goes much deeper than that."

"Mama, it can't. I can't risk everything over a few kisses from a man who's going to be gone before I can bat an eye. Nikolai is the one who'll always be here. Nikolai is the one who'll help Papa at plowing time. Nikolai will take care of everything. Bay just . . ."

"Which one makes your blood rush? Which one will make it rush when you're an old woman like me?"

Mariah looked up in anguish.

Acasta rose and paced the length of the braided rug, her arms crossed over her chest as though she had a chill, despite the heat. "I wish I knew what to tell you, child. I have been most fortunate. In your father I found both a wild, reckless lover—"

"Mama!"

A mild smile touched Acasta's lips. "You shock too easily, child. I think I failed you there. At any rate, Cornelius is somehow both slightly untamed and a sober, reliable husband. I wish you had found both in one man, but since you haven't, you have to decide what's best for you."

"No. All I have to do is wait a week or two. Then Bay will be gone—" Mariah swallowed back the catch in her voice and made herself continue. "He'll be gone and I can stop thinking foolishness. And when Nikolai proposes again after harvest, I'll say yes, because we'll both be ready."

"And if he doesn't ask you again?"

"I'll ask him," Mariah said. "See, I can shock you, too, Mama. Now, I'd better check on those biscuits and get Papa's dinner ready."

Mariah turned away, trying not to see the sad, knowing look on her mother's face. A lean, cocky figure standing just outside the open door, hat in hand, stopped her dead in her tracks.

A beloved smile flashed. "Doesn't your brother even get a hug?"

"Jimmy!" She threw her arms around him, everything else forgotten in the relief of having him home safe and sound. "Mama, it's Jimmy."

But her mother was already there, hugging him, tears

running down her cheeks. "Look at you. You look a year older, and it's only been two weeks."

"Did you finish up that job already?" Mariah asked.

"Have you had a decent meal since you left home?"

"Hold it. Hold it." Laughing, Jimmy shook himself free of the two women. "Let me get out of the sun first. It's been a hot ride."

"Does Papa know you're here?"

"Not yet. I came in along the creek."

Mariah gave him another hug and released him to her mother to pull inside. She gave the bell an enthusiastic ring to call her father in from the field, then took a minute to pull the biscuits out and arrange them on a plate. She set them on the table along with jam and butter.

"Now I know I'm home." Jimmy tossed a hot biscuit from hand to hand until it cooled, but refused to answer any questions about his adventures until his father arrived.

The two of them embraced. Cornelius thumped his son on the back. "You look good, son. Like you've grown up a little."

"That's what Ma said," Jimmy answered, puffing up a little.

"So, how did that job go?"

"Fine. In fact, more than fine." Jim reached into his pocket and came out with the leather money purse Mariah had given him for Christmas two years earlier. To her knowledge, it had never held more than six bits. Now he popped it open and spilled a roll of greenbacks onto the table. "Thirty-two dollars."

"Thirty-two dollars," Acasta exclaimed. "James, where did you get so much money?"

"Mr. Keenan, that's the man who hired me, he paid a bonus because we got the pens done so fast. He said it saved him five times that in lost shipping." He turned to his father. "It's for the mortgage, Pa."

Cornelius touched the bills almost gingerly. "They're your wages, boy. Are you sure?"

"Yes, sir. That's why I did it."

The money went into the screw-top tin on the third shelf, with the other cash.

"What happened to your horse?" Cornelius asked.

"Buck split a hoof just before I was going to leave. The

foreman said I could trade for one of their string, and if I get down that way again, trade back."

Something in Jimmy's manner didn't sit right with Mariah. Curious, she stepped back a couple of paces until she could see out the open door. She hadn't noticed before, but the horse tied over by the corral wasn't Jimmy's. The quick-looking chestnut stock horse appeared to be worth three times the old dun plodder Jimmy had ridden out on.

"I'm not sure," Jimmy answered his mother's query about his plans to return to Wichita. "It was awfully good money, and Mr. Keenan did ask me back. But I wanted to take care of a few things around here."

"Like Aurelia Martin?" her father asked.

Jimmy colored, but nodded. "Yes, sir. In fact, if you don't need me this afternoon, I'd surely like to ride over and tell her I'm home."

"I've done without you this long. I guess I can last out the day."

"But, James," Acasta began. "You've only just come home."

"Let the boy go, love," Cornelius said.

"I'll be back late. Don't wait up." Jim gave his mother a peck on the cheek. "We'll talk, Mama, I promise. And I'll tell you all about Wichita. You ought to see how they're throwing up buildings."

Mariah followed her brother outside and watched him check his saddle. It gave her a chance to look the chestnut over more closely. He was a fine animal, maybe even better than her first impression. Jimmy kept glancing up, a nervous little smile on his face.

"Could you get me a sandwich or something to take?" he asked.

Mariah obliged, going in to wrap a slab of ham in bread with some piccalilli relish for taste. She came back out and handed the concoction to Jimmy. "Your favorite."

"Thanks, Mariah."

"If that foreman traded this horse for Buck, he's a fool. How did you really get him?"

Jim's cheeks reddened under the peachy fuzz that passed as

his whiskers. "You always could tell when I was stretching the truth."

"How did you get him?" she repeated.

He considered her for a minute, then shrugged. "I won him on a straight flush. Spades."

Mariah relaxed. Jimmy's interest in cards and gambling had long been her mother's bane. He seemed to think being a card sharp went part and parcel with heading for the gold camps. No wonder he hadn't wanted to say anything in the house.

"What if you'd lost?"

"I didn't. And I sold Buck. That's where part of the money came from."

"Papa's going to figure out you fibbed the first time he takes a good look at this animal. How are you going to explain it to him?"

"I don't know yet. How are you going to explain fighting with that McKenzie in the middle of town, then dancing with him?"

This time it was Mariah's turn to color. "I've already explained. I take it you've already seen Aurelia."

"Stopped over this morning. She told me a lot of things have been going on around here, especially on Independence Day. I should have come back earlier. Are you sweet on him?"

"Mind your own business, Jimmy."

"Anything to do with a McKenzie and this family is my business." He slapped the stirrup down and moved to untie the horse. The tense silence drew out between them.

"So . . ." Mariah started tentatively. "If you've already seen Aurelia, where are you going?"

"Mr. Keenan runs a spread down south of Matfield Green. A couple of the fellows I worked with got sent over there. I figured maybe I could add to the mortgage money." He looked a little sheepish. "I held out a few dollars for a stake."

Mariah bit back the warning. It never had done any good before. "Oh, go on. Get out of here."

"You going to tell Mama?" he asked, sounding like the petulant kid brother she knew.

"No," she said.

"Thanks. Again." He gave her a quick peck on the cheek. "I'll see you later."

"Not too late. Mama will stay awake worrying."

Mariah watched him ride off, a smile touching her lips. Jimmy was home, pulling the wool over Papa's eyes and ducking out of chores to go off and get in trouble.

Somehow, it made her hopeful. Maybe everything *could* get back to normal after all.

Bay stood on the front porch of the house, looking out over the ranch. The boxy limestone outbuildings, so much lighter than the surrounding prairie, looked even more like monuments in the moonlight. He and Eli had ridden straight out from town, the mortgage papers burning in his pocket the whole way. Now Eli rested in one of the bunks down the hill, and Bay stood on the porch, where he'd been for the better part of an hour.

He could almost convince himself he'd stayed there so long because the porch itself attracted him.

It was magnificent, the kind of veranda his mother would have loved to dance on, if she'd lived long enough to see it built. She'd have loved the whole house. There would have been dinners and parties and cotillions enough to make the stones ring, and in another life, he could have invited Mariah. His mind put her on the veranda, gold and cream next to his mother's fiery Creole darkness. They'd have liked each other, for all their differences.

If *Maman* had lived. If she hadn't been driven to her grave by greed for the land, greed so great it didn't leave room for anything as inconvenient as love or consideration, greed so virulent it continued to threaten anyone who stood against it, friend or foe. Or family.

Bay breathed deeply, letting the familiar scent of the land he'd once called home wash away the images and calm the anger before he lost all control. He'd spent most of the afternoon planning what he would say and how. It could all vanish in a heartbeat if he let the fury win out.

His father was still awake. Through the front window, Bay could see where the light from the study washed the hall, and he'd watched the housekeeper say something to the person inside before going off to her own bed.

So it would finally be just the two of them, as it had been thirteen years ago.

Bay touched his jacket pocket, checking for the papers, then pushed the door open.

John McKenzie sat at his desk, account books spread out before him, his chin resting on his folded hands, eyes closed. For a moment, Bay thought he'd fallen asleep that way, and the part of him that was still his son softened for the tired old man.

Then those blue eyes flickered open. One brow lifted. "So you're back at last. I thought you must have run off again."

Bay ignored his father and walked over to the bookshelves that filled one wall. The books looked like they'd just been unpacked from crates. He touched a few. Perfect drama. Unused philosophy. Reams of unsullied poetry. The badges of substance for a man who lived nearly illiterate. John McKenzie could read. He just didn't take the time.

"What do you think of my library, boy?"

"People would be more impressed if you actually opened them." Bay took the smaller of the two pieces of paper out of his pocket, the one he'd carried all the way from Denver, and tossed it on his father's desk. "Here. I know you can always manage to decipher a bank draft."

John whistled appreciatively. "You've done well, I see. But then, you had a pretty good start with those horses."

"I gave them away. That's what you'd have gotten if I'd delivered them to the Rebs. With interest. Debt paid in full."

"There never was a debt. You're my son."

"So was Johnny."

"I had contracts to fulfill. You know that. I couldn't very well—"

"Pass by a dollar for your son's life. No, that would be asking too much. Tell me, did you keep selling to the Confederacy after I left?" Bay didn't really need the answer. He could tell by the way his father's eyes slid past him to stare at the globe standing in the corner.

"Business is business."

The cold-bloodedness of it destroyed Bay's resolve to stay

calm. He slammed the mortgage down next to the draft. "Well, here's some business for you."

It took John only a moment to puzzle it out, then a slow smile spread across his face. "You got it. You got the Hoag note."

"That I did." Bay retrieved the note, folded it, and slipped it back into his breast pocket. "Specifically to keep it out of your hands."

"What?"

"You heard me. My partner and I hold the note now, and we have no intention of pushing a foreclosure, whether the Hoags make a payment or not."

"What are you saying?"

"I watched you drive too many good people off their land. I came back to face you down about that and about what you did to Johnny and me, and what do I find? You're still at it. No more, old man. It's going to stop."

"By damn, it won't. I'm doing it for you."

"Like hell. You're doing it for yourself. You didn't even know where I was for the past thirteen years." Bay headed for the door.

"Ah, but I knew you'd come back. Sooner or later, you had to come back. You're too much like me to stay away."

Bay whirled. "I'm nothing like you, you son of a bitch."

"Maybe you don't want to admit it now, but you are," John said, stubbornly ignoring the epithet. "You always have been. Johnny might have been the oldest, but you were always *my* boy. You stood up for me. Fought for me. You understood how important the land was to us."

"Not to us, to *you*. I wouldn't give a tinker's damn for the whole mess. Or for you, anymore."

"Then get off this ranch," John snapped, finally angering.

Bay shook his head and leaned over the desk, his hands straddling the green blotter, his face inches from his father's. His voice rumbled out, low and threatening, between clenched teeth. "Not on your life. I'm not going anywhere. In fact, Eli and I are moving up to the house first thing tomorrow. Since you're feeling so damned paternal, that ought to make you happy. But we'll be keeping an eye on you, old man. You won't make a move on the Hoags or anybody else without me right on your tail."

"Go ahead," John growled. "You won't stop me. This is my ranch. You'll be a long time trying to keep me from running it the way I see fit."

"As long as it takes."

Bay stormed out the door, off the veranda and out across the grounds. He finally stopped at the stone building that housed the spring. The steady rush of the water pouring out of the ground drowned out the sound of his father, bellowing from somewhere inside. Lights came up in the back of the house.

Poor Mrs. Shaw.

Poor Eli. He was not going to be pleased at the prospect of staying a few more weeks.

For that matter, Bay wasn't too pleased with himself. Hanging around to rein in his father was not part of his plans. He'd let the old bastard get to him, let himself get mad instead of sticking to what he'd intended to say and do.

Part of the spring was captured by a pipe and funneled off to the house and barns. The rest ran out beneath the door in a passable stream that filled the stock pond at the bottom of the hill. Bay tossed his hat onto a stone bench outside the spring house, then stripped out of his coat and shirt and left them there, too, while he rinsed off the sweat. The icy water braced him and left his head clear.

"As long as it takes."

He recalled saying that about Mariah on Saturday night. He'd only been half serious at the time, but he wondered how much she had to do with what had just happened in the study.

No matter. Staying around a few weeks might not be in his plans, but it was the right thing to do. That counted for something. Maybe it would count with Mariah, too.

Chapter Nine

CLYDE STARTED YAPPING before Bay turned through the front gate.

So much for a discreet entrance. Bay whistled softly and the pup came out to sniff around Cajun's heels, then trotted alongside, escorting them to the house. The little traitor barked once more, then went over to stand by the front door as Bay dismounted.

When he turned, Mrs. Hoag was standing by the door.

"You," she said.

"Yes, ma'am." He couldn't read her face, but she didn't reach for the shotgun that he knew stood just inside the door, so he started toward her, hat in hand. "I thought it was time I came to apologize to you."

"For which incident, or do you hope to cover it all in one go?" Without letting him answer, she stood aside and motioned him inside. "You may as well come in out of the sun to make your little speech."

"Thank you, ma'am."

"I have some more of those ginger cookies you seem to like so well. Mariah baked them when James came home."

Bay settled in at the familiar wooden table while Mrs. Hoag put the kettle on to heat and arranged the cookies on a plate. The cutting board he'd mended sat on the table. He nudged a heel of bread aside and ran his thumbnail along the glued seam. He glanced up to find her watching him.

"It's holding fine." She took away the bread board and replaced it with a plate of cookies before she joined him at the table. "I'm glad you sent Mr. Stutt back. You seem to understand Mariah very well for as short a time as you've known her."

Bay popped a cookie into his mouth as a way of avoiding an answer. He didn't really want to get into a conversation about Mariah with her mother, of all people. He had few compunctions where women were concerned, but discussing his less honorable intentions with the lady's mother was definitely one of them.

"You've stayed beyond your week or two," Mrs. Hoag said.

"Yes, ma'am."

"For any particular reason, or are you hanging about just to bedevil by daughter?"

"My business isn't complete." He left it at that, interested enough in the second part of her question to set his compunctions aside. "Do I bedevil Mariah?"

She lifted one eyebrow, and Bay realized he'd seen Mariah direct the same expression of disbelief his way. "You know you do. In fact, it seems to me you pride yourself on it."

"I don't seem to be able to help myself."

"Don't be flippant, young man."

"I don't mean to be. You have a beautiful and amazing daughter. I find myself doing all kinds of odd things around her." Bay thought of the steely silence of his father in the days since he'd confronted him. And there was still an attorney to hire and more mortgage papers for the Jacks High Holding Company to secure. Odd and expensive.

Mrs. Hoag rose. "I don't keep the coffee on when everyone's away. Will tea be all right?"

"It would be, ma'am, but I think I'd better be going. I really did just come down to apologize face to face. I took advantage of your hospitality and for that I am most sorry."

"Accepted, because of the fine work you did while you were 'taking advantage.'" She waited. "No apology for kidnapping my daughter? For kissing her?"

"No, ma'am. Not even for pointing a gun at Thor." Bay rose and retrieved his hat from the peg near the front door. "And I suspect that means I'm no longer welcome."

Mrs. Hoag followed him out and stood watching as he untied

Cajun and mounted up. "So how long did you sit up on that hill before you figured out I was here alone?"

The question brought Bay up short and put a wry smile on his lips. "You saw me."

"I did."

"I watched your husband and Mariah drive off, but I had heard your son was home. I kept waiting for some sign of him."

"He left at sunup to go see his girl again. Mr. Hoag took the team over to help old Mr. Quincy pull a stump."

"Mariah went along for the outing, I suppose."

"Actually, she was going to get off about halfway there and pick gooseberries along the creek until her father comes back this way."

The hand Bay brought up to tip his hat partially blocked the grin that elevated the corners of his mouth. He took his leave a little briskly for manners. Mrs. Hoag's placid gaze made him think she really didn't understand his intentions toward Mariah.

Not that he understood, himself, but he did know exactly where he was going next.

The shade wasn't as thick as Mariah would have liked, but at least the patch of stream bank was cooler than the open fields. She picked steadily until she had a pie's worth of berries, then straightened and stretched.

With her mother feeling better and taking back many of the household chores, she'd had an unbroken week of working with her father and Jimmy in the fields. Her back hurt, her legs ached, and her feet, encased in her sturdy black leather shoes, felt as if they'd been boiled daily.

She could solve that last part, at least.

Checking carefully for the rattlers that always loitered in such places, Mariah made her way through the brush to the edge of the stream, set the pail aside, and sat down to peel off her shoes and stockings. She slid her feet into the water with a sigh. It would be better if the creek ran cool instead of balmy with the sun's heat, but its lazy swirl around her toes eased some of the pain.

A swish of movement among the pebbles mid-stream caught her attention. Crawdads. They didn't have many in the short stretch of creek that bordered their property, but now that she was looking, she saw evidence of a good crop along here. Big ones, too, big enough to make decent eating. Mariah untied her bonnet and dumped the berries into its full back puff, then she kilted her skirt up past her knees and waded out to try her luck. Within a few minutes she had a passable mess of the crayfish trying to clamber up the sides of the metal pail.

Enjoying her success, she snatched up a couple more crawdads and added them to the catch, then deposited the pail on the bank next to the gooseberries. Before her father came back, she needed to pick more berries for putting by, but for now, she just wanted to enjoy the water. Wading farther upstream to where the pebbles petered out, she worked her feet deep into the muddy bottom.

It felt wonderful.

She stood there, squishing her toes, watching the clouds of greenish grey silt curl up and float away, until the water ran a milky verdigris.

"I always liked to do that myself."

Mariah whirled to find Bay leaning against a tree, his arms folded across his chest. Such a turmoil of emotions, both negative and positive, ran through her that she couldn't think of a thing to say. She settled for pressing her lips together in what she hoped was disapproval.

"I enjoy the expression on your face when I first show up," he said with a grin. "Before you begin to frown, there's always an instant when you actually look pleased to see me."

Mariah waded for shore. "You imagine things."

"Maybe. But I still like to see it." Bay whipped the kerchief from around his neck, shook it out, and stepped forward to hand it to her. "You can use this to dry off."

Accepting the square of cotton, Mariah sat on the bank to rinse the silt off her toes and blot her feet and ankles dry. She'd just reached for her stockings when she realized Bay was watching with an amused intensity that set her blood pounding in her ears. She jerked her skirt free to fall over her legs and started to put her shoes on without stockings.

"You'll get blisters," Bay warned.

"I'm perfectly capable of dressing myself."

"Look, if it will make you more comfortable, I'll turn away."

"Now there's a case of shutting the barn door after the horse got out." Then embarrassed that she'd been the one to conjure up an image of the night in the barn, she yanked her stockings on.

With her shoes on, Mariah stood up to face him. "You don't strike me as the kind to go berry picking. Am I going to have to undergo another kidnapping?" *And more of your kisses and touches?* The idea seemed too appealing for comfort.

"I hadn't planned one, but I can if you'd like." Bay grinned as if he'd guessed exactly what had crossed her mind.

He stepped forward. She felt the now familiar anticipation ripple down her spine, and she fought it every inch of the way.

She needn't have. Instead of coming to her, Bay took off his Stetson and turned toward the gooseberry bushes, where he started casually flicking berries into the crown of the hat. A wayward sense of disappointment, combined with her unwillingness to admit to that disappointment, nearly brought a groan to Mariah's lips. She shook off the lethargy that held her waiting for him like a fool, snatched up her bonnet, and moved to the opposite side of the patch. She picked furiously, mad at herself and at him for making her realize once more how vulnerable she was to his charms.

Bay picked faster, matching her, and Mariah speeded up. It didn't take long for it to become a race, just like running the cattle had, with both of them charging through the bushes, stripping the stems bare as quickly as possible.

Inevitably it happened. Looking back at it later, Mariah couldn't be sure he hadn't planned it—or that she hadn't willed it. She reached for a cluster of berries at the same time Bay did. Their hands brushed and then tangled, and with one motion, Bay pulled her around the bush and into his arms.

"Instead of making me kidnap you," he said, with a wicked seductiveness in his low voice, "you could just let me kiss you. It's lots less trouble."

The first touch of his lips on hers shattered what remained of Mariah's self-delusions. This was what she wanted, all she wanted. Bonnet and Stetson and berries plopped to the ground. She matched the earnest searching of his hands, exploring the hard ripples of his form as thoroughly as he explored the curves of hers, anxious to brush away the clothing that dulled her touch. She found the top button of his shirt and began working it free. The skin beneath burned against her searching fingers.

"Oh, damn." With an agonized groan, he broke the kiss and trapped her hands between his.

When he pulled away, she felt as lost as the look in his eyes. "Bay . . ."

"Your mother is a very wise woman," he said.

"My mother? What does she . . . ?"

He kissed her fingers, still laced between his own. "I stopped by the house to apologize to her. She told me you were down here."

"She what?" Mariah was confused, even more so by the sensations dancing up her arm as Bay drew the tip of one finger between his lips. Her toes curled inside her shoes as she watched him and tried to keep her mind clear. "I don't understand."

"Neither did I, until just a minute ago," he said cryptically. He gave her fingertip another kiss and ran his tongue around it, then moved on to another. "You taste like berries. I think she assumed that if she treated me like a gentleman, I might actually behave like one. I guess she's right, or at least half right. A real gentleman would walk away right now." He took a deep breath, then let it out in a slow, resigned sigh that ruffled over her palm and did still more damage to her senses. "I want to call on you Mariah."

"You what?"

"Quite a talker, aren't you?" he teased. The second finger held his attention for another moment, and Mariah felt her capacity for speech slip farther away. "I have to go up to Topeka for a week or so. When I get back, I want to call on you. Properly. Flowers, buggy, clean shirt, talk with your father. The whole shebang. For as long as I stay around."

He was leaving. Mariah took a deep breath and found her voice. "How long will that be?"

Their eyes met over the destruction he continued to wreak on her fingers. "I don't know. A few weeks. Maybe a few months. I can't promise."

A few weeks or months of a lifetime of Bay's uncertain passions against stolid reliability from Nikolai. Kisses that swept her up in something heated and uncontrollable against kisses that left her feeling nearly unkissed. Mariah pulled her hand free and turned away, hoping that might help clear her mind, but the sensations he'd started continued to spread through the secret places of her body. She sighed. "When you're not around, I know exactly what to tell you."

"You've managed quite well a few times to my face," Bay reminded her.

"I wish you'd just believe that I don't want any part of you."

"I told you, I can't. Not when you don't believe it yourself." Bay slipped both arms around her waist and pulled her back against him. He nuzzled through the tangle of her hair and bared the back of her neck to his kisses. "Say yes, beautiful Mariah. Say I can be your beau."

The motion of his lips sent a shudder of willingness through Mariah, a shudder that turned into a slow, still-reluctant nod. "Yes. You can call on me."

She felt his victorious smile in the curve of his mouth against her skin, and it aggravated her as much as it pleased her. She prickled and tried to pull away, but Bay held tight.

"What makes you think I won't change my mind once you ride off today?" she asked.

"You won't," he said, nibbling at her earlobe.

She wouldn't. She tried something else. "My father is not going to like the idea of a McKenzie courting his daughter."

"He'll listen to you. And your mother." He traced a circle with his tongue over a spot just behind her ear that made her squirm with pure pleasure.

"He might," she said, "if we have a chance to tell him. If you're hanging onto me like this when he comes back, I won't get a word in before he shoots you."

Bay planted a final kiss in the curve where her neck joined her shoulder. "Then I suppose I'd better get going."

"I suppose you had."

She retrieved her bonnet and held it while Bay tipped his share of the berries out of the Stetson, then let him take her hand and walk her along the creek to where he'd tied his horse.

"I'll see you as soon as I get back. *That* I can promise."

And that would have to do, she told herself as she watched him ride off.

She could hardly complain at getting what she deserved. For all her efforts to be practical, she'd just agreed to let John McKenzie's drifter son make love to her and break her heart, if not worse. Now she had to figure out how to explain her insanity to her parents.

Mariah returned to her spot by the creek and checked the crawdads. One was about to clamber out, using his equally frantic brethren as stairs. She sloshed the pail to knock the wriggling ramp down and went back to her berry picking.

A couple of minutes later she heard a horse headed her direction, quickly. For an instant she thought—hoped—it was Bay riding back, then it struck her that the sound came from the other direction. She hustled out of the bushes into the baking sun just as Jimmy flung himself off his horse.

"Are you all right?" he demanded.

"I'm fine. What's the matter?"

"I saw him riding off. McKenzie."

"And?"

Jimmy glared at her. "And? For Christ's sake, Mariah, he's a McKenzie."

"He's not like his father."

"Oh, I bet. His daddy never tried this particular way of getting hold of our land."

"*Our* land? That's funny coming from you. You haven't helped out Papa more than two full days in the past week."

"I told you, I'm trying to win more money for the mortgage."

"And just how much have you won, Mr. Riverboat Gambler?" Mariah asked. Jimmy flushed, and she knew he'd been losing. "No wonder your friends want you to come back to work: they get all your pay. You're going to break Mama's heart."

"Those fellows are going back to Wichita tomorrow. And anyway, you're one to talk. Mama's going to have a fit when she finds out he was down here today doing God knows what with you."

"She's the one that told him where I was."

Jimmy turned beet red. "You liar. Our mama would not let you whore around with that—"

Mariah slapped him.

Jimmy backed up a couple of steps. A hand print whitened his cheek where she'd hit him.

They glared at each other, anger crackling between them, and then Jimmy relaxed. He touched his cheek gingerly and gave her a sheepish grin. "Shoot. You didn't have to hit me like that."

"Jimmy, I . . ."

"My fault," he interrupted. "I shouldn't have said what I did. It's just, we've been fighting McKenzie so long . . ."

"Bay's not like his father," she repeated. "He came down today to ask me if he can call on me. Out in the open. Properly. I said yes."

"Pa will never allow it. And what about Nikolai?"

"They're my problem. But I'd like you to go along with it." She saw the refusal spring to Jimmy's lips and tried to wheedle him out of it. "It means a lot to me."

Jimmy snorted. "I bet. I'm not about to tell Pa to let a McKenzie come around just because you like the way he sweet-talks you."

"Oh, you're not?" Mariah tried to keep the anger out of her voice, but couldn't. "Well, then you'd better just keep your mouth shut."

"Why should I?"

"Because if you don't, if you say one solitary word against Bay to the folks, or cause any trouble for him or me over this, I swear, I'll tell Papa everything you're up to. The gambling, the horse, everything."

Jimmy's eyes blazed. "That's no good as a threat anymore, Mariah. I'm a man full grown, and Pa can't say anything about what I do."

"Maybe not, but if Mama and Papa's opinions didn't matter to you, you wouldn't be hiding so much." *Neither would I,* Mariah noted with guilt. "I guess if you want any say in whether Bay comes calling or not, you'll need to straighten your own self out first."

"Maybe I will." Jimmy stalked back to his horse and mounted up. "Or maybe I'll just find a way to stop him myself."

Visions of a man lying battered wavered on the edges of Mariah's imagination, but she couldn't see whether it was him or Bay. "Jimmy, don't go off and do something foolish."

His answer was to spur his horse away, leaving her in a cloud of dust.

The look on Mariah's face when she and Cornelius pulled up in the wagon gave Acasta a sense of satisfaction tinged with concern. She finished shaking out the dish towel and went out to meet them.

"You should see what your daughter found for you," Cornelius said as he climbed down and reached to help Mariah. "Look in the back of the wagon."

Acasta was more interested in looking over her daughter, but she went around the back of the wagon to see what her husband thought was so exciting. "Crayfish. How lovely. We'll have them for supper. How was the berry picking, child?"

"Fine, Mama. I'll go start the preserves and put a pie in the oven to go with crawdads."

Her father probably didn't hear the accusation in Mariah's voice, but her mother certainly did. Bay must have told Mariah how he came to find her. Ah, well. The fact that she was mad about it proved to Acasta that she'd been right in telling him. It also made her wonder just what had happened down at the creek. That had been her one reservation about shoving the two of them at each other. The consequences of that much passion could be so great. But they'd be greater if Mariah was allowed to hide from it.

It took several hours for Mariah to get enough courage to broach the subject. With James and Cornelius both out in the field and the water steaming for the crayfish, she came and sat down across from her mother.

"He asked to start calling on me," she said with no preamble.

Acasta didn't pretend not to understand. "I suspected he might. I hoped he would."

"Why on earth, Mama? What ever possessed you?"

The confusion in your eyes, Acasta thought, but she didn't answer the question. "Your father will be . . . reluctant to say yes."

"That's what I told Bay." She smiled, finally. "He said you'd help me convince him."

"I will, child. You'll have to give me a chance to prepare him for the idea, though. I'll tell you when he's ready to hear it from you. You just leave it to me."

"Thank you, Mama."

To Acasta's mind, the whole thing was going well. She just had to make her husband see the method in her madness. Her chance came a few days later, when her husband came in to beg a cookie on his way back out to the orchard.

"Are the children busy?" she asked, pouring him a cup of coffee to go with the cookie.

"Clearing the firebreak again. It seems like we never get ahead of that grass."

"It is the prairie, dear." Acasta took a deep breath. "Sit down, Cornelius. We need to talk."

She began a carefully expurgated version of the story, but Cornelius still got up in the middle of it and started pacing the floor.

"Has she actually said anything?" Cornelius asked.

Acasta watched him make another trip to the door and back. "It's only a matter of time. I told you, I'm sure he went off to talk to her the other day, while you were over at Mr. Quincy's."

"I still can't believe you told him where to find her. You might as well have given him carte blanche to seduce her."

"Nonsense, Cornelius. In fact, if I know that young man, it had the opposite effect. It wouldn't surprise me if Bay decided to court her outright." A small fiction, but there was no reason for Cornelius to know his wife and daughter were conspiring.

"I understood that he'd be riding on, probably sooner than later."

"So he says. Mariah understands that, as well. That is one area in which he has been completely forthright. Unfortunately."

"What do you mean?"

"She thinks if she waits long enough, her problem will vanish." She smiled, a worried little half smile. "Left to her own devices, Mariah will put her head down, work herself sick until he finally does ride on, and then marry Nikolai because she thinks it's the practical thing to do. She will spend the rest of her life wondering about Bay. And should he, by some chance or intent, wander back through . . . Well, I've been thinking about this for days, and heaven help me, I cannot find another way. If he asks to call on her, I think we should let him. See what havoc he can wreak."

"Acasta, my love, I don't see how this will help."

"If he's going to break her heart, I'd rather it be over and done before she marries. Then perhaps she and Nikolai or some other man can go forward. Either way, it's better than dragging the heartache out for the next fifty years with what ifs. That would not be fair to her or to Nikolai." *And perhaps, just perhaps, Bay won't break her heart at all.*

"So," her husband said slowly. "You want to let him court Mariah just so she can get him out of her system."

"That sums it up nicely, yes."

"You make the arrangement sound like a dose of worm tonic."

"He is not nearly so unpleasant as worms, more's the pity."

"I'm not sure I can welcome him into my home."

"Then just tolerate him, husband. For Mariah's sake."

"I'll have to think about this."

"Of course, dear."

By the next morning, he had come around. Acasta informed Mariah and she raised the topic at supper. The family came to an agreement, almost too easily, that Bay could pay his visits, provided he minded his manners.

As Mariah served up bowls of apple pandowdy with cream, Acasta watched her son brood. James was angry, clear enough. The way he'd glared at Mariah while she presented her request had made Acasta think he would argue against a McKenzie ever setting foot on the property, but he hadn't said as much as one word. He just sat there, looking furious and not saying a word.

And that worried her more than anything that had happened in the past month.

* * *

Mariah straightened, a trailing stem of bindweed in her hand, and spotted Nikolai pounding down the road on the big dappled gelding. He lifted a hand in greeting, and she waved back before she dropped the weed into the bushel basket and stooped to pull another handful.

She'd been dreading this all week.

He slid off the gelding and flipped the reins around a fence post. "You should not work in the middle of the day when it is so hot."

"I got started early this morning and thought I could finish this end of the field before you came. Just the rest of this row and I'll stop."

Nikolai stepped over the fence—easy enough, considering how big he was. Starting at the end of the row, he weeded his way toward Mariah.

"There," he said when they met. He grabbed the basket and hoisted it over the fence, then helped her through. A moment later, he hung the empty basket upside down over a post, having dumped the contents well beyond the plowed fire-break that surrounded the entire farm.

"Come." Nikolai held out his hand. "I walk you back."

Nearly every man she knew, from Jimmy to old Mr. Quincy, had hands that showed the hard life they led—for that matter, she had her own share of blisters and callouses—but Nikolai's plate-sized palms were so thick and scarred by the rock he cut, they felt like boiled leather. She hesitated, then laid her hand across his. "Let's take the long way around."

"Ja. We need to talk." He curled his fingers around hers.

They walked all the way down past the corner of the property before Nikolai spoke.

"I went up to Elmdale this morning early. Mr. Lehmann told to me he has to have a yes or no by the end of the month. He cannot hold the land any longer."

"Oh," Mariah said. Nikolai's hand tightened around hers. She knew what he wanted her to say and what she ought to say, and she couldn't make either set of words come out.

"He told some other things, too," Nikolai continued. "Like how he was walking down to the livery after the fireworks to get his horse and saw us parked in the buggy. Except I was not in the buggy with you."

"Bay wasn't finished saying his piece and—"

Nikolai stopped, put a finger under Mariah's chin, and lifted it so she had to look him in the eye. "How long you think you wait before you tell me, Mariah?"

"Tell you?" Mariah tried to keep her voice level, despite the stain of guilt that crawled up from her neckline.

"That you kiss with him."

"I . . . he . . . it . . ." The grasshoppers, the horse, the stream, everything went absolutely still as she struggled for words. Mariah couldn't even feel her own heart beat.

"He forced you, ja? You tell me the truth, I make him pay."

"No." Her heart spasmed once, then settled back into rhythm. She took a deep breath. "He didn't force me."

The gelding stepped on Nikolai's toe. He growled and punched the animal on the neck. Mariah winced as the big horse jerked with a squeal. In two years she'd never seen Nikolai hit a living thing, and the vicious fury in that single blow terrified her. She froze, willing herself invisible, until he could bring himself under control.

Finally, he reached out to give the gelding an apologetic pat. The horse whinnied and pulled away, but Nikolai held on and pulled him closer, until he had the animal's muzzle tight against his chest and the horse relaxed. Staring past the gelding, Nikolai removed his hat, mopped his forehead on his sleeve, and settled the hat back. "Was that the first time you kissed him?"

"No." *Don't do this, Nikolai.*

"How many times before?"

"A couple of times." Just twice, but the sudden recollection of Bay's lips against her breast caught her off guard, poured through her like warm honey. She had to catch at the fence to steady herself.

"That is why you say no when I asked you to marry me."

"I told you the truth. I'm not ready. Not right now."

"Because of Mac-Kenzie," he said.

"Mostly because of me." *Because I want that feeling I just had thinking about him. As crazy as it is, as much as I know it can cost me, I want that.* "He's just . . ."

He finally turned to look at her. His blue eyes were icy. "Will you see him again?"

"Yes. I will see him. He asked to call on me until he goes, and I said yes."

His voice turned bitterly hard. "Do you lie with him?"

She felt her cheeks flame with guilt that he should have good reason to ask such a question. "No."

Nikolai started walking again, his head down in thought. Mariah followed. As they neared the gate, he stopped and blocked her way. "When he is here no more, you will be ready to marry me?"

"I hope so," she said in all honesty. "I do hope so, Nikolai."

His eyes narrowed as if he strained to see something just over the horizon and his lips pressed together in a grim, determined smile that made her flesh cold. "Then I wait. So long as you do not lie with him, I wait."

Chapter Ten

THE REST OF July passed with little rain, much heat, and no sign of Bay. During endless trips between the well and the garden with the water buckets, Mariah alternately hoped to see him ride through the gate on his tall blue roan and berated herself for putting so much stock in the word of a drifting son of a McKenzie.

When he still hadn't put in an appearance by the end of the month, she tried to resign herself to the idea that he'd gotten to Topeka—or wherever he'd really gone on his so-called business—and decided to just keep going. Tried and failed.

She headed off to Annie Richardson's quilting bee just after morning chores on the first day of August, anxious for a diversion. Jimmy rode with her, for once actually on his way to picnic with Aurelia *and* her family. Around them, the head-high grasses, beginning to yellow with the summer heat, rustled in the first licks of a morning breeze. The brightening sky picked up the showy pink of wild sweet william scattered along the creek bank, and the yellow of the sunflowers that flourished in the broken ground along the edges of the road. The clear colors contrasted with the glistening haze that lay along the horizon like an out-of-season Indian summer.

Not far from the house, a pair of horsemen appeared against the sky at the top of the hill. Her heart leapt and she straightened in her saddle to see better.

"It's not him," Jimmy said brusquely. "You know, if I was Nikolai and saw that look on your face, I'd break the son of a bitch in half. Maybe I'll tell him he ought to."

Mariah turned her horse across Jimmy's path, forcing him to

a halt. "You've gotten mean, little brother. You'd better remember our deal."

"I remember just fine." Jimmy wheeled his mount around her and lifted his hand in greeting toward the other riders. Moments later, the men reined in before them. Their overt stares made Mariah uncomfortable. She eased the sorrel back a little.

"We were just headed for your place," the shortest one said. He had greasy hair that hadn't seen a barber in a month of Sundays. "This the little honey you were telling us about?"

"Mind your manners. She's my sister," Jimmy said, bristling a little. "Mariah, these are my friends from Wichita. Otis, here. And the obnoxious one's Shorty."

Mariah nodded to each in turn as they tipped their hats.

"Pardon us, miss," Otis said in a mannerly way firmly at odds with his crusty appearance. "Sometimes we forget our manners around real ladies. The work we do, we don't see all that many up close."

"No offense taken," Mariah said. She gave Jimmy a sideways glance. "I thought you gentlemen had gone on back to Wichita."

"We did," Otis said. "But the boss sent us back. Thought since we were out and about, we'd see how young Jim here is doing, and let him know Keenan still wants him back on the crew. In fact, if you're interested, you could earn a dollar or two today."

Jimmy looked from Mariah's frown to his friends and nodded. "Give me a minute with my sister. I'll catch up."

"Sure. Nice to meet you, miss." Following Otis's lead, Shorty tipped his hat again before they turned toward the east.

"You're not going with them," Mariah began, but his lips went thin and his eyes narrowed.

"I sure as heck am. I want that money."

"For the mortgage or to go off and gamble?"

"For both."

Mariah tried a different tack. "Aurelia's expecting you."

That made him pause, but not for long. "I'll get over there late, that's all. Or I'll send a message. Depends on what this is about. She'll understand. She's the only one around here that seems to know what I really want. She thinks Colorado or Nevada or someplace sounds exciting."

"Then she's as big a fool as you are."

"I'm not a fool. I'm just tired of pouring my sweat into the ground and having nothing come back except corn."

"We have the land. A home."

"You want that, not me."

"How can you say that? This is all we have. Don't you want to give everything to hang onto it?"

"Like you, letting that McKenzie sweet-talk you?"

Mariah gritted her teeth. "I told you, Bay's not after the land. It's the last thing he wants."

"And I know what the first is."

"Shut up, Jimmy, before I have to smack you again."

"Just . . ." He bit back whatever he was about to say and began fiddling with the tie strings on his saddle fork, running them through his fingers. "Those fellows'll probably only stay around a few days."

There was something in his tone that made Mariah uneasy. She leaned toward him so she could see his face better. "Are you planning to go back to Wichita with them?"

"I don't know," Jimmy said. "Yeah, I suppose I am. If I stay around here, you and I will end up even more disgusted with each other."

"Oh, no you don't, James Frances Hoag. You're not going to make me feel guilty for you leaving. You were headed that way a long time before Bay came along."

"You're right, but the thought of you and him together makes it a sight easier to go." He dropped the tie strings and straightened to look her in the eye. His voice softened a little.

"The truth is, I hate working the fields, and I'm no good at farming. You're of more use to Pa than I've ever been. Shoot, you even plow a straighter row than I do. I can do more to help you and the folks keep the place if I make enough money to pay off the mortgage."

"When are you planning to tell Mama and Papa you're going? Or are you going to tell them you're headed for Aurelia's again and then just not come home?"

"Of course not," Jimmy said. He nudged his horse around to

the direction his friends had gone. "But I don't want to listen to arguments all week, either. I'll tell them the night before. Look, I've got to get. You go on and have fun at your bee. I'll see you back at the house this evening."

Mariah watched until he disappeared over the rise after his friends, her heart aching for the two drifters in her life. Then a flash of stubborn practicality made her straighten her spine and square her shoulders. The sun was shining, the meadowlarks were piping, and the haze, odd as it was, had a glittery sparkle that made her think of diamonds on the wind. This was Annie's day, and neither Jimmy nor Bay could ruin it. She wouldn't allow it.

She turned her horse north, toward the Richardsons' house and a quilting bee that promised a day's fun.

Late the same afternoon, Bay reined Cajun in next to Eli's mount on the top of a ridge just southwest of the Hoag place. Against the deep green of the trees along the creek, he could make out the barn and most of the tiny, sun-baked house. From a distance, the sprawling fields of corn and spring wheat anchored the farm's corners, with the smaller patches of tobacco, the orchard, and the garden in the center. Somehow it all reminded him of a quilt spread out for a picnic blanket in a meadow, a piece of civilization laid out over wild prairie that ran on for miles. But he knew that one or two seasons without the plow and you'd never be able to tell the civilized from the wild, except for the house. Mariah and her folks had picked a tough place to make a stand.

"You want me to go on down with you?" Eli asked.

Bay turned away from the view and gave his friend a wink. "Oh, sure. I always like to take along company when I go courting."

"Not to stay," Eli groused. "What kind of fool do you think I am? I just figured you might like me around in case that daddy of hers decides to pull out his bird gun. Besides, I'd kind of like to meet the gal who can get you to jump through the kind of hoops I've seen you take the past few weeks."

"She's not getting me to do anything. In case you've forgotten, the past two weeks were spent chasing around the state trying to out-wangle my old man." On arriving in Topeka, Bay had learned that the man he wanted to see had gone off hunting, and they'd had to run him down in Wichita to get some papers signed.

"Whatever. But she and I haven't ever been properly introduced. Heck, I've barely even gotten a good look. If I didn't know better, I'd figure maybe you didn't trust me."

"Only with my life and my money. Don't worry, you'll get your . . ."

A sparkle caught the corner of Bay's eye and he turned to look west. He'd been watching the haze all day. Riding northeast as they were, the thickest portion seemed to hang behind them. He had seen it climb up from the horizon, watching its color darken from milky white to hazy green and the pearliness increase as the day wore on, passing behind the mist.

He suddenly knew what it was.

Grasshoppers. The word of a plague had started spreading just before he and Eli headed out of Wichita two days earlier. Reports were coming in from the bare plains of West Kansas about hoardes of insects so thick the trains supposedly couldn't stop or start because of the crushed bodies on the rails. They ate the curtains right out of the windows and broke the limbs of trees with their weight. He'd discounted the stories as tall tales, the efforts of some newspaperman to concoct yet another story to thrill the readers in New York and Boston. He and Eli had ridden across the same plains only a few weeks before. Sure, there were hoppers, he told anyone who'd asked, but nothing like the nonsense coming over the telegraph wires. He and Eli had chuckled about the absurdity of the stories as they'd ridden the past couple of days.

But this was them. The sparkle was the sun on their wings. He suddenly knew it as surely as he knew his own name. As if reacting to his realization, the mist rose abruptly over them. The mass split and streamed toward the creek. The first large yellow and brown bodies thudded down and started stripping leaves off the wildflowers.

"Jeez-us," Eli said.

"Come on." Bay stabbed his spurs into Cajun's side and they raced down the hill.

Mr. Hoag stood before the house, gaping up at the sky, stunned shock on his face. He barely seemed to notice when Bay and Eli rode up. Behind him his wife glanced briefly in their direction.

"I'm not going to let locusts have the garden when Mariah's put so much into it all year," she said. "You two, come help us with this rug. Cornelius, I think you'd better bring in the animals before they panic. Then cut as many of the cabbages as you can."

His wife's matter-of-fact instructions set Mr. Hoag in motion. Cursing softly, he disappeared into the barn.

Bay strode into the house and began dragging furniture out of the way to get to the rug. Eli was right behind him but he paused in the doorway.

"Elias Hightower, ma'am. We haven't met."

"Thank you, Mr. Hightower, but the grasshoppers are following you in." She picked up a broom and swept the insects back out the door. Some of them clung to the broomstraws and she shook them loose before she slammed the door. "Take the quilts and blankets, too. Cover the tender vegetables first and we will harvest as much as we can."

Bay hoisted the rolled rug over his shoulder while Eli snatched up the bedding. Working as fast as they could, they covered the plants, anchoring the edges of the coverings with dirt and rocks. What wasn't covered in the first minutes soon crawled with wriggling bodies three inches thick. Mrs. Hoag attacked the cabbages with her broom, sweeping them clean as her husband cut the immature heads and poked them into a huge burlap bag that quickly swarmed with bugs as thick as those on the garden.

"Where's Mariah?" Bay demanded.

Mrs. Hoag looked up, and her face blanched. "Oh, dear lord. She should be headed home by now. She's out in the middle of this."

"James, too," Mr. Hoag said. "I'll go find them."

"No, sir," Bay said. "I will. You need to be here with your wife. Eli?"

"I'll stay here and help these folks out," Eli said. He grabbed a shovel. "I always had a strong back. Let's see if I can't stay ahead of these little devils." He laid to, in the steady rhythm of a placer miner, scooping the hoppers off the top of the covers and into the pile at the edge of the garden. "Do you have any kerosene in that shed?"

Cajun stood in misery where Bay had left him, the grasshoppers so thick on his hide he appeared to be dun colored instead of gray. He twitched and snorted as insects wriggled into his ears and investigated his nostrils. With a grunt of disgust, Bay brushed the horrendous mass away from the animal's face. Then he swept Cajun's back clear enough to see the saddle and swung up before the bugs had a chance to re-form. A couple of insects crunched under his seat and he had to hang on as Cajun crow-hopped twice. Some of the little fiends must have gotten under the saddle, too.

Mrs. Hoag had followed him away from the garden. She stood watching him, her face pinched and pale, nervously brushing the insects off her arms and skirts.

Bay let Cajun drift her way as he settled. "She'll be fine, ma'am. Locusts are nasty, but I've never heard of them eating people."

She rewarded him with a tight smile. Behind her, Mr. Hoag sloshed kerosene out of a can onto Eli's growing pile of hoppers. He dropped a match, and the smoke roiled up. The stench of coal oil and burning insects clogged Bay's throat. He turned back to Mrs. Hoag. She looked like she needed to retch and was holding it back.

"Depending on where I find Mariah, it might make more sense to take shelter someplace," he said. "If I don't find her, I'll come back and get help, but if you don't see us, she's fine with me. All right?"

She nodded. "Thank you, Mr. McKenzie. Keep an eye out for my son, too."

"Yes, ma'am," he said, though Jimmy Hoag's safety was the last thing on his mind. He turned Cajun toward the gate.

It took him two hours to find Mariah. Two hours of the damnable bugs crawling down his shirt, up his pants legs, and over his face. He tried tying his kerchief over his nose and tucking it into his collar, but they just wriggled underneath, which was worse. The shudders he got when one tried to creep into his ear almost shook him off the horse.

About an hour into the search, he spotted Jimmy Hoag on the other side of the creek, hightailing it for home. The boy didn't even notice Bay, small favors. That was one child Mrs. Hoag didn't have to worry about tonight. But where was her daughter?

He'd begun to think he'd missed Mariah and had turned toward the Richardsons' when he spotted her horse, riderless, tearing at him across a pasture. The sorrel's eyes showed huge and white-edged in the near dark as he ripped past, and his panic communicated to Cajun. Bay had to hold him back with brute force. When Cajun calmed, Bay urged him back along the route the sorrel had come—at least as far as he could tell. Every sign of the animal's passage had been obliterated in seconds under the shifting mat of grasshoppers.

Finally, just before the light faded completely, he spotted a blue calico bundle, huddled against a high bank along the stream's edge. Bay flung himself off Cajun, snubbed him to the stripped trunk of a sapling, and was at Mariah's side in seconds.

"Get them off me," she said between gritted teeth. She brushed at the creatures in jerky motions, shaking like she had a malaria.

Bay did what he could, but they swarmed back over her. It was the dress that drew them, he saw, with its pattern of tiny flowers and green stems against the blue ground. She looked like food. The little bastards were eating the clothes off her, never mind what he'd told her mother.

She flailed at her fraying skirts. "Get them off me," she repeated, her voice near hysteria.

He boosted her up on the saddle and swung up behind her. Cajun seemed to understand the urgency. He tolerated the extra weight without so much as a whinny and when Bay asked for speed, he delivered.

"Take me home," Mariah said, brushing at her face and arms.

Bay held her tight. She trembled so hard, he thought she'd fall apart in his arms. "The ranch is closer."

"Home," she repeated unsteadily. "Mama and Papa need help."

"Eli's there. And so's your brother. We're going to the ranch."

"No."

He tightened his grip as she tried to break free. "Stop it, Mariah. Cajun can't take much more and neither can you and I. The house is stone and tight as a jar. They won't get to you there."

She subsided against him as if suddenly exhausted, but her hands never stopped flicking at the insects. Bay helped as he could, shooing them from her face and hair as well as his own. He gritted his teeth against the feel of one or more creeping down his back inside his shirt.

They raced across McKenzie pasture land, past frantic cattle on the edge of stampede. Despite the darkness and the clouds of insects that filled the air, it was easy to spot the ranch house from a distance: a dozen bonfires blazed on the hill around the house and kitchen garden. As they galloped under the McKenzie and Sons sign, Bay saw men raking the hordes away from the barn and outbuildings and caught the same stench that surrounded the Hoag garden. Ignoring the turmoil, he wheeled Cajun up in front of the house and slid off. Mariah tumbled into his arms. A man appeared out of the whirling storm and led Cajun away.

Bay took the steps two at a time and pushed through the front door hollering for help. "Mrs. Shaw!"

The housekeeper stuck her head out of the library and her eyes widened. "Oh, the poor dear."

Between the two of them, they stripped Mariah out of her tattered, grasshopper-laden dress and petticoat in seconds. Bay pitched the garments outside as the housekeeper brushed the last few insects off Mariah's underthings and wrapped her in a throw. Mariah pulled it tight, as if it could both shield her and hold her together. The edges of the blanket trembled in her hands. She looked like she might collapse and she didn't say a word, just stared at them both. Bay wondered if she was in shock.

"There you go, dear. You don't want to go back out in that.

You'll be fine. Come along, let's get you into bed. You can wear one of my gowns." Mrs. Shaw gave Bay a stern look. "Push that rug back against the crack under the door, then see to it none of those nasty things stay alive in this house."

"Not if I can help it." Bay slapped at his back as one of his own pets slipped down toward his waist. "Mariah, go with Mrs. Shaw. Please."

Wordlessly, Mariah allowed Mrs. Shaw to steer her down the hall.

Bay rid himself of his personal infestation, then tracked down every last hopper in the front room, grimly stomping them into pulp. When he felt sure the house was safe for Mariah, he retreated to his own room and found some clothes that might serve him better: a tighter pair of jeans and a shirt wit a collar that fit too snug. He tore an old kerchief into strips, which he used to tie his pants legs at the ankles then headed down to see how he could help.

Mrs. Shaw passed him on her way upstairs with a tea tray. "She's shaky, but she's game," the housekeeper reported. "I think I'd have lost my mind with those creatures crawling over me. All she can worry about is going back out in them to go home."

"Make sure she doesn't," Bay said. "Even if you have to tie her down. Where's my father?"

Mrs. Shaw frowned. "Outside. You probably passed him coming in. I told him not to go. He has plenty of men to do the work, and he's not fit for it. But would he listen? No. Stubborn old coot."

Not stubborn, Bay thought as he crunched and slipped down the hill toward a distinctive bellow. Greedy. He probably couldn't stand the thought that the grasshoppers might eat something of his.

"You there, no slacking off." John McKenzie swung his cane like a general might wield a sword. "Shovel, boys. Burn the little devils to a crisp. There you are, son. They're trying to get in the grain bins. Get over there and help those lads."

Bay nodded and reached for a shovel.

Hours. They'd been at it for hours, the fires burning and McKenzie's hands working like dogs, and still the grasshoppers swarmed. Another burst hit the window glass like hail, and Mariah stepped back and pulled the borrowed shawl tighter around her shoulders.

Sometime long past midnight, she realized the fires were dying back. Exhausted men, sooty, sweat-drenched shapes in the flickering light, stood back helplessly as the weight of the tiny bodies smothered the flames. A few groups struggled on, pouring the last stocks of kerosene over the piles, but it was clear they'd lost. Gradually the men moved away into the dark. Mariah stood at the window, tears streaming down her cheeks.

Bay slipped through the front door, barely opening it, but the grasshoppers followed. He used his hat to beat off the ones that clung to his clothes, then pursued them until he killed every last one—including the two that made it to the potted palm on the far side of the room. Mrs. Shaw's steady footsteps came down the hall. She took up a broom that leaned by the door and began gathering the carcasses into a dust pan.

"Is there any sign of them letting up?" she asked.

"No." Bay twisted his head, trying to work out a kink that had developed from holding his neck so that no more bugs could crawl down his shirt. "Where's my father?"

"At his desk. He said I could go on to bed, so if there's nothing you need . . ."

"Just a glass of whiskey to wash this taste out of my mouth, and I know where that is."

"Yes, sir. I put the young lady in the rose room in the guest wing. I thought, considering everything that's passed over the last few years, she'd be more comfortable away from Mr. McKenzie."

"I'm sure she appreciates it. Thank you, Mrs. Shaw."

"Good night, sir."

Bay found his father's liquor supply and downed a tumbler of bourbon and branch water in one long draw and without bothering to sit. The whiskey's smooth fire cut the smoke in his throat and flowed right out to his fingertips. He poured another two shots' worth straight into the glass and carried it to the door of the study.

His father had turned his chair to face the window, and sat

staring out at the night. Bay stepped up behind him. With the fires out, there was little to be seen except the pale underbellies of the hoppers crawling over the glass and the black sky beyond.

"I thought you were going to bed," Bay said.

"I changed my mind." John lifted his cane and tapped the pane, and a score of hoppers leapt off into the dark. They regrouped in seconds. "I keep thinking there must be something we're missing, something that will chase them off and keep them off."

"I know, but I'll be damned if I can come up with it."

"You did well enough, lad, thinking to mud over the vents in the grain bins."

Bay sipped at his drink and rolled the liquor across his tongue. "I figured they wouldn't like lime mortar quite as well as they seemed to like the rags you were using."

"I didn't think of it." John whacked the window again, this time hard enough that Bay thought it would shatter. The glass cleared. "I *should* have thought of it."

"You hadn't seen them eat the clothes off someone already."

John leaned his cane against the wall and turned to face Bay. "I'm getting old. I never thought I would."

"Neither did I."

"Ah, lad, it happens when a man's not watching. It's natural, they say. I'll tell you the only thing natural about it: A son working beside his father, taking over when the old man gets tired. That's how it always has been and always should be."

Bay let the fantasy slide without commenting on reality. He had no intention of taking over the ranch or anything else, but it made no sense to argue the point tonight.

"I'll bet you made a fine officer for the Union," John said. "You got out there and pulled more work from those men than they ever thought they could give."

"They're a good crew." Bay felt his mind and his muscles start to relax under the influence of the liquor. "What are we doing, standing around congratulating each other on a job badly done? Come on. Maybe we'll both be brighter after a few hours sleep."

"Before you go, watch this." John reached for the coal oil

lamp on his desk and put the light out. The scene outside jumped into sudden, stark contrast, a whirling mass of wings touched by starlight.

"Bloody little bastards," Bay said.

John winced as he rose, but the corners of his eyes crinkled with amusement. "You're my son, even if you don't want to admit it."

Out fighting for his land, John had ignored the limitations of his mangled body, but now it appeared he was paying. Bay lingered, accommodating his father's painful hobble.

"Good night." It felt strange, saying that and meaning it for the first time in thirteen years.

"Good night, son." John paused in the doorway. "I never did ask, who was that woman you brought in earlier? I couldn't make her out for all the smoke and such."

"Mariah Hoag."

John raised one sooty eyebrow in interest. "Cornelius Hoag's daughter under my roof. I'll be. Imagine, out in that with nowhere to turn but to me and mine."

Bay could see the cogs turning, but he let that, too, slide. He was too tired to start a row, and besides, there was no way his father could damage the Hoags now. "Good *night*."

Bay headed upstairs for bed, stripping the buttons of his shirt open as he made his way down the darkened hallway in the guest wing. Light spilled out under his doorway. Mrs. Shaw must have turned down the bed and left the lamp burning, as she had every night he'd been in the house. It was no wonder she'd managed to stay on with his father and his tempers and meanness: not a thing bothered her. A locust invasion appeared to mean little more disruption than a summer rainstorm.

Just as his cramped muscles started relaxing with the thought of the cool, clean sheets, he saw the pinkish light under the door at the end of the hall. The rose room. Mariah. He veered toward it as surely as a moth toward a flame.

"Mariah?" She didn't answer, and Bay pushed the door open.

It was a night for staring out windows. Mariah stood before hers wrapped in a heavy plaid shawl over a modest nightgown, though the air felt hot as Hades to Bay. She stared out into the night, not moving, but he could see the reflection of the tears that streamed down her cheeks.

"Mariah?" he repeated.

"Everybody worked so hard," she whispered. "And they still couldn't stop them."

"We slowed them down where we had to. And there's still a crew working."

"How many men?"

"Six still at it, fifteen all together. Seventeen with my father and me. We're taking shifts. We'll go at it again in the morning, see if we can clear them out."

She drew a shuddering breath that made Bay's throat ache with her tears. "And at home there's just Papa and Jimmy."

"And Eli." *And your mother wields a pretty good broom,* he wanted to add, but that would only worry her more. "We got the garden covered before too many of them landed. That should help."

She turned toward him, her face streaked with tears and bright with pain and hope, and without realizing how she got there, Bay found her in his arms. She burrowed against his chest, her sobs muffled in the shawl and his shirt.

He stood as long as he could, but the liquor and the lack of food and the hours of riding and shoveling were taking their toll. After ten minutes or so, his legs began to shake. Carefully assessing his own intentions, he moved Mariah toward the bed and settled on the edge. He eased her toward the pillow, but she clung, and he found himself leaning over her, half embracing her.

"Mariah, you don't . . ."

"Hold me," she whispered. "Every time I close my eyes, I can feel them crawling on me again. Keep them away. Please keep them away." Her voice got higher and she began trembling again.

"Shhh." He stroked a wayward strand of hair from her cheek. "I'll stay a little bit."

It wouldn't be too hard being a gentleman tonight, Bay thought. He reeked of smoke and sweat and was too damned tired to get excited. He'd just hold her until she went to sleep, then slip out. He didn't even kick his boots off, just made sure his feet hung over the edge so he didn't ruin the duvet any more than his smoky clothes were already doing.

"Shhh. Sleep, sweetheart. Sleep."

The guttering lamp and the dull glow of sunrise woke Mariah, that and the sense that someone had just left the room. She sat up with a start, the weight of a single sheet falling away. Beside her, a smudged hollow marked the bed. She put her hand there and felt the warmth.

Bay.

Chapter Eleven

⁂

MARIAH HELD HERSELF very still, trying to recall how this had happened, *what* had happened. The images came to her sleep-befuddled mind in broken sections: the grasshoppers—oh, God, the grasshoppers—Bay finding her, the fires, Mrs. Shaw, and finally, asking him to hold her, feeling the comfort of his arms around her as she drifted off.

She remembered coming half awake sometime in the past few hours and hearing his sleepy murmur in her ear, "I'm still here. Shhh." Whether he'd lain awake beside her all night or fallen asleep himself, she didn't know.

A clock chimed somewhere in the house, the melody barely audible. She waited for the hours to strike, counting the tones off as they came . . . six . . . seven . . . eight.

Eight o'clock. It should be brighter. Mariah rushed to the window. The grasshoppers were still there, still scrabbling over the glass, still blocking the sun. She'd been so sure they'd be gone by morning. The tears welled again, and she swallowed them down.

They did no good. Not now.

Mariah found the plain gray wrapper Mrs. Shaw had laid out the night before and donned it, then headed down the hall.

A door popped open and Bay came out, pulling a clean shirt over his head. She dodged aside, but as soon as his head cleared the neck opening, he grabbed her by the arm.

"Where are you going in such a hurry?" he asked.

"I need to go home," she said.

"There's no one to take you right now."

"I don't need to be taken. Loan me a good horse. I'll be fine."

"Have you looked out there this morning?"

"Of course."

"Maybe you haven't had the best view." He tugged her downstairs and across the entry hall to the front door. "Look."

The view through the glass was disheartening. Down by the barn, several men worked steadily, raking grasshoppers away from the doors and beating at the stone walls with bags. On some of the outbuildings, she could see grayish-white smears around the shutters and vents, like someone had plastered the openings.

And over it all, a mask of yellow and brown, moving, shifting. The air seethed with iridescent wings.

"I'll be fine," she repeated less certainly.

"Did you notice that?" Bay pointed at something draped over the edge of the porch.

Mariah peered at the discolored lump and the bugs that swarmed over it. "What is it?"

"Your dress, or what's left of it."

The memory of a thousand clawed legs ran over her skin. Mariah shuddered and slapped at a strand of hair that brushed her neck. "If Mama can stand it, I can."

"Your mother has a house to retreat to when they get too thick, and three men around to help her. You'd be out on the hills alone again."

"I can do it," she said. "I have to. I watched invaders take our home once before. I can't let it happen again just because you won't take me home."

"Shhh." Bay slipped his arms around her waist and pulled her back against his chest, and his touch worked the same calming magic it had during the night. "You're not ready to go back out in that mess again, but I promise, I'll get you home as soon as you are. Right now, though, we both need something to eat."

"You cannot expect me to sit at your father's table. I can just see him, gloating and sitting there like one of those things," she motioned toward the locusts, "waiting for us to go under."

"He can't—" Bay began and stopped. He glanced away and shook his head.

"What?"

"Nothing. I don't think you'll even see him. If he's not out hollering at the crew, he's probably asleep—or at least he should be. Now come on."

She tried one last argument. "Mama and Papa will be worried sick."

"No." Bay explained the arrangement he had with her mother. "So until I say otherwise, you're in my hands."

"But I—"

He put his lips next to her ear and whispered, "You didn't seem to mind it last night."

Mariah reddened. "Hush."

"At least you can't accuse me of not being a gentleman this time."

"If you keep talking, I will."

"Then come to breakfast. I can't talk with my mouth full."

She conceded and allowed him to lead her to the dining room, where Mrs. Shaw quickly laid out plates of pan fried steak and flapjacks. Bay tucked in, but Mariah stared out the window.

"I wouldn't be wearing flowers this time," she said.

Bay laid his fork down. "You won't be wearing anything if you don't promise to stay put until things settle down outside. I'll have Mrs. Shaw take her dress back."

Mariah subsided again, and he went back to his food. She watched, finally noticing how tired he looked. His hearty appetite was at odds with the tight lines of his unshaven jaw and the deep circles under his eyes. Mariah realized the show was for her, and she reached out, wanting to smooth away the strain. The sound of Mrs. Shaw bringing in the coffee stopped her midway, but he captured her hand and pressed a more or less gentlemanly kiss to her fingers before he released her.

"I fell asleep, just so you know," he said, once Mrs. Shaw had gone. Mariah was of a mind to accept his explanation until his eyebrows went up with a mischievous tilt.

"You're incorrigible."

"Maybe. We can discuss it if you'd like, but right now, I'm

going to get back out there, like I should have three hours ago."

A few swigs of steaming coffee and he was on his feet. He stopped in the doorway.

"My father's study is one door down on the left. There are enough books in there to keep you happy for a year. Help yourself to anything, and I do mean anything, that you need."

"I'll keep myself occupied," she promised.

Mariah toyed with her food for a few minutes, then picked up the two plates and carried them into the kitchen.

Mrs. Shaw flushed and snatched them away. "That's my job, miss. You're a guest."

"More of a refugee, and one not used to having people wait on her. Give me an apron and put me to work."

"Absolutely not. Mr. McKenzie would have a fit."

"Mr. McKenzie—the young one, that is—said to ask for anything I need. I need to keep busy. Please, ma'am. I'll go crazy trapped in here, thinking about what's happening at home."

The housekeeper glanced out the bug-clotted window and sighed. She reached for an apron and held it out. "Come along then."

"Just when did you join my staff, young woman? Or are you stealing the silver?" John McKenzie's voice grated across Mariah's nerves. The serving dish in her hand rattled against the sideboard, but she managed to keep from whirling around like a child caught filching candy.

She wrapped her fingers around the platter firmly and collected herself before she turned. "Good evening, Mr. McKenzie."

"Well?"

She continued to ignore the question. "Mrs. Shaw thought you'd sleep longer. Supper will be a while."

"Tell her I'm not hungry."

"That doesn't surprise me, all the bile you must have in your stomach."

He actually chuckled, then hobbled over to sit down in the high-backed armchair at the head of the table. He looked like he was in tremendous pain, and his face seemed gray and drawn. Mariah felt a twinge of contrition over her biting words, but it faded when she saw his eyes, gleaming with interest and something she'd have to call acquisitiveness, as they impaled her.

"You do have a tongue on you." He reached for the bottle of Scotch that had already been set at his place. "But that's fine. I admire people who say what they think."

"I'm sure I could convince you to reconsider that position."

He laughed again, this time more heartily. "Mrs. Shaw!"

"Yes, sir?" The housekeeper stuck her head out from the kitchen.

"Take this bloody apron off this girl and haul your own dishes about. She's a guest in this house. She's to eat at my table, not wait on it."

"I tried to tell her, Mr. McKenzie."

Mariah would as soon pitch the platter at the man as sit down at a table with him, but there was no help for it. She was beholden for her shelter and board, and if he wanted her at his table, she would be there, with all the grace she could muster.

Mrs. Shaw gave her a sympathetic smile as she accepted the silver platter and the apron. She disappeared into the kitchen.

Mariah stood there for a moment, trying to dredge up enough of her mother's admonitions and lessons to make it through the meal without breaking her host's bottle over his head. The key would be to keep the conversation to safe topics. *Like the weather?* Mariah wondered. She ran through a conversation in her head: "Lovely locusts we're having, Mr. McKenzie." "Yes, indeed, and I figured out how to use them to drive you off your farm, too."

It was bound to be a very quiet meal.

When she finally turned to face John McKenzie, he was nodding.

"What?" she asked.

"Nothing, lass. Just watching you." He nursed the glass cradled in his fist. "You're a proud, stubborn family, you Hoags."

"Yes, sir."

"From what I see and hear, you're the proudest and most stubborn of the lot."

Mariah inclined her head, accepting it as a compliment instead of condemnation.

"You don't think much of me, do you?" John asked.

"I think quite a bit of you, unfortunately all bad."

"There we go. I could see you trying to figure out a way to be nice to the old man. I won't have it. I'd rather have you spit at me than that." He chuckled when she blushed. "Ah, so I hit it square on the head, did I? Well, come on and sit down. We'll do fine." John patted the table to his right. "I'm afraid I can't manage your chair."

"I can," Bay said.

In his quiet way, he'd come in through the kitchen. Mariah suspected Mrs. Shaw had something to do with that. His face was still damp, as though he hadn't taken time to dry well when he washed up, but he seemed at ease. Not at all like he'd rushed in to save her.

She gave him a grateful smile and accepted his help with her chair. His fingers lingered a moment against her back before he stepped away and took a seat across the table from her, on his father's left. His position made his father turn away from Mariah, and she silently sighed in relief.

John poured another four fingers of Scotch into his glass. "How is it out there?"

Bay shook his head. "We're holding ground. I sent out a crew to bring the herd in closer. Unless the grass is holding up better out away from the house, you're going to have to feed the stock anyway."

"I'll sell off all but the seed stock."

"Every ranch from here to Denver will be doing the same. You either have to beat them to market or hold out for a few months until the glut's past."

"Aye. I've thought of that, but grain and hay prices will jump now, if they can be had at all."

Mariah listened to the conversation intently. Everything that affected McKenzie would go double for the farm. The heartache she'd been suppressing all day by doing chores rushed back. When Mrs. Shaw carried in the big platter, now filled with a huge pot roast, new potatoes, and fingerling carrots, she could barely stomach the sight of such abundance. Heaven only knew what they'd be eating come winter.

Talking tactics all the while, Bay and his father managed to put down the biggest portion of the meal while she pushed a few vegetables around on her plate. Before she knew it, they'd finished.

Mr. McKenzie pushed to his feet and reached for his cane. "I'll be down at the barn."

"There's no reason for you to go," Bay said. "I just checked on everything."

"I know. Make that girl eat something before she goes to bed."

"I'll try," Bay said.

"You do that. I won't have her starving to death at my table." He paused in the doorway and gave Mariah another one of those odd stares. "I can see why you would do it, boy. I might have done, myself."

Bay reddened and turned, his mouth open, but his father had gone. A moment later, they heard the click of the front door latching.

"What did he mean?" Mariah asked.

"Never mind," Bay said, but his lips thinned. "It has nothing to do with you. He was right about one thing: You need to eat."

"I'm not hungry."

"You're not going to do your parents any good if you make yourself sick."

The truth in that statement won out over Mariah's mood. She stabbed a piece of carrot and choked it down. The second bite went down easier. Bay lazed in the chair opposite, his arms folded across his chest, watching her until she cleared her plate and laid her fork aside. She returned his steady gaze.

"For a man who doesn't want to be a hero, you keep managing to rescue me. Thank you."

His eyes flickered away from hers, like something in the distance had caught his attention. She glanced over her shoulder and saw nothing but a painting of a mountain at sunrise, a crescent moon hanging just above the peak. She rose and went to look at it. His chair scraped, and he stepped up behind her.

"Mount Evans, Colorado Territory," she read off the brass plate on the frame. "Have you seen it?"

He nodded. "Looking just like that. It's west of Denver."

And he wanted to see it again. Mariah's heart stopped, then picked up its steady rhythm again. "It's beautiful," she whispered.

"So are you."

The smallest movement, the slightest sway by either of them, and she could be in his arms. She waited for him to supply the motion, ready to surrender to the promise she felt in those words, but the seconds passed and they hung suspended those few inches from each other, until the moment broke on the sound of Bay's roughly indrawn breath.

He moved away. "I'd better hit the sack."

Mariah squeezed her eyes shut against the threat of tears, then turned to smile at him. "Me, too."

They walked down the hall side by side, so close she could feel his shirt cuff brush the fullness of her sleeve but never touching. He paused before his own door, his hand on the polished brass knob.

"Sleep well," he said.

No, not yet. She found a boldness she'd lacked a moment before. "I'm not sure I can."

Bay pressed his forehead against the door. His knuckles went white around the doorknob, and the tension in his arms and shoulders stretched his shirt taut. "If I come anywhere near your bed again, neither of us is going to sleep."

"I know."

He looked up, his eyes smoldering. His gaze swept over her body, stripping her right there in the hall, and she could imagine the rush of storm winds over her bare skin, stirring over the places where she burned for his touch. She stepped back under the assault.

"Not here," he said, his voice harsh with effort. "Not in my father's house when he thinks. . . . Go to bed, Mariah. Now."

All she had to do was touch him. It would release him, and she could lose herself in the things he would do to her. All she had to do . . .

So long as you do not lie with him, I will wait.

Her belly knotted with guilt, and she turned and fled. The hall echoed with the sound of two doors slamming.

Mariah loitered in the rosy morning glow of her room, asking herself unanswerable questions. How could she have been so brazen? Why hadn't she remembered Nikolai sooner? What if Bay had carried her to his bed?

Bay was at the dining table when she finally arrived, though by the looks of his plate, he'd beaten her by only a few minutes. As she slid into a place at the far end of the table, he gave her that look again, the same one he'd given her in the hall last night, with equally devastating effect. She stared down at her hands, folded in her lap.

"It won't do any good for you to sit down there," he said. "You could be in the next county and we'd still want each other."

"Don't," she said, but the way his eyes devoured her, she might as well have come to the table buck naked. Him, too, for all the games her mind played with the little bit she knew about how a grown man looked without clothes.

Mrs. Shaw came in with a plate full of eggs and fried potatoes and a steaming pot of coffee.

"I suppose my father's still out there," Bay said conversationally.

"No, sir." She glanced at Mariah and Bay, but didn't comment on their positions. "He came in a couple of hours ago, ate and went straight to bed. He said the worst of it's over."

"I can go home," Mariah said immediately, her mind back to what mattered.

Bay nodded. "Possibly. It was easing off yesterday afternoon, but I didn't want to get your hopes up. I'll go take a quick look around before we decide. You keep eating."

Mariah watched him from the dining room window as he circled the complex, talking to the men who still kept the outbuildings clear. Not much later, he headed back.

She met him at the front door. "Well?"

"It's looking better. There aren't a third of what were out that first day."

"Then I can go."

"If you're ready, I'll take you. Have Mrs. Shaw round you up some clothes. Pants and a shirt. Mine will be too big, but one of the men should have something to fit."

The housekeeper had followed her out into the front hall. "Mr. McKenzie! She can't go out dressed like that."

"Yes, I can," Mariah said.

Bay gave her a quick grin. "Tie the legs and sleeves as tight as you can bear them, and button the collar up tight. If you can stand gloves and a canvas jacket in this heat, that will help, too. And braid your hair down tight." He turned back to Mrs. Shaw. "Everything in neutral colors. I don't want them mistaking her for a posy patch again."

"Yes, sir."

An hour later, Mariah stood inside the front door, watching Bay lead his horse up the drive. The animal looked as unhappy as Mariah felt. Just watching the grasshoppers land on him, she began to shake.

"Are you sure you're up to this, Miss Hoag?" the housekeeper asked.

Mariah nodded. "The crack under our front door is about two hoppers high, Mrs. Shaw. I'd better *get* up to it. Now. On the count of three."

Mrs. Shaw yanked the door open and Mariah dashed out. A well fed, thumb sized locust landed on her arm, with enough force that she felt it through the canvas jacket. Mariah nearly screamed, but knew that if she did, Bay would make her wait another day to go home. Biting her tongue, she flicked the creature away, grateful that Bay had recommended gloves, thankful she could make the long ride in his arms, where she knew she'd be safe.

Bay nodded. "You're ready. Come on."

Bay chose their approach to the Hoag place carefully. Rather than take Mariah over the ridge, where she would look down on the whole place at once, he brought her up along the creek. Still, he could tell the instant she saw the corn field. She stopped breathing, and for a heartbeat, he thought she must be about to faint. Then she took a deep breath.

"Ride me all the way around," she said.

The fields looked like scythes had taken everything off a few inches above root level. At Mariah's request, they rode into the farmyard by way of the orchard. The trees stood as barren as if a winter storm had ripped them clean. One sturdy young tree stood with its lower branches propped, looking particularly grotesque. Bay recalled slipping the prop poles into place himself, beneath branches so heavy with peaches that they had threatened to break. Now only naked pits hung from stems, the green peaches having been chewed cleanly away.

"My garden," she whispered. She slipped off the horse. Bay tied Cajun to a fence post and followed her.

The linens lay mostly in tatters, devoured as thoroughly as Mariah's dress, the vegetables beneath clearly a loss. Though the rug seemed to be intact, Bay held out small hope for what lay underneath.

He squatted at the edge of the garden, where he knew onions had once grown. They'd thought those would be fine and hadn't covered them at all. Now nothing showed except a series of neat holes in the ground. Bay stuck his finger in one and dug around. A brown husk came up, the outer skin of an onion. The grasshoppers had eaten down the stem and into the bulb, hollowing it out, leaving only an empty mold in the ground. Mariah turned away, hugging herself, but she still didn't cry.

Bay rose and wiped his hands on his jeans. "Come on. Let's see how your folks are."

The front door opened as they rounded the house, and Mr. Hoag walked out. Mariah ran to him.

"Praise be," he said, holding her to him like a treasure. "When the sorrel came home . . ."

"I'm fine, Papa. Bay found me and took me up to the ranch house. How's Mama?"

"Better now that you're home, child." Mrs. Hoag came out in a worn wrapper. The hem of a nightdress hung below, and her cheeks had the feverish, unhealthy look Bay had seen when he'd first come.

Face pinched with concern, Mariah hugged her mother and led her back inside. Bay swung off Cajun and led him to the corral fence. Mr. Hoag followed him.

"I want to thank you, Mr. McKenzie. You kept your word. Believing that you would sustained my wife through this." Hoag offered a hand and Bay shook it.

"Your friend, Mr. Hightower, is out in the cave, I believe," Mr. Hoag said. "He's been another godsend. He and my boy managed to keep most of our food stores intact. And he thought to seal off the well before the grasshoppers fouled the water."

Bay nodded. He'd noticed the creeks running tobacco-spit brown from the dead grasshopper bodies that clogged them. Any open wells would be polluted for days, perhaps longer. And there sat his father with a spring running hundreds of gallons an hour, clear as melted snow. He gritted his teeth. The drought of '59 and '60 would not replay in this part of the country. People would have clean water, and plenty of it. He'd see to it himself.

"You go on inside with your wife and daughter," he said. "I'll find Eli and see if there's anything else we can do."

Hoag shook his hand again and disappeared, and Bay went in search of Eli. The cave, the homesteader's retreat against cyclones and used every day to keep foods cool, slanted into a rise not far from the creek. Bay pounded on the heavy oak door with the butt of his hand. He heard a sliding sound, then the door popped open. Eli stuck his head out.

"About time."

"Damned right." Jimmy Hoag pushed past Eli, his face set. "Where's my sister? What did you do with her for the past two days?"

"She's with your mother. We were up at my father's place. Out of this mess."

Jimmy's hands bunched into fists. "You son of a bitch. If I find out you've been messing with her . . ." He gave Bay a deadly glare and took off for the house.

Bay watched him go, then shook his head. "I'm getting real tired of men who want to beat on me for her sake."

"Not that you deserve it, of course." Eli took a whack at a grasshopper trying sneak past him, and pushed the door closed. He shook his head. "Two days with the girl up in that house. Her daddy's going to think about that in a few minutes. Maybe it's time we get out of here."

"Yep. All alone with her. Just her, me, the housekeeper, my father, and fifty million grasshoppers. Nothing happened."

"Not that you're likely to tell me anyway."

"Nothing," Bay said testily. "And we're not going anyplace until I know these people are all right. What were you two doing in there?"

"Checking on things, just to make sure they didn't get into the barrels. Let me finish up, then you can help me seal the door again."

A half hour later, Bay and Eli patted the last globs of mud over the cracks.

"It looks like you all did pretty well by yourselves," Bay said.

Eli looked at him cockeyed. "You seen the barn?"

"No."

"Come on." He led Bay back to the barn, pushed the door open, and stood back.

Bay felt the sweat pool between his shoulders. The barn looked like a crazed housewife had gone through it, sweeping it as clean as could be. Barely a trace of straw mussed the floor. He shot up the ladder to the loft. Stripped. Two cuttings of hay, gone. He stood there gawking, just trying to absorb it.

"The corn cribs are just as bad. He did have a couple of barrels of grain that we moved into the cave and saved." Eli said finally. "Look at the pitchfork."

Bay did. The handle was eaten halfway through, especially where salt and sweat stained the wood. A dozen thumb-sized monsters perched on it still, jaws working with determination. He swept them off with one gloved hand and ground them under his boot before he walked outside.

"I've never seen anything like it," Eli said, following him. "Nearly all his tools are ruined. We had to move all the tack and harnesses 'cause they were getting eaten, too. Half his chickens died from eating too much, and the rest are laying eggs that taste like grasshopper. The meat will be bad for weeks. And his hogs were eating them, too."

Bay closed his eyes and shook his head. He couldn't think of a thing to say.

After a moment, Eli cleared his throat. Bay looked up.

Mariah stood a few feet away, her eyes round and glazed with shock, so lost in her sadness she didn't seem to notice the grasshoppers that clattered past her cheeks and leapt to sample her clothing.

"Excuse me," Eli said, backing away. "I'll just go see about the cattle."

Mariah stared after him. "Papa says he worked like it was his place. He doesn't even know us."

"His folks had a farm once," Bay said, going to her. "He understands. How are you doing?"

"Mama's fever came back. She worked like she was possessed, right up until she collapsed yesterday morning. At least that's what Jimmy says. And then someone had to sit inside to keep the grasshoppers from crawling right into bed with her." She poked at the edge of what had once been a sheet with her toe and watched the insects shift away with unblinking eyes. "I shouldn't have listened to you. I should have come home."

Bay wrapped his arms around her. "If you had, your father might have two sick women on his hands. At least now there's someone here who's eaten and slept in the past three days."

"We're going to lose the farm," she said dully. "We'll need the mortgage money to buy food for us and the livestock. When we default, McK—your father will either buy the paper and foreclose or wait for the bank sale."

"No, he won't," Bay said. "Let's go back inside. I need to talk to all of you."

The tiny house steamed like a sweatbox, the result of every crack being sealed against the bugs. Bay and Mariah did what they could to keep any more grasshoppers from entering with them and the one gasp of fresh air that came in with them, but even so, Bay could see a few creeping on every surface. They clustered especially around the kitchen shelves and cupboards, after the food they could smell in the tins and canisters. Bay wondered briefly about what had happened to the bins of vegetables that used to sit under the counters.

From her rocker, Mrs. Hoag brushed a hopper off the lamp chimney on the table next to her and smacked it with a newspaper she held rolled in her hand. "Sit down, Mr. McKenzie. We can't offer coffee just now, but we have cool water. It's the one thing we seem to have plenty of, thanks to Mr. Hightower."

Bay hung his hat on the peg and joined Mr. Hoag at the table while Mariah poured tin cups of water from a covered pitcher. When she took a seat at Bay's side, Jimmy pointedly got up and walked out. Mrs. Hoag started to apologize for her son.

Bay waved it off. "All he knows of McKenzies is my father. I don't blame him, ma'am." He took a sip of the water. It was as cool and fresh and sweet as the first day he'd come to the farm, the only thing that hadn't changed.

"Bay says he has something to tell us," Mariah said. They all looked at him expectantly.

He set the cup down and took a deep breath, not at all sure how any of them would react.

"I have your note."

"I beg you pardon."

"I bought your note, sir. That is, a mining company that Eli and I own bought it." He waited for the explosion, but when the silence dragged out, he continued. "I found out my father was planning to have an out of state firm buy the paper, and I beat him to it. I was going to tell you in a few weeks anyway, but with this mess . . ."

Mr. Hoag's cheeks slowly darkened to purple and the veins in his temples stood out in pounding relief. He began to sputter, and when he finally spoke, his voice was hard and bitter. "No wonder you two worked so hard. Saving your own investment."

"Cornelius!"

"Papa!"

The smile that had started to light Mariah's face turned to an embarrassed flush, but she looked to Bay with real hope in her eyes for the first time in days. He nodded, and she reached to touch his hand where he still gripped the cup before she turned back to her father.

"Don't you see?" she said. "He's trying to help us. We can pay him back next year when the crops are better. He'll give us the time we need."

"I'll go one better than that." Bay reached into his shirt pocket and pulled out the heavy leather wallet he'd borrowed from his father's desk early that morning. He retrieved the carefully folded note and smoothed it out on the table. "If you have a pen and ink, I'll call Eli in and we'll sign it off paid right here and now. I can file it this afternoon when we ride into town to wire east for relief supplies. You'll have your property free and clear, and you can keep you mortgage money for the things you need to get through to next year."

"Oh!" Heedless of her parents' doubly shocked expressions, Mariah flung herself at Bay. She covered his face with kisses, the salt of joyful tears mixing with the sweet taste of her lips. "Oh, thank you. Thank you."

Bay enjoyed the tender assault, his hands gently spanning her waist, until his body started responding to the warmth of her. With her parents both staring in disbelief, he could hardly afford to let himself get aroused. He pressed a single chaste kiss to her forehead and eased her back toward her own chair, and tried not to recall the feel of her sleeping in his arms.

"Well," her mother said.

Mariah blushed again, but this time the smile stayed where it belonged. Bay gave her a wink.

Mr. Hoag rose and walked to the window. He looked out over the disaster that had been a farm three days earlier.

"I misread you, sir. I apologize."

"Accepted. I'm going into town," Bay said. "Eli has family in Ohio and we've both got friends from the army. I even know a couple of retired generals. They'll organize aid. You won't have to worry about food or supplies. No one in the area will."

"That is a kind gesture, as is your offer to release the lien on our property," Mr. Hoag said. "However, both are unnecessary. I've already made up my mind. We're going back to Virginia."

Chapter Twelve

❦

BACK TO VIRGINIA.

A dull throbbing filled Mariah's head, nearly blocking her father's continuing words.

"Mariah and my wife will leave as soon as Acasta is able to travel. Jimmy and I will stay behind for a few weeks to sell off the farm goods and then join them." He turned from the window to face Bay. "After that the farm is yours, Mr. McKenzie."

"I don't want it," Bay said. "I have no use for it."

"Then sell it to your father. I don't care."

I do, Mariah thought, but her chest was so tight she couldn't find the breath to speak.

"Blast it all," Bay said. "The only reason I bought your note is to keep his hands off it. I'm working to keep him from driving other folks off, too."

"I hope you're successful," Mr. Hoag said. "But we're still going home."

"No!" The word exploded from Mariah. "No. We can replant. Millet and cane will grow before snow comes. With the relief, we can make it."

"Not your mother," Cornelius said. "She cannot take another winter here, especially not under those conditions."

"I'd be fine, Cornelius."

"On rough cornmeal and millet gruel?" He moved to his wife's side and lifted one of her fine-boned hands. "I know where our daughter got her stubborn streak. You need good food and plenty of rest, my love, and you won't get it here. I will not watch you starve again."

Acasta tugged his hand close and brushed a gentle kiss over his knuckles. The pain and love in her father's eyes as he gazed down at her mother brought a lump to Mariah's throat. She remembered those years, too, the weeks of gritty brown bread spread with rancid lard and little more. Couldn't he see?

"That's why we have to keep our land, Papa," she urged. "Mama can go stay with Uncle Zachariah for the winter."

"I had already written him about that."

"I don't understand, then," Bay said.

"Neither do I," Mariah said. "If Mama's safe, then everything will be fine until next year."

"And then what. Another fire? A flood the year after? And then your brother will head off for the gold fields, and you'll marry, and your mother and I will sit here alone." His shoulders sagged in defeat. "I dragged you all out here because we lost everything at home and I wanted to have something to pass on. But the truth is, I'm not a very good farmer, and your brother doesn't want the place."

"I do," Mariah said.

"I know, darling, but . . ."

"You keep talking about home like it's someplace in Virginia. *This* is home. From the day that plow turned the first strip of sod. Heat and wind and grasshoppers and all, it's home. All I've ever wanted is to stay here." Mariah looked from her parents' dignified sorrow to Bay, but he gave her no clue to his feelings. It didn't matter. Only the land mattered. "I'm not going back. Jimmy and I will stay and work the place."

"Don't be ridiculous. Your brother has no more interest in farming than Mr. McKenzie does. Less."

"Maybe so, but he doesn't want to go east any more than I do. He'll stay."

"For how long, child?" her mother asked.

There was the problem, and Mariah knew it. Jimmy would likely take off after a month or two. But that didn't matter. "Long enough. He'll hold on until spring, at least. We can harvest a short season crop and get through winter together. By then Mama will be feeling better, and you'll be tired of Virginia. You'll see. You'll miss the way the clouds pile up on the horizon just before a storm, and the way the hills turn all purple and blue at dusk, and the sound of the wind rustling the grass, like someone's always walking toward you."

Acasta nodded slowly. "For all the trials and the starkness, it is a beautiful place at times. There is a part of me that calls it home, too."

"Then don't make a decision so quickly. We've had a setback, it's true, but we can get through this. You and Papa go back to Virginia for the winter. Rest. Get your strength back. Jimmy and I will take care of things here. And in the spring, we can all start fresh. Everything will be different, with the mortgage cleared."

Acasta turned to her husband. "Perhaps she's right, dear. We are both so disheartened right now. This isn't the time to make such a large decision."

"But what about James? I have no intention of leaving our daughter here by herself." Frowning, Cornelius shot a significant glance in Bay's direction. "And we have no guarantee that the boy will stick it out."

Mariah lifted her chin. "Let's ask him."

"If he says no, that's it," Cornelius said flatly. "We will do just as I said. Sell and go home to Virginia. The whole family."

"I understand, Papa." She understood that she would have to find another way.

She started for the door, but Bay stopped her with a few quiet words. "I'm not staying, Mariah."

She swallowed hard and took a deep breath. "I know. But some of us are."

Jimmy came running at her call, and it took only a few moments to explain. Apparently he'd already heard their parents' plans and had been biding his time before he announced his refusal. He backed Mariah with enthusiasm—until his father asked for his promise to stay with her on the farm until spring.

His long hesitation nearly made Mariah scream. *Come on, Jimmy. Please.*

Bay shifted noisily, his chair scraping against the floor. "I guess that's it, then, Mr. Hoag. I don't know what I'm going to do with the place, but if he doesn't want to help her . . ."

"I never said that." Jimmy leaned toward Bay, venom in his eye. "I'll stay, Pa. Promise. Mariah can count on me."

Bay excused himself shortly after that. He had things to accomplish before sundown, but more than that, it made him uncomfortable watching the Hoags hash out the details. He should have stayed out of it, kept his mouth shut and let the kid flounder instead of egging him into a promise as poor as that.

He found Eli perched on the corral gate, contemplating the few head of lumbering shorthorns the family kept, and climbed up beside him. They sat in silence for a long time.

"Things a little melancholy in there?" Eli finally asked.

"They're starting their good-byes," Bay said. "Hoag's headed east with his wife for the winter. Mariah and her brother are sticking it out."

"Whew," Eli whistled. "Bet it was her idea."

Bay nodded. "Can the boy handle it?"

"I think so. He seems to know what he's doing. I'm just not so sure he wants to do it. When we had breath to talk, he kept bringing up some outfit he was working for and how he was going to make enough money with them to help his folks out and then head on west to prospect. I told him about Montana and how you and I won the Jacks High."

"Great. He'll be gone in a week."

"I was just making conversation," Eli said defensively. He tipped his head toward the hills beyond the corral. "I've been sitting here watching the hoppers clear out. I can't tell if more of them are dying or flying, but they're going fast."

Bay surveyed the area. The air did seem clearer than it had even an hour ago when he and Mariah had ridden in. It made sense that they'd move on: There was nothing left to eat except the siding on the barn and house.

"I need to get to town while things are open," he said.

"I guess there's not much else I can do here. I'll go saddle up." Eli headed toward the house for his gear, but Bay kept watching the cattle, his thoughts wandering. The animals twitched at the bugs that still explored their ears and faces, but they had gone beyond the panic they'd displayed the first day.

In other words, they were doing better than him.

The emotion that had possessed him when Mr. Hoag announced his decision to leave felt an awful lot like panic, which meant he'd interfered not because Mariah wanted to stay, but because he selfishly wanted to keep her as close as possible for as long as possible. Any half-wit knew she'd be better off at her uncle's, especially if the kid took off on her, but the truth was, he wanted her here until he left. More than that, he wanted to know she'd still be here, within reach, when he came back.

And he would come back. He knew that now. He would come back over and over, whether it made sense or not, so long as she was here.

Two sets of returning footsteps crunched across the yard. Eli passed, lugging his saddle, but the gate squeaked as the other person stepped up on the first board. Bay glanced down to find a mass of golden blonde curls at his side, threatening to loop around his waist and thigh and bind him there. Chin resting on the top of the gate, Mariah looked out over the land, her face intently proud and possessive.

Bay's stomach twisted a little. He'd seen the look before, on his father, and he suddenly understood why the old man had tolerated her so well: He fathomed a piece of her Bay couldn't grasp anymore, the part that was tied to one piece of earth. He couldn't help but wonder just how far she'd go to hold her little chunk of ground, whether her determination would ever fester into obsession the way his father's had and make the land more important than anything or anyone else.

Mariah finally looked up, piercing him with her emerald gaze, even more brilliant in comparison to the devastation surrounding them.

"Thank you," she said.

"What for? You're the one that held on."

"You handled my father and Jimmy just right. Even me. You reminded me I'm doing this for myself, not anyone else."

"That's how it should be." Bay jumped down from the fence before he fell into those green pools and drowned. "You can't take on a thing this big for someone else's sake."

"Papa did," she said. She hooked one arm over the top board of the gate and hung there looking at him, her eyes on the same level as his. "I think maybe that's part of our problem. He wanted the farm for Jimmy and me, not for himself. He doesn't put his whole heart into it."

"And you can?"

"Yes." She started to add something, but changed her mind and pressed her lips together.

What? he wanted to ask, but his stomach twisted again at the thought of her losing herself to the land. "Good. I don't want you to turn around one day when things get hard, expecting me to be there. I probably won't be."

A vague flicker washed Mariah's face. "Don't worry yourself. You've warned me often enough. I don't expect a single thing from you." She hopped off the fence and gave him a sideways glance, strangely full of mischief. "Except maybe temptation and aggravation. You'd better make sure your canteens are full. There may not be any good water between here and town."

For all his talk of adventuring off on his own, it was Jimmy that got teary-eyed when the train pulled out carrying their parents east. Mariah heard him sniffling behind her as she waved and waved, refusing to turn because she might miss the instant the train vanished into the trees along the river.

When she could see no more, she offered him a hug, needing one herself. He squeezed her hard, surprising her with his strength. He was, as he said, a man full grown.

"They'll be okay," he said.

"Mama looked so tired."

"They've got a Pullman. The porter can open out a bed for her." He gave her another squeeze, then stepped away self-consciously when a couple of kids giggled and pointed. "She's my sister," he hollered after them, then turned toward the wagon and his horse at the end of the platform. He helped her up on the high wagon seat.

"This morning you let me climb up by myself," she pointed out.

"We're out in public now. Besides I'm supposed to take care of you."

"We're supposed to take care of each other," Mariah said.

"Let's see, you wanted to go by Beckett's while we were in town."

"We need a couple of new tool handles. Pa told me to buy hickory if they have it."

"And the seeds," Mariah reminded him.

"Carrots, beets, and turnips," he ticked off efficiently. "Are you sure nothing else will grow before frost? I hate turnips."

"You'll think they taste just fine long about January when the only other thing we have is millet," Mariah said. "Besides, we can use the greens this fall. I'll leave the wagon on Main, next to the print shop."

"See you in an hour." Jimmy swung onto his horse and tore off toward Cottonwood Falls, a mile and a half away on the other side of the river. Apparently from the haste he was making he had a lot more planned than a visit to the hardware.

Well, he'd done his share. In the past week, while she'd preserved or pickled every scrap of fresh food they had salvaged from the garden, he and Papa had plowed and planted forty acres of millet and started on the cane. It seemed to be doing him good, feeling responsible for her.

Mariah released the brake and headed after him at a more sedate pace.

Town looked as bad as anywhere else. She'd noticed that on the way through, but hadn't let it sink in. Now she needed to see. She turned off Broadway and drove past the Flowers' beautiful two-story home. The trees that had shaded the porch a month ago stood as naked as they would in the dead of winter. She didn't have the heart to stop.

A worse shock came at the general store. She'd expected that food would be dear, but the handwritten prices on the slate board were double or more what they had been a month ago and bound to go up. She gaped at the smallish basket of eggs that sat on the counter: marked "Fresh from Missouri. Guaranteed not to Taste of Grasshopper," they cost two dollars a dozen. She nearly choked when she saw they wanted fifty cents for a lone green pepper and an obscene twenty cents a pound for bruised green apples that smelled like they were half spoiled.

She began to have an idea of the value of the basket of

produce sitting on the counter at home. The boy who'd delivered it and a couple of bags of feed had been driving a wagon load of supplies around the area, all from Bay McKenzie to his neighbors, but she doubted anyone else had gotten fresh corn and summer squash. That would be the last such extravagance she'd accept from Bay. She quickly selected a new shirt for Jimmy, to replace the one he'd ruined fighting the insects, and counted out the dollar twenty-five.

Three men had settled on the liar's bench out front while she was inside. They tipped their hats as she left. "Miss Mariah."

"I hear your folks was on the train this morning," Mr. Patterson said.

Mariah stopped and eyed him with a grin. "Did you ever think of working for the *Leader*? You'd make a good reporter."

"Can't read nor write," he said. "Mebbe that's what makes me a good listener."

"Maybe." She considered a minute and decided she might as well feed the gossip with fact instead of fiction. "Mama wasn't up for a hard winter, so Papa took her back to Virginia for a few months. Jimmy and I are taking care of the place until they get back."

"You plantin'?"

"There isn't much choice, the way prices are already up. We managed to save a fair amount from the garden. We'll be eating a lot of kraut, but we'll be fine."

"Should think so, with Jensen and that McKenzie boy taking such interest in helping out." He gave her a wink, and his companions on the bench chuckled. "That was quite a load young Jack had sent out your way."

"It was for everyone in the area. *Bay* is a generous man, unlike his father."

"Bay, is it?"

"Yes," she said thinly. "He doesn't like to be called after his father. He doesn't think much of the name. Now if you gentlemen will excuse me."

"Good day to you. You be careful about your stock, girl. Them horse thieves are working that end of the county over pretty well."

The mention of the horse thieves pulled her back. "Have they struck again?"

"Just last night, down at Thurman." Mr. Patterson hitched his thumbs under his suspenders and leaned back, pleased to share his knowledge. "And they took a few over by Cedar Point the night before them locusts swarmed. Let me see, any more since the Johnsons' on Independence Day?"

"Nope. They tried at Murdock's, but ol' Rastus had his dogs out," said Mr. Vincent. "Still, that makes five places robbed for sixteen horses, by my reckoning. Whoever those fellows are, they're making a whole bunch of money."

"Does the sheriff have any idea who's doing this?"

"He ain't sayin' if he does or doesn't, and believe me, I asked," Mr. Patterson said.

"Well, if he don't, there's those that think they do," Mr. Isaacson said, interrupting his whittling. "For myself, I don't think some of the ideas make much sense."

"And a person always has to consider the source," Mariah said between clenched teeth. The men nodded sagely, and she took her leave.

No wonder Mr. Patterson had put Nikolai's and Bay's names in the same sentence. When she got her hands on Nikolai . . .

She didn't have long to contemplate what she might do. When she rounded the corner onto Main, she spotted her brother and the suitor in question standing next to the wagon, deep in conversation. She crossed the street and came up on their blind side.

"You say all the folks have been robbed since McKenzie got to town?" Jimmy was asking.

"So." Nikolai fished a piece of paper from his pocket and showed it to Jimmy. "See, I wrote the days. The thefts, they all happen when he is in town, but when he is not, nothing. Here, he went away and no horses stolen. Then he comes back, and two times. You see?"

"*I* see," Mariah said stepping around the wagon. "I see plenty."

Nikolai at least had the sense to look sheepish. "Mariah."

"You promised," she said. "How dare you pander this nonsense all over town."

"It is not nonsense. I more than speculate, now." Nikolai waved his paper in her face.

"Let me see that." Mariah snatched the sheet away from him and scanned it. "This is coincidence. Bay and Eli are not that kind. Besides, last I heard there were three men involved."

"Only some of the time. Maybe they have a friend who takes the horses away to sell."

Jim had been looking over Mariah's shoulder. He took the paper from her and handed it back to Nikolai. "I'm not much on McKenzie, myself, but Mr. Hightower seemed like a right kind of fellow. You ought to show this to the sheriff. Let him look into it properly."

"Ja. I do that." Nikolai fished out his pocket watch and flicked the case open. His mouth twisted in chagrin. "But now I am supposed to pick up new chain at the hardware for Mr. Clements. I been too long already."

"I'll come with you. I have a few things to get, yet."

"You mean you still haven't been to the hardware?" Mariah asked.

"Don't worry. I'll still make it back before my hour's up." Jimmy started down the street. "Come on, Nikolai."

"I will be one minute," Nikolai said. He loitered at Mariah's side until Jimmy reached the corner. "Your brother says your mama and papa went home. I am sorry. If you need anything, you tell me this time, ja, not Mac-Kenzie."

"We needed you when the grasshoppers came. Bay was there to help us, he and his friend both. Where were you? No, never mind, I have the answer to that. You were putting together that fool list and talking all over town."

Nikolai's face darkened. He gripped her arm and pressed her back against the wagon. "Did I not tell you we might have extra work the last time I visited? You know this, and you let Mac-Kenzie come around you. I even hear that you spend two nights at his ranch." His fingers crushed her arm and he leaned close, threatening. "Should I stop waiting now?"

"Turn loose of me," Mariah said quietly, fighting to keep a tremor of fear and fury out of her voice. "Now, Mr. Jensen."

He released her immediately, looking contrite. "I am sorry. I forget myself."

Without a word, Mariah climbed up on the wagon seat, slapping his hand away when he reached to help her. She picked up the reins.

When she reached for the brake handle, Nikolai grabbed it. "I cannot think of him around you without I get crazy."

"Don't you ever touch me in anger again," she snapped. "I will not tolerate it. You can tell Jimmy I started without him and why. Now, take your hand off that brake."

He did, and she popped it free. The wagon rumbled off down the road.

"I am sorry, Mariah," he called after her. "I will come on next Saturday and we will talk. I am sorry."

She didn't answer. A good two miles passed before she might have been able to, before she stopped shaking and could pull her thoughts together.

This whole thing was getting out of hand. Not only was Nikolai perched on the edge of violence, he was trying to infect others with his suspicions. The more people he talked to, the more likely to believe the worst. Lord knew enough people in the area stood predisposed to find the worst in a McKenzie, any McKenzie, and his drifter friend.

And there was that paper. Taken at face value, the paired lists of dates damned Bay and Eli outright. There had been an instant when she'd first seen the black pencil scratchings that they'd made perfect sense, that she'd thought maybe, just maybe, Nikolai could be right.

If she could feel that way, knowing Bay as she did, what would the rest of the county believe? More importantly, what would the sheriff believe?

Hoofbeats pounded up the road behind her, and she twisted to see Jimmy racing to catch up, tool handles bouncing crazily across the back of his saddle.

"Are you all right?" he asked, slowing the chestnut to a walk alongside the wagon. "Nikolai told me what he did. He's really sorry."

"He should be. As strong as he is, he could have broken my arm."

"He's upset about you and McKenzie," Jimmy said.

"That's no excuse. If he ever so much as looks like he's

going to touch me like that again, that will be the end of him." The wagon bounced over a rut in the road, emphasizing her statement.

Jimmy reached behind to untie the handles and toss them in the bed of the wagon with a clatter. "He'll be fine once McKenzie's gone. And I have a feeling that won't be long, once the sheriff sees that list of Nikolai's."

"Bay is *not* a horse thief. The man owns a mine. He has money enough to buy and sell our farm. Why would he need to steal horses?"

"Mines go broke," Jimmy said.

"That's odd talk coming from you. But even if you were right, why come here, where people know him? There must be thousands of horses between Montana and here. Or Denver and here."

"You don't even know where he came from."

"He moves around a lot," Mariah said.

"Why *did* he come here, anyway?"

"To settle things with his father. Then he's going to ride on, and you and Nikolai and the sheriff can look for a different robber."

"I guess we'll see about that pretty quick," Jimmy said. "Any settling he wanted to do with his pa is done."

"Why? What happened?"

"About the best thing that could." A satisfied grin spread over Jimmy's face. "A rider came barrelling into town to get Doc and the preacher right after you ran off. John McKenzie fell over dead this morning."

Chapter Thirteen

BAY RAN A thumb down the spine of Ben Franklin's *Autobiography*, the scent of leather rising from the uncreased cover. He slipped it back in its place and scanned the yards of books that filled the shelves, not sure what he was searching for, just knowing that he wasn't finding it in his father's study.

In the few hours since the foreman's shout for help and the realization his father was gone, he'd caught himself making this useless search twice. With a shake of his head, he turned back to the desk and the letter to his father's attorneys he was trying to compose.

A knock at the study door interrupted him before he had time to scratch through another sentence.

"Come."

Mrs. Shaw pushed the door open. "I'm sorry to disturb you, Mr. McKenzie. There's someone here you need to see."

Bay set aside the pen, grateful for the excuse, and glanced at the clock on the mantel. Too soon for the doctor, he thought, rising, then he caught a glimpse of drifting gold curls over the housekeeper's shoulder.

"Thank you, Mrs. Shaw," Mariah said, stepping past the woman into the room. The door closed silently behind her.

She looked windblown, and her cheeks glowed red with the heat. Her skirts carried the unmistakable crumples of riding astride, and when she moved into his arms she smelled faintly of hot horse and saddle leather, but the sense of relief that came with her touch felt like the first sun after a brief but bitter winter. He clung to it, to her, savoring the comfort as well as the sharp desire that followed on its heels.

"I thought maybe I could help," she said after a time.

"You are helping." Bay shifted back so he could perch on the edge of the desk, but kept her within his arms. "I was going to send a message over after things got more settled."

"Jimmy heard the news just after we put Mama and Papa on the train. He didn't much want me to come up here, but I convinced him if he'd like supper any time before midnight, he'd better take the wagon and loan me his horse." She reached up and brushed a strand of hair off his forehead. "What happened?"

"He found out the foreman had overridden one of his orders. He started giving him hell, like he always does, and then he got an odd look and folded up. For a minute, we thought his legs had given out, but . . ." Bay squeezed his eyes shut and swallowed, trying to ease some of the muscles that closed his throat.

"Are you going to take him into town?"

"No. My mother's buried up on top of the hill. Under that sycamore." Through the window he could just see the men working next to the bare, grayish tree, digging the new grave alongside the carved limestone marker. "When she died, we were living a mile or so away down by the creek, but he laid her here. He had the house planned even then, right down to the color of paint on the walls. It was going to be his manor house, like the one on the hill above the fields he worked as a boy. He laid out foundations a couple of years later. After he'd gotten his hands on another thousand acres."

"He was a very determined man."

A wry chuckle escaped Bay. "Ah, Mariah, trying not to speak ill of the dead. Don't hold back on my account. He was a mean, greedy son of a gun with no regard for other people."

"Bay! He was your father." She added softly, "Besides, he's no threat anymore."

"True on both counts." Bay gave her a squeeze and released her. "Anyway, look what his determination got him: exactly the same amount of land as any of us get in the end."

Mariah stepped back a little and gave him an assessing look, but if she had an opinion, she kept it to herself.

"Mrs. Shaw is going to need some help," she said. "Getting him dressed and such."

"She said she'd wait until after the doctor comes out to sign the death certificate."

"It's awfully hot. Maybe we should get started."

"You don't have to do that. You didn't even care for the man."

She raised up on her toes and leaned forward to press a kiss to his cheek. "I'm not doing it for him."

Bay watched her go, then retreated back to the documents on his father's desk. This time the letter came easily, and he moved on to the papers in the strong box he'd found earlier in the bottom drawer.

It was Mariah, he thought, her and her infectious practicality. The body needed laying out. The papers needed sorting for the lawyers who would descend soon. They each had their chores.

The doctor came eventually, saw what he needed to see, said the polite words most folks expected him to say, and made out a death certificate before he left. Bay added the black-edged form to the bundle for the lawyers, then went in search of Mariah. He found her in the kitchen with Mrs. Shaw. Both women looked solemn and worn. The ruddy glow in Mariah's cheeks had faded to pallor.

"Everything's ready as soon as the men finish with the coffin," Mrs. Shaw said.

"They're done," Bay said. "At least the hammering stopped a while ago."

"Good." Mrs. Shaw wiped her hands on her spotless apron. She must have put on a fresh one as soon as she'd come downstairs. "I'll go down and tell them to bring it in. I can use the walk." She slipped out the back door.

Mariah poured two cups of coffee from the pot on the stove and handed one to Bay. He gulped down a mouthful and grimaced at the burn in his gullet.

"Tastes good," he said.

"I bet you haven't had anything to eat since breakfast."

Bay thought a moment, then shook his head.

She marched straight to the pantry. When she returned, she bore a tray loaded with bread, cheese, butter, and a jar of pickled onions. "There's a roast in there, but I'm not sure how old it is. Maybe when Mrs. Shaw—"

"What you have is fine."

As she sliced and spread, Bay topped off his cup of coffee, then leaned against the counter, watching her work.

"What about you?" he asked.

"I'll have something at home," she said. "I need to leave right away if I'm going to get back before it's pitch black."

"I don't suppose it would do for you to stay the night."

Her quick glance told him she'd thought of the same thing, but she shook her head. "Not unless you want to arrange some more grasshoppers to convince Jimmy I had to."

"Then I'd better walk you out."

One of the ranch hands, sitting on the porch steps, jumped to his feet as Bay and Mariah pushed the front door open. By the time they crossed the veranda, he'd fetched her horse. He checked the cinch and handed the reins to Bay. "Do you want me to saddle Cajun up for you, Bay . . . that is, Mr. McKenzie?"

"Bay will still do. No, thanks, but could you find Eli and ask him to ride Miss Hoag home?" Bay turned to Mariah as the cowboy hustled off. "I'd like to take you, but—"

"You belong here," she said. "I don't even need Eli to go along."

"I'll feel better if he does." He checked the cinch automatically, even though the cowboy had just done it. It made busy work for his hands, when what he really wanted was to grab onto Mariah and convince her to stay. Instead of kissing her, he laced his fingers together and gave her a leg up.

She tugged at her skirts to make sure her ankles stayed covered, then looked down at him. "What time is the service?"

"I asked for Reverend Dodd to come early."

"Then I will, too."

Mariah returned the next morning just as the sunlight brightened from gold to brilliant white. The banker and a few businessmen who'd profited from John McKenzie over the years showed up with the preacher. She watched Bay stand like a statue through the ceremony under the sycamore, and afterwards, when the visitors all collected around the dining room table to weep their crocodile tears, she pitched in to help Mrs. Shaw and serve as hostess, seeing that their glasses and plates stayed full. She was pleased to see Bay tuck in with his usual appetite.

Finally, they all climbed back onto their horses and into their buggies and headed back to town. Bay wandered back in from seeing them off and caught her hanging out the dining room window, shaking the crumbs off the tablecloth.

She glanced over her shoulder. "Would you like to talk now?"

His laugh caught her off guard. "You are a wonder, Mariah Hoag. Yes, I would. Let's go for a walk."

She folded the linen, hung it over the back of a chair, and let him lead her outside into the afternoon heat. They strolled over the crest of the hill, far beyond the house and outbuildings, out of sight of the sycamore and the sad mounds of earth beneath.

"I've been trying to figure it out," he said finally. "How I feel. Why. The best thing you've done for me in the past two days is not expecting me to grieve."

"You thought he was mean and unprincipled. It's hard to grieve that."

"But he wasn't always. I remember him when his arrogance was pride, and his greed was determination to make the best of life in a new country. My mother used to tell me how taken she was with him and his energy and plans."

They wandered down over the hill, headed west, as if it was the most natural direction for him. Mariah waited for him to say more.

"The house in New Orleans used to shake with the dancing and laughter. He was the grandest man I ever knew, and we all worshipped at his feet, especially *Maman*."

"I saw a little of that in him during the grasshopper plague," Mariah said. "I imagine he could charm the down off a goose when he cared to."

Bay nodded. "One day he got this idea to head west, to carve out his own place. He took the money *Grandpére*—my grandfather—loaned him, dragged us here, and built a soddy. Somewhere along the line, having his own place turned into founding his own dynasty. He was going to have the grandest outfit in the state, and damn anything or anyone that got in his way. He poured every penny into land and the best stock, and he made it so miserable for people to live around us that they'd sooner sell out or, better yet, forfeit so he could claim their land—I don't know how he missed that plot you're on. *Maman* died within a year. They said it was fever, but looking back, I think it was shame. And loneliness. The few neighbors we did have didn't want much to do with us, even then."

"And then the war came," Mariah said. "And your brother left."

"And I found out I didn't want to have much to do with my father, either. Or his almighty land."

"But now it's yours." She'd heard the banker say that over lunch, and had been trying not to get her hopes up all afternoon.

Bay's frown told her she'd been wise. "Oh, he saw to that, all right. One of the codicils on his will is dated for the day after I showed up here. We hadn't exchanged ten words, and he was busy trying to bring me back into the fold and build a fence so I couldn't get loose again. The old son of a gun probably died just to keep me here."

I would, too. Mariah ignored the ache in her chest. Bay's grieving mattered, now, not hers. "So you're still angry at him."

"Yep, still. Or maybe I'm mad all over again. I'm not sure from minute to minute."

"You'll figure it out," she said. "Or maybe you'll let it go, but eventually you'll sort it through, and then you'll know whether you need to mourn or not. Meantime, it looks like you have a ranch."

"Only long enough to find a buyer."

Mariah stopped and took a deep breath. The stench of the grasshoppers had faded. The air tasted sweet again, and the grass was starting to put out new tips. She could smell the green under the dust for the first time in days. A little rain and the millet would sprout. "I don't understand that."

"I know."

"But you've done so much to help people since the grasshoppers. The water. The supplies. Starting the relief drive."

"It needed to be done. Partly to make up for what *he* had already done to them."

High overhead, a sliver of new moon hung pale in the mid-day sky. If he found his buyer quickly, Mariah thought, he might be on his way by the time it came around like that again.

"Hire someone to manage the ranch for you," she said. "Like you did for the Jacks High. You could come back now and again to check on things." Lord, what was she doing inviting him to ride roughshod in and out of her life for years to come? She'd spend her life waiting, and she'd never find any peace, with Nikolai or with anyone else. It was crazy, and she wanted it anyway.

She held her breath as Bay scanned the hills, weighing, assessing. He drew in a deep breath as if ready to speak, then pressed his lips together. The wind ruffled his hair across his brow, and he lifted her hand up to brush a kiss across her wrist. "Let's go back to the house. You should head home pretty soon."

The needed rain came in a pair of afternoon thunderstorms that rumbled across the sky in dark bands.

The second of the storms blew Nikolai through the front gate on Saturday, weighted down though he was by remorse. Mariah listened to his apology and his promises that he would be patient, warned him once about ever touching her again in anger, and then let the matter drop. He grinned with relief and pitched in to split a couple of armloads of kindling. He even managed to get through a whole afternoon without mentioning either Bay's name or horse thieves. At least not to her: she caught him and Jimmy with their heads together twice.

She bided her time, until Nikolai had finished supper and headed home and she was washing up. "What's he spouting now?" she asked her brother.

"Nothing."

"Come on, Jimmy. I saw him pull that paper of his out and show it to you again."

"He's done some more checking around. He says you told

him McKenzie and Mr. Hightower were staying at the Doolittle House on Independence Day."

"That's what Bay said."

"Well, they were there the night before, but they checked out that morning."

"They probably took a room someplace else."

"Nope. Nikolai asked around. They weren't in town at all. In fact, he found someone who claims he saw them over by Cottonwood Station late that night, not far from where Johnson's horses were stolen."

"I don't believe it."

"Why not? He's a McKenzie, with a McKenzie's love for things that belong to someone else. Land. Horses. Women." He stared pointedly at her.

"I'm not Nikolai's," Mariah said.

"You used to be."

"No, I wasn't. We courted, that's all. We still court." Mariah ran a dish towel over the cast iron skillet and set it on the warming shelf. "Part of the problem is that you don't know Bay."

"I know him well enough. Everybody that knew him before says he was just like his father, enjoyed pushing people around. You've heard the stories."

"I know, but he's not that way now." She spotted some dried food on a butter knife and dunked it back in the water. "He's going to be calling here sooner or later. When he does, I'm going to invite him to stay for supper."

"I won't have him on the property."

Mariah rounded on her brother, dripping hands planted on her hips. "*You* won't? Who did Papa put in charge?"

"You," Jimmy said begrudgingly. "But he meant the farm work, not for things like this. As a matter of fact, he told me to watch out that McKenzie doesn't take advantage of you."

Mariah flushed at the idea of her father talking with her brother about her possible seduction, but she wouldn't let it stop her. "Fine. The easiest way to keep an eye on him is to be at supper, because I *am* inviting him. And you will be civil."

Jimmy snorted, but he slumped down in his chair. "Yes, ma'am."

* * *

Within a few days, the fields turned palest gold, then green with new millet. The cane, which Mariah and Jimmy had finished planting in eighteen straight hours of backbreaking effort the day after John McKenzie's burial, came in close behind. The garden, put in the day after that, sprouted in tidy rows that promised enough root vegetables over winter to break up what looked to be a very limited diet. Mariah allowed herself to breathe more easily.

Except that as the crops grew, chores shifted from plowing and planting to the everyday drudgery of hoeing and weeding and watering: the kind of work that had to be done over and over.

The kind Jimmy loathed so much.

Mariah began to catch him scanning the tattered pages of a pamphlet on gold prospecting he'd ordered a year ago from the back of a dime novel. On Thursday he left it on the table after dinner, and Mariah picked it up. The list of recommended gear, on page four, had prices written alongside in Jimmy's hand, with the total circled at the bottom: One hundred forty-one dollars and thirty-five cents. He couldn't have anywhere near that much put aside, but she knew that wouldn't stop him if he decided to go.

"Give me until harvest, Jimmy," she whispered to the empty house, laying the pamphlet aside. "Just until harvest." She tied on her bonnet and followed him out to where they'd left off the hoeing.

Bay showed up around mid-afternoon the same day, three single blue asters in his hand. He presented them to Mariah with a flourish and a bow that made Jimmy grimace and move down the row. Clyde rose and stretched, then trotted over to have his ears scratched.

Bay winked at her as he ruffled the pup's fur. "I found the poor things growing practically out of a rock, and I couldn't decide whether it would be more of a kindness to pick them or leave them be."

"I didn't think we'd have any more flowers until spring."

"There'll be plenty more," Bay said. "The wild plants are tougher than corn and wheat. There are places that the prairie's up nearly a foot in the past couple of weeks, and a few pockets where you can't tell anything happened at all."

"I guess you won't have to sell the cattle so fast after all." She hoped.

"Maybe," he said, and the quick, one-sided smile that followed his concession stirred enough optimism to make it hard for Mariah to concentrate. "Your fields look pretty good, too."

"The rain helped."

"Well, now. We've talked about the weather and the crops." He reached for her hoe. "So much for convention. Do you suppose your brother would mind if we go put that lovely bouquet in water?"

"No, sir," she said quite clearly, so Jimmy would hear. "He won't mind at all." She didn't even bother to look her brother's way, certain he'd just be glaring at them anyway.

Bay put the hoe over his shoulder, and they walked back to the house in silence, Clyde following close on Mariah's heels. She took out one of the julep glasses, filled it with water from the pitcher, and stuck the flowers in.

"They look awfully puny in there by themselves," Bay said.

"They're beautiful." Mariah gathered the skimpy nosegay together and sniffed. "They even smell good to me right now. Thank you."

"You're welcome. But we're getting conventional again." Bay took the glass out of her hands and set it in the middle of the table. "Don't you know why I brought them?"

"For manners?" She guessed.

"Nope." He pushed the deep brimmed bonnet back off her head, then took her wrists and guided her hands up around his neck. She had to step closer to reach. His chin was smooth and slightly pink from a recent shave—probably after lunch, considering how the minty smell of shaving soap clung beneath his jaw. "To have an excuse to get you in here away from your brother. So I could kiss you."

Which he proceeded to do, lowering his head to brush her lips, then deepening the kiss possessively until Mariah lost track of breathing and grew giddy. He slid his hands the length of her arms and skimmed his palms down the curves of her body, not the bold way he had before, but gently, as if recalling something to mind. As his arms went around her waist, she sighed and lifted into his embrace.

"Do you realize it's been better than a month since I've done that?" he murmured against her ear.

That didn't seem right. She tried to remember, but the nips he took at her earlobe made it difficult. "It can't be that long. I've been up at the ranch. We . . ." She flushed at the recollection, and her voice came out a whisper, as though she was afraid Jimmy might hear, clear out there in the field. "We spent the night."

"Ah, that we did, my pretty." Bay put on an actor's overdrawn voice and scattered a dramatic string of kisses down her throat. His voice softened. "But we didn't kiss, not then and not when you came up to help with my father. In fact, we haven't kissed since down by the creek, that day before I left for Topeka. Not a proper kiss."

He moved back to her mouth to demonstrate another proper kiss with thorough care, apparently intending to make up for the lack right then and there. Mariah encouraged his efforts for a few delightful moments, until his hands began moving over her with the brazen familiarity that set her on fire and made her think of the things he'd done to her and the highly improper things she wanted him to do. She broke the kiss, but with reluctance.

"Jimmy will come in after us in about another minute," she said. "Besides, I need to water the garden and get supper started. You'll stay, I hope."

The corners of Bay's eyes crinkled with humor, as if at some personal joke, but he set her free. "I was counting on it. And I'll earn my board hauling water. Remind me how much goes on what."

They each grabbed a bucket as they went out the door, and Mariah outlined the garden's needs as they strolled to the pump. Out in the field, she could see Jimmy whacking away with his hoe, pretending he wasn't watching their every move with proprietorial intensity.

"How are you two doing?" Bay asked.

"Oh, fine. We had the big crops mostly in before Papa and Mama left, you know, and—"

"That's not what I mean." He gestured toward Jimmy. "Is he going to stick it out?"

Mariah bent to spill a little water into the top of the pump to prime it. The movement hid the uncertainty on her face.

"Long enough," she said firmly.

Bay frowned in Jimmy's direction, but took the bucket without comment and hung it from the end of the spout. With his strong muscles working the pump handle, it took only a few strokes to bring the water splashing out in a cool stream. Mariah watched for a few minutes, then retreated into the house to make supper.

By supper time, Jimmy seemed to have resigned himself to Bay's presence. His eyes narrowed every time Bay teased a laugh from Mariah, but he kept his conversation civil and his opinions to himself right through the pound cake Mariah sliced for dessert. He even stayed inside when she walked Bay out to his horse.

In the half light, Bay wrapped his arms around her and pulled her close. "Look over my shoulder."

Mariah did. "What?"

"Is he pointing a gun out the window?"

She swallowed her giggle and said solemnly, "No. Out the door."

"Damn." He kissed her. "Well, if I'm going to get shot, I may as well enjoy my demise." He kissed her again, this time more ardently. "I can hardly blame him. Heck, if he knew what I was thinking about all through dinner. . . ."

"Bay McKenzie!"

"I'm trying to behave. Truly, ma'am." He moved his hands lower, spreading his fingers to cradle her buttocks and pull her a little closer. His face grew serious. "I don't understand the effect you have on me. I've always been able to—"

The heavy crunch of a booted foot on gravel stopped him. Mariah started to pull away, but Bay held her, though he shifted his hands slightly to move them back to a more seemly spot at her waist. Jimmy stalked past, headed toward the barn.

"Got to check on the stock," he growled. "Good night again, McKenzie."

"I'll be out of here in a minute," Bay said amiably, but he waited until the barn door smacked against the siding before he released Mariah. He touched a fingertip to his mouth then drew the kiss across her lower lip. "He's right. I'd better say good night before I get myself into trouble."

"Good night," she managed in return as he mounted up. She climbed up on the gate to watch until his silhouette disappeared into the prairie shadows.

She was still there when she heard Jimmy come out of the barn behind her. The whinny of a horse made her turn. Jimmy had the chestnut saddled. He threw the reins over the horse's head and swung up.

"Where are you going?" she asked.

He patted the horse on the shoulder. "To let this fellow run. I'll be back in a little. Don't worry."

A little turned into late. Mariah woke to the squeak of the bootjack as he undressed in the next room sometime past midnight. She bit her tongue and lay in the stifling August night.

Just let him stay until harvest. Just until harvest.

Chapter Fourteen

"It's NOT GOING to work." Jimmy shoved his plate away and propped his elbows on the table. "The money won't last with prices shooting up the way they are."

Mariah carefully laid her fork across the edge of the plate. Five weeks. It had been only five weeks. She should never have let him go into town alone this morning.

"Then we'll make do with what we have," she said calmly. "Besides, Papa's probably settled in and found work by now. He'll be able to send some money before we get short. Or we'll take relief if we need to."

"But we don't need to. I saw Otis in town today."

"Oh?" She stared at her hands, willing them not to shake.

The dishes rattled as Jimmy tapped his toe against the table leg. "They still want me on the crew. I'm going back to work for Keenan."

"No." Mariah leaned toward her brother. "You promised, Jimmy. You *promised*."

His gaze flickered away from her, and he shrugged. "I promised you could count on me. You can. I'm going to take care of you."

"You're going to take care of your stake, you mean." She reached over and yanked the folded miner's pamphlet out of his pocket. "A hundred and forty-one dollars worth of stake."

He snatched it back. "You're too nosy for your own good. It's not like I'm running out on you. I'm doing what I need to do to take care of you."

"Just how do you do that from Wichita? There are eighty acres of millet and cane to harvest. Do I do that by myself?

And what about the hay we need to get in? It's a short cutting, but I can't do everything by myself."

"Otis told me he worked it out for me to stay on the Matfield Green spread with him and Shorty through fall roundup. I can get home to check on you now and again. And he said they'll let me off for harvest."

"I'll need help before then."

"I don't think you'll have much trouble finding someone," Jimmy muttered.

"It's not Bay's job to rescue me every time I need a hand. He doesn't want the responsibility, and I have no intention of forcing it on him."

Jimmy got a sour look. "Listen to yourself. 'It's not Bay's job.' If you're so all-fired anxious to make a go of this place, you'd better start thinking sense and go to the man who feels it *is* his job."

"Meaning Nikolai."

"Darned right, Nikolai. He's crazy in love with you, God help him, in spite of the way you carry on with McKenzie. If you said the word, he'd do the whole harvest."

"The word he wants is a yes," Mariah said.

"Then give it to him. Marry him. He's your best chance at what you want. Not Bay McKenzie." Jimmy slugged back the dregs of his coffee and pushed to his feet. He paused with his hand on the door latch. "And not me. The sooner you figure that out, the better off you're going to be. I'm going to go check over my gear. I want to leave first thing after chores in the morning." The door thudded hollowly as he left.

She knew that set in his jaw, the same one Papa got when his mind fixed on something, and it wouldn't do any good to talk. A body might just as soon talk a snapping turtle into turning one loose.

The worst of it was, he was right.

Nikolai was her best chance at the life she wanted, the life she'd clung to for years. Her head told her that as clearly as Jimmy did.

Nikolai. She closed her eyes and could see him in the fields at spring plowing, walking the long rows behind his big gelding. Sitting at the table talking to her father. Showing her the land he wanted to turn into a home.

When she thought of Bay, she pictured him staring out across the fields, his bridle in hand. Kidnapping her just to say his piece. Looking at her in that heated way of his while he warned her he was moving on.

"Stay, little brother." She sent the thought toward the barn, hoping it might land in Jimmy's skull to become his own idea. "Give me time, please."

He didn't. He couldn't. Watching him sling together his gear the next morning was like watching a prisoner on the day of his release. When he mounted up, the chestnut, sensing Jimmy's excitement, arched its neck and sidestepped.

Thirty-seven days, Mariah thought, watching him settle the animal. She'd counted it out on the railroad calendar that morning while the flapjacks browned on the griddle. He'd lasted exactly thirty-seven days since they'd put Mama and Papa on the train. She had already decided not to mention his defection in a letter, not until she had to. They would just insist she come to Virginia, without giving Jimmy a chance to change his mind, without giving her a chance to decide what to do.

And she would do something. She wouldn't turn loose of her home, not now.

Jimmy leaned over and planted a kiss on her cheek. "I'll be back to bring you some money as soon as I get paid. If you see Aurelia, just say I'll talk to her soon."

"Didn't you bother to tell her?" *Would Bay bother when he decided to ride off?*

"She hasn't been too happy with me lately. I'll see her when I come back. It won't be too long." He gave her his puppy dog look, the one that had worked his whole life. "Don't be mad at me."

"Don't ask me for that today," she said. She hugged herself, trying to contain the fear and the overwhelming sadness that threatened her veneer of calm. "You just do what you feel you have to. So will I."

What she had to do.

The knowledge of just what that was trailed Mariah through

the fields all day and through the evening chores as well, sticking as close to her thoughts as Clyde stuck to her heels while she hauled and fed and watered and weeded.

What she had to do was marry Nikolai, and the sooner, the better.

It was the only thing that made sense, the only chance she had at holding on. Nikolai would continue to board at Mrs. Totten's on the days he had to report to the quarry, coming out to work the farm at the end of the week, not so very different from what he planned to do with his own property. They weren't so far out that he couldn't come home occasional nights during the week if need be. They'd buy their own farm one day, of course, after the land and Mama both healed and she and Papa came back to Kansas to stay. Everything would work out fine. Mariah laid out each detail in her head, the scene essentially unchanged from the plans she'd made for the past year or more.

Unchanged, except that she had changed. Changed so much that she had actually considered clinging to the vague hint of a possibility of a hope which was all Bay could offer.

"Damn you, McKenzie." She spoke the words aloud, startling the chickens that clustered around her ankles begging for their supper. "And damn you, too, James Frances Hoag. Well, you've made your choices, both of you. And now I've made mine."

Practical. She was being practical, that was all. The ache that ran from her head down through her shoulders and into the center of her chest came from doing Jimmy's work along with her own. That was all.

"Sit," she ordered Clyde. She flung the contents of the tin basin across the yard, then watched the hens scramble for the cracked corn and kitchen scraps. The pup whimpered at the bounty he wasn't allowed to touch, but followed her reluctantly back to the house.

Nikolai arrived late on Saturday, covered with rock dust and apologizing.

"A block hung up. She would not break free," he explained, whacking at his britches with his hat. Grayish white clouds of powdered limestone billowed around his legs, matching the streaks on his face and arms. "I had no time to change clothes before I come. Maybe I should not go inside."

"You're fine," Mariah said. "I'm glad you came."

He bobbed his head. "I wash, anyhow, before I come in."

She listened to the sounds of his rinsing and splashing from inside, next to the big black stove. The glowing warmth of the stove and the scents of the food cooked on it had always meant home. Tonight she needed their familiarity to remind her why she was about to break her own heart and agree to marry Nikolai Jensen.

A few minutes later, he came to the table, blonde hair towel-damp, face and hands sparkling clean. "Is better, ja?"

"Much. You looked like a plaster statue."

"Sometimes when it rains just a little, I feel so." He watched her dish corncakes, bacon, and carrots onto the plates. "Your garden grows good."

"These are the thinnings," Mariah said, waving her spoon over the tiny new carrots cooked with brown sugar and caraway seeds. "We had a mess of baby turnips the night before Jimmy left."

"You miss him?" Nikolai asked.

"More than I thought, considering how often he went gallivanting off. It's so quiet at night, and—" Mariah stopped dead, staring at Nikolai. "You knew he was gone."

"Ja, sure. I hear in town."

"You did not. I haven't seen anyone to tell them, and he didn't even tell Aurelia. But he told you, didn't he, before he told me?" she demanded. Nikolai's reddening ears were as good as a confession. She slammed his plate down in front of him. "If I find out you put him up to this, to back me into a corner . . ." A corner she'd nearly accepted.

"I would not do this," Nikolai protested. "I worry that you are alone with no one. That is why I come so dirty. There are more horses stolen nearby. Some two nights ago."

"If you're going to claim . . ."

Nikolai scowled and waved her silent before she could say Bay's name.

"Ja, I know. You believe him, Mac-Kenzie, and say I am

jealous." A whole slice of bacon disappeared into Nikolai's mouth and he chewed it like he wished it was Bay. "So I show the sheriff the paper with the days written and I tell him the other things. He does not think it is only rumor or because I am jealous."

That piece of news pushed Jimmy and Nikolai's possible plotting to a distant second place. Mariah deposited her own plate on the table carefully and sat down across from Nikolai. "What is he going to do?"

He frowned. "He can do nothing. Just like he could do nothing when the father was bothering you."

"John McKenzie was a snake. He pushed the law, but there was never any proof that pointed straight to him."

"The sheriff says the same now. 'No proof.' But some of the men who lost horses are not happy with this answer. They make a committee and come to see me to ask what I know."

A committee. He meant vigilantes. "Nikolai . . ."

"And they tell me something I have not heard before." He speared a forkful of carrots and sopped them around in the syrup. "At least two times, the stolen horses go straight toward his ranch."

"But not *onto* the ranch."

"Maybe. They lose the track in cattle, or in a stream. But this committee, they watch now. They watch tonight. They know it is him, and they will catch him. Then you will know what kind of man he is. You will see that you should marry me and forget Mac-Kenzie. Please, some more corncake?"

A half moon hung high in the sky, but Mariah rode like it was full sun. The little sorrel's flying hooves ripped up the miles between the farm and the McKenzie ranch house, good fortune steering them away from gopher holes hidden by the dark. It had taken so long to ease Nikolai out the door. Too long.

Oh, lord. Vigilantes. Anything might have happened.

She'd sat at the table and watched Nikolai plow through his usual three helpings of everything, so cocksure he had finally nailed Bay that he had no further reason to be jealous.

She'd wanted to smack him. Instead, she had sat there and

smiled and nodded, carefully pumping him for every detail he possessed about the men who were after Bay. She'd even tolerated a kiss before he'd finally gone on his way, smiling and smug, convinced that he'd been right all along. As soon as she'd seen his horse's pale haunches disappear to the north, she'd thrown a saddle on the sorrel.

The complex of buildings finally appeared ahead, apparently calm. She barely slowed going through the tall gate.

"Where's Bay?" she called to the man on watch.

"Up at the house, miss. Shall I get him?"

But she was past already, and hurtling off the pony a moment later. The French doors into the front parlor stood cracked, inviting the night chill in. She took the porch stairs two at a time and pushed through the doors calling, "Bay?"

The study door swung open, and she flung herself into his arms, nearly sobbing with the relief of finding him with both feet solidly, safely on the ground.

"What on earth?" He hugged her tight, but she could feel the gentle tremor of a chuckle. "It's okay, Eli. It's a friendly sortie."

Mariah pulled away, embarrassed at her display in front of Bay's friend when everything seemed so calm. "They think you two stole all those horses. Now there are vigilantes after you." She explained the situation and Nikolai's part in it in terse sentences.

Bay swore a soft vow at Norwegian masons with less sense than their horses.

Eli didn't take it as lightly. "That's what we get for hanging in one place so long. Nesters don't take to men like you and me, whether we do anything or not. I say we get the blazes out of here, while the getting's still good."

Mariah held her breath, waiting.

Bay shook his head. "They'll just assume they were right."

Eli grumbled a moment, but gave in. "Well, then, I'd better go take care of that matter we were talking about."

"Thanks," Bay said. "Mind making sure things are buttoned down tight while you're at it?"

As the men laid a few quick plans, Mariah drifted into the study, where she sank gratefully onto an overstuffed chair. Her eyes burned from tears that hovered close to the surface, and she rubbed at them. The mantel clock in the front room began to chime, and she rested her head against the chair back, letting the bells resonate through her. He was still here, and he would stay for now. For now. But how much longer?

Bay leaned against the bookcase, smiling, watching Mariah. The way she sat, with her head back in surrender, she made a tempting sight. The arch of tawny throat begged to be kissed, demanded that his hands trace the curve down to the lift of her bosom. She sighed, with no idea of the turmoil she caused him, the way he got aroused just by looking at her. Not that he had any business letting himself get that way. Even if this so-called committee didn't show up tonight, his ear would be tuned for them. He had no cause to get himself in the middle of something in which he couldn't participate fully. But the temptation . . .

As the last of the nine tones faded, he cleared the lump from his throat. Mariah jumped a foot, her eyes wide.

"Sorry," Bay said.

"How do you sneak up so quietly?" she asked when she'd composed herself.

"All us horse thieves can do it. They teach us in school." His smile faded. "What were you doing storming up the hill to save me?"

"It was my turn," she said.

"If those fellows are really in a hanging mood, it was also damned dangerous."

"I do dangerous things sometimes, remember?" She said it glibly, but if she was trying to protect herself, her words had the wrong effect.

Lightning flashed in his mind's eye. "Oh, yes," he said, his voice suddenly husky. "I remember, beautiful heathen."

Mariah colored and rose, her arms folded across her chest as though trying to hide remembered nakedness. "I should never have told you that story."

"Probably not. But I've been glad that you did more times than you can imagine." He grinned, trying to appease her, but she continued to frown. He pulled her into his grasp, trapping her folded arms between them. Touching her at all was a risk. He'd tried to tell her at the house that night, how whenever he got near her, he came perilously close to losing every vestige of control. A dozen times he'd been tempted to push her to the floor or the grass or whatever convenient surface had presented itself.

Apparently recognizing the fact didn't change it. His body started responding even before he dipped his mouth to find hers and coax a kiss from her, before he felt her arms go around his neck and pull him closer. He swept the curves of her torso with his palms, finding the swell of her hips and fitting her against him. Mariah moaned softly.

The unwilling, reluctant sound of it brought Bay to his senses, reluctant as he was to hear it. He pulled away while he still had the wherewithal, telling himself it was the right thing, for himself as well as Mariah. She'd had a rough night. She was scared, despite her show. And he had a herd of aggrieved neighbors out to tack his hide to the wall.

Still, it took him a minute to get himself together, a long moment when they stared at each other, something beyond the immediate needs of their bodies thick between them.

"Come on," Bay said firmly, when the heaviness in his groin and the dullness in his brain had both started to ease. "Let's find Mrs. Shaw and have her get a room ready for you. I'll send someone to let Jimmy know you're safe."

"There's no need for that," she said with that same odd sound in her voice. He wondered what arrangement she'd made, but let it slide.

Mrs. Shaw took the explanations with her usual equanimity and led Mariah off to the rose room.

Bay followed them partway, veering off into his own room before he could see the door close behind Mariah. He'd kept his old room in the guest wing, despite Mrs. Shaw's suggestions that he take the master bedroom. Now he wished he hadn't, so he'd be farther from Mariah, wished he didn't know what she looked like in that bed, tousled with sleep, wished . . . wished.

Mrs. Shaw's sturdy footsteps passed his door, headed back to her quarters. Mariah was there alone. Cursing softly, Bay stripped off his shirt, then spilled the contents of the pitcher into the bowl of his washstand and began splashing the chill water over his face and chest. When he finished, the carpet around his feet was soaked, but the throb in his loins had faded to a dull ache. He blew out the lamp and collapsed into the wing chair in the corner, closed his eyes, and waited for the rest of the madness to leave his body before he went out to walk the grounds.

He was never sure if he'd dozed or if she'd moved that silently, in revenge for his own habit of sneaking up on people. All he knew is that something disturbed him, a flash of light as the door opened and closed or perhaps the elusive scent of her. His eyes popped open. He searched the blackness and couldn't find her, yet he knew he was lost.

"Damn you, Bay McKenzie," she whispered.

Bay opened the drapes with a jerk, spilling moonlight across the floor in a beam that lit Mariah like day and left him in the black shadow of the corner, nearly invisible.

"Damn you," she said again.

She heard him stand, but couldn't see him until he cut across the moonbeam. She put up her hand. He stopped, an inch beyond her fingertips. His eyes were mirrors, reflecting her own image back at her. What she saw was need, pure and raw, and she knew he must see the same thing. The fact that he stopped anyway made her want him more.

"I almost made a mistake tonight," she said, admitting it aloud for the first time. "I almost forgot about the lightning. I almost traded it for safety."

"I can't give you that, Mariah." His voice was taut. "I can't give you what you need."

She finally stretched her arm that final inch and laid her fingertips against the bare skin of his chest. "Yes, you can."

Bay shuddered once, then curled his fingers around her wrist and dragged her to him, until all she could see was the wall of his chest and the pulse pounding at the base of his throat and his mouth, descending like a cyclone that would draw her away from the land. He enveloped her, and Mariah tried to push away with a last convulsion of self-preservation that died when his lips touched her.

And touched and touched, not her mouth, but her cheeks and her eyes and her temples, searing over her face until Mariah splayed her hands over his chest in surrender. Finally, he met her lips, tangled his tongue with hers so she couldn't tell one from the other. His hands slipped restlessly over her form, fitting to one curve then the next, testing, arousing.

Just when she knew she couldn't stand it anymore, Bay moved on, leaving her lips to trail kisses down her neck. He nuzzled aside the collar of her dress to nip at the slope of neck into shoulder. One hand slipped up along her waist to rest just below the rise of her breast. Teasing, Bay traced the lower curve with his thumb, then slowly, so slowly, took the weight of her breast in his broad palm and slipped his thumb up to circle the crest.

The center of her melted. Dizzy with the sudden evidence of what she had nearly forsaken, Mariah buried her forehead against Bay's shoulder. He smelled distinctly male, a mixture of castile soap and saddle leather and his own scent that only made her senses whirl more.

"Bay," she pleaded with a voice so husky with need she didn't recognize it.

Bay's answer was to reach for the buttons at her collar, and tug a trio of them open to expose more of her shoulder to his searching mouth. He pushed the collar aside. His teeth closed over her skin, his tongue flickered, a seductive torture that sent shivers of pleasure coursing down Mariah's spine. More buttons, more gentle torture while he exposed the swell of her bosom, until his fingers dipped into the widening vee of her neckline and brushed across both sensitive peaks. Soft cries caught in Mariah's throat. Her lips moved hungrily against his skin; she tasted the salty sheen of perspiration that bloomed there.

"I want to see you in the moonlight, Mariah." Bay formed the words against her ear, almost soundless, and they rang in her mind and heart like a command. "Undress for me."

Barely able to keep her feet, Mariah peeled away her clothes. Bay stepped back a little, watching her with enough heat to set the house on fire—dangerous heat, beyond human control. Shoes, stockings, dress, petticoat landed at her feet, but her fingers froze over the ties of her camisole and drawers. She thought Bay would rescue her, either help her pull the garments away or release her from this exquisite lunacy, but he waited, as motionless as she, and finally she tugged the ribbons and the rest came easily. Before she could think anymore, she stood before him, trembling.

It occurred to Mariah she should try to hide herself behind her hands, but she just stood there, arms at her sides, wanting, waiting. Her trembling threatened to shake her off her feet.

"Please, Bay."

Bay stepped forward, reached out to touch her lips with one index finger, then traced the line from there down the center of her body, between her breasts, down across her belly, to rest in the thatch of golden hair that crowned the juncture of her thighs. It was a simple act, but Mariah's flesh felt branded.

"You're not a heathen, Mariah. You're a pagan goddess." Bay caught her with an arm around the waist and scooped her up. "My goddess."

His bed creaked with the weight of their bodies as he stretched out beside her. Now his mouth traveled unrestricted over her breasts, flicking, sucking, back and forth from one to the other until she felt on fire herself, was sure the mattress beneath her would smolder and burst into flame and consume them both. Flailing for something to anchor herself, she found Bay, pulled him up so his face was close to hers.

Bay kissed her again, leading her deeper into her need with darting tongue and clever wandering hands that claimed her. Parts of her body she had no name for ached, and he found them and touched them too, until she cried out softly, senselessly. She began to shadow his movements with her own hands, letting him lead her explorations, learning the feel of his body along with her own.

Face. A day's growth of whiskers roughened her palms, smoothing into the line of his neck, curving into his shoulder.

Shoulders. All edges and sweeps of corded muscle, down onto strong arms or into carved ridges of back that tapered into waist and the subtle mound of jeans-covered hips. Bay's hands flattened beneath her own hips and carried her closer, and she felt a hardness against her belly that terrified and excited. She moved against him, and he set a gentle rhythm, encouraging her with his hands.

"Help me. Oh, please, Bay." She knew what she was asking for, knew also that if she didn't have it soon, she might die. She didn't see him strip away his jeans, but they disappeared, and then he was over her, his knees pushing her thighs apart.

"Let's see how ready you are, goddess." Spreading her gently with his fingers, Bay positioned himself against the core of her need. The liquid feeling between her thighs spread, and he smiled with satisfaction. "Very."

He settled into her, moving slowly, letting her own moisture ease his way. Mariah stirred restlessly beneath him as she realized how large he was, how tight the fit of her body to his. Bay stopped, waited a heartbeat, then tentatively pushed again. A small groan escaped her lips.

Bay froze. "Mariah, look at me."

She opened her eyes, found his face inches from her own, looking strained.

"Are you a virgin?" Bay asked quietly.

Every scrap of her being focused into one aching, swollen spot, but she managed a nod. A shudder racked Bay, driving him deeper, and she gritted her teeth against the stretching invasion.

"I thought . . ." With calloused fingertips, Bay brushed a wisp of hair from Mariah's face and kissed her nose. "Never mind. I should have known. I should have gone about this a little differently, but for the life of me, I can't stop now. I'll try not to hurt you, goddess. Put your arms around me."

Every muscle trembling with the effort of holding himself back, Bay bucked his hips gently, withdrawing a fraction, then pushing a little beyond. Back, then forward again, and again, and suddenly he slipped past the pain and deeply into her with a low shout of accomplishment.

Mariah gasped and stiffened, suddenly too full, too stretched to feel the pleasure in this, but then Bay began to shift his hips slowly from side to side. The rocking motion soothed. She relaxed and let Bay's strong hands hold her, guide her into the motion he wanted.

The motion *she* wanted, though she didn't know it until she found it. The rightness of it burned through Mariah and brought the pleasure back again full force.

"Oh, yes," she said in delighted surprise. Instinctively, she hooked her heels behind his knees and lifted to meet him.

This time it was Bay who groaned, and then he delved deeper, finding still more pleasure in her, generating a tension in Mariah's body that she didn't comprehend. She reached for understanding, matching his rhythm, clutching at his hips to pull him into her so he could help find that one answer. It eluded her, staying just beyond reach.

"Follow me, goddess," Bay murmured against her ear. His hands wandered over her skin, to where her breasts crushed against his chest.

The feel of Bay's roughened fingers across her nipples answered the question, released the tension. Pleasure cascaded through Mariah in waves, pulsing the length of her spine. She arched like a bow beneath him, until she felt her spine would break, and she didn't care.

Only Bay's hoarse shout held her together, that and the feel of him going rigid above her. His back and buttocks tightened beneath her hands, and she gathered him into her until the tautness left his body.

Bay caught his weight on his elbows and held himself suspended above her, waiting for the final pulses to subside. His kisses drifted lazily over her face and down her neck.

"You make a beautiful pagan," he said. He pressed into Mariah, set off another round of tremors within her that gradually subsided. His kisses moved lower. "Beautiful goddess."

"Oh, Bay, I . . ." *I love you*, she wanted to say, but she knew the words would shock him as much as they had her when she'd finally admitted them to herself, alone there in the rose room. He was leaving, that was part of the danger of the storm, that it would consume her and blow on over the horizon. She couldn't say the words aloud, even if she knew they were true.

"Mmmm?" Bay asked, his mouth full of breast, suckling yet another spasm of pleasure out of her.

"I . . . I don't know. I can't think."

"Good." He flicked his tongue over her nipple again and chuckled as she swore softly and arched against him. Mariah felt the stir of his renewed desire, still deep within her, and the fact of his wanting her set her alight all over.

She'd been a virgin. Bay silently berated himself for reading so much into Jensen's boasting and her own seductive story. She'd really meant a storm.

But if there was a storm in that room tonight, it was Mariah herself, all flashing light and restless clouds in his arms. He wanted her again, even now, wanted to pin her soft fury beneath his body and discover all over that he was the first.

The first.

The reality astounded Bay and left a lingering smile on his lips. For all the women who'd passed in and out of his life, none had bestowed such glory with their gift. None but Mariah.

"Goddess," he whispered, and he took her again and revelled in the way she thrashed and called out beneath him when he carried her past the edge the second time.

Afterward, when she slept and he was about to doze, her frantic dash up the hill and the reason for it finally came back into his head. Damn it all, where was his mind?

He took one look at Mariah, sprawled beside him, her back an erotic curve of bare skin, and he knew. It was with her, where it had been for weeks.

And now it had to be elsewhere. He flipped the covers over her and slid out of bed. Moving silently, he grabbed for his boots and clothes and dressed in seconds.

Eli was in the front hall when he got downstairs.

Bay took his gunbelt off the hook in the front hall and buckled it on, then pulled his pistol and gave the barrel a quick spin. Six cartridges. He slipped the Colt back into the holster and reached for the tie down. "Anything happen in the past couple of hours?"

Eli raised one eyebrow. "You tell me. I came up to get you a little while ago. Jesus, Bay. Right in the middle of all this?"

"Shut up, Eli. Just tell me if anything happened."

"I took Gid Willis down to help me with that little problem in the south end. We think we spotted some riders over Coon Creek way. That's what I was coming up to tell you when I heard you—"

"Nothing. You heard nothing."

Eli cleared his throat. "My mistake. Anyway, we hightailed it back in case they headed this way, but we haven't seen a trace of them yet. You up to this?"

The cobwebs had cleared remarkably quickly. Bay nodded and reached to douse the lamp. No use giving anyone a good silhouette to fire at. "Let's go out and arrange a proper reception for the gentlemen."

Chapter Fifteen

THE MAN AT the front gate pulled back to the house as soon as the riders were spotted coming up the valley. Bay and Eli met him on the porch.

"Are you certain the others know they're not to fire unless I do?" Bay asked.

"Yes, sir." The boy—he wasn't much older than Mariah's brother—answered too quickly. "Rolley told them. He's got them spread out all around, with the men he thinks are most levelheaded in charge, just like Eli said."

"How about you?"

"No, sir. I mean, I won't draw unless they do."

"Unless *Eli or I* do." Bay poked the kid in the chest, shoving him back a good six inches. "If you want to stay alive, you'll be real clear on that. They're after me, and possibly Eli, but I intend to convince them they've made a mistake."

The cloud of dust turned off the road and careened through the gate. Eight or ten horsemen, Bay guessed by its size. In seconds the group pulled to a halt in front of them, the horses steaming and snorting in the yard.

Eleven, he counted quickly. Manageable, provided everyone kept calm, but the grim expressions and the number of weapons didn't give him a lot of confidence. Neither did the ropes looped across a couple of saddles.

Holding his hands well out from his sides, Bay stepped to the edge of the porch.

"Good evening, Creelor. Michaels." He nodded to the two in front. They both nodded back. "What can I do for you gents?"

"We got some questions for you," Creelor said.

"You're on *my* property in the middle of the night," Bay pointed out evenly. "I'd like an explanation before I start answering any questions."

"This is about the only spread in this part of the county that hasn't had horses stolen," Michaels said. A couple of men behind him seconded him.

"I'm not so sure of that," Bay said. "We're just now starting roundup. I haven't had a chance to compare the tallies to my father's records."

"Enough of this folderol." A man Bay didn't recognize nudged his mount forward. "A pair of my horses disappeared three nights back. The trail faded out on Cedar Creek, headed this way. Tonight we had a little better luck. Asa Smith lost a team but a couple of us managed to follow them. And the *three* fellows that took 'em." He looked significantly at Bay and the two men behind him. "They rode right up along Coon Creek. Onto your land."

"That's open range. Anybody could bring horses across there." And anybody with a grudge could leave them there to be found. Jensen, for example. He wasn't with the crowd. Bay kept his eyes on the angry stranger. "I'm no horse thief."

"So you claim. The evidence says otherwise." A mutter of agreement wove through the group.

"Never heard a horse thief admit it," a voice called out from the back.

"Not until his neck was about to stretch," another said.

The shift from group to mob was sudden and deadly. Bay felt the hair rise on the back of his neck even though he'd expected it from the start. At the edges of his vision, his own men moved and closed in, surrounding the horsemen.

Not one of the riders noticed. In fact, they seemed to be staring past him. Damn that kid, if he started a war . . .

"Go on back inside, miss," Eli said.

"No."

Mariah. Bay blocked the impulse to turn to her, to shove her inside, out of danger. If he moved quickly, one of them might fire. He kept his voice calm. "Mariah, get inside."

"No. These gentlemen need a few things pointed out to them."

She passed him to stand barefoot on the bottom step, nightgown and wrapper white as a shroud. She stared up at the man who was a stranger to Bay.

"He didn't steal those horses any more than you did, Thomas Fitzsimmons."

"But . . ."

"But nothing," she snapped. "You said Mr. Smith's horses were stolen tonight. I got here before nine o'clock. Bay and both these men were here when I arrived. They couldn't have taken them."

"He could've gone back out," Creelor interrupted. "He had plenty of time."

"He didn't go out," Mariah said.

"Begging your pardon, Mariah." Michaels tugged at his collar, clearly uncomfortable. "How can you be sure?"

She lifted her chin, and her voice, when she spoke, carried so well, she might have been reciting memorized verse in a grammar school program. "Because he was with me the whole time. In bed. I'll swear to it in court if I have to.

"Nikolai Jensen's making fools out of every one of you," she continued over their stunned silence, disdain dripping from her words.

"Not as big a one as you're making of him," a voice answered. Another mutter ran through the crowd, this time followed by lewd snickers. Bay fought down the urge to drag one of the men off his horse and demand an apology. They still had guns at hand. Men could still die if he lost his head.

Fitzsimmons leaned forward and gave Mariah a once over. "I can't see as you'd swear to something like that if it weren't true. In fact, I have a hard time figuring you'd admit it if it was. I thought your parents raised you better than this."

"I doubt that your mama's very proud of you tonight, either, Tom."

"I'm just trying to protect my property," he grumbled, but he lifted his hand away from the pistol at his side and rested it on his knee. Michaels followed the lead, then the others, none looking straight at her. Bay's own men backed off quietly at a signal from the foreman.

Bay went to Mariah's side and slid his arm around her. It

might not show, but she was shaking like a leaf. Several of the men on horseback looked like they'd still be willing to string him up, if for a slightly different reason.

Bay let his teeth show in a cold, feral grin. "Time you gentlemen went home." *Before I yank every one of you down and bust you into pieces. Holier than thou herd of sheep.*

"Come on, fellows. We're done here." Fitzsimmons turned his horse toward the gate.

"Right behind you." Creelor touched his heels to his horse. The animal pushed forward, jostling Bay into Mariah. Bay shoved her out of reach just as the man's hand swept downward, his quirt slashing across Bay's neck.

"Whoa, boys, whoa," Eli called as several guns came up on both sides.

Bay grabbed for Creelor, ready to pound him into a pulp, but Michaels beat him to the man, snatching him by the coat and yanking him backwards, nearly off his horse. "What the hell are you doing?" Michaels demanded.

"Son of a bitch ruined a good girl," Creelor yelled. "Her pa would horsewhip him if he was around."

"Fine, but you ain't her pa and you almost got yourself shot with that stunt. Didn't you notice he's got better than a dozen men on us?"

Creelor looked around and noticed Bay's crew for the first time. He swore.

"I don't need them," Bay yelled. "Get down here and we'll have it out. One on one." God, he ached to hit someone. This jackass would do just fine.

Unfortunately, Creelor chose that moment to get some sense. He wheeled his horse away. The rest followed, slower than they'd ridden in, streaming down the hill and off into the night where such mobs belong.

Eli was the first to move. He tapped Bay's left shoulder. "You'd better get that taken care of."

Bay shrugged his hand away. "You and Rolley pick out a couple of men and follow them. Make sure they get off my land, and that they split up and go home and don't give anyone else any trouble tonight. I want two men on the gate and two up on the hill behind the house. The rest of you get back to sleep. And thanks."

His neck started smarting about the time Mariah finally convinced him to go inside. She paused to light a lamp, and he caught a glimpse of himself in the hall mirror as she steered him toward the dining room. Crimson soaked the shoulder of his shirt, and the wound just above his collar gaped open like he'd taken a shallow slash from a bayonet. He should be hurting worse.

Mariah yanked open a drawer in the sideboard and snagged the first clean cloths she could find. She pressed them to Bay's neck.

"Hold these," she ordered.

"Mrs. Shaw's not going to like me bleeding all over the good linens," Bay said, but he clamped his hand over the embroidered napkins. The pressure transposed the sting to a raw throb that seemed more reasonable considering how his neck looked.

"They're yours," Mariah said. "You can bleed on them if you like. Come on, I'll get Mrs. Shaw to help."

The kitchen, however, already blazed with lamplight. Mrs. Shaw, looking as formidably calm as ever, came out of the pantry bearing a basket with rolled bandages, liniment, and a needle and darning thread. She drew a pan of steaming water off the still-hot tank on the stove's side, added some liniment to it, and dropped in the threaded needle.

"I don't need stitching," Bay said.

"Hush," Mariah said. She pushed him down in the chair and peeled away his shirt, then nudged his hand away from the napkin.

He sent his mind elsewhere as the two ladies examined and poked and prodded and reached some kind of consensus, at which point Mrs. Shaw disappeared back into the dining room. She returned with a glass and a half-empty bottle of his father's scotch whiskey, poured out three fingers, and handed it to Bay.

"You may want this, Mr. McKenzie," she said.

He tossed the liquor back, and for an instant, the inside of his throat felt nearly as raw as the outside. As the burn mellowed to numbness and spread out from his belly, Mrs. Shaw said,

"My eyes aren't what they used to be. I think you should do it, miss."

Mariah looked from her to Bay and back again. "I've never sewn up a person. Just a couple of piglets. And a cat one time. Papa chloroformed him."

"Did they live?" Bay asked with a sense of bravado based in some part on whiskey.

"Yes," Mariah said. "But Mama—"

"Then I will, too."

"You'll do fine, miss," the housekeeper agreed.

Frowning, Mariah rinsed her hands in liniment water and picked up the needle. Bay curled his fingers around the leg of the table and braced himself. "Go ahead."

Whatever her misgivings or lack of experience, she sewed him as efficiently as she sewed her dresses. Bay winced as she pulled the first loop snug. Her stitching wasn't so bad, but the liniment leached off the thread and set the already raw flesh afire. To distract himself, Bay watched Mariah's reflection in the window glass. Her lips thinned as she bent over him, her face growing tighter, her eyes more pained each time she had to jab him, and he forced himself to smile, to reassure her she wasn't killing him. She finally tied the last knot and snipped the thread. While she wiped her hands on a towel, Bay leaned toward the window to get a better view of her handiwork. The stitches were small and neat, just tight enough to close the lips of the wound.

"Very tidy," Mrs. Shaw said, squinting.

"That's a better job than most Army surgeons could do," he said.

Mariah wrapped her arms around herself and turned to the stove, as if she hadn't heard them.

Bay wanted to reach out, catch a handful of her wrapper in his fist, and pull her back onto his lap, but Mrs. Shaw stood there between them, still squinting at his wound.

"I can deal with the dressing," the housekeeper offered.

"Thank you. I, uh," Mariah looked around distractedly. "I suppose I need a breath of fresh air."

"I shouldn't think you'd want to go outside again dressed

like that," Mrs. Shaw said quietly. "The hands might still be out and about."

The words were said without any note of condemnation, but Bay recognized that the woman was telling them she knew what had passed between Mariah and him, and had known of it before Mariah's self-damning testimony. Mariah realized it, too, in the same instant. She turned bright red, and Bay absorbed the fact that she could announce her fall from grace to a horde of men without shame, yet be brought up short by another woman's simple reminder of modesty.

But she mastered her discomfort before Bay could think what to say, straightened a little, and gave Mrs. Shaw a kindly smile. "You're right, of course, thank you. I'm afraid I had forgotten myself in all the excitement."

She returned to Bay's side and helped clean him and wind the strip of bleached cheesecloth bandage around his neck. A few minutes later, the two women pronounced him fit for sleep and escorted him up to his room. There was a brief, uncomfortable silence in the hall as Mrs. Shaw waited expectantly for Mariah to step past and head toward the rose room.

Again, the kindly smile touched her mouth, this time firmer, more certain. "You really must be exhausted, Mrs. Shaw, being awakened abruptly in the middle of the night like this. I'll see to Mr. McKenzie now. You can get some rest."

This time, the housekeeper's eyebrows went up a quarter of an inch. "Yes, ma' . . . I mean, miss. Goodnight." Lips pressed firmly together, she headed back toward her quarters.

Her footsteps had barely faded when Bay pulled Mariah inside the room and pushed the door closed with a firm click. "You are truly amazing, woman."

Mariah's lips twitched a little as she looked up at him. "Woman, not lady."

"Yes, lady. The bravest lady I know. You didn't have to do that. We could have handled them."

"For tonight. And tomorrow they would have still believed you stole the horses. Now maybe they'll stop." She pressed her lips to the edge of the bandage, so gently he wondered if he'd imagined the touch until she did it again. "Am I terrible, Bay? I was terrified they were going to kill you, but now that it's over, all I can think of is lying in your arms again. To *know* that you're safe."

Bay backed to the bed, and sat down, tugging her along. "I'm safe."

She surged into his arms, carrying him backwards into the tangled sheets, covering his face with quick, desperate kisses.

"It's all right, sweetheart," he murmured against the frantic assault. He tasted salt on her lips and realized silent tears coursed down her cheeks. "Everything is going to be all right. I'm fine. We're fine."

Slowly her kisses changed, grew hungrier, more demanding. Her touches grew more intimate. Bay let her explore, let her strip away his jeans, and helped her peel the white gown over her head, revealing her more beautiful than ever. Desire rippled through him, washing the throb in his neck to distant awareness. In one motion, Bay rolled, carrying her to her back, where he thought he could regain control, but it was too late. She drew him into her, and this time it was Mariah who set the pace, and Bay had to rush to follow as she raced like a cloud before the wind.

"Stay," Bay said. "Sleep in with me."

"I can't."

Streaks of pearly gray touched the sky, but the light barely penetrated the depths of the bedroom. Mariah groped her way around the bed, unwilling to put match to lamp wick and break the spell of the dawn. "I have animals to feed and the cow to milk. I need to get home."

The dark shape on the bed that was Bay stretched and yawned. "Let your brother take care of things for once."

"Jimmy's not at home," she said. Somehow, a lot of the pain had gone out of that fact. "He left two, no three days ago to go back to work for that outfit of Keenan's."

Bay sat up, his bare legs dangling. The bandage gleamed, an odd white strip around his throat. "You said something last night, but I didn't . . . I'm sorry, Mariah."

The honest sadness in his voice counted for more than he could know. She found her clothes on the carpet, a pale mound laying right where she'd stripped them off. Had she really been so brazen? She sorted out her shimmy and drawers, and turned away to don them.

"What are you going to do?" Bay asked.

"Go home and milk Peach."

He came off the bed in one step and turned her to face him. His voice was harsh. "You know what I'm talking about."

"Yes, I do, but that's all the answer I have right now. I'm going to go home and milk my cow and feed my chickens and weed and hoe and water, just like I do every day." Mariah shrugged out of his grip and bent to retrieve her petticoat. "You told me once to take things as they come. Well, I am. Just let me continue."

He caught her hand and pressed a kiss to her palm. His eyes had a pinched look, but he smiled. "I'll go get your horse."

In less time than it took her to get her buttons lined up, he was dressed and out the door. Mariah sighed, then finished dressing and went outside herself. Her jacket hung neatly from the rack by the front door. Mrs. Shaw must have found it in the study.

From the veranda, the curve of eastern horizon showed clear pink, like the inside of a sea shell Mariah's aunt had once shown her. She waited there in the glow, conscious of the looks cast her direction by the cowboys that moved around the yard. Some were curious, others openly appraising, but every one of them looked elsewhere the minute Bay came out of the barn leading the two horses. She met him halfway.

"Give me a minute, and I'll go get my hat," he said. "I must have left it in the study last night when you came charging in."

"Where are you going?"

"I thought I'd ride you home. I can help with your chores."

She took a deep breath. "I'd rather you didn't."

"Now you're being stubborn."

"I'm being practical." She took the reins out of his hands and checked her saddle. "I can't let myself get dependent on you, Bay. You've told me time and time again that you're not going to be around for long."

"But right now I am."

"And I'm glad. I truly am." She reached up and stroked his jaw just above the strip of bandage. His whiskers, so rough against her cheek and breast, felt like silk velvet beneath her fingertips. Her chest tightened with the ferocity of what she felt, and she had to turn away. "Give me a leg up?"

He did, and when she looked back down at him, he was his old self, standing there in his Levi's and his half-open yellow shirt, a shock of jet hair hanging over eyes that laughed at her. He looked just like he had that first day. He could find his hat and be ready to ride off, Mariah thought. Nothing had changed.

"So, when am I allowed on the property?" he asked.

"When you stop feeling guilty for not locking me in my room last night," she said.

He gave her a sheepish grin that said she was right. His fingers curled around her ankle, warm through the thin leather of her high button shoes. "Teasing aside, Mariah, it might be a week or so before I come down. We're in the middle of roundup, and I want to take some cattle to market as soon as we're done."

Selling off stock. "Then I'll see you when I see you." *If you come back.*

Nothing *had* changed.

"Have Mrs. Shaw see to that bandage," she said.

She wheeled the sorrel around and rode off before the tears could catch up to her.

They would both come back. Despite her protestations of independence, Mariah kept going by telling herself that Bay and Jimmy would both be back to offer whatever help they could. Particularly, she still held onto her faith that Jimmy would bring home his pay. Meantime, she needed to bring in cash on her own. It would keep her going that much longer. It might even give her enough to hire on a man to harvest if Jimmy let her down. On Thursday morning she hitched up the wagon, packed the past month's worth of butter in a keg of cold, salted water, nestled five dozen eggs into a straw-filled basket, and headed for town.

She knew word of her fall from grace must have spread—men were deadlier gossips than any woman she'd ever known—but she wasn't sure what that spread would mean. Her first clue was the looks she got driving through town:

shocked stares or blatant turning away. The men on the liar's bench fell silent when she pulled up in front of the general store. She nodded anyway as she passed.

Then it took her a good quarter of an hour to attract the clerk's attention. Finally she planted herself square in his path and he had to acknowledge her.

"I'm sorry, Mariah." He glanced at his feet, the shelf, and his fingernails in quick succession. "What can I do for you?"

"I have a load of good, sweet butter out in the wagon," she said. "What are you paying today?"

"I'm afraid we just bought, and with money being so tight, we can't take more. People simply can't afford to buy."

"Eggs? Fresh from under the hens."

"Overstocked. I'm sorry to disappoint you," he added, still not meeting her eyes. Behind him, one of the town matrons cleared her throat with pointed disapproval.

"It's fine," Mariah said tightly. "I'll find other buyers."

She found them, too, at the hotels and boarding houses where she could call at the back door, away from the customers' eyes. They even paid better than the store, but in the end she was left with nearly five pounds of butter floating in the keg.

"Somebody wants this," she muttered. Then she saw a wagon going by carrying bags marked "Kansas Relief." She followed it to the courthouse.

Inside, people milled about outside the Register of Deeds, organizing the first shipments of flour, meal, and dried apples. Mariah pushed her way through the knot, ignoring the whispers that trailed behind her. The two men running the operation were too harried to notice whether the donation came from a socially fit person or not and accepted the butter with thanks.

On her way back to the wagon, Mariah spotted a familiar figure carrying a package down Broadway. She called out, "Annie!"

Annie Richardson cut between two wagons and crossed to Mariah. They exchanged hugs.

"Mail order?" Mariah asked, pointing at the package.

"My new corset," Annie whispered. "I got it to go with my wedding dress."

"You're still getting married, then? I wasn't sure after all that mess with the grasshoppers."

"Henry says we might as well. We'll just get married first and harvest millet after. Papa wanted us to wait another year, but Mama and I wore him down. So it's two weeks from Tuesday."

"I'm so happy for you. I'll be looking for my invitation."

Annie went pale, and her bottom lip started trembling. "Oh, Mariah. Papa made me throw yours out."

Mariah didn't bother to ask why. She knew. Everyone in town knew. She saw Mrs. Watterson staring at her and Annie, her face frozen into sour disapprobation, and she straightened her shoulders. "You'd better run on. Your father won't want you talking to me either, especially out in public like this. I'm soiled goods."

"It's true then?" Annie's eyes widened and the color came back into her cheeks in a rush. "You and that McKenzie?"

"Me and that McKenzie."

"And you *told* everybody?" Her voice was a squeak of disbelief.

"I told the people who needed to hear it." Mariah raised her voice so Mrs. Watterson would be sure to hear, too. "Those men were ready to hang him for something he didn't do, but I doubt anybody's talking about that part."

Annie shook her head. "Papa wouldn't even tell me where the story came from. Henry had to find out. Now Papa just says he won't have someone so proud of her immorality in his house."

"But he'll have his vigilante friends in, won't he?" Mariah snapped. "I'm sorry. He's your father and he's doing what he thinks is right for you. But it seems pretty hypocritical to me. They want to lynch Bay, and they're fine gentlemen. I love him, and I'm a sinner. And I do love him, Annie, heaven help me, I do, and that's the first time I've said it aloud."

"There's no justice in it. I think it's terrible, and so does Henry, even though we always thought you and Nikolai would . . . Have you even seen Nikolai since all this happened?"

Mariah stared at the fancy lettering of the return address on her friend's package. "I wouldn't know what to say to him. He . . . He thought he was doing the right thing, too. Lord save us from righteous men."

"They're not all bad. Henry isn't. He understands that you're my best friend in the world, whatever anyone else thinks. After we're married, you're welcome in our house any time. We already decided that together."

"Oh, Annie, thank you." Mariah swallowed hard to keep the tears at bay. Mrs. Watterson was still frowning. "You'd better go, really. I don't want to cause trouble for you now. Your wedding should be a happy day."

"I wish you could be there." Annie gave her another squeeze and started to turn away, then stopped. "*Are* you proud of what you did?"

"No. But I'm not ashamed, either."

"Good," she said. Suddenly, her eyes twinkled with mischief, the old familiar Annie from school, never quite what the teacher expected. She leaned closer, her voice barely a whisper. "Neither are Henry and I."

With a wave and a good-bye, she hurried off up the street. Mariah stood there for a moment, astonishment changing the lump in her throat to laughter. A broad smile lit her face as she faced Mrs. Watterson. "Lovely day for gossip, isn't it?"

The woman harumphed and marched away.

The ride home was easier for Annie's revelation, but the note pinned to the door of the house pretty much ruined Mariah's improved mood.

Bay had come and gone while she was in town. His note, scrawled in pencil on a scrap of envelope, said that and something worse, at least as far as her peace of mind was concerned: he'd come to tell her good-bye. Just for a few days, according to the note, but reading the word in his bold, angular hand made her heart twist in agony. Mariah read the whole thing through again, looking for some clue as to which direction he'd chosen—not west, please not west, for if he started off that way, he might keep going—but he didn't say. He didn't even close the note properly, just signed his name in slashing letters that trailed off the edges of the scrap.

"Take things as they come," Mariah reminded herself,

adding her mother's favorite, "Don't borrow trouble from tomorrow."

This was the choice she had made for herself. Time to learn to live with it. She crumpled the note, stuffed it into the pocket of her coat and turned to unhitch the team.

"Welcome home, Mr. McKenzie. Eli." Mrs. Shaw appeared at the dining room door wiping flour-coated hands on her apron. "I hope your business went well."

Bay hung his gun belt on the peg and nodded. "Well enough. It was a long ride to make that fast."

"Yes, sir. I didn't know you were coming back today, so supper will be a little late."

"Right now all I need is fresh coffee. I get tired of Eli's after a couple of days. We'll be in the study."

"Yes, sir." She disappeared.

"Since when do you get tired of my coffee?" Eli demanded as he followed Bay into the study.

"Since I got used to better. When did she start calling you Eli?" Bay laughed as his friend turned three shades of red, none of which matched his beard. "Come on, let's go over those sale records again."

Two hours later they scraped the last flakes of apple pie crust off the china plates. Bay leaned back in his chair and lifted a cup of strong coffee, brewed with the dab of chicory his father had always demanded. "A man could get used to this."

"Um-hmm." Eli nodded, but his mouth pursed in a way Bay had come to recognize as disapproval.

"That's it." Bay slammed the cup down. A chip flew off the saucer and spun across the desk. "You've been doing that to me for a week now. Say your piece."

"What?"

"That look. Like you think I'm growing rockers in place of feet."

"Well, it has been a long time since I heard anything about moving on. I kind of figured you'd at least think about heading on west while we were riding this time, but nope. Here we are, right back where we started. We were supposed to be in Sante Fe by now, remember?"

"That was before this ranch landed in my lap."

"That's not the only thing in your lap."

"I'm not going to discuss Mariah with you. I told you once I'd make her understand how things are. I did, and she does. She's not what's keeping me here."

"Phhht. I'll remember that one." Eli got up and went to the small framed map of North America that hung in the space between the windows. He put one finger on eastern Kansas and traced a path south toward Texas, and then across to Santa Fe. "We could still do it with good weather to spare if we cut down this way."

Bay shook his head and stabbed a forefinger down on the sale lists. "We've still got this mess with the horses. Unless we get out from under the suspicion, it will follow us. It could sour anything we take on down the road."

"And after that, you'll want to find a buyer for this place," Eli muttered to himself. "And then who knows what you'll think up." Eli traced the southern route backwards and forwards a couple of more times. "Why don't you just admit you like having her to warm your bed?"

Only seven years of friendship and words that hit way too close to home kept Bay from knocking his friend through the window. "Eli, shut up."

Unconcerned, Eli strolled back to the table and polished off the dregs of his coffee. "You could set this place up like we did the mine. Hire a manager for a share of profits. Do what you need to do to make sure she's here when you come back this way, if that's what you want, and we'll hit the road."

The same suggestion Mariah had made. The same one he'd been turning over in his head for weeks and was so close to accepting. He hadn't gone straight down to the farm when they got back because he wanted to be able to tell her something sure. Anything sure. She deserved that much.

"I'll stick around and help you as long as you need it," Eli continued as he headed for the door, "but sooner or later, I'm headed for Santa Fe. I sure do hope you decide to come along."

Bay could see the route in his mind's eye. He'd ridden most of it before, after the war, taking the longest possible way to Montana Territory. The sweeping west Texas plains. The first view of the mountains. His hand drifted to his belly, heavy with Mrs. Shaw's dinner. He was already going soft, but not so much he couldn't get lean again with a few weeks in the saddle.

And Mariah would still be here.

"Shall I clear the plates, Mr. McKenzie?" Mrs. Shaw interrupted his daydream. Bay gave her a nod, and she moved efficiently to gather the dishes onto the tray she'd left on the sideboard.

It took him a moment to realize she had finished and was standing there, watching him with those level brown eyes. "Is there something you wanted, Mrs. Shaw?"

"Yes, sir." She reached into her apron pocket and handed him a sheet of plain blue paper, neatly folded and addressed with his name. "That would be my notice, sir. I'll give you plenty of time to find a replacement, of course. In fact, I took the liberty of jotting down the names of a couple of other widow ladies who might make you a good housekeeper, there at the bottom of my letter."

As she talked, Bay flicked the note open and scanned it. "Very straightforward. Only you neglect to mention why."

"Personal reasons," she said. Her eyebrows went up a quarter inch as she reached for the tray.

He'd seen that look exactly once before, when Mariah had announced her intentions to see him to bed. "That won't do, Mrs. Shaw. I want the truth."

She set the tray down. "I worked for the elder Mr. McKenzie for over ten years, since Mr. Shaw died. I saw him do a lot of things I didn't approve of. But never once did he take advantage of a woman."

Now it was Bay's turn to raise an eyebrow. "Excuse me, Mrs. Shaw, but bull."

"Not the way you have, Mr. McKenzie. He may have taken land, but he never took a woman's good name. Now, if you'll excuse me."

"I will not." He trailed into the kitchen after her. "Are they talking about Mariah in town?"

Of course they are, you jackass. He didn't need Mrs. Shaw's nod to tell him that, once he stopped to think. He listened to her story, as mad at himself as at the gossips who spread the tale.

He'd been so caught up in his own concerns he hadn't considered the impact of the tale the committee men would pass on to their friends and families. That came out of his father's training, one of the few things Bay had held to through the years: McKenzies never gave a damn about common gossip. But Mariah would.

And only one thing would put a stop to it.

Now he had something sure to tell her.

"Mrs. Shaw, I am a Grade A fool." Bay headed back the way he'd come, grabbing his hat as he passed the dining table. Behind him, he heard Mrs. Shaw snort.

"That's a fact."

Except for the ruffle of chill wind from the north, the prairie was unusually still. Mariah stood in the door, listening to the stirring of the animals in the barn and pen, but beyond the edges of the yard there seemed to be nothing but night-dark sky and the shadow of rolling hills. Even the coyotes were silent.

"How about you, Clyde?" She glanced down at the dog, who thumped his tail twice. "Sing for me."

Instead, he licked the toe of her shoe.

"No?" she said. "Well, at least you're here, which is more than I can say for the other males I know. Come on in, boy. You may as well eat your supper in here where you can see it."

Clyde complied, his face a satisfied doggy grin as he pushed his dish of table scraps around the floor.

"Don't count on this every night," Mariah warned. "You know Papa doesn't like you coming inside. If I spoil you, he'll be unhappy when he gets back. And listen to me," she added to herself. "Less than two weeks alone and I've taken up chatting with the dog. Well, why not? Nobody else will talk to me, will they, boy?"

After she washed Clyde's dish and set it back outside filled with water, she dragged the big tin washtub out into the center of the room. She'd poured a couple of buckets of well water in earlier. Now she tipped the boiling contents of the kettle in and refilled the kettle for another shot of hot water. With just herself to wash, she didn't see the point of filling the tub, but she wanted what little water she had to be hot. As the kettle heated, she moved about gathering towels and soap and a warm nightgown, piling them on the seat of a chair pulled next to the tub.

Clyde watched for a few minutes, then ventured over to sniff the tub. He put his paws up on the edge and stuck his head down to lap cautiously at the water.

"Get out of there." Mariah nudged the pup away. "You have perfectly good water outside. Go on, time you went out anyway."

As she opened the door, Clyde's ears went up. He darted past her and out into the middle of the yard, where he stood staring off at the gate, every muscle attuned to whatever was out there. Mariah heard a horse whinny and reached for the shotgun.

Then the dog bounded off, tail wagging, and Mariah relaxed. Whoever was riding in, Clyde recognized them as friend. She smoothed at her hair, hoping to see Bay's lanky blue roan.

Instead, a moonlit gray giant of a horse appeared, with another giant on its back, and Mariah's stomach clenched.

He slid off his horse, tied the reins to the top rail of the stock pen, and walked slowly over to Mariah. His face was solemn, but he wore the clean white shirt and black pants he always wore when he came calling. He took off his hat.

"We need to talk, Mariah," Nikolai said. He pronounced the words clearly, as though he had rehearsed them.

"Nikolai, I . . ." Mariah hesitated. Her mouth was dry and her heart raced, but she credited that as much to guilt as to fear. As he stood there, hat in hand, she saw none of the anger that had flared in the past, and she felt suddenly foolish. This was Nikolai. He wasn't going to hurt her. And she owed him an explanation. This was as good a time as any. "Come on in."

She hurried ahead of him to clear the chair of her nightgown and push the tub back in the corner. When she turned, he was hanging his hat on one of the pegs just inside the door. Her everyday bonnet hung on the next peg, and she saw him run his fingers down the strings, almost like a caress, before he pulled the door shut.

"Did you have supper?" she asked. "I just fed the leftovers to Clyde, but I could fix you some bacon and eggs."

He nodded, and started toward the table.

With some sense of relief, Mariah turned to the familiar chore of cooking. The task would give her a few minutes to collect herself, to think. She took her time slicing bacon while the skillet warmed on the stove, various apologies and explanations forming and dissolving in her mind, as they had been all week.

"Do you cook for him, too?" Nikolai's voice came from right by her ear, vaguely slurred.

Mariah started to turn, but his arms went around her, one at her waist and the other around her chest. He held her there, trapped between him and the table, her back against the solid wall of his body. Liquor fumes, sour and thick, wafted over her shoulder. He'd been drinking. That's why he had spoken so carefully before. If she'd smelled him first, she'd have slammed the door in his face.

"Do you?" he asked again. "When he comes to you, do you fix him supper and breakfast?"

"Nikolai . . ."

"I been thinking about you all week. What I would say to you. What I would ask. But I see you now, and all I can think is, do you cook for him, too?"

He wasn't hurting her, just holding her. Mariah twisted a little, so she could look up to see his face. He still had that solemn look, but here in the light, his blue eyes looked flat and cold. Beyond anger.

She curved her fingers tighter around the handle of the knife. "Nikolai, turn loose of me right now."

He shook his head, dipping his head so his lips brushed her temple. "The people in town, they talk about you. You know what they say?"

She didn't answer.

"Answer me, Mariah," he ordered.

She kept her voice calm. "That I was with Bay. That I came out in my nightgown and said I'd been with him all night. They were going to lynch him, because of what you had been telling them. I couldn't let that happen. Even if I'd had to lie, I wouldn't have let that happen."

The skin around his lips went taut and white. "But you did not have to lie, did you?"

"No." She was sorry. She wanted to tell him so, but some instinct told her that he'd read an apology as weakness. She could not afford that right now.

"Do you know what else they say? That you make a fool of me. That you been laying with Mac-Kenzie for a long time and think to trick me to marry you."

"That's not true."

He pulled her a little tighter against him, still not hurting her, as though he was comforting himself with a hug. His chin rested on top of her head and his voice rumbled through her skull. "All week I tell myself this. All week I keep working, pretending I do not hear them talk about you, hear them laugh at me when I go past. All week I try to forget that you act so nice and let me kiss you, and then go straight to his bed."

She felt it the moment his mood shifted, as clearly as she'd heard the men at Bay's turn into a mob. His voice grew bitter; his grip tightened to the point of crushing.

"Tonight, you be in my bed."

Chapter Sixteen

MARIAH BROUGHT THE knife up and slashed, drawing the sharp blade across the back of Nikolai's arm. He grunted with surprise, but kept his hold.

She slashed again. He batted her hand away and grabbed her wrist with his injured hand and squeezed. She fought to twist free, but Nikolai simply held on and squeezed harder. Her hand went numb, and the knife clattered to the floor. He swung her around to face him, holding her easily by both wrists. His blood ran over her hand, sticky and warm.

"That is not nice, Mariah," he growled. "I want you to be nice to me, the way you are to him. The way the girls are when I pay them."

She knew her face showed shock and disbelief when he chuckled. "Ja, I go to whores sometimes. There are always some for the men at the quarry. For two years, I been wanting you. But I think, my Mariah, she is a good girl, so when I need a woman, I find a whore. One of them has blonde hair. Not so pretty like yours, but enough like that I can pretend. I been pretending for two years, because I thought you wait until we are married. For two years I go to a whore, when I could have had you. Now you are whore and I will have you."

She kicked him. Hard. Right between the legs.

Jimmy had told her once that would hurt a man. He hadn't lied. Nikolai's knees buckled. He grabbed for his crotch.

Free, Mariah scrambled for the shotgun. She reached the door before Nikolai could straighten. She whirled, the gun at her shoulder, her thumb on the hammer. Nikolai stumbled to a stop an arm's length from the muzzle of the gun. Hate distorted his face.

"You want me to pay?" he sneered. "I pay. You don't need gun. The others will pay, too, when I tell them. You will make lots of money."

"Get out of here," she said. *Aim at a man's chest*, her father had told her and her mother when he'd had to leave them alone. Mariah lowered the muzzle of the gun a few inches, so it pointed at Nikolai's heart. "You bastard. You get out of here. I swear I'll shoot you." And she could, this time. She could.

Outside the door, Clyde began barking again.

Nikolai must have seen the determination in her face, must have recognized her fury. The sneer left his lips. He put his hands out to his side, palms forward in surrender. "I go. You don't have to shoot."

Mariah stepped aside, making room for him to pass. She kept the gun square on him.

"You don't shoot me in the back," he said again. He opened the door.

A fist landed in the middle of his face.

Nikolai reeled backwards, clutching at his nose.

Bay stepped through the door. His sweeping glance took in everything, and his face darkened.

"Get on my horse, Mariah. Get out of here."

"Not without you."

"Mariah." Bay's voice crackled with authority. Without ever losing her sight on Nikolai, Mariah backed toward the corner.

Damn, she wasn't leaving, and Bay didn't have time to convince her. Jensen moved forward, a look of grim pleasure on his bloody face. He held his huge fists high, like a prize fighter. "Ja. Ja. Maybe she like to watch me break you, Mac-Kenzie."

"Try. Come on and try, you son of a bitch."

Jensen launched himself, quick for a man his size, but he swung high. Bay ducked in under his fists, landed three heavy blows to his midsection, and bobbed away before the big man had time to react.

God, it felt good. He'd wanted to beat this bastard to a

bloody pulp, even before he saw Mariah standing there with that gun and those wide, scared eyes. Now he'd just as soon kill him.

Bay swung again and heard the whoof of air as he hit Jensen's stomach. Then Nikolai connected, the pile driver blow Bay had expected he'd pack. Bay's head exploded with pain and he felt his knees start to give. He turned the collapse into a dive, hitting Nikolai at the waist. His momentum carried the mason backwards. They hit the table and went over. Bay clung to Nikolai, buying a moment for his head to clear.

With a roar, Jensen pushed to his feet, dragging Bay along. His fingers locked around Bay's throat. "You make her whore."

Bay felt the pressure build in his lungs and head. He locked his fists together and, reaching for strength he wasn't sure he had, hammered them straight up into Jensen's chin. The shock jolted up his arms and made the muscles in his shoulders bunch and scream.

Nikolai crumpled like he'd been shot. Bay pounded him as he folded, driving all his rage into each blow, wanting to hit him until he couldn't hit anymore. But Jensen just lay there, his eyes rolled up. Bay backed off, gasping for breath, and waited for him to come up, waited for him to move, so he'd feel justified in bashing his head into the floor.

"Did you kill him?" Mariah stepped out of her corner, gripping her shotgun.

Bay saw Jensen's blood-stained shirt move with even breaths. "No, more's the pity."

"But he . . ."

"He's out, but he's going to wake up in a minute. If you won't go by yourself, I'm getting you out of here. Where are your clothes, your underthings? Do you have a carpet bag?"

"In there." Mariah pointed toward her bedroom. "Mama took the only bag we had."

"Keep that shotgun on him."

A tiny chifforobe stood in one corner of the lean-to room. Bay stripped it, dumping the meager contents into the center of her bed. He flipped the corners of her quilt up and rolled the whole mess into a tight bedroll arrangement, then tucked the bundle under one arm and went back to the front room. Jensen twitched spasmodically, like a frog on a gig.

"The skillet." She pointed at the stove, where the first wisps of smoke rolled up off a cast iron skillet. "Take it off the stove. I don't want the house to burn down."

He complied, using the corner of her quilt for a potholder, then grabbed Mariah's coat and pitched it to her. "Get out there and get on my horse."

As she clambered onto the roan, he jammed the shotgun into the empty rifle scabbard on his saddle. What a damned fool he'd been, coming over unarmed. He tied the unwieldy roll of clothes on the back of his saddle, then took a moment to run Jensen's horse off before he swung up behind Mariah. From inside the house, a groan and the sound of a chair tipping over told him the giant was awake. For just an instant, Bay considered going back in to beat Jensen back into unconsciousness, but that would be for his own satisfaction. Right now, he needed Mariah to be safe.

"Let's get the hell out of here."

They were a good half mile down the road when she started to shake in after-reaction. Bay coaxed Cajun to a steady lope and wrapped his arms around her tighter.

"He was going to rape me," she whispered finally.

He'd known it, from the moment he'd put the presence of Jensen's horse together with the sound of her voice, ordering him out, but the words triggered Bay's fury in a new way. If he'd actually heard them earlier, he'd have killed Jensen in cold blood, no hesitation. As it was, he had to fight down the urge to turn Cajun around and go back to do the job.

She must have understood, because she tightened her grip on the arm he had around her waist. "You stopped him."

"*You* stopped him. I just beat him up after you were done. How did his arm get so hacked up?"

"I used the kitchen knife." She told the story, her voice gradually growing stronger. Bay forced himself to listen without exploding, keeping his mind on the fact that she was safe in his arms. That he could make sure she stayed safe.

They rode in silence for a long time after she finished, until finally she looked around. "You missed the turnoff to the house."

"We're not going to the ranch. We're going to town."

"But I—"

"Who are those people you and your folks stayed with on the Fourth?"

"Mr. and Mrs. Flowers."

"Will they take you in, even with the gossip?"

He could sense her blush, despite the dark. "Yes. They're good people. But I have animals to feed and—"

"Shhh. I know." He nuzzled beneath her hair to plant a kiss on the back of her neck, inhaling the scent as strands tangled around his face. "Always so practical. The animals will be taken care of, I promise." *And so will you.*

A few hours sleep, a good scrub, and a hearty breakfast at a table with other living, breathing people all went toward healing Mariah. She hadn't felt she needed healing until the process started. The tears caught her unawares; she hadn't known they were there, right under the surface. She'd been too preoccupied with getting to town, and how the Flowerses would react to the midnight intrusion, and why Bay insisted on riding off after he had her settled. Then suddenly she found herself alone in the comforting folds of one of Georgina's feather beds, with the tears streaming down her face.

Now she felt better, steady enough to face the world—or at least the congregation at church—though she still worried about Bay. She sat at the kitchen table, enjoying the warmth of the cookstove, waiting for him to come back.

"He said he'd be here by eight," Mr. Flowers said. It was past that now. "I, ahem, is he reliable, Mariah?"

She forced a smile and patted his gnarled hand. "In his own way, Mr. Flowers."

At half past, the knock finally came. Mrs. Flowers went to answer the door. The rumble of Bay's voice drifted down the hall as Mariah cleared her dishes from the table.

"Things took a little longer than I thought," Bay offered when he stepped into the kitchen a few minutes later. He was clad in what appeared to be a brand new tailor-made suit and a fresh white shirt complete with starched collar and silk cravat—and looked as easy in them as in his work clothes, despite the bruise on his cheek and the battered look of his hands. He turned down the cup of coffee Mr. Flowers offered. "I hate to be rude right off, but I need to talk to Mariah alone before we start to church."

"The front parlor's best for privacy," Mr. Flowers said.

Mariah accepted Bay's arm as far as the parlor, where he pulled the sliding door shut. "Who's milking Peach?"

"I sent a couple of my men over to take care of things."

A couple, Mariah thought, in case Nikolai was still there. "You went all the way back to the ranch?"

He nodded. "Where did you think I was headed?"

"I wasn't sure. I thought maybe . . ." Her voice trailed off and she had to start again. "I thought you went after Nikolai."

His face turned dusky under the tan. "Not until I get you taken care of."

"I was fine here. Not that I'm saying I want you to go after him, but I . . . You don't have to take care of me."

"There we disagree. I got you into this mess."

"You did no such thing, Bay McKenzie."

"I didn't leave you a lot of choice."

"You tried. You warned me off at every turn."

"And did everything I could to make you ignore the warnings."

"You pursued me," she admitted. "But when it got down to brass tacks, I came to your room, as you may recall."

"Recall?" Bay brought a hand up to cup her chin. "Christ, Mariah, I haven't been able to think of much else for the past week. I've never had such a gift in my whole life." He touched his lips to hers, and she felt the instant flare of his excitement. Her own flesh began to pulse deep within the places he had shown her with his touch that night. She slipped her arms around his neck as his hands began the familiar dance down her body, and for a heady moment, she wondered if he intended to take her right there on Georgina Flowers's Persian carpet— and if she had the wherewithal to stop him if he tried.

But he pulled away before that crucial border was crossed

and led her to a chair. Before she quite realized what was happening, he was on his knee, his hat in his hand.

"You gave me your self, your reputation, your security. I only know of one way to give any of that back to you. Marry me, Mariah."

Yes. The word teased Mariah's lips, threatening to leap forth even as she gaped at Bay in disbelief. "Whe . . . What?"

"Marry me," he repeated. "Today. Right now."

"You're crazy."

"That's what Eli said."

"You told him? Before you even thought to ask me?"

"No. I'd definitely thought about it when I told him." Bay raked at his hair with his fingers and settled his hat back on his head. His lips curved up in a wry smile as he hoisted himself back onto the settee at her side. "I told a bunch of other people, too, most of whom are over at the church right now, waiting for a wedding to happen. I guess it never occurred to me you'd say no."

"I didn't."

"Then you're saying yes?"

"No. I don't know what I'm saying. For pity's sake, Bay, give me a minute to think. You've had all night."

"Actually, since supper yesterday. I was coming down to ask you last night when . . ." He turned to stare out at the street, where people were heading for church. A muscle twitched beneath his clean-shaven jaw. "No one knows what happened last night except Mr. and Mrs. Flowers. I want you wearing my name before Jensen starts talking, so that any other man that assumes what he did will think twice. I want to marry you in front of the whole town, so they all know how I value what you gave to me. I even convinced the good reverend to marry us at the beginning of the regular service so we'd have the biggest crowd."

He turned back to her. "Mariah, I can't give you back your name, and God knows McKenzie isn't the one you'd choose for yourself. But it can protect you. I can protect you."

"In other words, you're going to rescue me again."

"Like I should have last week." He grinned. "The saints

preserve us both, I'm gong to do the right thing by you, Miss Hoag."

But are you going to stay? She desperately wanted to ask the question, but she was afraid of the answer, terrified that he'd lie and say yes, or tell her the truth and say no.

She squeezed her eyes shut. "I don't have a wedding dress."

"Is that a yes?"

She opened her eyes. Bay glowed. He looked smug, cocky beneath the bruises. That McKenzie smirk was big as ever. His gaze drenched her in the warmth of liquid silver. And where was love in all this? *The same place it was when you went to his bed, you fool, in your own heart.* Nowhere else. Nothing had changed.

"Yes."

He bounded off the settee and shoved the door open. "Mrs. Flowers! Did you find that dress?"

Her borrowed wedding gown had borne enough pins to start a dress shop; she'd had no bouquet; her best friend had to openly defy her father to stand up for her in front of a congregation who, by and large, believed she was going to burn in Hell; and the best man frowned all the way through the ceremony. She hadn't even been given away by her own father or brother—Mr. Flowers had performed the act in her father's name while Georgina shed her mother's tears in the front pew.

But far worse than any of that was the look in Bay's eyes as they rode back toward the ranch in his father's handsome rockaway carriage.

The smugness had disappeared during the ceremony, about the time he'd had to say "I do." Now he sat there beside her barely able to carry the threads of a decent conversation with Mrs. Shaw or her. He kept staring past Mariah out the carriage window, toward the west, and with every passing mile, her chest squeezed tighter around her heart.

They finally rolled under the McKenzie and Sons sign and up the hill to the house. The driver, the same young man Mariah remembered from the front porch the night the vigilantes had come, hopped down and pulled open the door.

Mrs. Shaw climbed out first. "I'll see to things inside. Welcome home, Mrs. McKenzie."

The driver echoed Mrs. Shaw's welcome as Bay helped Mariah down.

She smiled. "Thank you . . ."

"Gideon Willis, ma'am. Gid will do fine. I'll carry your things in."

"Thank you, Gid."

Bay escorted her to the veranda, where one by one, the other men came to introduce themselves. Some she recognized from the trouble they'd caused her family, some only from her past visits to the ranch. She tried to give them all the same warm greeting, all the while conscious of Bay's hand on her shoulder, and of his silence. He spoke once, to introduce the foreman, Pete Rolley. This time she couldn't stay silent.

"Mr. Rolley and I have met," Mariah said. "He used to drive your father's cattle through our fields for sport."

The foreman's cheeks darkened with his flush. "Sorry about that, ma'am. We were just following orders. I hope you won't hold it against us all."

"Whether she does or not, you'll follow her orders, now," Bay said.

"But she's a wom—Yes, sir. I'll make sure the men understand."

"Good. Is there anything I need to know about that won't wait until tomorrow morning?"

"No, sir. We're in good shape. You enjoy your . . . that is, congratulations to both of you." He stepped back with the other men, but instead of dispersing, they all stood around, looking at the porch expectantly.

"Mrs. McKenzie," Bay said softly.

Mariah looked up at this man, her lover, who was now her husband. His eyes were dark as slate, unreadable in the deep shadows of the porch. He turned her to face him, and his mouth came down to hers in a chaste kiss. The men chuckled, then broke into a cheer as he picked her up and carried her stiffly through the front door.

He kicked the door shut, then set her on her feet. Outside, the men drifted away, and the house grew silent except for the ticking of the clocks and the distant sounds of Mrs. Shaw in the kitchen. Mariah kept waiting for Bay to do something, to say something, anything, that would take away the horrible chunk of lead that was growing in her chest, filling her soul, but he just stood there, looking at her in the unblinking way he had stared out the window of the carriage, his hands rigid at his sides.

"You don't have to pretend," she said softly, striking the first blow. She took off her bonnet and hung it on the hat stand, and started unbuttoning her coat. "I mean, I know you wanted to convince your men and all, but I'm quite aware this isn't a real marriage."

"Not real," he echoed.

"You married me out of a sense of honor. I won't ask for any more than that. I won't ask any more of you than I did before."

"Where is this coming from?"

"You look . . ." Mariah hesitated over the word. *Trapped.* She hung her coat and changed her tack. "You barely said a word all the way here. I know you don't want to—"

"I didn't talk because I would have embarrassed us both to death."

"What? Why?"

"Shhh." His warm breath fanned over her face. "All I could think of were the things I want to do with you. The way you look with your hair tumbling around your bare breasts. How you tighten around me when I'm deep inside you."

A firestorm rushed through Mariah. The lead melted and pooled between her legs. She gasped. "Bay . . ."

"I didn't talk because it was all I could do to keep myself sane, to keep my hands under control. I looked down at you in the church while you were saying your vows, and I don't know, something broke. I swear to God, I could have had you right then and there, or in the carriage in front of Mrs. Shaw, and it wouldn't have mattered to me. It took everything I had to make it this far, and now I'm half afraid to touch you. Afraid I'll hurt you, scare you, from wanting you so much."

A deliciously carnal chuckle bubbled up in Mariah's throat, a release of all the festering doubt. She reached for the button at her collar and turned to walk away from him. "I will be upstairs."

She was at the head of the staircase, her waist half undone, when his footsteps came pounding up behind her. His grip was rough on her wrist as he dragged her into the bedroom. He pushed the door shut and propelled her back against it, his body hard and urgent, his hands scalding in their need and heat. His fingers tangled in her hair, holding her still for the plunder of his kisses. Hairpins tumbled to the floor in a jangling rainfall.

Craving the feel of flesh against flesh, Mariah reached for another button. Bay tore her hands away and pinned them over her head, holding them easily in one of his. The pose lifted her breasts and left her bodice gaping. He smiled down at her exposed bosom, a wolfish gleam in his eyes.

"That's one of the things I was thinking of. Taking you like this. Standing against a door somewhere with all your clothes on." With his free hand, he worked open the remaining buttons and spread the opening of her dress. Her camisole came down with one jerk, leaving her breasts bare above the edge of her corset. His head dipped and his mouth closed over one nipple. Mariah moaned and shut her eyes. He worked the peak with his tongue and lips, laving it, suckling, making it pucker and throb until she couldn't bare it and thrashed away from him. He tugged her back and turned his attentions to the other breast.

Her breath came in short rasps of pleasure. "Bay, please . . . I want . . ."

"What do you want?" he demanded. He flattened against her, his wool jacket and stiff shirt front painful pleasure against her swollen nipples. Still holding her pinioned, he worked a knee between her legs, lifting until she rode his thigh. "This?"

"Oh."

He dragged her skirts upward. "This?" He reached the hem of her skirt and slipped his hand beneath. His fingers found the open crotch of her drawers and brushed through the mat of curls. "This?"

She arched, grinding herself against his leg, as crazed with need as he professed to be. He flattened the palm of his hand along her belly and pressed her back, controlling her motions.

His long fingers slipped down, searching for a spot of pleasure, finding it, slipping past and inside her. "This?"

A shudder racked Mariah's body and she felt the pool of lead, now white hot within her, stir and flood over his fingers.

"Ahh. This," he said. He moved his fingers back and forth, each stroke taking him deeper, taking her closer to the edge. She knew what lay over the precipice now, knew and wanted to fall.

Her spine tightened unbearably with the need. She stepped into space. The spasm started low and exploded outward, engulfing her in waves of heat and vertigo, making her body pulse with the effort of flying until she spiralled down and landed, breathless, against Bay's chest.

He released her wrists as the last shudders rippled through her. His kisses feathered over her eyelids. "Look at me, Mariah-goddess."

She did, and felt him move his hand away from her. She thought he was going to enter her, and she let her hands slip to the waist of his trousers, ready to free him and help him to the same unspeakable pleasure.

"No," he said. "Not yet. Not until I do that to you again. A different way."

"I can't stand it again."

"Yes, you can." He brought his hand up, still slick with her moisture, and holding her eyes, very deliberately sucked his fingers clean. "You taste good."

The firestorm struck her again. She hadn't know a man would do such a thing, hadn't imagined it was possible, but she understood immediately what he meant to do. And she wanted it, oh, God, she wanted it. She moaned, a low animal noise that reverberated deep in her belly.

Bay nodded, a knowing smile curving his mouth. He kissed her, sweeping her mouth with his tongue. She tasted herself on him, salty and exotic, and began to tremble.

"You're going to like this as much as I do," he promised.

He stepped away from her, backing to the center of the rug, and beckoned her forward. All the urgency seemed to have gone out of him and lodged in her, making her legs wobble as she walked to him.

He removed his coat and tossed it toward the chair. It missed and slithered to the floor. He pushed down his suspenders, then reached for his cravat. It wouldn't come. He fumbled with the knot, the only sign that he might still be aching like she was. He finally tore it and his collar away.

"Help me with my shirt."

She obeyed as if in a daze, working open his buttons, feeling herself waver like the horizon in a summer heat wave. He peeled the sweat-damp linen over his head and flipped it away, then kicked off his boots. She reached for his fly once again. He caught her hands and put them at her sides.

"Now you."

He knelt and unbuttoned her right shoe, then reached up under her skirts to peel down her stocking. He worked slowly, drawing out the project to its nerve-twanging limit. Her trembles grew to shaking, then to wracking shudders. She had to steady herself with a hand on his head. He repeated the operation on her left shoe and stocking, then rose and started to work on her dress. Slowly, so slowly.

"It was faster when I did it," she said between gritted teeth.

"Why didn't you say you were in a hurry?" Bay yanked. She heard a button pop, and her dress dropped away. His hands glided around her back. Seconds later, her corset fell loose to her hips. He stripped it and her shimmy and drawers away with one long push.

He stood back, looking at her. His face grew taut with desire. "You're even more beautiful in daylight."

"Bay." Her voice was a rising plea for relief.

"I could do it right here, with you standing up. No. I don't think you would last." He spoke as if to himself, though she knew every word was designed to excite her. It worked. She could see herself, him kneeling before her. She could feel him kissing her . . . *there*. She swayed with need, and he smiled. "The chair? That would be good, but I have something else in mind for that. A couple of things, in fact."

Her imagination failed utterly. "The bed," she whispered.

"Ah, yes. The bed." He stepped closer. His hands splayed across her bare hips, pulled her to him. She could feel the play of hair across her nipples, and his hardness against her belly.

He kneaded her bottom, stirring new sensations between her legs. "Do you want to lie down with me, beautiful lady?"

"Oh, yes, Bay. Now."

He scooped her up and lay her down on the coverlet, then stretched out beside her. She moved to him, her touch anxious, searching, arousing. She needed him on top of her to anchor her to the ground. She grabbed at his waistband and pulled him closer.

Again, he pushed her hands away. He propped himself on one elbow, looking down at her. "If you do that, I will never get to what I promised you."

"It's all right," she vowed. "It can wait until next time."

"Maybe 'it' can, but I can't. I've been thinking about this all day. All week. That's half the reason I'm so crazy with wanting you. I want you to let me do this for you, Mariah."

"Then let me touch you. I need to."

"I'll explode. I only look like I'm in control of myself." He found her hand and placed a kiss in her palm, then guided her fingers to the edge of the cherry wood headboard. "If you want to hold something, grab this. Understand?"

She nodded, then closed her eyes and waited.

"Besides," he whispered, very close to her ear. "I already have plans for the next time."

His teeth closed on her earlobe. Mariah flinched. He tongued the spot just below. She shivered. He found her mouth and drew her lower lip between his teeth, and she moaned softly. He moved down her body taking lush, open-mouthed samples of every part of her, adopting the rhythm he'd used undressing her: slow, torturously so, and the more she responded to his gentle assault, the more drawn out it became.

By the time he dipped his tongue into her navel, she was sweating and tense with anticipation. She tried to take his head, to steer him lower, but he shifted away. She heard him strip off his trousers, then he knelt between her legs. His hands slipped between her thighs, massaging her, opening her.

At the last minute, she lost courage. She tried to close her legs, to protect herself. But he was there, blocking her. He pushed her legs farther apart, opening her even more.

His low chuckle stirred air across her belly and down, over

moist, sensitive flesh. Bay followed it's the path, nuzzling the curls between her legs before his tongue swirled across her and found the sweetest spot.

So sweet, it was almost painful. She scrabbled against the mattress, trying to escape the wicked invasion. At the same time her heels dug in, lifting her to him and the deliciousness that was his mouth. She heard her own cries, guttural, primal, as the tension built inside her. Her limbs seemed to move of their own accord, thrashing, flinging her about. She felt her muscles tighten, and she thought how much she loved him and called his name.

And then he was moving over her, into her, driving himself deep in a single, long thrust that sent her careening into her release. Her body clenched, and she felt him buck and stiffen above her. She grasped at him, finally, pulling him into her, letting her hands dance over his skin the way his did on hers. He buried his face in her shoulder. His hoarse shouts tangled in her hair. His body throbbed within hers, warm, wet, heavy, releasing him.

Oh, God, please let him stay. She wrapped her arms around him and held him as tightly as her strength would allow.

Slowly, Bay relaxed, settling into her, bearing his weight on his elbows. He moved his hips in a tight circle, forcing one last pulse of pleasure, a final gasp from her lips. His laughter hummed against her throat.

"You're my wife, Mariah. My *wife*. It is real."

Bay padded downstairs barefoot, an unfamiliar thing. He registered the textures of the rugs and bare oak floors, acutely aware of them for the first time, his senses honed to a razor edge by Mariah and her loving.

She loved him. She'd called it out in the middle of passion, along with his name. He wasn't sure if she'd known what she was saying, if she remembered saying it. But he remembered hearing the words, just as he remembered the powerful need that they bred, to be inside her. He'd spilled at the first stroke, as though he'd been a raw kid with a woman for the first time, but it had been enough, because of those words on her lips.

The study door stood open. He went in and ratted around on

the big desk until he found what he wanted leaning against the inkwell. He stuffed the paper into his shirt pocket.

He wandered through the dining room, past two carefully laid place settings of the best china and crystal, and into the kitchen. Mrs. Shaw was up to her elbows in bread dough.

"I wasn't sure if you'd be up this early," she said.

He pinched a morsel of dough away and popped it into his mouth. It dissolved, yeasty, on his tongue. "We're not, but we're starving."

"I'll have breakfast to you on a tray in fifteen minutes. Just let me put this to rise."

No raised eyebrows. Bay got the urge to test her. "Just knock and set it outside the door. And if we're not down by one o'clock, bring dinner up, too."

"Yes, sir."

Bay stood for a moment, watching her lift the dough into a crockery bowl and pat it into a tidy mound. As she flipped a clean tea towel over the bowl, her square hands shone with the lard she'd rubbed on to keep the dough from sticking.

He reached into his pocket and pulled out the creased sheet of blue paper, his name on one of the outside folds. He propped Mrs. Shaw's notice of resignation up tent style, just at the edge of the circle of flour.

Without a word, she wiped her hands on her apron and picked up the note. The stove was only a few steps away. She grabbed the lid handle, pried the front burner lid off, dropped the paper in, and turned back to him.

"Do you think Mrs. McKenzie would like some marmalade with her biscuits?"

"It is real," he had said. And yet it seemed so unreal to Mariah at times, like when she awoke on the third morning of her marriage and he was gone and she had no idea when he'd left.

She sat bolt upright at that first realization, her heart thundering in her ears. Every instinct screamed out that she had to find him, had to keep him from leaving. She curled her fingers into the coverlet and forced herself to sit, to breathe, and to think.

That last was the hardest, but eventually reason came back. Bay wasn't gone, not really. Something on the ranch had pulled him out of bed early, that's all. He hadn't wanted to wake her. Mariah told herself that, over and over, until she finally believed it, then she rose and dressed. She raked through her tangled hair and pulled it back in a braid that started to fray before she even got the end tied.

She intended to go straight to breakfast, but at the foot of the stairs, the front door beckoned. She went out on the porch and scanned the yard, looking, though she wouldn't have admitted it aloud, for Bay.

The dull, coppery disk of the sun gleamed through a thick autumn haze that lay over the hills. The crew's chores and breakfast might be over, but the day's real work had clearly just begun. A few men were saddling their horses in the corral; others huddled in the chill, jackets buttoned and collars turned up, listening to instructions from the foreman. Bay was with neither group. Mariah gathered her shawl tighter and continued to search for her husband, scanning beyond the yard and stock pens.

Finally, a pair of specks on a hill far to the south caught her eye, so far that if it had been another man, she might not have known who it was. But Bay, she recognized, and Eli, she assumed from a gleam of red hair. She stared hard, until she was sure her eyes weren't playing tricks: They were riding back. The tension oozed out of her shoulders.

When they got closer to the house, Bay spotted her and waved, and she saw the flash of white teeth in his tan face. He said something to Eli, then galloped Cajun ahead.

Moments later, he held a chair for her, then took the one at the head of the dining table. Mrs. Shaw entered with a tray containing two heaping plates of fried eggs and cottage fries, a platter of cinnamon buns, and a stack of newspapers that she laid at Bay's elbow before she went back to the kitchen.

Bay dug into his food with gusto. "I'm starved. Mrs. Shaw wasn't up when we left."

Where were you? "I would have cooked your breakfast," she said instead. "All you had to do was wake me."

"After last night?" Bay asked with a suggestive lift to his

eyebrow. "Anyway, we left too early. Even Eli wasn't too happy when I hauled him out of bed." His manner was so relaxed that Mariah let it go. He'd gone for a ride, that was all.

He cleared his plate before she was half finished and turned to the papers, spreading one out on the table before him. Mariah watched him as she ate, enjoying the play of emotions over his face as he read each article.

"Anything worth knowing?" Mariah asked.

"Someone else pontificating about herd law, as if we need to worry about that right now." He turned back to the front page. "Another carload of relief supplies came in."

"I hope it was more than clothes and cornmeal this time." She took a final bite of cinnamon bun and chewed it slowly. "Bay, we've got to do something about the farm."

Bay folded the newspaper in quarters and laid it aside. "Yep. Rolley needs those men back at work. I told him to bring your stock up here for now. Clyde and the chickens, too."

"Thank you, but I'm just as worried about the crop. People are starting to go hungry. There are forty acres of millet down there that someone could harvest and eat."

"Do you want to find a tenant?"

"I've thought about that, but when Mama and Papa come back next spring, they—"

"Mariah . . ."

"I know. You don't think they will, and down deep, I'm not sure I think so either." Mariah sighed. "But if they do, I want the place ready for them. And I don't want to have to put someone off if they do come back. I'm thinking we can find someone to harvest in exchange for half the grain. The rest could go to the Relief."

"Do you think there's enough to make it worthwhile?"

"Unless something's happened since Saturday, it's a fair crop."

"All right, then. Draft a notice, and we'll list it in a couple of the papers."

"Meantime, I want to start riding down every morning to take care of the garden."

Bay lifted one eyebrow doubtfully. He reached for Mariah

and pulled her into his lap. "Tired of lazing in our bed already?"

Just then, Mrs. Shaw came out of the kitchen. Mariah reddened to her toenails, but the woman didn't seem to notice, even though she must have heard. "I happened to glance up and see a rider coming up the hill," Mrs. Shaw said. "I'll go answer the door."

She had barely reached the hall when a door slammed.

Mrs. Shaw said firmly and very loudly. "You stay right there, young man." Footsteps pounded down the hall.

Bay shot to his feet, nearly dumping Mariah in the process. His hand went automatically to his sidearm and he headed for the hall, calling over his shoulder, "Stay back."

Before Bay reached the door, Jimmy pushed past Mrs. Shaw in a jangle of spurs and a cloud of dust. Bay relaxed.

So did Mariah. "Hi, Jimmy."

Her brother looked from her to Bay, then swung without warning. "You son of a bitch."

Chapter Seventeen

∞

Mariah saw Bay's arm go back, saw one instant of hesitation, and then he blasted Jimmy. Her brother's head snapped back and he stumbled against the door frame.

"Stop it! Both of you." She ran between the two of them and grabbed Jimmy's arm before he could get his feet under him. His eyes blazed, full of pain and hatred.

"You dumb kid," Bay hollered. "I ought to knock the living daylights out of you."

"You just did," Mariah snapped back. "What were you thinking? He's just a boy."

"I am not," Jimmy yelled. He pulled up the corner of his kerchief and blotted at his split lip.

"Should I call for help, sir?" Mrs. Shaw asked.

Bay shook his head. "We're fine. Thanks for the warning, Mrs. Shaw. I was just a little slow reacting."

She nodded and went off toward the kitchen.

Mariah faced off with her brother. "James Frances Hoag, what did you think you were doing?"

He glared at Mariah, and she could feel his disgust, all directed at her. "Me? I ride home to see if you need me, and those fellows squatting on our farm tell me you've moved up here to be with him. Christ, Mariah. If you've got to whore for someone, why a McKenzie?"

Bay yanked Mariah aside and stuck his face right in Jimmy's. "Apologize to your sister. Right now, or I swear, it won't matter to me if you are family. I'll beat your brains in."

"Bay!"

"You're no kin to me," Jimmy growled. He clenched and

unclenched his fists, as if he were warming up to punch again.

"He is, too." Mariah wedged back between them. "We're married, Jimmy. Married. Husband and wife." She repeated herself until reluctant understanding dawned in her brother's eyes.

"He . . . you?" Jimmy stuttered over whatever he was trying to say. He shook his head. "Aw, shit." He turned and stalked toward the front door.

"Jimmy!"

"Get back here," Bay ordered.

"For heaven's sake, leave him alone." Mariah ran after her brother. She caught up with him on the front porch and touched his arm.

He shrugged her off as if she had leprosy, but he stopped.

"What is the matter with you? The man married me."

He gave her a sideways look. "When?"

"Sunday."

"About a week too late, don't you think?" He flashed a sour grin at Mariah's sharp intake of breath. "Yes, sister dear. I heard. From Shorty last night. And he heard it from some fellow I don't even know. Do you know what it was like, hearing from strangers that my sister had slept with that bastard and then announced it to half the town?"

Mariah turned away, her hand to her mouth. Tears scalded her throat. "No wonder when you heard I was up here . . . I'm sorry, Jimmy. You must have been mortified."

"*You* are the one that should have been mortified. You should be now, married to that thieving McKenzie."

"He's not a thief." She whirled on her brother, the accusation against Bay overriding her own embarrassment. "He's not. That's the point. That's why I had to come forward when those men showed up here, even if it meant confessing in public."

"And I suppose he told you how grateful he was," Jimmy sneered. "Why did it take him a week to get around to marrying you?"

"He had to go away for a few days."

"I'll bet. Do you know where he went?"

"No. He had business, that's all."

"He was . . ." Jimmy glanced around and frowned. Bay's

men were watching, as they had been since Mariah had come out on the porch behind her brother. "Come on. There's something you need to know." He took her by the arm and led her off the porch and down around the house out of the crew's sight.

She dug in her heels when Jimmy tried to drag her behind a bare lilac bush. "Stop it. Just say what you have to say."

"I don't want anybody hearing. No telling what he'd do, to me or you, if he knew."

"That's nonsense. Bay wouldn't hurt me, or you either, if you'd just show some sense and behave—"

"We saw him down in Wichita last week," Jimmy blurted, cutting her off.

"We who?"

"Otis and I, and some other fellows. We had to go down ourselves, and there he was."

"So. Bay's business must have been down there."

"It's not even so much where he was as who he was with." Jimmy was practically gloating, but he took another quick look around, and dropped his voice low. "McKenzie and Hightower had their heads together with these two drovers from Texas, real serious-like. I ducked out of sight before they saw me, but I asked Otis to slip up behind them and listen in. They were doing a little horse trading."

A little horse trading: Bay had used those exact words himself, that first day. For just an instant, Nikolai's list of the thefts and dates danced in front of Mariah's eyes. She shunted it aside. "For Pete's sake, this ranch raises horses."

"Blood stock, mostly. Not the kind of animals they were talking about."

"How do you know?"

"Otis said the Texans mentioned twenty or thirty head. Nobody buys that much blood stock at one time, much less to trail back through the Indian Territories to be cow ponies."

"Bay's probably planning to sell off some of his working stock. He's cutting the crew back now that round-up is done."

Jimmy went florid. "You won't listen to me. You never would listen to anyone about him. And now look. People are talking about you for fifty miles around."

"The talk will fade. Jimmy, I'm sorry you had to find out what happened that way, instead of me telling you, but you've got to remember that everything I did, I chose for myself. Bay is my husband now, part of the family. Family members support each other."

"I said it once already, he's no kin of mine." He released her and started toward his horse. "Not after what his father did to us. Not after what he's made of you."

Mariah followed, knowing there was little she could do until he calmed down. "Come back tomorrow. I'll ride out with you. We'll talk all this through."

"Not while you're living under his roof. I won't come around this house again, Mariah. When you come to your senses and leave him, let me know." He mounted up and sat there, looking at her, his expression flat and angry. "Don't wait too long, though. As soon as I get my stake together, I'm heading for Colorado."

She made herself watch him ride down the hill and out the gate. He turned north.

One of her drifters gone. *Oh, please, let the other one stay.*

Bay sucked at the fresh split on his knuckle and watched his wife staring after her brother with hurt-filled eyes.

He felt like hell.

Using his fists to defend the McKenzie honor got old fast. He'd done it too many times as a kid, whenever one of the other boys had pointed out his father's sins.

Now he was at it again, and while the honor of the woman outside represented a higher cause, he still didn't like it. Not that hitting a man didn't feel good at the time, especially drilling Jensen. Bay flexed his fist and felt the satisfaction ripple through him. That one, he'd do again in a heartbeat. More thoroughly.

Hitting Mariah's little brother had been a simple reaction to being attacked. The kid had had the right, maybe even an obligation, believing what he did, and Bay had simply stopped him. He wished he hadn't, for Mariah's sake—but then again, he didn't much appreciate the tales Jimmy was carrying home from Wichita.

He'd thought he'd learned better ways to handle his pride: He hadn't been in more than three or four brawls since he'd gotten out of the Army. Yet here he was, two in less than a week, with one other narrowly avoided. They might be justified, they might be his own damned fault, putting Mariah in the situation he had, but they still brought up the shame of the old days. They reminded him he was back in his father's territory, on his father's land.

Face it, McKenzie, you're right back where you started, just like Eli said. Same name, same place, same bad habits.

Mariah finally turned and started into the house. Her eyes met his and he caught the glint of tears before she swiped them away with her fingertips. He met her on the porch and put an arm around her slender waist.

"He loves you," he said.

"I know. He's just trying to protect me." She let her head rest on his shoulder. "He's probably headed off to talk to Nikolai. I didn't have a chance to tell him what happened. I hope they don't get each other riled up."

"They won't. I rode over to the quarry yesterday afternoon. Jensen's gone."

Mariah stared up at him. Her eyes got round. "Bay, you didn't . . ."

"I didn't, though not for lack of intention. He left town on his own. Just packed up his gear and rode off Sunday morning without even quitting."

"He was probably embarrassed when he sobered up."

"Crap. He wasn't that drunk. He's a coward, that's all. That's why he attacked you instead of me in the first place." At the thought, Bay's knuckles tingled again. "At any rate, he's gone, and without telling anyone what he tried. If the Flowerses keep it to themselves, at least you won't have that talk to deal with."

He gave her a squeeze. "And in the interest of your reputation, I think it's time we took a ride over to Bazaar. Let the neighbors know what a lovely bride I managed to corral."

She straightened and brushed herself off, and once more he marvelled at the way she put things behind her. "Thank you, sir. And on the way, we can stop down at the house and I can see what kind of farmers your cowboys have been."

* * *

Over the next weeks Bay turned Mariah's life inside-out a dozen new ways, not the least of which was the discovery of a previously untapped lazy streak. With the millet contracted out and a score of ranch hands taking care of her animals at the ranch, it didn't much matter when she got up. She could give herself over to Bay and his loving all night and sleep half the day if she wanted, which seemed to suit them both just fine.

He was usually up and around, often out riding, when she awoke. Her only pressing duty was the garden, and that would end soon. They'd had a light frost the second week of October, but now they were having a streak of Indian Summer and she was coaxing every last day's growth out of the season. When the next cold snap came, she'd harvest everything and haul it up for Mrs. Shaw and the crew cook to put by in the spring house. By February, even the ranch's relative bounty would stand a little stretching with fresh vegetables.

One morning, Bay leaned in the doorway, watching her brush her hair.

"How much longer is that going to take?" he asked.

"I'm not sure." Mariah tugged until her scalp smarted. She had to blink back a tear. "I've never had such awful tangles in my life."

"And all in the back, too. I wonder how that keeps happening," Bay asked in mock innocence. He reached for the brush. "Maybe I should help."

"You'd just put more in, which is exactly the problem. Go on downstairs and have your breakfast. I'll work better without you making cow eyes at me."

Bay laughed. "I do not make cow eyes, and I had breakfast hours ago. I'll tell Mrs. Shaw you'll be another ten minutes. After that, I come haul you down, tangles and all. It's almost noon. I don't want you getting bony from lack of food."

"Piffle." Mariah shot her husband a frown that turned into a smile as the door closed behind him. It was only just past eight: She'd heard the clock chime. Besides, if he didn't keep her up till all hours of the night, tossing her head against the pillows until her hair matted, she'd be up at dawn.

Finally, with a ripping sound and a sacrifice of a small wig's worth of hair, the rat's nest at the nape of her neck unravelled. Mariah disposed of the knot and brushed till her hair shone, then left her wayward curls to manage on their own. She'd tried again of late to corral her hair into the sedate, contained styles a married woman was supposed to wear, but a wedding hadn't changed her hair any more than it had changed Bay.

When she reached the dining room, he was finishing his coffee and one of the multitude of newspapers for which he carried subscriptions: Kansas City, Denver, all three Chase County papers, including the brand new *Courant* and the occasional *Scalping Knife*, and one from New York that came in fat bundles, apparently every month or so. He read two or three every morning, which pleased Mariah to no end. She liked watching him. It gave her time to study his face unobserved, to memorize every line and fleeting expression, so that she'd have them in her heart when he left.

He caught her watching him today, and gave her a wink. "Any plans for what's left of the day?"

"Nothing special. Just the garden. I'm going to take Clyde along. He's been moping around the past few days."

"That's a show he puts on for you. I caught him chasing rocks for Gid Willis. He was having a good old time."

"He misses Jimmy. So do I."

"I know, sweet. If you want me to try and get Jimmy back up here to talk to you . . ." He let it drop when she shook her head. "Anyway, I'd like to start showing you the accounts this afternoon. Everything's pretty much in order now that fall branding's done, so it's a good time for you to get an idea of how this outfit runs."

Most of the men she knew of didn't let their wives into anything beyond the household accounts. This was the closest Bay had come since the wedding to saying he'd be leaving, and despite her supposed resignation to the fact, Mariah's stomach churned violently, threatening to relieve her of her breakfast. She looked him in the eye and nodded. "I think that's a good idea. Keeping the books will give me something to do once we close up the farm."

So after she got back from her chores at the farm, she

cleaned up and appeared in the study, ready, if not happy, to plow through the fat ledgers.

Only one problem: her tutor wasn't there. When asked, Mrs. Shaw said he and Eli had headed out just after lunch, but neither she nor the foreman had any idea where they'd gone or when they'd be back.

"I think they just got an urge to ride for a while, ma'am," Rolley said. "If there's anything I can take care of for you . . ."

"No, thank you."

Clyde followed her back to the porch, and they waited.

An hour later, when Bay still hadn't returned, Mariah shooed the dog off and returned to the study. He had clearly planned to honor his promise: The ledgers were out and a neatly tied portfolio of legal documents sat on top. She untied it, pulled out the top document, and sat down. For an instant she thought her eyes had crossed, and then she realized the problem was language, not vision.

The papers were in Latin, or at least enough to confuse things, mixed into some of the most convoluted excuses for sentences she'd ever seen. She put the document away, retied the portfolio, and set the bundle aside. This would have to wait for Bay.

But ciphering, she understood. She opened the top ledger and found the place where Jack McKenzie's miserly precision shifted to Bay's bolder slashes, then went back to the first of the year.

The books were a tribute to clear accountancy, at least to Mariah's unpracticed eye. She could actually make out what money had come in, and where it had gone, and why. Given enough time, she could understand this ranch's fortunes for as many years as they had ledgers. She could even learn to keep the books herself.

Mariah flipped to the present month. A sheet of paper was tucked into the binding. She started to lay it aside, then noticed the writing on the back. *B. McKenzie, Room 23*. She turned it over.

It was a letter, written on stationery from the drover's hotel in Wichita, and dated for a few days after the committee had ridden out here with their ropes. The writer, a Fred Linden or Lindner, she couldn't make out the signature, said he had found the buyer Bay was interested in. *Meet me at the Red Dog for a drink this evening and we will work out the details.*

The words in the letter stood out: *We will work out the details.* They sounded more like those of a black marketeer than an honest and aboveboard trader.

Jimmy and Otis had seen Bay at a saloon, talking to a couple of drovers from Texas about horses. Stolen horses, Jimmy said.

Why hadn't Bay mentioned he'd been in Wichita?

Mariah stuffed the paper back into the ledger and slammed the book shut. This was just the kind of jumping to conclusions for which she faulted Jimmy and Nikolai. If Bay was in Wichita that week, it was to sell his own stock. And if he hadn't mentioned that he'd been in Wichita, well, he'd come home to that mess with Nikolai and the wedding, and by the time things settled down, the trip hadn't seemed any more important to him than it had to her. After all, she'd never asked him about it.

That's all there was to it.

She believed her reasoning, too, until later, after Bay came in and they started to go over the books together. When he opened the ledger and saw the paper, he frowned.

"You know what?" He flipped the cover closed again. "We should look at the deeds and all the legal folderol first. This part will seem simple afterward."

By the next morning, when they finally got back to the ledger, the note had disappeared.

Bay moved around the room quietly, slipping into his long johns and the heavy clothing it took to stay warm in the middle of a late October night.

Damn, he hated this sneaking around, but there was no way Mariah would understand.

He looked at his wife lying bunched under the covers. The room was chill and dark. The quilts and blankets added for fall obscured the curves he had grown used to holding, but the sight of her still filled him with a sharp need to crawl back in bed and wake her.

Just a couple more of these crazy expeditions. Then it would be over, and he could talk to her, explain himself. And maybe, just maybe, they could work out the kind of life he wanted to have with her.

If she could forgive him.

If he didn't get himself killed first.

Now that the first crack had appeared, it seemed to Mariah the whole edifice had been ready to crumble all along. First the note, then the realization that Bay was leaving their bed, not just before dawn as she'd believed, but as soon as he thought she was asleep. She lay there, making herself take even breaths, and listened as he dressed and walked out. The sound of Eli's hushed footsteps on the hall runner was louder than any sound Bay had made.

How do you sneak up so quietly?

All us horse thieves can do it. They teach us in school.

When time had passed and she was sure the two of them had ridden off, she lit a candle, found a warm wrapper, and headed downstairs. Her stomach roiled and lurched, and she had to rest on the stairs for a few minutes until the nausea passed.

Mrs. Shaw kept Bay's old newspapers in a basket next to the back door, where they could be used to start the fire or cut into squares for use in the privies. When her stomach settled, Mariah carried her candle into the kitchen and scrounged through the basket for back copies of the *Leader*, which she hauled into the study. She quickly lit a lamp and spread the papers out in order.

A few minutes later, she sagged back in the chair. The dates were damning, a continuation of the pattern Nikolai had noted during the summer. No, it was worse. Not only had the thefts stopped completely during the week after the vigilante raid—the time period Bay had been in Wichita—the robberies afterward started up again the day she had first awakened to find him gone.

If she'd really been asleep tonight, he could easily have gotten out without waking her. How many other nights had he done so? How many of the times he'd claimed to have gone for a morning ride had he actually been out all night?

The night the vigilantes had come, she'd awakened to find

him gone and the men riding into the yard. She had assumed Bay had just left the bed.

Now she wasn't sure. She wondered if he'd let her stand there, in front of men she'd known half of her life, and speak her sins as truth when they were really a lie.

Maybe it was all a lie.

Mariah blew out the lamp. The candle's solitary flame flickered, throwing shadows against the wall, as bizarre and elusive as the truth in all this.

With sudden clarity she knew she had to get out of this house before Bay came home, to sort things out in her own mind before she faced him and asked the questions she needed to ask.

She hurried upstairs to dress, but carried her shoes until she slipped out the front door. Clyde shook himself out and came over to nuzzle her elbow as she sat on the bottom step to button them up.

Moving quietly so as to avoid questions from the night watch, Mariah went to the barn. The sorrel nickered to her from the stall nearest the door on the left. Across the aisle, the two empty stalls for Cajun and Eli's horse simply confirmed her need to leave. She worked in the clear light of the full moon to saddle her mount, then led the sorrel out into the night and up the hill between the outbuildings and trees, sticking to a path that kept her out of sight of the man at the front gate. Not until she was out in the whispering dry grass, where she could no longer see any trace of the ranch complex did she climb onto the sorrel's back.

A cluster of cattle across the gully stirred and trotted away. She looked down at the dog with his dangling tongue and perked ears.

"Come on, boy. Let's get out of here."

Home.

The coal oil lantern in the middle of the table blazed its brightest, Mariah's effort to chase away the sadness that hung around her shoulders like a tattered shawl.

The house was nearly bare. Any furnishings the mice might shred for nests had long been moved up to the ranch for safekeeping, but the wooden items, like table and chairs, the old china cabinet, and the stripped bedsteads, still stood in their places. She'd also left enough supplies in tins on the shelf to put together a simple meal when she came to garden. When the stove warmed up enough to heat the kettle, she'd go pump water and fix herself some tea.

For now, though, she jut wanted to think. That's why she'd come here, out of some sense that the land that had provided the center of her life for so many years could help her find that center once again. She had hoped a long ride would clear her head, but Clyde had acted oddly the whole way, stopping intermittently, ears forward, to listen to something only he could detect. His behavior hadn't especially frightened Mariah, but it had kept her alert when she'd wanted to let her mind drift. So she had kept riding until she'd come home.

Now, of course, Clyde seemed fine. He lay stretched out in front of the door, his chin on his paws. With a sigh, she stared at the flickering orange flames visible around the burner lids.

Mariah huddled deeper into her coat. She didn't want it to be true. She didn't want to hear Bay tell her she'd worked it all out correctly, to see the guilt in his eyes. If that's what she had to face tomorrow, she'd rather he just keep riding tonight. Head west. Never come back, not even to say good-bye.

Clyde popped to his feet and started pacing back and forth in front of the door, head cocked and eyes alert. He whined twice

"What is it, fella?"

He barked and pawed at the door. Frowning, Mariah opened it. Clyde roared outside, sounding full alarm. With the door open, Mariah could hear the approaching drum of horses. She reached for the shotgun by the door out of habit.

Her hand closed on empty air. The shotgun was up at the ranch, on a rack with a dozen finer pieces. She'd been stupid coming off by herself at night without a gun. She latched the door and fetched the poker.

Half a dozen horses ripped through the front gate. Outside Clyde stationed himself in the middle of the yard and barked furiously into the night.

"Shut that damned dog up or I'll shoot him," a man growled

A low call and a whistle silenced the dog. After a pause, Jimmy shouted, "Who's in there?"

Mariah sagged against the door in relief. "Me, Jimmy." She flipped the latch up and raised her voice to be heard outside. "It's just me. Mariah."

Jimmy and Otis burst through the door.

"Shit," Jimmy said.

Otis pushed on past Mariah. He was carrying a set of saddlebags, and he began stripping the last of the food from the kitchen shelves and stuffing it in the pouches.

"Stop that." Mariah started after Otis but Jimmy grabbed her.

"What are you doing down here at this time of night? Did you leave him?"

"Of course not," she said with more certainty than she felt. "I felt like a ride. Why is he taking our food?"

"We need it. We're headed out."

Mariah took a closer look at her brother. A sheen of sweat covered his pale face. "What's going on?"

"We're just in a hurry, that's all."

"Real big hurry, thanks to your brother there," Otis added. He stuffed a final tin into the saddle bags, fastened the buckle, and slung the bulky load over his shoulder.

"Jimmy?" Mariah backed away from her brother. The position gave her a better view out the door, and she made out Shorty, sitting on his horse. A half dozen riderless mounts, each on a makeshift rope hackamore and a long lead, stood steaming and stamping behind him. She recognized Gabriel Lee's prize mare, and felt her world crumble.

"Oh, God, Jimmy. Dear God, it's you. It's been you all along."

Chapter Eighteen

"I SURE DO wish you hadn't figured that out, miss, I mean ma'am," Otis said. "But I reckon you were bound to. You're going to have to come with us now."

Jimmy whirled. "No."

Otis's pistol appeared almost magically in his hand. He leveled it at Jimmy. "You're a downright disappointment tonight, boy."

Mariah recognized the fear that gleamed in Otis's dark eyes, the kind of fear that left him just a shade more rational than a trapped rat. He'd kill either one or both of them without compunction, and she was scared, more scared than she had been since the war.

She forced herself to meet Otis's gaze. "You don't want to take me with you. Bay will chase you down."

"I kinda figure he'll already be after us," Otis said, rubbing at his chin. "That is, if he manages to convince the sheriff it wasn't him out there tonight. Might be harder without you to say you was in bed with him. Anyway, the way I see it, McKenzie's likely to hold back a little, knowing his wife's with us. Maybe he'll even think you're part of the gang. What do you think, Jimmy? Wouldn't that put a twist in his drawers?"

A smile flickered at the corners of Jimmy's eyes, and Mariah knew she'd lost him, even though he frowned again and said the expected words. "Hell, Otis. She's my sister. Let her be."

"Can't do that. She's the best card we got right now and I always hold my best card." Otis waved his pistol toward the door. "That pony of hers is too slow. Go on and grab her saddle and throw in on that black mare so we have a mount for her later. For now, ma'am, you ride behind me, until I see for sure Jimmy-boy's got his nerve back."

Off in the distance, a dog barked.

Something about the sound bothered Bay, but he couldn't put his finger on it.

"They're running toward your land, McKenzie," Creelor said with satisfaction.

"It's west of here," the sheriff said. "That's the direction I'd run, if I knew someone was out to hang me. If it isn't clear to you we're not chasing Bay, here, anymore, maybe you'd better go on home."

Creelor grumbled, but kept his place in the posse. They pounded on up the hill. Fortunately, this pasture hadn't been grazed since the hoppers, and the men they were chasing were riding hard and carelessly: The trail of beaten down grass stood out like a macadam road, even in the moonlight.

From the top of the hill, the barking was clearer yet, but on a night like this, with the air so crisp, sounds might travel miles. Bay craned to hear over the horses. Down below, he could see the roof of the Hoag barn on the other side of the creek. The trail ran right to the farm.

"Clyde," he said abruptly. "Eli, is that Clyde?"

"Sounds like him," Eli said. "But why would he be down here?"

Bay refused to ask himself the same question as he raced ahead of the others. From the way the road was torn up, the gang must have turned into the farm. Bay swept the area, saw the empty yard and the swath of trampled grass that picked up again on the other side of the gate, and decided they were gone.

The front door of the house shuddered from the impact of Clyde bouncing against it. Bay checked through the window, saw nothing to disturb him, and tripped the latch. Warmth poured out the door as Clyde bounded out and danced around his feet.

"What are you doing here, boy?"

Clyde flopped over to have his belly rubbed.

Bay took a match from the holder just inside the door and reached for the lamp. The glass chimney scorched his fingers.

They weren't far gone. He lit the lamp and adjusted the wick. The house looked just like it had the last time he'd ridden down with Mariah, except for the bare kitchen shelves. A fine mist of cornmeal and coffee dusted the counter and floor, as though whoever had stripped the shelves had done so in a hurry.

Not Mariah, he told himself. She'd have cleaned up.

But something, some instinct, told him she'd been here. He closed the damper on the stove to put the fire out.

The posse pulled into the yard and Eli stuck his head in. "Everything okay?"

"Check the barn," Bay said.

A minute later, Eli was back. "That little sorrel she rides is out there. Fresh bridle and saddle marks on his hide, but no tack in sight."

The sheriff stepped in behind Eli. "Looks like Mariah was in on this with her brother. No wonder they were able to match the thefts to your schedule so well."

Bay's gut twisted. Heaven help him, he'd considered the same idea for a moment, but having another man say it aloud let him hear how ludicrous it sounded.

"Mariah wasn't a part of this," he said flatly.

"But all the signs say she met them here."

"They *found* her here and forced her to go along. Look, I left her in our bed, and don't have the faintest idea what she was doing down here in the middle of the night, but I can tell you this: If Mariah had planned to meet Jimmy here, she would never have lit the stove and left it burning hot. It's wasteful. They've taken her, and the longer we stand around here debating it, the farther they get ahead of us."

The sheriff pulled a stogie from his vest pocket and rolled it between his fingers, releasing the bitter scent of tobacco. "You've been right so far, McKenzie, little as any of us wanted to believe you. We'll assume you're right again." He jammed the unlit cigar between his teeth and walked out to where the rest of the makeshift posse still sat on their horses. "Mrs. McKenzie has been taken hostage. Let's go get the lady back."

Mariah shivered uncontrollably. The skirts of her wool dress hung around her legs in damp disarray, soaked in their pre-dawn crossing of the Cottonwood River. She wrung at them with fingers stiff from cold. The hilltop a few hundred yards away was bathed in sunlight, but Otis held them to the wooded valley of the Cottonwood, where the sun hadn't yet penetrated. Her only satisfaction was that he was surely just as miserable: His horse had stumbled into a hole mid-stream and dunked them both nearly to the waist.

"I've got to get dried out," she whispered to Jimmy when they stopped for a break. "I'm freezing."

"I know. I'll talk to Otis. There's no reason we can't ride out in the sun for a while, as long as we stay off the tops of the ridges." He glanced around. Otis had hiked up the hill to check for pursuers, while Shorty sorted through the meager supplies they'd taken from the house, looking for something they could eat without cooking. Jimmy walked Mariah a few yards away, where the sounds of the creek would cover their words a little. "I'm sorry you're in the middle of this."

"What happened back at Lee's?"

He broke a twig from a chokecherry bush and tossed it aside. "There was an extra man on watch that we didn't expect. He caught us by surprise, and Otis shot him."

"Oh, Jimmy."

"I tried to stop him. The fellow went down, but when we went to check, he'd crawled off or something. Otis is mad at me for maybe leaving a witness who could identify us." He ripped another twig off the bush and stared at his fingers as he broke it into quarter-inch pieces that fell and collected on the toe of his boot.

"I'm a witness now."

Jimmy's head came up quickly. "He won't hurt you, Mariah. I'll make him let you go just as soon as we're sure we got away clean. I promise."

Just what were his promises worth these days? He continued to fidget with the stick, growing more agitated.

"I wanted to help out with the mortgage." His words were a plea for forgiveness that infuriated Mariah.

"Those were our neighbors. You stole from them."

"Otis and Shorty were doing it before I came along," he said as though that excused him. "And it seemed so easy, all that money."

"Especially with Bay taking the blame."

"That was all coincidence, to start. But after he started hanging around you and Nikolai showed me that list of dates. I just thought . . ." He dropped the final bit of twig and dusted his fingers together. "All we had to do was keep track of Bay and leave his horses alone while Nikolai spread the notion he was behind it all."

"Did Nikolai know?"

"Nah. He really thought Bay was the one."

At least Nikolai had one point in his favor—better than her brother. Mariah shook her head. "Why, Jimmy? Why couldn't you just—"

"Let's get out of here." Otis came scrambling back down the hill, slipping on the dew-slick grass. "Now. I spotted riders headed this way."

"How many?" Shorty asked.

"I didn't stop to count. Get that damned mess cleaned up and get on your horse."

Shorty jumped to stuff things back into the saddle bags. "McKenzie or the sheriff?"

"How the hell do I know? Maybe both. Jim, get that mare ready." Otis grabbed Mariah by the wrist. His fingers bit into her flesh. "We got to ride lighter and faster."

As Jimmy quickly checked the saddle over, Otis yanked his bandanna off and grabbed for Mariah's other wrist. She wrenched out of his grip. He swore and lifted his arm to backhand her.

"Leave her be," Jimmy said.

"She'll run off."

"No, I won't," Mariah said. Whoever those riders were, she didn't want to be at Otis's mercy when they started shooting. "If you really want to get away, leave my hands free. I can ride faster than you can lead me." She held her hand up, solemn oath style. "I promise I wont' try to run off." *Not until there's a good chance of escaping, anyway.*

"I'll see to her," Jimmy said.

Running his tongue over stained teeth, Otis stuffed the

kerchief into his pocket and motioned Mariah toward the horse. "You'd better, Jim-boy. I'd hate to have to shoot her."

Bay took a pull from his canteen. His eyes swept the wooded bottoms where he knew Jimmy and his friends rode with Mariah. Just like the war, he told himself. See it in the same way. They're the Rebs. You have to stop them.

He pointed along an intersecting stream. "We can beat them to that far bend if we cut across that way."

"Not once they figure out what we're doing," Eli said. "They'll just take off away from the river the other way, and then we've got ourselves a race all the way to Denver."

"And them with a change of horses." The sheriff shook his head. "I say we just keep after them. Slow and steady. They'll make a mistake sooner or later."

Bay took another swig of water and screwed the cap back on the metal flask. "We can do both. Sheriff, if you take Creelor and the others and keep trailing them, Eli and I can cut around and set an ambush."

"You can't make it that fast," Creelor said. "Not without being seen."

"They'll be watching you all. It's pretty clear they spotted us already and are hoping we haven't seen them. That's why they're still hugging the trees instead of cutting out cross country. You just keep up the same pace. Stick to them like hounds. But don't let them get a clear look. If they can't count you, they won't know we've split up."

"You've got to get across that cut without them seeing you," Creelor said. "What if you don't make it in time?"

"We'll make it," Bay and Eli said together. Bay added, "But not sitting up here."

"All right," said the sheriff. "Go. We'll keep our distance so they won't move any faster."

"Make sure you stay back until I get Mariah. I don't want her in the middle of cross fire." Bay looked straight at Creelor and touched the side of his neck where the other man had slashed him. "She's my wife, not some damned fool's horse."

The sheriff nodded. "I understand. Go on. And good luck."

Bay wheeled Cajun around and spurred him to a gallop. Eli fell in alongside.

"Do you have more of a plan than bushwhacking them?" he hollered over the pounding.

"Not much."

"Jeez-us."

Otis chose a path that straightened the sweeping oxbows of the river's course, a broken line that bypassed farms and connected the outside edges of the curves. Behind them somewhere, lost in the same trees that hid them, rode other men, hunters, ready to run them into the ground.

Mariah did everything she could think of to slow her horse without making it look like she was working against their escape, from sloppy hands on the reins to brushing needlessly close to branches, so the snagging branches would disturb the mare's pace. Otis was too involved with watching over his shoulder to notice, but she caught Jimmy glancing her way a couple of times. He'd noticed the subtle sabotage, she was certain, but he didn't say anything.

Oh, Jimmy. Little brother. Letting them catch us means you hang. He had to know that. For herself, that reality sat hard on the heels of her desire to be out of this mess, safe in Bay's arms where she could apologize for doubting him for those horrible hours.

If she could find a way to accomplish that and let her brother and his so-called friends escape, she'd do it in a heartbeat. Better that than wiring back to Virginia to say Jimmy was dead. That would kill Mama, sure as a knife in her heart.

"We shoulda changed horses," Shorty groused. "We still could."

"Not yet," Otis snapped. He swiped at his cheek with the crumpled bandanna. Mariah watched him, leery of the way he sweated and twitched and cursed beneath his breath. He was getting more dangerous by the minute, falling apart now under the pressure of pursuit. "Soon," he amended. "I want to be sure we're enough ahead to have time to make the change. Their horses've got to be wearing down. Just let me catch one more glimpse of them, just to see they haven't gained on us, and then Colorado, here we come."

"There they are," Shorty hollered a few minutes later. "I see 'em. Right there, just below where you can see that white streak on the bluff."

Mariah turned with the others and caught a fleeting glimpse of men and horses, filtered through distance and a tangle of bare branches. She couldn't even count the men at this range, much less identify them, and yet an impression settled on her that Bay was not one of them, an impression that left her bereft.

What if Otis was right? What if Bay thought she'd been in on the thefts with Jimmy, had been helping Jimmy make him look guilty? What if the whole town thought she'd been in on it? Even if she got away, she wouldn't be able to go back to the farm.

But none of that would matter if she didn't stay alive. She caught the malignancy in Otis's gaze as it raked over her, and she understood: She'd die before him. Her fingers seemed to vanish as numbing fear washed through her body. She looked down to find them, to make sure she still held the reins.

When she looked up, Bay was there.

The image of his fury-lined face froze in her mind, then shattered as he and Eli, rifles raised, exploded from the thicket that had concealed them. The clearing erupted as the horses reared away from the attackers and scattered. Otis screamed in rage, reaching for her, reaching for his gun.

"Go!"

The mare shot away at a dead run before Mariah absorbed the sound of Jimmy's voice and the slap of his hand across the horse's rump. Instinct threw her forward, low against the mare's sweaty neck as the animal plunged past Otis and through the low brush along the bank, down into the river. Gunfire exploded behind her, shot after shot, wrenching at her insides, and the only thing she could do was run, give Bay one less thing to worry about. She clung to the black mane, letting the mare have her head, and they raced upstream in the shallows.

Finally the gunfire stopped and there was only the sound of the river and another horse in the water behind her. Mariah twisted to see. Water fountained up from driving hooves as Jimmy's chestnut pounded past, riderless.

"Jimmy." Mariah searched the swirling brown water frantically. She spotted Jimmy floating at the edge of the river, the current tugging at him, trying to sweep him away. She turned the mare toward him. "Jimmy. Oh, no, Jimmy."

She dove off the mare and reached for his boot just as the water worked him free. He slipped, and she threw herself across his body and pushed and pulled and lifted until his head and shoulders rested on the bank. The current, relentless, dragged at his legs, but Mariah dug her heels into the chalky silt and clung to him, her fingers twisted into his shirt.

Blood welled from his head, matting his hair and running down to soak the ground, so much blood that a thin stream of red trailed into the water and downstream. She felt for a pulse, found it, and knew he was alive.

Alive to hang.

The bushes rattled somewhere downstream. Mariah hitched Jimmy a little higher on the bank and reached for his pistol, still in its holster. She didn't know who had won the gun battle, and she had no intention of volunteering herself until she did. The pistol, though soaked and muddy, might make a man stop and think. It might even fire. She shrank down in the flimsy cover of the denuded brush, one hand on the gun, the other on Jimmy, and held her breath as whoever it was got closer.

"Mariah. Damn it, where are you? Mariah!"

"Over here. Bay, help me. Please help us."

The branches parted and he appeared, rifle in hand, his face a mask of agonized fury. He got to her in two steps and fell to his knees, one hand cupping her cheek. "The son of a bitch got off two shots your way. I saw your horse and the blood in the water and I thought . . ."

"I'm fine," she said. "Help Jimmy."

He turned his attention to her brother, checking quickly for a pulse. "Young fool."

"He saved me, Bay. He made sure I got away."

"He almost got you killed to start with." Bay ran his fingers expertly over Jimmy's skull. "And me, too."

"But in the end, he helped me. He put himself between Otis and me, and now they'll hang him. Don't let them, Bay."

Eli crashed through the brush to join them. "Those other two are dead. The sheriff will be here before long."

Mariah grabbed Bay's arm. Her voice shook, pleading. "He's my brother. They'll hang him."

"If he lives that long," Bay said harshly. "He's bleeding like a pig and he probably swallowed a lot of water. I can't take care of him with you yanking on me. Get her out of here, Eli."

Eli tugged her to her feet and away from Jimmy. "Come on. You can't help him now, not in the state you're in."

"Bay, please."

He glanced up at her, his eyes softer. "Go on, Mariah. I'll do what I can."

Eli left her at the edge of the clearing with a warning that she might not want to look at Otis and Shorty and walked back along the trail to wave in the rest of the posse. Within a few minutes, the rumble of the approaching horses drowned out the whine of the flies already buzzing around the two dead men. The sheriff and the others dismounted and gathered around the bloody shapes. Mariah blocked out their jubilant conversation, listening only for some sound from the riverbank.

It came, finally, the rattle of Bay pushing through the bushes. He was alone, and as the sheriff and Eli started in his direction, he shook his head.

"I'm sorry, Mariah. He's gone."

"But he . . . Oh, my god, Jimmy." Her words turned into a wail of grief. She ran toward the river.

"There's nothing you can do." Bay caught her and pulled her to him, crushing her against his wet shirt. "The current pulled him right under. I couldn't get to him." He started telling the sheriff some story about Jimmy getting shot and washing down river. "I don't see how a man could last that long under water."

Wet shirt. Current. Under water. Through her sobs, Mariah struggled to put it together. Bay was soaked to the skin. She tried to look at him, but he wrapped his arms more tightly and pressed her head to his shoulder so hard she couldn't move.

"It's all right, sweetheart," he crooned. "This is the time to cry. Sheriff, can we sort this out later in town? I think my wife's had more than she can take today. And I need to get us both dried out."

"Surely. I understand. I'm sorry about your brother, Mrs. McKenzie. I just don't know what happens to ruin a boy like that. It's a tragedy for everyone. We'll ride the river on the way back, see if we can't bring him home for a proper Christian burial."

Bay must have nodded, because the sheriff moved away, calling out orders. "Somebody cover those fellows up and get them onto horses to take back. You two go round up the strays. I don't know about you fellows, but I want to get home."

"I'll just stay here with Bay and see if I can help out," Eli volunteered. Under his breath he muttered, "What's going on?"

Bay edged Mariah away from the activity, keeping his grip all the while. He pressed a kiss to the top of her head. His voice was barely audible over the breeze. "Listen to me. He's fine, but you have to keep up the show until they're gone. Understand?"

"Yes," she said against his chest. It wasn't so hard. The tears came naturally enough, out of her joy and fear for Jimmy.

It took a good half hour for the sheriff to get everyone under way, during which time Eli got a blazing fire going and scrounged some coffee and a battered pot out of Shorty's kit. One of the men offered a blanket to Mariah before he left. She accepted gratefully and huddled on a log as near the flames as she could bear, letting the heat dry her clothes and seep into her bones. It seemed like she'd been cold and wet for weeks. Bay hovered close by, turning to let his clothes dry, front and back.

Finally, she and Bay and Eli were alone in the clearing. They waited in silence several long moments, watching after the others, listening to the hoofbeats fade and then to the sounds of the river and the birds.

"All right. They're gone." Bay held out his hand to Mariah. "Come on."

He led her and Eli back down to the riverbank, but took them twenty or thirty yards upstream from where she'd left Jimmy, to a spot where the bank was undercut a little. The remains of a good-sized tree lay in the cut, washed-out roots and all, its skeleton bleached silver by the sun. Mariah was almost past it before she spotted Jimmy's foot. She scrambled over and pulled the branches away.

He lay there, bloody head wrapped with a strip of Bay's yellow shirt, hands and feet tied with bandannas, looking miserable. But alive.

Mariah sank down in the gravel next to him, fresh tears streaking down her cheeks. "You little idiot."

"It's just a little graze," Jimmy grumbled. He struggled to sit up. "Turn me loose."

"Whoa, whoa, whoa." Bay kicked the snag into the river and squatted next to Jimmy. "I thought we had this clear. Those men wanted to hang you, boy. The only reason they don't still is because they think you're dead. I might still disabuse them of that idea."

"Bay!"

"Be quiet, Mariah. This boy needs to find out just where he stands. I'm so damned mad at him, I could string him up myself. He stole horses. He tried to get me hung for it. Then to top it off, he let those slimy sons of bitches take his own sister hostage." He poked Jimmy in the chest. "Do you have any idea what would have happened to Mariah if your friends had decided they wanted a woman?"

Jimmy sagged back against the bank. Tears spilled down his face. "Christ, Mariah. I didn't even think that far. They would've had to shoot me first, you've got to believe me."

Mariah saw what Bay was doing now, and she hugged herself to keep from reaching out to soothe Jimmy. She and Mama had done too much of that. He needed to face the hard consequences of his choices, painful as it was to watch.

"Scared?" Bay asked.

"Yes," Jimmy sobbed. "Please. I promise I'll keep straight. No more stealing. No gambling. None of that. I swear, I'll never hurt another person in my whole life. I just don't want to hang."

"That's better. Now maybe you'll satisfy me on a few points," Bay said. "What happened at Lee's last night?"

Slowly, Jimmy got himself under control. He repeated the story he'd told Mariah, adding a couple of details.

"That's just about what that boy of Lee's told us," Eli said.

Bay nodded. "Next, if I decide to turn you loose—and that's a big if—where would you go?"

Mariah bit her tongue.

"Montana," Jimmy said. "I hear they're still finding gold there."

"Some," granted Bay. "Silver, too. What will you do for money for a stake?"

"Work. Honest work. I told you, no more stealing or gambling." Jimmy squirmed upright. "You going to let me go?"

"I shouldn't." Bay reached for the bandanna at Jimmy's ankles and worked the knot out, then started on the one at his wrists. "But your sister has this fool idea you might turn out to be worth something, and I'll be damned if I can figure out a way to hang you and still keep her in love with me."

Eli hoisted Jimmy to his feet and steadied him as he wobbled. "I bet you have a dandy of a headache."

Jimmy touched his head. "Yes, sir."

"At least you have a head," Eli said. "That's more than that friend of yours has. Let's see what we can do to get you cleaned up and dried out. You can't be riding off like that. I bet I can rustle up some kind of meal out of what I took out of that fellow's saddlebags. It was a godawful mess, but . . ." Eli's voice faded as he and Jimmy headed for the fire.

Bay rose and helped Mariah up. She looked up at him. "That was cruel."

"He had to learn."

"Not that. Telling me he was dead."

"I'm sorry. I just didn't know if you could act, and if they'd caught us, they might have assumed we were in on the whole thing. It was the only way I could see on that short notice."

"It worked," she said. She wrapped her arms around his waist and burrowed against his still-damp chest. "Thank you. Thank you for giving me my brother back."

"It's not much of a present. He'll never be able to come home. He won't even be able to write to you, not under his own name."

"I know. But he's alive."

"And so are you. Let's go sit by the fire. You're starting to shiver again."

Fed and dried and patched to the best of Eli's ability, and with a roll of Bay's money tucked into his sock to buy food and gear, Jimmy followed the afternoon sun away to the west.

"I love you," he told Mariah fiercely before he mounted up. "I know I let you down, but I do love you. Ma and Pa, too. Make sure they know."

"I will."

Mariah watched until he faded into the distance, then walked down to the river. Bay followed her, leaving Eli to pack up and see the fire was out.

Gravel crunched as he caught up with her on the bank. They stood there a moment, watching the brown water swirl past.

"Why did you let Jimmy go?" she asked.

"You heard what I told him. I want to keep you loving me."

A smile touched Mariah's lips. "You sound pretty cocky, Mr. McKenzie. How do you know I do to begin with?"

"You dropped the secret on our wedding night." He stepped in behind her and folded his arms around her waist. The scent of river water clung to his clothes beneath the smoky aroma of the fire. "Were you leaving me? Is that why you were down at the farm?"

Her smile faded. "I heard you get up in the middle of the night. I saw the note from the man in Wichita. Everything Nikolai and Jimmy said started making sense. Why didn't you just tell me?"

"I didn't want you to know what I was doing until I was sure." Bay shook his head. "Wild accusations against your wife's brother are not a prescribed recipe for marital bliss."

"It's better than thinking it was you. Better than not knowing whether you're going to be there the next time I turn around."

Bay whipped her around to face him. His fingers dug into her arms, but his face was tight with guilt. "That's where the doubts came from?"

"It made them easier. You never told me when you'd leave, or how. Just that you would. I kept telling myself it was all right, that whatever time I had with you was enough. But it wasn't. It isn't."

"I already figured that out for myself," he said. He released her and paced a few yards down the bank and back. "Look, Mariah, when I told you our marriage was real, I meant it. I must not have made that clear, either."

"No," she said. "You didn't. I thought you just meant the physical part."

"Then let me set you straight." He gathered her to him and kissed her, a kiss as full of promise as it was passion. "I love you, Mariah. I don't know if I'll want to stay in Chase County forever, but I can promise you this: I will have you at my side always, wherever I am. I will never, *never* go any place without you."

"But what if I don't ever want to leave? This country is so much a part of me, I don't know if I *can* leave." She took a deep breath and crossed her fingers. *Please don't let me down now.* "And what about our children? I certainly don't intend to raise our children anyplace else."

"Then we'll work things out. Maybe travel and come back, like you told me to do. We'll just do it together, and . . ." Bay's voice trailed off and he stared. "Children? Are you telling me . . . ?"

"I think so. I've been sick to my stomach for a couple of days. I thought it was nerves, but while I was drying out, I counted days in my head. My last cycle was before the vigilantes came. I'm way past my time."

Bay's whoop echoed off the bluffs on the both sides of the river and came back to her ears a dozen times, enough to erase the last doubts. He picked her up and spun her around, then set her down, his face grave. "I should be more careful."

Mariah laughed. "After the past twenty-four hours? If he hasn't shaken loose yet, he's not going to."

"A boy? No, you wouldn't know. It doesn't matter anyway." He whooped again.

"What the heck's going on?" Eli demanded, stomping over to join them.

"Fatherhood," Bay said. "It looks like I'm going to be a father."

"Jeez-us." Eli stood there a minute, blinking. "Well, I guess that puts the kibosh on Santa Fe so far as you're concerned. Damn, but I hate to travel without a partner."

"Jimmy's headed west," Bay said.

Eli's eyebrows went up and then down, and a slow smile spread across his face. "I guess I could kind of keep an eye on the boy for a month or two. Keep him on the straight and narrow. Maybe I can even convince him to try Santa Fe first." He offered Mariah his hand. "I'll let you know where we end up."

"That would be wonderful. But you don't have your gear with you."

"I can buy new in Marion, same as your brother." Eli turned to Bay. "You know what's important out of my things. I'll let you know where to send it. Give the rest to Gid Willis. He's a good kid."

"I'm going to miss you, pard." Bay cuffed him on the shoulder.

"Oh, I'd venture I'll make it back this way now and again. I've kind of grown to like Eliza's cooking. Well, if I'm going to catch him, I'd better hightail it. See you down the road." He pushed back through the brush, and a moment later, they heard the sound of galloping hooves.

Bay stared after him, and for just an instant, Mariah could see the longing in his eyes. Then he turned and blessed her with the McKenzie smirk in all its crooked glory, five lines by the right eye, three by the left.

"Eliza?" He raised one eyebrow. "Mrs. *Shaw*?"

"And Eli," she said. They broke into peals of laughter.

Bay wiped a tear from the corner of his eye and caught her around the waist. "Come on, wife. Let's go home."

Epilogue

"Now that was a blasted waste of time," Bay grumbled. He stood on the porch another moment, swatting his hat against his leg to knock the snow free.

Mariah held the door open while he finished brushing himself off and came in, then she pushed it shut firmly. "I can't believe how fast the weather changed this afternoon. What happened?"

"Rolley dragged us all over creation looking for some steers he claimed had gone missing. Turns out they were in that batch we sold last month, and all of us dragging around out in the snow." He hung his coat on the peg and unbuckled his holster with fingers stiff from the cold. "I don't know if he's going dotty or just forgot this one time, but I swear if he pulls a stunt like that on me again, I'll have him mucking stalls with a tea spoon. I don't know what's going on around here, but the past week . . ."

Bay's tirade trailed off as he turned to find Mariah eyeing him with a disconcerting mixture of humor and concern.

"What?"

"Oh, nothing," she said in a way that made him suspect that it was more than nothing, though he had no idea what. "I'm sorry you had such a bad day."

"And I'm sorry I'm grousing at you. You didn't have anything to do with it."

Mariah turned away to finger the doily that covered the hall table, but Bay caught a glimpse of her smile in the mirror. He stepped up behind her and slipped his arms around her thickening waist. The bulge of her belly neatly filled the cradle of his hands. He tapped his fingertips against the taut skin and grinned at the gentle shift beneath his palms as the baby moved. "Hello, little one. Your mother is up to something."

Mariah covered his hands with the warmth of her own and he watched her smile broaden mischievously in the mirror. "Just having a baby."

"That's not what I'm talking about. You've got a look . . . Why the fancy duds?" He tugged on the long scarf that draped down from the neck of her soft wool Mother Hubbard to help disguise her condition. For his part, he wouldn't mind if she wore silk cut to show everything. Each swelling curve managed to both strike him with awe and fill him with desire.

"It's your birthday," she said. "I thought I'd try to look pretty for you."

"That doesn't take your best gown. However, I suppose that means I should dress for dinner to match you."

"That would be lovely."

Bay slipped his hands over her belly and up to catch the weight of her breasts in his palms, savoring the lush fullness that came with her pregnancy. "Come tie my tie for me."

She pushed his hands down with wifely firmness. "If I do that, we will never eat dinner and Mrs. Shaw will be mad as the dickens. She spent all day baking you a cake."

Bay sighed ostentatiously, but released her. "Fine thing, when a man has to run his life by how the housekeeper might feel. I'll be down in five minutes."

It was more like fifteen, because he decided his wife's efforts deserved a smooth jaw and shaving with the cool water in the basin took forever. Finally he headed downstairs, tugging his collar into place as he went.

Mariah was pacing back and forth in the hall, one hand at her back. "That was a very long five minutes."

"I assume that means you and junior are hungry as usual."

"Ravenous." She took his arm and they headed toward the dining room. "Speaking of junior, we really should start picking out names, unless you plan to follow your father's lead and find a way to name all your sons after yourself somehow."

Bay snorted. "Hardly. I think passing on the McKenzie name

is enough of a burden, don't you?" He reached for the dining room door and pulled it open. "What happened to the lights. I thought Mrs. Shaw—"

"Surprise!" a dozen voices shouted. Sulphur fumes filled the air as matches flared in the dark. A herd of laughing faces, male and female, wavered into view. Within seconds, candles blazed all around the room and someone was reaching to light the brass chandelier over the table. Crystal and silver sparkled against the white linen, bouncing the light around the room in rainbow shards.

Bay stood, stunned, looking from the people to the spread of food that covered the sideboard.

"Don't look so blamed shocked," Len Michaels said, stepping up from the back of the group. "We just came to celebrate your birthday." He stuck his hand out. "That's what neighbors do."

Bay took Len's hand and gave it a firm shake. He had to clear a lump in his throat before he could speak. "And fine neighbors you are, too."

"That's what we were just saying about you."

The men in the group surged forward, thumping shoulders and shaking hands until Bay felt like his arm might fall off.

Mariah rescued him. "I hate to rush you all, but with Bay taking so long, I'm afraid Mrs. Shaw's food is getting cold. Shall we sit down?"

Grinning like a fool, Bay escorted his wife to her place at the foot of the table. "Now I understand what that goose chase was about. I'll have to give Rolley a bonus."

"You might also consider forgiving Gid for leaving the stallion's stall open," she said, stepping in front of her chair. "I put him up to it in order to have time to write the invitations out."

As he eased her chair against her knees, he leaned forward. His words were low and suggestive and directed to her alone. "There are terrible punishments for conspirators."

She looked up, cheeks flushed but eyes sparkling with merriment. "I'll just have to bear up."

* * *

There was something to be said for marrying money, Mariah concluded, surveying the parlor with satisfaction. A body could accomplish so much, from seeing that hungry neighbors got food to arranging a birthday party for one's husband that could surprise the daylights out of him.

Dinner passed amid much conversation and laughter, and afterward the men gave up their cigars to join their wives in the parlor—although they drank whiskey while the ladies took sherry. As soon as their glasses were empty, Mariah had them dragging aside furniture and rolling the rug. Two of the ranch hands appeared, scrubbed and shaved and carrying a fiddle and a squeezebox, and the dancing began.

A little later, as Bay was spinning her through a slow waltz, she caught him watching his mother's portrait. "I know it's a painting, but I keep thinking I see a new lift to her smile."

"I wish I'd known her," she said.

"Me, too." Bay glanced down at her, his expression tender. "She would have loved you very nearly as much as I do."

By midnight, she felt herself beginning to fade. Bay signalled the musicians to play one final waltz before he and Mariah escorted their guests upstairs and saw them settled into the guest wing.

Back in their own room, she settled onto the edge of the bed to unbutton her shoes. She was getting so round that she had to hoist each foot onto the opposite knee to reach the buttons. "I'm glad we'd planned for everyone to stay. I'd hate to see people driving home in the snow this late."

Bay pushed the curtain aside and looked outside. "Actually, it's stopped now. But I'm glad they're here, too. A passel of guests is just what this house needs." He dropped the heavy velvet swag and started to remove his coat. He stopped suddenly and reached into his inside pocket. "Your little surprise made me forget one I had for you. While we were out dragging around today, I rode on over to Birley for the mail. There's one here addressed to Mariah Emmeline Hoag McKenzie."

"Mama." Mariah grabbed the letter out of his hands and ripped it open. She scanned the pages quickly, picking the important bits out of her mother's neat, spiderweb penmanship for Bay. "She claims she's doing much better. They're coming back in a couple of months. Mama wants to be here to help with the baby. Then she says they'll see about staying." A few lines of her father's heavier hand filled the space beneath her mother's signature. She read the message and winced. "Papa sends his love and says he didn't mention it before, but 'that husband of yours has some explaining to do about how soon the baby's due.'"

Bay looked up from his own letter and laughed. "I told you he'd calculate it out sooner or later. It's a good thing I married you so quick."

"After some of the things my mother told me, I'm not sure he has the right to say a word." She folded the letter and laid it on the bedside table. She knew she'd read it over again later, probably a dozen times. "Who's the other one from?"

"Eli." He held one sheet of stationery out to her. "Part of it's for you. From your brother."

Mariah felt the tears burn her lids before she even took the note.

"He's doing fine," Bay said quietly. "I read it and the note from Eli before I decided to give it to you."

Jimmy's message was brief. *Dear Mariah, First off I want you to know that I'm keeping all my promises, even about gambling. Eli grumbles about not playing poker, but he says it's probably better for him, too. He makes sure I don't fall in with the wrong people or do anything stupid. I'm learning. Knowing I can never come back made me realize how big a mess I made of things, especially when I think of Aurelia. It kills me to know that she thinks I'm dead and that there's no way you or I can tell her otherwise. I wrote the folks last week, so they know I'm all right. I hope they can forgive me. I'm working odd jobs now and again. Eli tells folks I'm his cousin. I'll write you by the name of Frank Hightower from here on out, and you can send mail to me in Santa Fe. I hope someday I can see you again, because I really do love you. J. PS—Tell Bay I owe him.*

As she read, Bay stripped off his coat, tie, and shirt, then sat down on the bed beside her. His arm was a warm, comforting weight across her back. Mariah swiped away a tear and looked up at him. "What's Eli say?"

"Pretty much the same thing. The kid seems to be doing fine. Really trying to get back on track."

"You sound as relieved as I feel."

"I am. For all I knew, turning him loose could have cost someone else down the road." Bay crawled around behind her and began to rub her neck and shoulders. "It looks like it won't."

"I'm glad." She relaxed into the gentle kneading. "I should be doing that for you. It's your birthday."

"That's why I get to do what I want." He pushed the mass of her hair aside and touched a kiss to the back to her neck, then chuckled at her shiver. "You know, if some fellow had told me last spring that within the year I'd have a beautiful wife, a child on the way, and more friends than fingers, I'd have laughed in his face and laid him twenty-to-one odds. But here I am. I've never felt so at home in my life."

Mariah smiled with satisfaction and pulled the scarf from around her neck. "I suppose that means I won't have to face that court-martial for conspiracy."

Leaving off the message, he reached over her shoulders to unbutton the top buttons of her wrapper. "Oh, no. You've already been tried and convicted *in absentia*. This is the sentencing."

The warmth of anticipation replaced that of comfort. Mariah sighed dramatically. "The wages of sin."

"Mmm-hmm. Unless you're too tired . . ." His teeth closed over the delicate skin at the curve of her neck, where he could do the most damage to her ability to fall asleep any time soon.

Mariah sighed again, this time with a shudder of surrender.

"I'll take it that means you're wide awake," he said, chuckling. He shifted around so that he half-knelt on the edge of the bed, facing her. His gaze held hers while he flicked open another button and slipped his fingers into the gap to skim the rise of her breasts. "I'm a kindly judge. I'll let you pick your own punishment."

"Well," she said, as though she had to think of something, as though the thought hadn't been floating in her imagination all evening. "You never did show me the second idea you had for that old chair."

Author's Note

THE MEETING BETWEEN Bay and Mariah and their later trials during the grasshopper plague were inspired by and adapted from the true accounts contained in *Pioneer Women: Voices from the Kansas Frontier*, by Joanna L. Stratton (Touchstone Books, 1982), and other sources.

Researching any area far from home is always a challenge, but the process can be made easier by a helpful person at the other end. It was my good fortune to stumble onto one of those people. Barbara Livingston gave me more information and support than I could have imagined. Thanks, Barb. I hope I got it right.

I'd also like to express my appreciation to the volunteers of the Chase County Historical Society and all the other wonderful historical societies around the country who have taken the time and care to preserve their local heritage. The rest of us are richer for your efforts.

I enjoy hearing from readers. Please write to me at 321 High School Road #353, Bainbridge Island, WA 98110.

If you enjoyed this book, take advantage of this special offer. Subscribe now and...

Get a Historical

No Obligation

If you enjoy reading the very best in historical romantic fiction...romances that set back the hands of time to those bygone days with strong virile heros and passionate heroines ...then you'll want to subscribe to the True Value Historical Romance Home Subscription Service. Now that you have read one of the best historical romances around today, we're sure you'll want more of the same fiery passion, intimate romance and historical settings that set these books apart from all others.

Each month the editors of True Value select the four *very best* novels from America's leading publishers of romantic fiction. We have made arrangements for you to preview them in your home *Free* for 10 days. And with the first four books you receive, we'll send you a FREE book as our introductory gift. No Obligation!

FREE HOME DELIVERY

We will send you the four best and newest historical romances as soon as they are published to preview FREE for 10 days (in many cases you may even get them before they arrive in the book stores). If for any reason you decide not to keep them, just return them and owe nothing. But if you like them as much as we think you will, you'll pay just $4.00 each and save at *least* $.50 each off the cover price. (Your savings are *guaranteed* to be at least $2.00 each month.) There is NO postage and handling—or other hidden charges. There are no minimum number of books to buy and you may cancel at any time.

FREE
Romance
(a $4.50 value)

Send in the Coupon Below

To get your FREE historical romance and start saving, fill out the coupon below and mail it today. As soon as we receive it we'll send you your FREE Book along with your first month's selections.

Mail To: **True Value Home Subscription Services, Inc. P.O. Box 5235
120 Brighton Road, Clifton, New Jersey 07015-5235**

YES! I want to start previewing the very best historical romances being published today. Send me my FREE book along with the first month's selections. I understand that I may look them over FREE for 10 days. If I'm not absolutely delighted I may return them and owe nothing. Otherwise I will pay the low price of just $4.00 each; a total $16.00 (at *least* an $18.00 value) and save at least $2.00. Then each month I will receive four brand new novels to preview as soon as they are published for the same low price. I can always return a shipment and I may cancel this subscription at any time with no obligation to buy even a single book. In any event the FREE book is mine to keep regardless.

Name _____

Street Address _____ Apt. No. _____

City _____ State _____ Zip Code _____

Telephone _____

Signature _____
(if under 18 parent or guardian must sign)

Terms and prices subject to change. Orders subject to acceptance by True Value Home Subscription Services, Inc.

0070-0

Diamond Wildflower Romance

A breathtaking new line of spectacular novels set in the untamed frontier of the American West. Every month, Diamond Wildflower brings you new adventures where passionate men and women dare to embrace their boldest dreams. Finally, romances that capture the very spirit and passion of the wild frontier.

__TEXAS ANGEL by Linda Francis Lee
0-7865-0007-7/$4.99

__FRONTIER HEAT by Peggy Stoks
0-7865-0012-3/$4.99

__RECKLESS RIVER by Teresa Southwick
0-7865-0018-2/$4.99

__LIGHTNING STRIKES by Jean Wilson
0-7865-0024-7/$4.99

__TENDER OUTLAW by Deborah James
0-7865-0043-3/$4.99

__MY DESPERADO by Lois Greiman
0-7865-0048-4/$4.99

__NIGHT TRAIN by Maryann O'Brien
0-7865-0058-1/$4.99

__WILD HEARTS by Linda Francis Lee
0-7865-0062-X/$4.99

__DRIFTER'S MOON by Lisa Hendrix
0-7865-0070-0/$4.99

__GOLDEN GLORY by Jean Wilson
0-7865-0074-3/$4.99 (February)

Payable in U.S. funds. No cash orders accepted. Postage & handling: $1.75 for one book, 75¢ for each additional. Maximum postage $5.50. Prices, postage and handling charges may change without notice. Visa, Amex, MasterCard call 1-800-788-6262, ext. 1, refer to ad # 406

Or, check above books　　Bill my:　☐ Visa　☐ MasterCard　☐ Amex
and send this order form to:
The Berkley Publishing Group　Card#_____
390 Murray Hill Pkwy., Dept. B　　　　　　　　　　　　(expires)
East Rutherford, NJ 07073　　Signature_____ ($15 minimum)
Please allow 6 weeks for delivery.　　Or enclosed is my:　☐ check　☐ money order

Name_____
Address_____
City_____
State/ZIP_____

Book Total　$_____
Postage & Handling　$_____
Applicable Sales Tax　$_____
(NY, NJ, PA, CA, GST Can.)
Total Amount Due　$_____

FREE Romance

(a $4.50 value)

Send in the Coupon Below

To get your FREE historical romance and start saving, fill out the coupon below and mail it today. As soon as we receive it we'll send you your FREE Book along with your first month's selections.

Mail To: **True Value Home Subscription Services, Inc. P.O. Box 5235
120 Brighton Road, Clifton, New Jersey 07015-5235**

YES! I want to start previewing the very best historical romances being published today. Send me my FREE book along with the first month's selections. I understand that I may look them over FREE for 10 days. If I'm not absolutely delighted I may return them and owe nothing. Otherwise I will pay the low price of just $4.00 each: a total $16.00 (at *least* an $18.00 value) and save at least $2.00. Then each month I will receive four brand new novels to preview as soon as they are published for the same low price. I can always return a shipment and I may cancel this subscription at any time with no obligation to buy even a single book. In any event the FREE book is mine to keep regardless.

Name
Street Address   Apt. No.
City   State   Zip Code
Telephone
Signature
(if under 18 parent or guardian must sign)

Terms and prices subject to change. Orders subject to acceptance by True Value Home Subscription Services, Inc.

0070-0

Diamond Wildflower Romance

A breathtaking new line of spectacular novels set in the untamed frontier of the American West. Every month, Diamond Wildflower brings you new adventures where passionate men and women dare to embrace their boldest dreams. Finally, romances that capture the very spirit and passion of the wild frontier.

- __TEXAS ANGEL by Linda Francis Lee
  0-7865-0007-7/$4.99
- __FRONTIER HEAT by Peggy Stoks
  0-7865-0012-3/$4.99
- __RECKLESS RIVER by Teresa Southwick
  0-7865-0018-2/$4.99
- __LIGHTNING STRIKES by Jean Wilson
  0-7865-0024-7/$4.99
- __TENDER OUTLAW by Deborah James
  0-7865-0043-3/$4.99
- __MY DESPERADO by Lois Greiman
  0-7865-0048-4/$4.99
- __NIGHT TRAIN by Maryann O'Brien
  0-7865-0058-1/$4.99
- __WILD HEARTS by Linda Francis Lee
  0-7865-0062-X/$4.99
- __DRIFTER'S MOON by Lisa Hendrix
  0-7865-0070-0/$4.99
- __GOLDEN GLORY by Jean Wilson
  0-7865-0074-3/$4.99 (February)

Payable in U.S. funds. No cash orders accepted. Postage & handling: $1.75 for one book, 75¢ for each additional. Maximum postage $5.50. Prices, postage and handling charges may change without notice. Visa, Amex, MasterCard call 1-800-788-6262, ext. 1, refer to ad # 406

Or, check above books   Bill my: ☐ Visa   ☐ MasterCard   ☐ Amex
and send this order form to:
The Berkley Publishing Group   Card#_____ (expires)
390 Murray Hill Pkwy., Dept. B
East Rutherford, NJ 07073   Signature_____ ($15 minimum)

Please allow 6 weeks for delivery.   Or enclosed is my: ☐ check   ☐ money order

Name_____   Book Total $_____

Address_____   Postage & Handling $_____

City_____   Applicable Sales Tax $_____
                          (NY, NJ, PA, CA, GST Can.)

State/ZIP_____   Total Amount Due $_____

Stories from
THE BARN

Stories from
THE BARN

JOHN GRAY

Stories from the Barn
Copyright © 2023 by John Gray

This is a work of fiction. Names, characters, places and incidents are the products of the author's imagination or are used fictitiously. Any resemblance to actual events, locales, or persons, living or dead, is entirely coincidental.

All rights reserved. No part of this book may be used or reproduced in any form, electronic or mechanical, including photocopying, recording, or scanning into any information storage and retrieval system, without written permission from the author except in the case of brief quotation embodied in critical articles and reviews.

Cover art by Shanna Brickell
Book design by Jessika Hazelton

Printed in the United States of America
The Troy Book Makers • Troy, New York
thetroybookmakers.com

ISBN: 978-1-61468-783-2

For David Kissick
teacher, mentor, friend.

CONTENTS

HOPE 1
   The Barn 3
   Silent Boy 9
   The Coat 15

FAITH 21
   The Stones 23
   Path to Heaven 27
   Snowflake 33

LOVE 39
   Peter's Punishment 41
   The Letter 47
   Two Old Souls 55
   Just Another Love Story 61

INSPIRE 67
   Let Go of Your Leaves 69
   Fortunatus 75
   Sparrow 81

THE HAYLOFT 87
   Piper & Samuel 89
   Little Things 97
   Pen Pal 103

EPILOGUE 111

HOPE

The Barn

Driving through the country I came upon a barn. It was incredibly old and falling down and looked sad to me. I frowned as I stared at it, thinking, "Poor, poor barn."

Just as I turned to go the barn spoke, saying, "Don't do that. Don't look at me with such disappointing eyes. You know nothing about me silly man."

I glanced around certain someone was hiding in the shadows and playing a joke, but there was no one there; just the shambles of the weathered barn.

I couldn't tell you why, but I smiled in that instant and decided to play along, saying out loud, "OK Mr. Barn. What don't I know?"

The barn responded, "You see me only as I am today but imagine for a moment what I was before; big, strong, something of great value. I protected animals under this roof. Children used to play in the hay in my loft. I saw so many baby cows brought into this world not three feet from where you are standing right now. I was a great barn once."

Before I could speak the barn continued, "The boy who grew up on the farm that used to occupy this land, kissed his very first girl by the light of a lantern, right here, 53 years ago. I did great things, saw great things. So, spare me your sad glances please."

I was quiet for a moment and then realized the barn was right. What I was looking at today was a lie, a small final chapter in a great and complex story. This barn was young and strong once long ago.

Just then I heard rustling in a thatch of hay near my feet and saw a bunny with three tiny babies moving about. Up above I noticed several bird nests resting in the crooked beams of the failing structure; one of them filled with hatchlings only a few days old. They were calling to their mother for breakfast. I realized in that instant this old barn, now more on its knees than standing tall, still had purpose even in this diminished state. Barely hanging on yet refusing to fall.

Finally, I spoke, "You're right Mr. Barn. I was wrong; I only saw you as you are now. I'm sorry. I'm Sorry. I'm..."

At the Shady Acres Nursing home, a middle-aged woman asked her teenage son, "What did your grandfather just say?"

The boy just stared at his *Pa* with a mixture of gratitude and concern. This was the man who taught him how to swim, fish and skip stones so many years earlier.

The teen then said to his mother, "He mumbled something about an old barn and said he was sorry. I couldn't follow it mom. He seems out of it today."

The boy then noticed his grandfather was looking out the window at something, so he moved closer, right alongside, and looked too. Across the road from the nursing home was a big field that used to be a farm. Tumbleweeds had their way with it now. Yet up on the hill was the one thing that still told the story of what once was. An old barn fighting time and, like the old man now staring at it, hoping others could see passed the broken pieces of today to the beauty, strength and purpose that used to be. The boy now understood what his grandfather was saying.

When the boy left the nursing home, he asked his mom to wait while he snapped a photo of the old barn.

"Why do you want a picture of that?" she asked.

The boy didn't respond, he just looked back toward the nursing home and his grandpa's window and smiled.

One year later the old man died. There was a funeral and speeches and kind words about a life well lived. The following morning a plate of cookies was dropped off at the nursing home to say thank you to the staff for their years of care for the old man along with a single framed photo delivered by a teenage boy.

The woman running the home looked at it and grinned, saying, "I know just the place for this."

STORIES FROM THE BARN

If you stop by Shady Acres, you'll find it hanging in the foyer, greeting every guest as they walk through the front doors to visit the seniors who call this place home. It's a photo of an old falling down barn with a brief stanza below that reads—

"Cast not your gaze on what you see, but what I used to be. This weathered shell has stood the storm with grace, love, and glee.

I once was strong, useful, beautiful and will be once more. When I break the chains of this tattered life and knock on heaven's door."

Silent Boy

Angela worked weekends at the Hallmark store. The popular card shop was in one of those outdoor shopping plazas that offered everything from shoes, to toys, to cafes where you pay $5 dollars for a gluten-free muffin.

It was just after Thanksgiving when she first noticed him, a little boy in slightly shabby clothes who always wore a red knit cap and carried an empty canvas shopping bag—the kind you lug groceries in. He'd come into the store and snake his way to the back where they kept the ornaments. He never said a word; he'd just focus on one area for a few minutes and then leave as quietly as he came in.

More than once, Angela asked him if he needed help, but the boy looked away as if to say, "Please leave me alone."

So, she did. He certainly wasn't causing any harm.

* * *

One day around the 10th of December, Angela was stocking Christmas cards when the same silent boy came in and made his pilgrimage to the wall of ornaments. She pretended to be focusing on the cards she was restocking but, in truth, she was watching him.

It was then she realized he wasn't looking at all the ornaments, just one in particular. Which one? She couldn't tell from her angle, so she waited until the boy left with his empty sack before taking a closer look.

The ornament showed two children standing in front of a blackboard with the words, "The reason for the season" written in white chalk. The little girl on the ornament was pointing toward the words and the little boy was doing something odd with his hands. Honestly, it didn't make sense. For the life of her, Angela couldn't imagine why the quiet boy was so enamored with that specific ornament.

A week later, not long before Christmas, Angela was working the register at the Hallmark store when the boy came in. She waved hello and he didn't respond, just making his way back to the ornaments only to leave a few minutes later with his empty bag.

Angela was feeling sluggish, so she told a co-worker she was going to the cafe next door to grab a cup of coffee. She got her usual drink and as she headed back to Hallmark, she heard a clanging sound coming from outside one of the nearby stores. It was the silent little boy who visited her store so religiously. He was taking the top off the metal garbage can and reaching deep inside to grab something. At one point, he tipped so far that his feet left the ground and Angela was certain he'd fall right in. Then he shifted his weight and popped back out and clenched in his tiny grip was an empty soda bottle.

She watched him tuck the bottle into his canvas sack and then move on to the next garbage can a few stores down. All the time Angela had worked in this shopping plaza she had never noticed how many trash cans there were.

By the time he reached the end of the plaza, the boy's sack was bulging full of empty bottles. He then sat on the bench and, a few seconds later, a city bus pulled up and he disappeared with a "swoosh" of the closing doors.

Soon it was Christmas Eve and Angela was working at the store when the little boy in the red cap appeared on schedule—only this time he wasn't alone. He was with a woman in her early 40s and a little girl a couple years younger than him. He marched back to the ornaments; only this time, he took his favorite one off the shelf and brought it to the cash register.

The silent boy pulled $9 in quarters, nickels and dimes out of his pocket and carefully counted it out on the countertop. He then spoke to his mother and sister using sign language and Angela noticed, for the first time ever, the boy was smiling.

"Excuse me," Angela said to the woman, "I have to ask. He's been coming here for weeks looking at that ornament. He's deaf?"

The mother answered, "No, he's autistic, non-verbal. So, he signs. And, yes, he loves that ornament, but I told him if he wanted it, he'd have to pay for it, so he did, one empty bottle at a time."

It was then that Angela realized the boy on the ornament wasn't doing something strange with his hands; he was signing something to the little girl.

"What is the sign he's doing?" Angela asked the boy pointing to the ornament now resting in his tiny hands. The silent boy took his middle finger on one hand and pointed it to the palm of the other.

The mother said, "That's right honey. Jesus."

The mom looked up at Angela and added, "The boy in the ornament is doing the sign for Jesus."

As the family turned to go, Angela remembered the words on the ornament's blackboard—*the reason for the season*. Her heart tumbled a bit as a special little boy took his sister's hand and led her safely into the world.

The Coat

Brian lived in the nicest house in the nicest neighborhood on the hill. Every upstairs window facing west had a view of the big city below, where he spent so many waking hours grinding away as a lawyer. He and his wife joked that they should have named their dog *Billable Hours* instead of Rocky.

There was more money than time to spend it, but Brian did his best to waste it where he could, including buying a new winter coat every single November whether he needed it or not.

He parked in a private lot adjacent to the law firm and the one-hundred pace walk from his reserved space to the office door took him by the back end of a homeless shelter that had no shortage of customers.

One day, a handsome middle-aged man in a brown wool coat caught his eye. It wasn't the man, so much as the expensive jacket he was wearing that caused Brian pause. Brian stared at the jacket wondering why it drew his attention; then it hit him. The jacket looked exactly like the one he had donated to *Good Will* two years prior.

The man and two others stood shoulder to shoulder warming themselves by an old steel barrel that had wood burning in it. The man in Brian's coat was laughing and chatting away as he rubbed his weathered hands together to generate more heat. Brian dismissed the moment and went about his day only to see it repeated the next morning and the one after that. Same man. Same coat. Same happy demeanor.

Often on that ride into work Brian caught himself looking in the rearview mirror at his own sad eyes. I say "sad" because despite the expensive car and house with the view, Brian's life had become an endless pursuit of more. More clients, more money, more things they didn't need for the house that love did *not* build. Not this house anyway. The very plaster in the walls were a mix of worry, stress and late-night arguments with his wife over things he'd missed because he was always at work.

The funny thing is, it wasn't always this way. Back when he and his wife were first married, before the money, they lived in a tiny apartment near the park. Their small bedroom window looked out on a sugar maple tree that turned the most beautiful colors each fall.

They lived on mac and cheese and the place was always freezing, yet somehow, they were happy. Certainly, happier than they were now.

One morning after parking the car and starting his walk to the law office, Brian couldn't help himself when he saw that homeless man in his jacket laughing away with his friends by the fire, yet again.

Brian put down his expensive briefcase filled with important things and quietly approached saying, "Excuse me, I see you here almost every day and, well, I think you're wearing my old coat."

The man looked at the beautiful wool, ran his fingers over it, smiled and said, "You want it back?"

Brian told him no, saying he just came over because he noticed the man a few times before.

Brian turned to go, but curiosity stopped him, and he decided to ask a simple question to the stranger in his old coat, "How can you be so happy? I mean no disrespect, but you're standing outside a homeless shelter in a coat you could never afford, and you always seem ... happy."

The man stepped away from the others to give them privacy and leaned in so only Brian could hear, answering, "Sir, if I seem happy it's because I'm grateful. When the recession hit, I lost my job and health insurance. Then I got sick, and the doctor bills wiped out my savings. The landlord carried me for a few months but eventually put me on the street."

There was humility in his voice, as he continued, "I'm happy because people like you donated this warm coat. I'm happy because people at this shelter gave me food and a place to sleep and let me use the computer to apply for jobs and I found one a year ago. I'm back on my feet again but stop by here most mornings to help others who find themselves where I used to be. And on the chilly days we have this wonderful fire to warm us. I'm grateful for that too."

He saw Brian staring at the fire now and whispered, "Sir. Can I ask ... why aren't you happy?"

Brian's eyes met the man's as he replied, "I used to be."

The man in his coat smiled warmly and responded, "If you don't like the road, you're on, change your road."

"Is that the advice you give the others?" Brian asked.

The man smiled and nodded yes.

* * *

Brian skipped work that day, instead taking his wife out to a long overdue lunch. I won't tell you he quit his job, but things changed after that. He worked less, volunteered his legal services at the homeless shelter and sold his expensive house on the hill, choosing to live a small brownstone right near the park instead. It was not as grand, but the view of the duck pond and children playing in the park was more than a fair trade. And many nights, I'd swear you could hear laughter again, along with the scent of ten dollar wine and Kraft mac and cheese.

FAITH

The Stones

It was a weekly ritual Alice thought no one even noticed. Wednesday morning Mass at her local church and then a cup of tea at the diner across the street. She liked it there because it was never crowded, and her favorite corner booth was often empty.

The bill was always the same too, $1.75, to which she'd leave an even three bucks, more than covering the tip. And there was something else she did, not always, but often enough that a young waitress noticed.

One morning the pretty girl, wearing a blue apron dotted with flour, worked up the courage to ask, "Ma'am, I don't mean to intrude, but you've been coming here for almost a year now and I wanted to, I mean ... well, I'm wondering about the stones."

Sometimes when she thought no one was looking, Alice would reach into her pockets and take out several small, smooth stones, no bigger than a silver dollar. One was as white as a snowflake, two black, another grey and the last one the color of rust.

Five stones that she'd rub in her hands as she looked out the window at the busy world and then line up in front of her on the table as she sipped the lemon apricot tea. The waitress wondered if this sweet woman who sat alone might be half mad but was relieved when she smiled warmly and offered a seat and story the waitress would not soon forget.

"My life is wonderful now, blessed you might say," Alice began, "But it wasn't always this way. The road here has been hard and each of these stones represents those rough patches."

"This first black stone is from the spring of 1980, when my husband Ben lost his job. It was hard not having his income but for the first time Ben spent real, quality time with our two children. For four months he made lunches, drove them to school, sat with them to do homework; things he didn't have time for before. It changed him in a good way. He, of course, got another job, but he always made time for us after that, and this stone reminds me of what a blessing his firing was."

Alice continued, "This other black stone is for me, and a health scare I had a few years ago. I, too, had lost sight of my priorities, but hearing from a doctor that I might not be here in a year has a way of shaking you awake to what matters."

"This grey stone is from before you were born. On Oct. 4, 1987, a freak snowstorm knocked out power for 11 days and forced us to pull together in ways we never did before. Without TV, we played Scrabble by candlelight and talked for hours. Believe me, we were happy to get the lights back, but I'll treasure that time as a family always."

Alice picked up another stone and said, "The white stone is for my granddaughter born last year; seven weeks premature. It was touch and go for a while, but those nurses and doctors never left her side and she's happy and healthy now—my perfect little angel."

She reached for the waitress's hand, adding, "And this last stone is from a neighbor of mine. That year I was dealing with health problems, we fell behind on the yard work and, without anyone asking, the man across the street showed up with his teenage son and raked our entire yard. It took them hours. Somewhere under the leaves he found this stone and left it in the mailbox for me. I thought it looked like a heart, so I kept it to remind me of his friendship."

She squeezed the waitresses hand gently and finished, "Hard times can be the best times. These stones remind me of that. They keep me on the path."

A bell rang and the waitress excused herself to go to grab someone's order. When she returned to the corner booth to thank the old woman for sharing her story, she was gone. Just an empty teacup, three dollar bills folded in half and small rust-colored stone holding the money in place. She put it in her pocket and smiled. It was the nicest gift she'd ever received.

It has been a tough couple of years for so many—lost family, lost jobs, lost homes. Just remember storms pass, ice thaws and, in the end, love wins.

Path to Heaven

There once was parking lot with a church on one side and tattered old row houses on the other. Every day, the elderly priest from the church would hobble down with his cane and read the morning paper on a bench there. And every day, a young girl from one of the homes would play hopscotch on the cracked pavement of the lot, near to where the priest was sitting. Her parents never took her to church, but she knew what a priest was and sometimes said hello to the old man.

One day, as she was chewing on her second-to-last piece of her favorite butterscotch candy, the child saw the priest holding his rosary and praying.

Without invitation, she walked directly over and asked: "Father, how do you get to heaven?"

The priest smiled thoughtfully and said in a soft voice, "Do good deeds but seek no credit." He could tell the child was confused so he told her this story instead.

Two men stopped at a gas station at the same time on the same night. They both noticed a man in a broken-down pickup truck with a child in the front seat. There was faded writing on the truck's door, that said, *Yankee Way Paving* although most of the letters were weathered away to the point where you could only make out the Y and A in the word "Yankee".

The man from the truck approached each driver separately, looked sheepishly toward his own feet, and told them he was out of gas and asked if they would give him ten dollars, with the promise that he'd pay them back with interest someday. He added that he was a proud man so he hoped they could show discretion and not tell anyone of this act of kindness.

Each man looked at the child in the front seat, the stranger's daughter no doubt, and felt sorry for the guy, so they gave him the money and their home address so he could someday pay it back. They also promised to trust him and keep quiet about this act of charity.

A month went by and the first man who lent the money never spoke of it or gave it a second thought. He felt good about what he did and decided if he never saw the money again that was fine.

The second man, who helped the stranded motorist, couldn't help but tell several friends what he did and how generous he was. When the money did *not* show up in the mail, he got angry, assuming he'd been tricked or lied to. He even tried tracking down this *Yankee Way Paving* to demand his money back but was furious when he learned there was no such company listed anywhere in the state. He promised himself that if he ever ran into that man again, the one who asked for help, he would give him a piece of his mind.

Fifty years later, on the very same night, both the men who lent the money to the stranger died. To their shock and surprise, when they arrived at the gates of heaven, they saw the same old pickup truck parked out front and the stranger they had helped so long ago was the one who greeted them. He hadn't aged a bit.

The man with the pick-up welcomed the first man, the one who had kept his word and never boasted about his act of kindness, then let him in heaven immediately.

The second man hung his head in embarrassment, as the gentleman said, "I told you I would repay you some day and you didn't believe me."

He continued, "I asked for discretion, and you used the act of kindness to puff yourself up."

He told the man to reflect on his life and choices, then handed him a bucket and sponge, saying, "I'd like you to wash my truck. When it's clean I'll know you understand the lesson I was trying to teach."

The first man, who had already been let into heaven, stepped back outside the gates, and asked, "Can I help him?"

Together, the two strangers took up sponges and set out to make the dingy old truck spotless. As they washed the door with the faded lettering on it, the second man, the one who had messed up and was not allowed into heaven, began to laugh loudly. It was right there the whole time: Y A WAY Paving.

"Yahweh" he said. "Yahweh Paving."

"I don't get it. Ya what?" said the first man.

The second man then explained that Yahweh is the Hebrew word for God.

"Wait. So, the guy we helped that night was God?" the first man asked, adding, "Hmm, I thought he'd be taller."

Both men laughed and when the truck was clean, they walked into heaven together.

The little girl stared into the old priest's eyes, pondered his story for a moment, then reached into her pocket and wrapped her tiny fingers around her last piece of butterscotch candy, handing it to him.

"This is a gift Father. You don't owe me a thing and we'll never speak of it again," she said with a wink and a smile.

Then, off she went, skipping her way toward heaven.

Snowflake

Everyone saw her but nobody really noticed or wondered why she was standing on the marble steps looking up at the cold December sky. She had what looked like a scroll rolled up in her hand.

Her blue eyes, which could pierce you like a sword, stared intensely toward the clouds, waiting for something. But what? Then she closed them and there appeared in her mind a beautiful child with curly red hair in a long white coat. She was perfect, all but for a wristband she was wearing. There was writing on the plastic band, but the coat's sleeve covered just enough so you couldn't make it out.

The perfect child with the perfect hair was in a park watching the world around her. A homeless man on a wrought iron bench shared his last piece of bread with the pigeons; a mother fixed the wool cap secure on her baby nestled in his carriage; a young couple clearly in love walked arm-and-arm on the cobblestone path.

The little girl's name was Jessie and she smiled as she turned her attention away from the people in the park and drew in a deep breath of the chilly air, waking her lungs. Then she fixed her eyes on the sky and waited.

Finally, she saw it. It had to be two stories up, gliding over the treetops and making its way down. Jessie started running toward it, trying to get underneath but it kept changing directions. Finally, as it got close to the ground, she zeroed in, stuck out her tongue and caught it.

"First snowflake of the season," she said. "Magic!"

The snowflake melted on her tongue just as she had melted the hearts of the doctors and nurses who had spent the last six weeks caring for her. One of those nurses, just a couple years out of college, was named Nancy.

Nurse Nancy took Jessie's hand, and said, "There, you got your snowflake. Now a deal's a deal kiddo. We have to get back or doc's going to kill me."

The girl with curly red hair squeezed the nurse's hand tight, looked up and said, "It's all gonna be alright now."

The sound of a bus's air brakes shook her awake from the memory and the woman on the marble steps opened her eyes. She drew a quick breath of the unforgiving winter air before going back inside the building and up to the pediatrics wing of the hospital.

She changed into her white coat, grabbed a stethoscope and clipboard and started making her rounds. Her first stop today was room 316 and a little girl named Brynn. "Brave Brynn" is what they called her on the floor since she came in with that terrible cough that turned out to be something much worse. Brynn was due for surgery later that day.

Her favorite doctor now stood in the doorway with something in her hand—a piece of paper all rolled up.

"Before we take you to surgery, I have to show you something my dear, something special," the doctor said.

The doctor handed Brynn the scroll and she opened it on her lap in the hospital bed. It was a drawing of a child with curly red hair and long white coat in a beautiful park catching a snowflake on her tongue. Brynn studied the drawing carefully and noticed the child's wrist band, asking what it was.

Doctor Jessie Danvers reached down and gently touched Brynn's wrist, where she too wore a hospital band, and then explained the rest of the story.

"When I was your age, Brynn, my heart didn't work so good and doctors had to fix it," Jessie began.

"I had heard that the first snowflake of the season was magic, so I got my nurse to bring me to the park across the street from this very hospital. I was patient and waited and then caught that first snowflake. The legend about the first snowflake must have been true because soon I got better and the day I left the hospital I drew this picture and gave it to the nurse who took me to the park that day—Nurse Nancy."

Brynn looked down at the drawing her doctor Jessie had drawn all those years ago and said, "You got better and grew up to be a doctor?"

Jessie smiled and nodded, then said, "This morning, as I stood outside on the hospital steps worried about you, Nurse Nancy saw me and came out and gave it back to me. I didn't even know she still had it."

Brynn, perhaps truly nervous for the first time since she was brought here, locked eyes with Jessie and said, "I'm going to be OK, right doc?"

Jessie blinked back a tear, swallowed hard and said, "You bet you are. Now get your coat. The weatherman says it might snow today and we are going to the park."

Brynn smiled and asked, "First snow of the season?"

"That's right," Jessie answered, "Let's go!"

Three weeks later, the little girl they called Brave Brynn went home and a doctor with curly red hair and piercing blue eyes found a gift waiting on a now vacant hospital bed. It was a new drawing of a child in the park, tongue out, eyes on the sky, catching a little magic.

LOVE

Peter's Punishment

It was his mom's favorite candy dish that started this. Peter was messing around with a football in the house when it got away from him, hit the dish and shattered it. He didn't have time to come up with an excuse or plead guilty to the crime, because she heard it from the other room and pounced, calling out, "How many times, Peter? NOT in the house."

The 13-year-old could only hang his head and await the sentence. His mother was an expert at doling out the harshest punishments—raking dog poop, cleaning out gutters, there was no end to her backyard tortures.

It had snowed all night, a rare Valentine's Day storm, so he was surprised when she said, "Go shovel out Mrs. Milch's house across the street."

Abigail Milch was about the meanest, ice in her veins, rust bucket of a person that Peter and his friends had ever encountered. If you set foot in her yard, she yelled. If you waved, she snarled. She even turned the porch light off on Halloween as if anyone would dare knock on her door looking for a Snickers bar.

"You've got to be kidding", Peter said to his mother. "Mrs. Milch?"

"NOW," she barked back.

Peter grabbed the shovel and marched across the street to certain doom. Yet, what happened next would change him forever. He started shoveling as quietly as possible, hoping the old curmudgeon wouldn't hear him. With each toss of the snow, he'd spy those shut blinds, praying for no sign of life inside. Peter was about to finish when he heard the snap of a lock and the front door creaked open a few inches.

Peter was ready to bolt when a gentle voice came from within, "Can you come here please? It's all right child. I have something for you."

As Peter stepped into the house, the warmth of a fire and smell of hot cocoa embraced him. The old lady handed him the cup and returned to her chair by the fireplace.

"Thank you for shoveling me out, Peter; very kind of you."

He answered honestly, saying, "Actually you should thank my mom; she's the one who…wait, how did you know my name?"

Instead of answering, she motioned toward an antique hutch in the corner. Peter sipped the cocoa, walked over and noticed an array of framed photos neatly arranged on two shelves. The pictures on the top row were of a little boy he didn't recognize. He could tell from the yellowing of the paper and clothing on the child that they were old. They showed the boy from birth, to toddler, to elementary school, and then nothing. The progression stopped.

The next shelf looked much more familiar. It was Peter. One from about four years ago and another the year after that. Then two more that were taken recently; candid shots of him waiting for the school bus or playing in the front yard with his friends.

Peter found the courage to ask, "Ma'am, why do you have photos of me?"

The old lady explained as best she could. "The boy on the top shelf is my son Jeremiah. He was my only child. Perfect and so loved."

Peter interrupted, "Why do the pictures stop?"

Abigail gazed at the fire and continued, her voice quivering with pain, "Because he died. One day he got a fever and it turned into an infection and we just lost him. He was only seven. It destroyed my husband. He started drinking. He blamed me. Two years later he left."

She told Peter that eventually she packed away the memories of her son like a bad dream and moved to this town, this street, shutting herself in.

"I just stopped," she explained. "Stopped talking, loving, living."

The old woman looked over at Peter with tears in her eyes now, continuing, "Then one day I saw you, Peter. You looked just like my Jeremiah. I know it was probably wrong to take your photo without permission, but it always broke my heart not seeing my son get older and have friends. Looking at the pictures, the ones of you, made me happy. Made me think of what could have been. I'm sorry."

Peter wasn't sure what to say. None of this day was what he expected. He excused himself and returned home, not sure what to think. As he came into the house and took off his hat and scarf, his mother saw something different in his face. It was as if he aged two years in that short visit with Mrs. Milch.

After a long silence, he finally asked, "Mom. Why'd you send me over there?"

His mother put her hands on his shoulders and said, "She seems so lonely. I don't know, hon; I thought someone doing something nice for her would help."

When Peter didn't answer, his mother asked, "I saw she had you come inside. What did you talk about?"

The corners of Peter's mouth inched up almost forming a smile, as he replied, "Her son and what could have been."

The next day Peter slipped a Valentine's Day card under his elderly neighbor's door.

Abigail Milch sat by the hutch in front of her pictures and read it aloud,

> *Dear Mrs. Milch, I wanted to thank you for the hot cocoa and telling me about your son. I'm not mad about the pictures but I got an idea. Maybe I could come by and help with chores sometimes. If you had me around that might be better than a photo. Your friend, Peter.*

For the first time in years, Abigail opened the blinds and let the sunshine in. The light hit the hutch in the exact spot where she had carefully placed the nicest Valentine's card anyone had ever given her.

The Letter

For an old and dying man he was still quite clever, hiding the letter in the place he knew only the new homeowners would find it. Sure enough, a week after closing on the turn-of-the-century Victorian, Sarah and Jacob went to the basement and opened the washing machine to do their first batch of whites, discovering the letter carefully taped inside the lid.

"Congratulations," it began. "If you are reading this correspondence then two things are most certainly true: my life is over, but you two are just beginning. I made certain in my Last Will and Testament, that when my home was sold, they would only entertain offers from a young couple that was in love. That would be you two. Let me tell you why you were chosen."

The letter continued, "The Worthington's built this house in 1902 and filled it with warmth and children. When they died, my wife Gloria and I, not two weeks married, purchased this home in 1951 and tried our best to do the same. We never did have kids but believe me when I tell you during these past 70 years there was love in every corner, cupboard and floorboard. I lost my sweetheart a few years ago and stayed here in the house as long as the good Lord let me, missing her every hour of every day."

Sarah smiled at Jacob and squeezed his hand as the letter read on. "I know you don't know me, but I want to ask you for three favors. They're small things, I promise, but if you perform them, I believe the two of you may get a gift in return."

"The first will come in late spring. There's a beautiful birch tree in the front yard, with an old bird house hanging from the limb. Each day put a fresh cup of sugar water inside the birdhouse and watch what happens."

Spring came and Jacob did as the letter asked. By the third day, as the two of them enjoyed their morning coffee on the front porch, Sarah pointed and said, "Oh my.

Look." There were hummingbirds buzzing around the tree to drink the water. They were beautiful and the two of them watched the birds with wonder.

The letter continued, "My second favor is an easy one. In the study on the west side of the house there is a big bay window. Please don't wash the second pane down on the right-hand side. Come October go sit in that room, watch the sunset and you'll understand why."

October came, and as instructed, Sarah and Jacob went into the study and waited for the sunset. As the orange glow sank deep into the horizon, a momentary burst of light came through the window and the one pane they were told not to clean revealed a secret. In the glass was the impression of a heart someone had traced with their finger.

"That heart is Gloria's," the letter explained. "Many years ago, I told her I'd clean the windows, but I missed a single pane. She teased me by drawing a heart in the dust and the impression never left. You can only see it in the fall, which is appropriate because that was her favorite time of the year. I could never bring myself to clean it and I hope that heart reminds you of what it taught me: that there is beauty in imperfection."

The third and final favor in the letter was the strangest of all. The previous owner wrote, "I know it's asking a lot, but once a month on the eleventh day could you take a single yellow rose and leave it on the stone wall out back at dusk? It would mean the world if you could do me this small kindness. God bless you two. Don't ever stop loving each other."

The single-page letter was signed with just two letters: J.F.

Sarah and Jacob did as the old man had asked and placed the yellow rose on the stone wall just as the lightening bugs were coming out to play. They waited and nothing happened. Then, the next morning, Jacob noticed it was gone. The following month, on the same day, the 11th, they placed the rose again and sure enough the next morning it had vanished like the morning mist.

By the third month the suspense was killing them, so after placing the rose on the wall they vowed to stay up all night and keep watch. Just as they were losing hope, the sun peeked over the pines, and they were awoken by the sound of a pick-up truck making its way along the dirt road that ran behind their property. A man in a wool cap and a weathered brown jacket got out and retrieved the rose.

Sarah and Jacob scrambled for the keys to the car and were quickly in pursuit. It was still dark out, but they followed the taillights of the truck as it went over a hill and suddenly disappeared. Surely it didn't vanish, so they re-traced their steps and noticed a small, unmarked road hidden by a large bush. They drove up the road and it led to an old cemetery.

After parking, the two of them walked slowly past the headstones, not sure what they were looking for but knowing they would understand it when they saw it. Sure enough, they came upon a well-kept grave with a single yellow rose resting on top.

The man who delivered the flower, emerged from the shadows and explained to the young couple that he was simply keeping a promise he made to a dying friend.

"If ever there was a rose on that stone wall behind your house, I was told to bring it here," he said.

Sarah and Jacob stepped closer to the grave and suddenly everything made sense. The grey stone was etched with a huge heart and inside were the names Gloria and Jedediah Fitzgerald. Surrounding the heart, also carefully etched into the stone, were an array of beautiful hummingbirds.

The man explained to the astonished young couple, that hummingbirds and yellow roses were two of Gloria's favorite things in the world. He told them she died on November 11th, the 11th day of the 11th month. Her husband Jed brought the flowers to her grave each month on the date of her death. That, of course, stopping when he closed his eyes for the last time and joined his bride in heaven.

Sarah and Jacob drove home without saying a word, their hands locked together the entire way. They hadn't clenched their fingers that tightly since their wedding day. They promised each other, at that moment, to

STORIES FROM THE BARN

always honor the old man's letter and never forget the lessons within.

That spring, they planted a dozen rose bushes in the front yard and when they bloomed a few weeks later, all those who passed by quietly wondered what one young couple could possibly want with so many yellow roses.

Two Old Souls

For a man who didn't like dogs it made no sense that Frank lived so close to the animal shelter. On a clear night when the wind was still you could hear the animals barking from their kennels clean through his double-pane windows. Sometimes he'd sit on his porch and nurse a Sam Adams beer, watching the fools come and go from the shelter. They'd walk in empty handed and leave a short time later with some scraggly fur ball under their arm.

"Idiots," he thought. "Nothing but an eating, pooping and barking machine; that's what dogs are."

He didn't much care for cats either. Yeah, it was fair to say Frank was a crusty old coot proving the adage, that while the good die young, the miserable can hang on forever.

He had no use for pets and never planned to get one until that hot July day when he ran out of beer and patience and decided to march over to the shelter and give them a piece of his mind. That's when he met Walt.

The shelter was set up like most, with a large front desk and rows of cages stretching behind. They laid things out like a crescent moon so a person looking to adopt could start on the left side and walk in a circle all the way around, making certain to see every available creature.

Frank, a retired Navy veteran who spent the 15 years since his wife died being mad at the world, pushed through the front door loaded for bear. His surly mood only got worse when he saw there was no one minding the desk and the phone was ringing.

"Where the hell are you people?" he grumbled, "No wonder you have so many animals making so much noise when nobody is here to help a customer."

Not that he was a customer—he was just there to yell at some poor fool.

Finally, a young man appeared from a side door and asked if he could help.

Frank launched into his complaint about the endless barking coming from the shelter and the kid interrupted, "Oh you should talk to Connie; she's the manager. Follow this hallway all the way around and you'll see her office near the back."

Frank could tell this guy was useless, so he pressed on as instructed, eventually finding an office. The door was mostly shut and had a piece of copy paper taped to it with the words, "Big Cheese" scribbled in black marker.

"Is that supposed to be funny?" he thought to himself. He knocked hard and a pleasant face opened the door and asked how she could help.

"Your dogs are barking too much, and I can hear them from my home down the block," he told her.

Connie smiled and said, "Dog you mean. Singular."

Frank was confused, so Connie added, "One dog is barking non-stop. Just one."

Connie opened the office door, and lead Frank to a row of cages, stopped and pointed.

"This is your culprit," she said. "Walt Kowalski. Isn't that right, Walt?"

The dog turned when he heard his name and let out a loud painful shrill.

"Yes, that's the bark I've been hearing," Frank said. "Now I need you to shut that thing up because…"

It was then Frank caught himself and stopped, asking, "Wait. Walt Kowalski. Why do I know that name?"

Connie laughed, "Oh sorry, we don't actually know his name. The staff here started calling him that after the guy from that movie *Gran Torino*. Remember the Clint Eastwood character who was always angry and telling people to GET OF HIS LAWN?"

Frank smiled for the first time in days, answering, "Yeah, I know that movie."

Connie continued, "That's how this little guy is. Nobody will adopt him. He's too miserable."

Frank stared at the dog and saw something familiar in his eyes. The animal didn't look angry; he looked hurt. Hurt by a world that let him down and landed him in this place.

Connie told Frank that they placed him in three different homes, but his first owner died and the two homes that followed didn't have the patience for him.

It was then that she noticed something odd. "You know he hasn't barked since you got here. Strange."

Maybe it was because Walt was staring into Frank's eyes at that moment and saw the same kind of hurt looking back at him.

* * *

Frank left the shelter and the barking soon returned, carrying on well into the night. The next morning Frank came back to the shelter to yell at the dog personally and again, the moment the mutt saw Frank, the barking stopped.

This went on for the better part of a week and it seemed the only time Walt stopped yapping was when angry old Frank was glaring through the cage at him. The workers at the shelter found the daily ritual quite amusing to watch. Then, it happened.

"Oh Jesus, Mary and Joseph," Frank said. "If this is how it's gonna be you might as well come with me, you miserable mutt."

Frank borrowed a collar and leash and walked Walt Kowalski the 200 feet from his lonely cage in the shelter to his new home with Frank.

"This is just temporary", he told Connie at the shelter. "To get him to shut up."

Connie just smiled, like a magician hiding a secret.

A few months after taking Walt home, Connie brought her lunch outside to the shade of a maple tree growing in front of the shelter. As she sat on a blanket and took out her sandwich and drink, off in the distance she heard laughter and caught sight of a once grumpy old man and miserable dog playing tug a war with a piece of rope. An empty bottle of Sam Adams sat next to a water dish and for a moment both the man and dog looked like they were children again.

Just Another Love Story

Calista wanted so badly to be a writer; yet she was off to a horrible start, breaking one of the cardinal rules right out of the gate. To conjure up something brilliant, a writer needs privacy, yet here she was with her laptop open on a cold Saturday in November at the most popular coffee house in town.

The place was crowded, and you could tell it was freezing outside by the frost on the windows and the way people reacted when they swung open the door and got hit with the unforgiving November air.

Calista was sipping some kind of pumpkin spice drink. It was *the special* the barista had scribbled on the chalkboard hanging above the register—a little too sweet for her taste but, still, it gave her something warm to hold while she contemplated how her story should begin.

At the next table was an old man who looked like he fell out of a black and white movie. He wore a long black wool coat, had the cap of an Irishman and some kind of old pipe that he liked to carry but rarely smoked. It seemed to give him comfort just to hold it. He had a kind face full of wrinkles, telling even the casual observer that this was a man who had lived a life and seen some things.

He seemed to be waiting for something, then his eyes rested on Calista's open computer and the blank screen. "Writer's block?" he asked.

Calista smiled and replied, "Is it that obvious?"

The man smiled warmly, as she continued, "Yes. I want to write a great love story but I'm not sure where to begin."

The old man nudged his chair closer and whispered, "Well you need two things—a hero and a woman worth fighting for."

Calista paused thoughtfully and then said, "And you know something about this hero business?"

The old man smiled, "Oh child, I know everything."

Then he told her a charming story.

"I once knew a boy named Patrick Fitzgerald. He was a tough lad who loved work and sports but had no time for women. He'd see each of us fall for this girl or that one and tell us we were fools to fall in love."

Calista sipped her drink, and her eyes urged him to continue.

The old man obliged, saying, "Every year in the small town I'm from, up in Maine, they had a carnival—you know, rides, games, cotton candy for the kids."

Calista could imagine it, saying, "Go on."

He did, continuing, "Everyone went and one particular evening, I was with Patrick when I thought he was struck by a lightning. We were standing there, the bunch of us boys, when we saw a group of girls. But he wasn't looking at them, he was looking at *her*."

"Who was she?" Calista asked.

"A beautiful woman with hazel eyes, hair black as a witch's cat, wearing a long white scarf and a smile that could light the darkest night," he said, "So, we walked over and when she laid eyes on Patrick it was as if the rest of the world vanished."

Calista was smiling now.

The man pressed on, "They talked for hours and later I saw them holding hands. They say there's no such thing as love at first sight, but don't you believe it."

"So, they fell in love, that's the story?"

The old man laughed. "I didn't get to the hero part yet, now did I?"

He then added, "Right before the carnival closed, she wanted to go on the Ferris wheel, so up they went. You could see the whole town when the wheel stopped on top. As the moonlight gleamed across her perfect face, he leaned in to kiss her, but her scarf got in the way. She untied it from her neck when suddenly a gust of wind blew it from her hand. The scarf drifted down, coming to rest in a tree a good 30 feet off the ground."

Calista then asked, "So did he kiss her?"

The man replied, "First things first, the lady needed her scarf back."

"He didn't?" Calista responded.

"Yep. Patrick could tell she loved that scarf so when they got off the ride, he took off his jacket and climbed the tree to retrieve it. The branch that was holding it was too thin for his weight, but he shimmied out anyway, grabbed the scarf and yelled *I GOT IT* just as the tree snapped."

"Was he OK?" she asked.

"Well Patrick fell hard and broke his leg in three places. They say to this day he still doesn't walk right. But he got the kiss, the scarf, and the girl and they lived happily ever after."

Calista turned back to her computer and said, "I think I know where to begin now with my story. Thank you, sir."

Just then the bell over the coffee shop's door rang and a beautiful older woman appeared.

"That's my date," the old man said with joy, as he stood and slowly walked away.

Calista was about to start typing when she heard a dragging sound, looked up and saw the old man walking with a very bad limp. She watched him hug the woman waiting at the door, like it was the last time they'd ever embrace, and noticed she was wearing an elegant white scarf.

"Son of a gun," Calista whispered to herself.

As the perfect couple went to leave, Calista called out, "Thank you, Patrick."

The old man turned and gave her a nod and the hero made his exit.

INSPIRE

Let Go of Your Leaves

"It's November—let go of your leaves," the woman said.

The man sitting next to her in the coffee shop looked up from his laptop, trying to figure out who she was talking to. She just looked over the smiled.

"I'm sorry, were you talking to me?" he said.

"Yes," she replied. "I said it's November—let go of your leaves. Don't you know they should be gone by now? That's October's business."

The man was convinced the woman was losing her mind, so he said, "Listen. I'm kind of in the middle of something here so if you don't mind."

The woman replied, "Not at all. I just overheard you talking on your phone and see the way you are banging away on that laptop with such anger… I just thought someone needed to tell you. Sorry. I'll leave you be."

The man went back to his computer, the woman to her cup of mint tea and there was silence for a half-minute before he shut the laptop and said, "I know I'm going to regret this, talking to a crazy person, but what business of yours is my business and what the heck are you talking about with this leaves stuff?"

She put down her tea and showed the man she wasn't crazy at all.

"Listen, you're right. Your business is your business," she began. "But I heard you talking to someone about your ex-wife, right?"

He nodded yes and she continued, saying "And something about your son and her being late dropping him off, correct?"

"Yes," the man replied.

She pressed on, "And now you plan to drag her back to court the same way she did it to you when you were repeatedly late with a drop-off or pick-up. How my doing so far on my eavesdropping?"

The man smiled, "Pretty good. Go on."

The woman leaned in so only he could hear. "I never got married, never met the right person, but my twin brother did. He thought he had the perfect wife and life but sadly he was wrong, and it ended pretty badly."

The man slid his chair closer now whispering, "And?"

She went on: "And somewhere in between the court dates and lawyer fees, he lost himself. He stopped being the good, decent person he used to be—you know, the brother I knew and loved. His ex was no saint, believe me, and he had reason to be angry when they split but she had her beefs, too. He wasn't perfect. Soon though, both of them started using that anger and resentment to rip each other to shreds every chance they got."

The man then asked, "How?"

She pressed on, "Oh, if either one was late, straight to court. If someone needed an extra week to pay a bill they were supposed to pay? Straight to court again. They were so busy trying to hurt each other that they didn't realize they were only hurting the child, and neither could move on with their life."

The man started thinking about how he had been behaving lately and wondered if this stranger in the coffee shop had a point.

"So how did he get passed it?" he asked softly.

"That's the funny part," she continued. "One day, just like this one, he met me for coffee and said, *I can't do this anymore, this being so angry with her. I'm wasting time and money, and nobody wants to date me because I'm always miserable'*. So, he stopped. He let the anger go like a tree dropping its leaves."

The man thought for a moment, then asked, "Just like that?"

She finished her tea with a gulp and looked sharply toward the store's front window as if she'd been waiting for someone and they just arrived. "Yep, just like that. And she's been happy ever since. Listen, I have to go but it was nice chatting with you. Good luck."

As the woman pushed open the shop's front door, a tiny bell hanging above made a loud clang just as a bell went off inside the man's head as well.

He stood up in the shop and called out, "Wait. You said *she*. You said *she* has been happy ever since."

It was too late. The woman was already outside on the busy sidewalk. The man approached the door and looked through the front window seeing a man in his late forties pull up in a car and a little girl hop out and take the hand of the woman who had just been sipping tea a moment before.

He watched the woman give a quick wave to the man behind the wheel and in an instant, put it all together. There was no "twin brother", she was talking about herself the whole time. She was once divorced and bitter and found a way to let the anger go. That's why she spoke up when she heard him on the phone earlier. She knew the disease that inflicted his soul because she recognized the symptoms. What was initially taken as an act of rudeness was kindness in disguise.

A moment later as he opened the door to leave the coffee shop, a cold wind smacked him across the face. He tightened his scarf, tucked his hands in his wool pockets, looked up to the unforgiving sky and said, "It's November—let go of your leaves."

Fortunatus

Jamie was tired. Long day, long week. I'd say long life but being just a day shy of her 30th birthday there was still more road in front of her than behind. Being a single mom money was tight, so after working at the hospital all day she did housekeeping at the Marriott all night. Tonight her 8-year-old daughter Olivia tagged along, not just good company, but a hard little worker putting out fresh towels and mints while Jamie did the rest.

Once a room was done, she'd check the tip envelope left conspicuously on the dresser to see if the guest remembered her. Tonight, was a good night because the envelope in the last room she cleaned had three dollars inside. Jamie didn't see it as money but what the money could buy, in this case the small chicken for her birthday dinner.

Turning 30 depressed her. This was not the life she planned. As she slipped the tip in her pocket, she noticed doodling on the hotel stationary, the same word written over and over again: "Fortunatus."

She thought it might be an anagram when, "What's this mommy?" Olivia asked, holding up a small funny shaped piece of white and blue cardboard she'd found on the floor.

"It looks like garbage Liv, throw it away."

For some reason Olivia thought differently tucking it in her coat pocket.

"This is a lucky room, Mom," Olivia added. "Today is January 24th and this is room 124. Get it? One, twenty-four."

They both smiled at the coincidence and made their way downstairs.

Jamie was thirsty so she ducked into the store in the lobby to buy water, Olivia choosing to sit just outside playing Nintendo. As Jamie walked in, she was passed by a man who looked lost. She found her water quickly, but a little boy beat her to the counter plopping down a greeting card that had a pretty rose on the front. The child was excited having found such a nice card in the $.99 cent section.

Outside the store the man who passed Jamie, saw Olivia on the bench, smiled and said, "What 'cha playing?"

Without looking up she responded, "Mario Kart."

The man continued, "My son loves that game. He's in the store buying a…"

Olivia cut him off, "I'm not supposed to talk to strangers. Sorry."

The man nodded in agreement, backing away silently.

Back in the store the little boy was heartbroken when the clerk said, "$3.99 please." Someone had put the card back in the wrong spot and the boy only had a dollar.

As he turned to go, Jamie announced to no one in particular, "I didn't want chicken anyway," handing the little boy her tip from cleaning the hotel room, so he could purchase the card.

"Wow, thanks lady," he exclaimed as he bolted from the store, card in hand.

Jamie collected her daughter; they locked arms and took two full spins around the hotel's revolving door before vanishing into the night.

The next day after school Olivia stopped by the hospital to surprise her mom for her birthday. After a long hug the two made their way past the ICU, looked through the window and said at the same time, "I know him."

Inside the room was a woman who had just come out of surgery, a man holding her hand and boy laying on her bed at her feet. The boy looked up from the puzzle he was working on, whispered something to his father and they gestured for Jamie and Olivia to come into the room.

The man was Peter, his son Kyle, and the woman in the bed was Sarah, Peter's wife. Sarah just had a cancerous tumor removed and though her outlook was grim Peter was so thankful for his time with her and their beautiful son.

Jamie glanced at the *Get Well* card on the bed stand with the rose on the front.

"My son says you helped him buy that?" Peter said. "Very kind of you."

At the foot of the bed Olivia asked Kyle what he was working on?

"It's a gift for my mom," he responded. "She loves the ocean so I got this jigsaw puzzle of a sailboat in the ocean, only I can't finish it. I lost the last piece."

Olivia smiled at her mother, reaching into her jacket pocket.

"You were in room 124 at the Marriott, weren't you?" Jamie asked Peter.

Before he could answer Olivia handed Kyle the odd shaped piece of cardboard she'd found the day before, his eyes growing as big and blue as the ocean in his puzzle. It was a perfect fit. Turns out, it was a lucky room after all.

The drive home was quiet; Olivia proud of what she'd done and Jamie feeling a bit ashamed. All day she'd been feeling sorry for herself and here was this man and child facing such hardship and with such grace. Meeting them was a gift.

"Oh, I meant to tell you something Mom," Olivia said, breaking the silence.

"I asked my teacher about that word scribbled on the paper at the hotel. It's not a sonogram or whatever you called it. "Fortunatus" is Latin, it means blessed," Olivia added.

Jamie squeezed Olivia's hand just as the front porch light to their small but precious home came into view.

As she pushed away a tear from her cheek, Jamie said to her daughter, "Fortunatus indeed sweetheart."

Sparrow

His real name was Oscar, named after the poet Oscar Wilde, but everyone at school called him "Drakes." They were mocking him with that name. You see, at twelve Oscar had developed a bad case of acne so his face got red and bumpy. One of the bullies on the school bus said those bumps reminded him of a Drakes coffee cake and the nickname stuck.

The bullying started in middle school, kids making fun of his weight, face, the way he talked. His parents intervened but that just made things worse because the other kids added the word "snitch" to his resume.

"Just hang in there," his mom would say. "It gets better; high school will be different."

Then it wasn't. Freshman year was even worse. He never swung back at the taunts or went to a grown-up for help again; Drakes just suffered in silence.

Now it was June and he decided to end the school year and all this misery with a bang, or should I say a drop. A long drop off the local railroad bridge to the murky water of a local river where his grandpa taught him to fish.

Crappies, he called those fish. Crappy indeed—the fish and his life.

Drakes rationalized that he could end this daily and unending torment with one step off that rusty bridge. He did not see it as suicide. To him it was just skipping ahead to the end of a very bad movie. That's when he looked out his bedroom window and saw something that changed everything.

Drakes' window faced west. He thought he was watching his last sunset before going to the bridge, when he spotted a memory swaying left to right in the evening air. It was a birdhouse he made in the second grade and had hung from the branch of a maple tree several years prior.

It was simple, made of old roof shingles, with a door just big enough for a sparrow to fit through. Seeing the birdhouse made him smile because he was still "Oscar" to everyone back then. Each child at school was told to paint the birdhouse however they liked. Oscar decided the best way to get feathered guests to go in was to write the word "birds" on the side; only he had a habit of writing his "d" backwards like a "b", so his house had the word "BIRBS" in big letters along the side. Can you imagine? His classmates couldn't stop laughing.

Now on this, his darkest of days, Drakes' gaze fell on his old birdhouse at exactly the moment a tiny baby bird fell out. He saw it drop like a stone to the thick grass below and thought for sure it was dead.

Drakes planned to make the bridge by dark, but he couldn't leave until he made sure that poor bird was okay. After all, he didn't want to leave it to the bugs.

Before he got to the spot where the hatchling fell, Drakes heard the baby chirping frantically. He scooped it up in his soft hands and tried to put it back in the nest. Then, he remembered something he'd heard once; if a baby bird carries the scent of a human the mother will reject it. So, what to do?

Drakes brought the bird inside, found a shoebox and filled it with grass and shredded newspaper. He looked up a wildlife website on his computer and learned the bird could survive on water and seeds.

For the next three weeks, he nursed the bird and watched it slowly gain strength and grow. Drakes noticed the bird had dark feathers with a white chest, prompting him to say, "Hey, since everyone calls me Drakes after the coffee cake, I think I'll call you Yodel after those chocolate treats with cream inside."

If a bird could smile, this one did. Then, exactly three weeks after that bird hit the grass, Drakes took his new friend out into the yard, placed the box on the lawn and waited. Sure enough, Yodel flapped his wings and flew away.

It occurred to Drakes at that moment he'd forgotten to go to the bridge to take that final step weeks earlier and the truth was, now, he had no desire to. He also didn't feel much like a "Drakes" anymore; his name was Oscar.

Life seemed to get a little better each day after he saved that baby bird and the bullies lost interest in him, as bullies often do. Still, whenever he was feeling down or unsure of his footing, this special young man thought of a quote from his namesake Oscar Wilde.

It was six simple words. "Be yourself, everyone else is taken."

THE HAYLOFT

Piper & Samuel

It was exactly 47 steps from the first floor of the *St. Thomas Home for Boys* to the loft high above. They used it for storage, and no one was supposed to go up there. Not one for following the rules, it was Samuel's secret place to sit alone and escape the chaos of the house.

From the window facing west you could watch the sun set over Arlington Manor, a gated community with the most expensive homes in town. Samuel wondered what it was like to live in a place like that—perfect homes, perfect families, perfect lives.

The kids from Arlington Manor rode the same school bus as Samuel, but they had no idea he was an orphan because he deliberately walked six blocks away from the home for boys, to catch the bus. To the wealthy Arlington crowd, he was just another kid from the city.

Father Mills, the man who ran the home for boys, told Samuel to be proud of who he was, to carry it like a shield, but Samuel was embarrassed and didn't want kids feeling sorry for him. Especially a little girl named Piper.

Piper was 13, the same age as Samuel. They not only shared the bus ride to school but had many of the same classes together. Long blonde hair with the greenest eyes he'd ever seen. She also had a big heart. That was Piper.

As luck would have it, after boarding the bus in the morning, the driver took the kids right by the orphanage on the way to Jefferson Middle School. More than once, Samuel noticed Piper staring at St. Thomas as the bus rolled by. If they caught the red light, she'd press her nose against the glass, her face taking on a serious look, as if her eyes were searching for something in the windows there. Every time she asked Samuel about his own home, he would change the subject quickly, making her wonder why he was being so elusive.

One day on the bus ride home, Samuel wished Piper a nice weekend and hopped off at his usual stop. It was not until the bus pulled away that Piper saw Samuel's history book laying on the bus floor, having fallen out of his backpack.

She knew they had a history test on Monday, and he'd be lost without it, so she screamed to the driver, "STOP!"

By the time Piper got off the bus, Samuel was already around the corner, so she quickly gave chase. A few moments later she stopped in her tracks when she saw him race up the steps to the *St. Thomas Home for Boys*.

Piper backed away into the shadows, unsure of what to do, but knowing in her heart that Samuel would be embarrassed if she knew. A lesser child would have run to the others at school and said, "Guess what I know?" But that wasn't Piper.

The next week and every week after, Piper kept her secret and the two of them carried on as normal. When the holidays drew near, Piper noticed the windows of St. Thomas were not decorated like most of the town. There was a single wreath on the door but nothing else to tell you Christmas was coming.

That Sunday as her family left church, Piper approached Father Mills and asked him why the home for boys didn't celebrate the holidays like everyone else?

The priest smiled and replied, "We do sweetheart, we just don't have money for fancy decorations. Every dime is spoken for, and food is more important than tinsel."

That night Piper went to the attic of her home in Arlington Manor to see if her family had any extra decorations. She didn't realize, until that moment, that if you looked out the window toward the east, you could see the top of the St. Thomas home.

Piper's father asked her what she was doing in the attic, and she told him she wanted to help those boys in some small way.

"You know, Piper," he told her, "Most people are happy to help; you need only ask them."

Piper smiled like a girl with a plan.

The next day, she rode her bike to Main Street with a wish list in her pocket. She asked the florist if he would donate poinsettias to St. Thomas, next stop being the baker, asking for a big cake. Piper visited the man who sold Christmas trees to see if he could spare a few. This went on all day. Business after business, unable to say no to those big green eyes.

Soon there were trucks arriving at St. Thomas delivering all manner of wonderful things.

Perhaps the best gift though, was the one Piper purchased with her own money. It was a snow globe with a boy inside, standing on top of a mountain, his arms reaching up toward the sky. When you shook it, silver snowflakes drifted magically above him.

Piper wrapped the globe and gave it to Samuel as they sat on the swings in the schoolyard on Christmas Eve. He shook the globe and as he watched the snow fall, he said, "It was you. All that stuff that came to the boy's home. You know, don't you?"

Piper swallowed hard and replied, "How did you…?"

Samuel looked down at the globe in his hands and replied, "The man from the florist shop said a little girl asked him to deliver this."

Piper tried to explain but Samuel quickly turned away.

Before walking off he turned back and said, "I didn't want you to know."

After a momentary pause he said in a hushed voice, "Thank you for my gift."

Then he was gone.

That night, Samuel climbed the 47 steps to the loft of St. Thomas and stared sadly out the window. He hated it when people felt sorry for him.

There was a knock on the door and Father Mills, aware of Samuel's troubles, came in, asking, "This about Piper?"

Samuel didn't answer, he just let out a sigh.

That's when the priest said, "She doesn't feel sorry for you Samuel. She is you."

The look on the boy's face told the priest he didn't understand, so he took a seat by the window next to him, sharing the rest of the mystery.

"She's adopted Samuel," Father Mills explained. "She lived in a home just like this one until she was seven years old."

"I didn't know," Samuel said.

The priest got up to leave and added, "She's not ashamed of it mind you, but it's not something she talks about. Of all people, I think you'd understand."

As the priest reached the door, Samuel called out, "Merry Christmas Father."

The old man smiled and replied, "Don't stay up too late."

Samuel turned his eyes back out the loft window and toward the west and the house he could see far off in the distance was hers. He noticed a light on in the very highest room. It was Piper, alone in her own attic, looking east toward Samuel.

The boy shook the snow globe Piper gave him as a gift and smiled when he saw real snow start falling outside. The big fluffy flakes drifting across the night sky and suddenly the distance between them seemed to vanish.

Little Things

Skip Miller was the longtime maintenance man at St. Mary's church. That is how he got his teenage daughter Jennifer a part-time job answering phones in its rectory. She was a pretty young lady, with no shortage of boys vying for her attention.

Most days on the job, she found herself telling callers the weekend mass schedule or taking messages for the pastor. But today was different. It was the first of the month, which meant a parade of widows would be coming in with their checkbooks to arrange special masses for the people they'd loved and lost.

To have a mass offered in someone's name, it simply required a $5 donation. The money collected was then used to buy flowers for the altar. The widows always came in on the first of each month because that is when their retirement checks arrived. Grocery stores, pharmacies and church rectories were always busy on the first of the month.

Most women would ask for one or two masses for their loved one, but not Molly Sullivan. Molly was the exception. She would arrive shortly after 9am, sit patiently until it was her turn, then hand over a check for $50 dollars, just enough to have the 4 p.m. mass every Saturday and Sunday in her husband Arthur's name. By year's end, she'd spend $600 making sure the congregation remembered someone, who to her, was the most special person in the world.

This was the fourth month in a row Molly handed young Jennifer a check, prompting the girl to say, to the normally quiet widow, "He must have been a real keeper for you to honor him this way. Flowers, candy, the whole nine yards."

Molly took a seat across from Jennifer in an antique mahogany chair, and replied, "Is that what you think love is, sweetheart? Flowers and candy and spending lots of money? That couldn't be further from the truth."

Jennifer sat up straight in her chair, looked the old woman dead in the eye, then asked sincerely, "So, what is love?"

Molly rested her purse in her lap, smiled and responded: "Love isn't a series of grand gestures, but the little things most of the world doesn't even notice. Love is having a husband who didn't want a vegetable garden but was willing to kneel next to you on hard stones in the dirt to help you pull the weeds from yours."

She continued, "Love is a person who'd get up early, even though he worked late the night before, to start *your* car on a bitter cold morning and clear the snow off your back window, so you wouldn't get into an accident."

The thought made Jennifer smile, as she said, "Go on."

So, Molly did, "Love is a person who, in all the years you've known him, has never driven a new car, because he'd rather spend the money on you and the kids. Love is someone who wouldn't argue about visiting the in-laws, and ignored the slights and digs hurled his way, because he knew that this was your family, and he didn't want to make you upset. Love is someone who calls in sick to work when you're sick, so you can rest, and he or she can take care of you."

Molly took a deep breath and continued: "Love certainly isn't asking someone to marry you on the Jumbotron at a baseball game, showing off for everyone at such a private moment. Instead, it's a person who will gently take your hand in his and say, *I can't live this life without you.*'"

Molly reached over and touched Jennifer's hand now. "I was young, just like you, a long time ago, and I wasted time on boys who dressed the part of the perfect man but were more interested in pleasing themselves," she said. "Then I met Arthur and I saw what real love looked and felt like."

Jennifer smiled warmly now, saying, "Yeah?"

Molly pressed on, adding, "It's not always pretty; sometimes it's downright messy, but it's always real. Look for authentic over athletic."

Molly stood up now as if ready to leave, adding, "Anyone can say they love you, dear, but your true love will show it to you with a million little things."

As Molly turned to go, Jennifer's phone buzzed on the desk in front of her. She glanced down and saw the name of a boy she'd been dating.

"Boyfriend?" Molly inquired with a smile.

Jennifer nodded yes, and before she could speak Molly added, "Tell him you're working, and if he wants to see you, he should ride his bike over here and ask you out proper. And don't chase him dear. He should chase you!"

Jennifer turned the phone over so she couldn't see the screen any longer, then looked up at Molly and said, "The little things, right?"

Molly made her way to the rectory door, and before closing it behind her, said, without looking back, "The little things are the big things. Remember that, and you're home free."

Pen Pal

Rosa Ramirez sat patiently in the lobby of a high rise building with a yellow legal pad on her lap and a pen in her hand. Her appointment, the one that everyone told her was impossible to get, was at 10 a.m. and at exactly that appointed hour an executive assistant to the CEO came to bring her to the penthouse.

Forty seconds after the elevator doors closed, they opened again, and Rosa was led to a large conference room with chilled bottled water in a silver bucket and fresh flowers waiting on the solid cherry table.

She didn't have time to sit before Polly Prendergast, one of the richest women in the country, came in to shake her hand.

"Do you know why you're here?" she asked Rosa.

Rosa hesitated, then answered, "Because I asked you for an interview for my English class paper."

What Rosa didn't know is everyone wanted to interview Polly Prendergast—Forbes, Time, the Wall Street Journal; but she turned them all down flat. So why was she giving such rare access to a high school girl?

Polly smiled then reached into a leather briefcase producing a single white sheet of paper, then read aloud, *Dear Mrs. Prendergast. My classmates and I were told to write a paper about someone we admire, dead or alive. Most kids chose Rosa Parks, Abraham Lincoln or Tom Brady, but I want to write about you. To do that I need to meet you and ask one simple question. You were once poor just like me and now you're rich. How did you do it? I'd like to know so I can become rich and help people. Sincerely, Rosa Ramirez.*

Polly looked up from the single-spaced letter and asked, "Sound familiar?"

Rosa nodded, "Yes ma'am."

Polly placed the letter carefully down on the table in front of her and said, "That's why you're here."

Polly smiled then and asked, "So, are you ready for my answer?"

Rosa leaned in, pen in hand, her big brown eyes waiting anxiously. That's when Polly told her a story.

"When I was exactly your age, I went to summer camp on Lake George. One night 21 one of us campers went down to the lake just after dark. When we reached the water, we started swatting away the mosquitoes. I told the group that if we went out on the dock, away from the trees and weeds, it wouldn't be as buggy. Five kids said they were afraid to do that and left."

Polly continued, "When we reached the end of the dock, we were all startled by some fish jumping in the lake; they were going after the bugs on top of the water. This scared another five kids and they also left."

Rosa then said, "So now there were 11 of you left? On the dock I mean."

Polly nodded, "That's right."

She continued, "The mosquitoes were still bothering us a little so I suggested we get into the warm water and dunk ourselves so they couldn't get us. Even though the water was shallow, and we could stand there, five more kids said no and left. So now there were just six of us in the water."

Rosa kept writing, as Polly said, "After a moment someone saw something dark shoot by above our heads. I told them not to panic, it was just a couple of bats eating the bugs that were flying above the lake. I told them the bats had better radar than NASA and we were in no danger of them bumping into us, but five more kids got out of the water and went to the shore."

Rosa quickly checked her math, using her fingers to count, then said, "So it was just you left?"

Polly smiled and said, "Correct."

There was silence in the room now and Rosa looked confused by the meaning of the story.

Polly then explained, "You asked how I got here? After high school some of my friends decided to put off college for a year and party instead, they felt they deserved a break. I went to college, that was the dock."

Polly continued, "When things got hard at school some kids quit and went home, that was the scary fish."

Rosa continued taking notes, as Polly pressed on, "When I graduated college the best jobs that were available required me to go away to places, I'd never been to before and didn't know a soul, that was the lake."

Rosa interrupted asking, "And the bats bothering you?"

Polly looked her in the eye and said, "The bats are the nonsense on social media. They are family and friends telling you your dreams are crazy or you aren't smart enough. They are anything that distracts you from your goals. Let them eat the bugs and just ignore them."

Rosa considered what Polly said and asked, "Is that all I need to know to be successful? The dock, the fish, the water, the bats…"

Polly got up from her seat and said, "No, one more thing. When I left the lake that night and went back to the cabin, I had a leach on my leg. Everyone screamed and panicked but do you know what I did?"

Rosa shook her head no, as Polly finished her story, "I took some common table salt and sprinkled it on the leach, and it let go of me."

Polly then said to the young girl, "As you go through life, hang on to the people who really care about you and let go of the leaches."

Rosa smiled and said, "So I should always keep salt handy?"

Polly walked her to the elevator saying, "That and a good attorney."

Before the elevator doors closed, to take Rosa away, she called out, "Any more advice Mrs. Prendergast?"

Stopping the closing door with her hand, she said, "Yes. Be kind to people when there's nothing in it for you. Floss every day and no matter how busy you get, call your mom."

With that the doors closed and a high school student no one ever heard of got the scoop of the year, all scribbled down in barely legible notes on a yellow pad.

A few months later, Polly sat in her penthouse office, looking out the window, thinking of the young lady who stopped by for chat; curious if the advice she gave took hold.

What she couldn't know, even from that lofty perch, was that four hours north of Manhattan, at a summer camp in the Adirondacks, Rosa Ramirez asked 20 friends if they wanted to go down the lake after dark.

Epilogue

Thank you for sharing your time with me to read these short stories. If there is a single thread that runs through them, it is *hope*. Hope for a better tomorrow. Hope that we can all do better at reaching out to each other, especially during the difficult times.

This past year was a difficult one for Courtney and I, as we lost our sweet puppy Keller. Our special little man made both of us better people and reminded us every day that there is so much to be grateful for.

A portion of the money you spent on this book is being donated in your name to help victims of domestic violence. Together we can shine a light on a dark world and make it a brighter place.

That's most certainly what our Keller would have wanted.

So, for Courtney, myself and my pups… God Bless.

-John